Praise for Faye Kellerman's
New York Times bestselling mysteries

"Always fun to read, Faye Kellerman has written yet another page-turner featuring Decker and Lazarus, a 'Mr. and Mrs.' for the ages. [. . .] Another great Kellerman read with a full spectrum of action and surprises!"

Suspense Magazine on *Murder 101*

"Master storyteller Kellerman reboots her long-running Peter Decker/Rina Lazarus series. Retired from the LAPD, Decker is now working for the police department of the sleepy college town of Greenbury. Transplanting Decker allows Kellerman to bring in new characters and a new vibe to this outstanding series while still keeping the important family dynamic. Excellent as always!"

RT Book Reviews (4 1/2 stars) on *Murder 101*

"One of the finest."

Los Angeles Times on *Stalker*

"Hard-hitting details, vignettes of Jewish life, and uncomfortably close glimpses of a cold-hearted psycho make this an entrancing page turner. Not to be missed."

Library Journal on *Day of Atonement*

"In a class with the most literate, facile, and engaging writers in the business."

Associated Press on *False Prophet*

BONE BOX

By Faye Kellerman

BONE BOX
THE THEORY OF DEATH
MURDER 101 • THE BEAST
GUN GAMES • HANGMAN
BLINDMAN'S BLUFF
THE MERCEDES COFFIN
THE BURNT HOUSE
THE RITUAL BATH
SACRED AND PROFANE
THE QUALITY OF MERCY
MILK AND HONEY
DAY OF ATONEMENT
FALSE PROPHET
GRIEVOUS SIN
SANCTUARY • JUSTICE
PRAYERS FOR THE DEAD
SERPENT'S TOOTH
MOON MUSIC
JUPITER'S BONES
STALKER • THE FORGOTTEN
STONE KISS • STREET DREAMS
STRAIGHT INTO DARKNESS
THE GARDEN OF EDEN AND OTHER CRIMINAL
DELIGHTS: A BOOK OF SHORT STORIES

With Jonathan Kellerman

DOUBLE HOMICIDE
CAPITAL CRIMES

With Aliza Kellerman

PRISM

FAYE KELLERMAN

BONE BOX

A DECKER / LAZARUS NOVEL

wm
WILLIAM MORROW
An Imprint of HarperCollins*Publishers*

HarperCollins
PUBLISHERS
— Since 1817 —

This is a work of fiction. Names, characters, places, and incidents are products of the author's imagination or are used fictitiously and are not to be construed as real. Any resemblance to actual events, locales, organizations, or persons, living or dead, is entirely coincidental.

BONE BOX. Copyright © 2017 by Plot Line, Inc. All rights reserved. Printed in the United States of America. No part of this book may be used or reproduced in any manner whatsoever without written permission except in the case of brief quotations embodied in critical articles and reviews. For information, address HarperCollins Publishers, 195 Broadway, New York, NY 10007.

First William Morrow premium printing: August 2017
First William Morrow paperback international printing: February 2017
First William Morrow hardcover printing: February 2017

Print Edition ISBN: 978-0-06-242497-6
Digital Edition ISBN: 978-0-06-242525-6

William Morrow and HarperCollins are registered trademarks of HarperCollins Publishers in the United States of America and other countries.

17 18 19 20 21   QGM   10 9 8 7 6 5 4 3 2 1

To Lila, Oscar, Eva, Judah, and welcoming Masha
And as always, to Jonathan

BONE BOX

🌿1

The eye sees what it wants to see—and sometimes more.

Late summer in Upstate New York was glorious: warm but not hot with humidity kept in check. Deep in the woods, the sky was a blazing blue through the canopy of green trees with singing birds and humming insects, brilliant enough to turn the most curmudgeonly into optimistic fools. Rina stopped on the trail, breathing in air that would soon turn cool then cold. Back in Los Angeles, she would have never attempted a solo hike, but Greenbury was a small town, and somehow that made it feel safe.

Wearing a backpack, she made sure to keep to the trail. Cellular reception was spotty at best and as she walked deeper into the forest, it all but disappeared. The temperature dropped a few degrees and the vegetation turned thicker. Some of the oaks and maples were hinting at the fall colors to come; autumn was her favorite time of year. As she walked through the woods, she marveled at the way the light sparkled against the ground, the contrast between sun and shade. The stunning displays of nature were providing her with many Ansel Adams moments. Why not take advantage?

She took off her backpack, fished out her phone and a bag of camera attachments. One thing that was great about a phone was the nearly limitless amount of photographs she could take and delete and take again.

Having walked the trail about a half-dozen times, Rina was familiar with the terrain. Every time she shot photos along Bogat, she tried to pick out something new. Last month had been insects; she'd captured over a hundred snapshots of beetles, spiders, butterflies, and other winged creatures. Today she was aiming bigger, specifically for the magnificent, majestic trees and the interplay between light and dark. She found just what she was looking for in the form of a giant, old oak—a huge trunk with leaves shimmering in a gentle breeze, a thousand facets of broken light like the sun reflected off a lapping lake. Trouble was the oak was some distance away off-trail. Although she had a zoom lens, she wanted up-close-and-personal shots.

It isn't that far away, she told herself. *Go for it.*

Taking out an old-fashioned compass, she made a note of her coordinates. It was very easy to get disoriented in the woods. Everything was green and lush and looked the same even if you were paying attention. But she was emboldened because as she walked closer to the oak, there was a clearing and some phone reception.

Off-trail, she had to be particularly careful about falling. Tree roots were thick and rocks abounded.

As she inched forward, she looked around until she found a great spot to set up. She stepped forward and backward to get the ideal frame, the forest floor beneath her feet feeling spongy. Odd because it had been at least a few weeks since it had rained.

She took a giant stride backward to zero in on the tree and felt a sudden snap under her foot. At first, when she looked down, she thought she had stepped on a twig. Then she realized it was something different and in her confusion, it took a few seconds to register.

A skeletal hand with human fingers.

It had been several hours since she had eaten, but her stomach lurched and her gut felt leaden. Her head went light as her heart started pumping full force. She managed to stay upright, but she was finding it hard to breathe. Talking herself off the ledge.

Old bones, Rina. No one is here. You're safe.

She brought her hands to her mouth and tried to calm down.

Go back to the trail.

Don't run. Walk.

Then she heard her husband's voice in her head.

But . . . first document this.

The attachment was already on.

It was easier to look at the horror through the filter of a lens. She snapped pictures not only of the hand but also of the surrounding area. She was feeling more and more anxious, so she stopped. Stowing the camera attachment, she took out her phone. Her husband's mobile went straight to voice mail.

She took out the compass, slowly making her way down the hillside and back to the trailhead. As she walked, she kept trying her phone.

No reception.

Okay. At least you're on the trail.

Keep going, keep going.

Don't run. Walk.

Her perfect day had turned sour. But she didn't dare wallow in pity.

Deep in those woods, it had once been an inconceivably hideous day for someone else.

The calls kept going to Peter's voice mail, so Rina tried Tyler McAdams, her husband's sometimes partner in crime solving, which really wasn't a tall order in such a small town. When he answered, she explained what had happened. The first thing out of his mouth was "Where the hell is Bogat Trail?"

"Didn't you live here for a year?"

"Two and a half but who's counting? Have you personally ever seen me in a windbreaker or a parka?"

"I don't think I have."

"That's because cashmere snags when caught on a tree branch. My idea of hiking is going from the law school to Widener. I repeat. Where is Bogat Trail?"

"Just call up Peter. Tell him I'm in my car at the trailhead. He'll know where that is. And tell him to call me. I can't get hold of him and by now, I've left so many messages, his voice-mail box is full."

"He's in a meeting with Radar and one of the college proctors. There was an altercation at one of the bars last night; punches were thrown and a window was broken. The owner is not happy."

"The semester just started."

"Exactly. Just stay put, Rina. I'll go interrupt him."

A few minutes later, her husband's voice cut through the line.

"What in God's name are you doing at Bogat Trail by *yourself*?" he thundered.

Rina paused before she spoke. "I've been on this trail alone at least a half-dozen times."

"Well, you never told *me* you were there."

"I'm certain I did but you never cared because I never found any human remains before."

A pause. "Go home. We'll talk later."

"I'm not going home, because you need me to show you the spot. I copied down the coordinates from my compass."

"Then I should be able to find it myself. Just go home."

Rina sighed. "Look, sweetie, I know your anger is coming from a place of concern, but it wasn't my fault I found bones and this call isn't about me, okay?"

A long pause. "You're right. You're sure the remains are human?"

"Unless there are monkeys here, I saw human finger bones."

"Are you okay?"

"No, but thanks for asking." Rina felt her throat clog up. "Just get here as soon as you can."

"I'm leaving now. It'll take me about twenty minutes."

"Is Tyler coming with you?"

"Probably."

"You drive because he hasn't a clue where Bogat is."

"I'm sorry, Rina. It must have been awful for you."

"It was, but I'm breathing normal again." A pause. "I took pictures."

"You took pictures? Of the bones?"

"Of the bones and the area around the bones. After the initial shock, I figured I might as well do something useful."

"Are there people around?"

"No one, but I'm protected. I'm in my car eating a tuna sandwich with the windows slightly open and the doors locked."

"Close your windows."

"Not when I'm eating tuna. But stay on the phone with me."

"Of course. We're walking out to the car now. Did you happen to see anything else while you were up there?"

"Like a potential murder weapon? No. How's your day been going? I heard about the trashing of the bar."

"Stupid kids. Other than that, uneventful."

"Same here until this."

"What were you doing up there?"

"Enjoying a beautiful day. I found a magnificent oak and I was hoping to take some pictures of it. Oh well, I'm sure you'll get lots of pictures of my tree now. I didn't smell anything putrid, Peter. Whatever was buried rotted a long time ago. How long does it take a body to decompose?"

"If the weather's warm, it can take weeks. Longer if the ground's frozen, but it isn't. Thaw was months ago."

"So the body's been there for a while?"

"I don't know. There haven't been any recent missing persons reported, but I'll check the archives; maybe some local girls have gone missing. I'm turning on the car's ignition. You're going to Bluetooth. I may be cut off."

A moment later, the line was reconnected.

"Are you there?"

"Still here," Rina said.

"Hi, Rina."

"Hi, Tyler. Thanks for giving Peter the message."

"No problem. How are you doing?"

"Better than when we first spoke. Are you calling out SID?"

"Mike Radar is assembling a team," Decker said. "He'll call in a coroner and depending who's available and how far away he or she has to come from, we'll have the whole crew up there in a couple of hours. There's still a lot of daylight left."

"I passed a lovely meadow on the way. It was still filled with flowers. I'm sure the trail will be closed for a while. How sad. I mean it's way sadder for the person buried up there. I'm kind of rambling. I guess I'm still a bit shaken up."

"I'm shaken up and I'm not even there yet," McAdams said.

"Said by the man who has been shot twice."

"That was so last year."

Rina laughed. "Just stay on the phone with me until you get here."

It was the second time she said that. She was more shaken than she was letting on. Decker said, "Again, I'm sorry if I was gruff with you. It scared me, thinking of you alone up there, miles from civilization." When Rina chuckled, Decker said, "What's the joke?"

"I was just thinking. Despite all those spooky Grimm's fairy tales, it's probably still safer in the woods than in so-called civilization."

The forensic teams were relegated to hand tools and brushes in order to preserve the integrity of the bones. It didn't take long before the hints of a skeletonized body emerged. Decker spoke to the coroner, a man in his forties from Hamilton Hospital about thirty miles away. His name was Jerome Donner and he mostly dealt with assigning death certificates to natural causes. He wasn't ideal, but since Greenbury was not near Boston or New York, he was as good as it gets on short notice.

"No soft tissue left so far. There is hair and nails, which can outlast soft tissue by a long stretch."

"Long dark strands. Female?"

"Can't tell from the position of the body. I have to wait until I get the bones in the lab."

The body was curled in a fetal position. An unusual way for a body to be buried, but it did require a smaller grave.

Donner turned to Rina. "You didn't notice the hand sticking out right away?"

"No. I just stepped back, heard a crunch, looked down, and saw the fingers." She made a face. "Sorry if I ruined the crime scene."

Decker put his arm around his wife. "Why are you still here?"

"Because I want to be here." She stared at the open grave. "Can you age the skeleton?"

"Not easily," Donner said. "I'll try once we get it into the morgue. You've got the hair. Dead hair, but at least we have a length and a color."

"Probably a woman," Decker said.

"Probably." The coroner looked up. "Aren't these things usually women?"

Decker's shrug was noncommittal. He said, "Once all the biological material is removed, we can poke around and see what else we can find."

"Like a purse with ID?" Donner asked.

"In a perfect world."

"Paper by itself would disintegrate. Paper in a purse or wallet would take longer. Even if we can't find ID, maybe we can get bits of clothing."

"How long do clothes last before disintegrating?" Rina asked.

"If it's an artificial fiber, it could be a while. If there's a purse and it's made from plastic, then we get lucky."

McAdams came over. "Reception's really spotty, but I finally did connect to Kevin. He's going to pull all the missing person cases going back around five years. I told him it could be anyone, although with long hair it's probably female."

Decker nodded. "The body could be local or from anywhere. This is prime dumping ground."

"But she wasn't dumped, she was buried," McAdams said. "Someone took the time to dig a deep hole and cover her up."

Rina said, "If it was a random killing, would a random killer have taken the time to bury the victim?"

"If he wanted to hide his handiwork and he had the time, sure," Decker said. "Some killers get a big thrill out of the burial. But I know what you're thinking: that the killer could have been someone close to the victim who thought it was disrespectful to leave her in the open."

"Any indication of how the victim was killed?" McAdams asked the coroner.

"Nope."

"How long do you think it'll take to remove all the bones?"

"We'll be working through the night."

Decker turned to Rina. "Let me walk you back to your car."

"Sure. You want my other tuna sandwich? I think I might even have two of them left. I always come prepared with lots of food when I hike."

"I'll take the sandwiches. Cool it with the hiking for a while."

"Winter's coming anyway."

"Let's go, darling."

While they walked back, they made small talk. Then there was silence. Rina broke it. "She could be a student from the Five Colleges of Upstate. How far is the campus? A fifteen-minute drive?"

"Not even." Decker was quiet. Then he said, "Do you know anyone who has been at the colleges for a while? Someone who might remember missing girls from years ago?"

"Tilly Goldstein has been at Hillel for over twenty years as administrative director."

"How old is she?"

"In her late fifties. Want me to ask her about missing students?"

"Sure. She'll ask you why. You can tell her about the bones, but tell her to keep it to herself for the moment. And just ask her and no one else. I need to keep track of who we talk to."

"Of course. I'll call her when I get home."

"Thanks."

"Anything else I can do?"

"There's a lot you can do, but unfortunately you can't do it in public."

Rina smiled and hit him.

"What?"

"What *what*?"

"It just means I'm still interested. At my advanced age, isn't that a compliment?"

She took his hand. "I suppose it is a compliment. When exactly is this little tryst supposed to take place?"

"Certainly not tonight. Can I hold you to it at a later date?"

"I'll have to see if my calendar is open."

Decker smiled. "As they say in our former city, have your people call my people."

❧ 2

Despite having just a few hours of sleep, Decker felt refreshed. He woke up at seven, smelled the coffee, showered, shaved, and dressed, arriving in the kitchen with a spring in his step. Last night was a long one. He hadn't expected Rina to wait up for him, but she did and that was very, very nice.

"Good morning." Rina gave him a kiss. "You look good."

"Considering . . ."

"No qualifiers. You look good. Take a compliment. Your bones didn't make the papers yet."

"They were still working when I left at two. Kevin and Karen took over for me." He poured himself a cup and sat down. "I should give them a call. See what's going on."

"Absolutely."

When Decker called, reception at the site was poor. He found out that the coroner's office was still working on unearthing material, but that would soon be over and they could scour the grave for evidence. He told them that he was on his way and hung up.

"Did they find anything?" Rina asked.

12

"Not yet. But the coroner's office is almost done. I should get up there and see if there is anything left in the hole."

"I've already packed some food for you and Tyler. I called Tilly last night."

Decker stood up as Rina sat down. So he sat down again. "The Hillel lady."

"Yes. She remembered two missing women in the last eight years and they both made the news." Rina picked up a scrap of paper on the table. "One had been from Clarion College—Delilah Occum—and the other had been from Morse McKinley—Yvette Jones." She handed the paper to Decker.

"Okay . . . hold on." He took out his phone and checked the names against a list that was e-mailed to him by Kevin yesterday. "I have Delilah Occum at the top of the heap." He looked down. "I don't have Yvette Jones, but the list only goes back five years." He showed Rina the compilation of names.

"Wow, that's a lot of people."

"It's from upstate and down through the greater tristate area. It does not include New York City, which is an entity to itself. When did Yvette go missing?"

"Don't know."

"Hold on." He took out a laptop and plugged her name into the search bar. A moment later, the results popped up. "Seven and a half years ago." He read the article. "She was coming back from a free lecture at Morse McKinley and never made it back to her dorm." He pressed several buttons and closed the laptop. "I'll check it out once I get to the office. Did Tilly know the girls personally?"

"I don't know. We're having lunch today at the Vegan Palace. I'll ask her for details."

"Thanks. And you told her to keep quiet—"

"Yes, yes."

"It's probably irrelevant anyway. There are lots of people digging, so the news is bound to hit soon." He stood up. "I'm off. Have a good lunch munching on rabbit food and tofu."

"I will, Mr. Me Want Steak Caveman."

Decker smiled. "You've got my number down."

"We can do a barbecue tonight while the weather's still warm. Invite Tyler. He is also a steak man."

"Is he worth a ribeye?"

"I suppose it depends on what he produces today."

"The kid's been okay. More than okay." Decker slipped on his jacket—more for professionalism than for warmth. The mercury was predicted to be in the low eighties. "I was reading an article in the *Wall Street Journal*. Do you know what the top firms pay Harvard interns for the summer?"

"Around three grand a week."

"For ten weeks. That's thirty grand. You know what he made this summer?"

"Around ten grand?"

"Not even. What a fool."

"Look at the workload, Peter. I dare say that the two of you have been spending way more time on the Xbox than at the station house."

"Not anymore. Cold cases are a bitch. If it's one of the college girls, that means she's not local. I'm going to have to track down people who probably won't remember much. Students are transitory. Professors leave for better opportunity. Evidence—if there was any to begin with—gets old and lost."

"If anyone can do it, it's you."

"You're such a cheerleader," Decker said. "Why are you always so positive?"

"Inborn genetics, supplemented by exercise and the right diet. Try some tofu, Caveman. It'll not only help your arteries, it just might change your disposition."

Once the bones were gone, Decker could comb through the grave proper. There was nothing much retrieved for his effort except sweat. No ID, no purse, no wallet, no cell phone, no laptop. No books or schoolwork. No intact clothing, but there was a piece of cloth; one small, silver hoop earring; and one light gray button that might have been white at some point. He handed them over to the Scientific Investigative Division for analysis.

All morning, Decker, along with Greenbury PD, searched the surrounding area, looking for something that perhaps the killer dumped or lost on the way to the victim's burial. There were lots of rusted beer and soda cans, cigarette butts, and snack wrappers left over from summer hikes and picnics.

After the items were bagged and tagged, Decker and McAdams drove to the station house. Once there, Decker turned on the computer and read about Delilah Occum: she had disappeared from Clarion College three years ago.

"She was a brunette so she's definitely in the running. She was last seen wearing a black coat, a red mini dress, and heels." Decker looked up and directed his question to McAdams. "Did the fabric look red to you?"

"I couldn't tell a color, pard. Too dirty. The button doesn't look like it came from a black coat."

"Which would make sense," Decker said. "It's hard to bury a body in winter. The ground is frozen." A pause. "When did Delilah disappear?"

"Lemme look it up." McAdams clicked onto her file. "Right after Thanksgiving vacation."

"I wonder what the temperature was." Decker clicked the keyboard. "Huh . . . first snowfall wasn't until almost Christmas. I suppose theoretically you could bury a body, especially if the forest floor was covered with stuff to keep out the cold."

McAdams said, "To me, the button looks like it came from a blouse or a shirt."

"I agree. What about the other college student—Yvette Jones?" Decker brought up the file on his computer. "Also a brunette."

"So she's a contender."

"Yep. Yvette's roommate remembered seeing her in the morning . . . she was in the dining hall for lunch—cameras caught her leaving at two-fifteen. Then she went to a lecture at Murphy Hall: Investment for the Socially Conscious. She was caught on camera wearing jeans, a light-colored sweater over a light-colored blouse, and sneakers."

"The button was light colored."

"Yes. Yvette was five four, one twenty-six, brown hair, brown eyes. We have our files obviously, but the school didn't turn them over to GPD until a few days later. I'm sure they also have their own files with their own information. We should find out."

"Think they'd keep old files like that?"

"If they didn't, they would be negligent. These are still open cases." He leaned back in his desk chair. "Let's see what the coroner has to say. Give him a call. He should have the bones laid out later in the afternoon."

"He's in Hamilton right?"

"He is. Do you want to grab lunch before we go? We've got time."

"No, I'm fine. I'm still digesting breakfast."

"What did you eat?"

"Three eggs, bacon, hash browns, orange juice, and three cups of coffee?"

"The Iris Special at Paul's truck stop?"

"How would you know Paul's truck stop, Old Man? There isn't a shred of food that hasn't been contaminated with bacon."

"I was called out to the place last winter. Two hyped-up truckers got into it. Nothing serious, mostly tired guys letting off steam, but someone thought it was prudent to call in reinforcements. I'm sure I'd be called down a lot more often if the place had a liquor license."

"The reason why college kids have passed it up. That and it isn't in walking distance from the schools."

"No, it's definitely not a college hangout. Do you go there a lot?"

"All summer long. Paul's makes an apple pie to rival my own."

"Not your usual crowd, Harvard."

"Some truth to that. The place is packed with long-distance haulers named Billy, Bud, Bubba, Cletus, Dwayne, Jessie, Jimmy, and lots and lots of Juniors. Sometimes the names are followed by Ray, Lee, or Boy as in Jonny Boy or Billy Boy. But the rednecks and I have reached a real truce. They call me Mr. Lawyer and ask me legal questions so that they can sue their employers for workman's comp. The waitresses flirt with me and call me honey, and I leave them big tips. The place has Wi-Fi. I sit at the counter and surf the Net. Other than your house, it's my home away from home."

❧ 3

Rina was early, but Tilly Goldstein was even earlier. That was a good thing. Vegan Palace was already crowded and it was good that Tilly had snagged a table. The woman had blue eyes, short curly gray hair, and glasses that hung down from a chain around her neck. Today she had on a yellow, summery dress with short sleeves exposing thin arms and baggy skin. Rina slid into the chair opposite Tilly. Immediately they were handed menus by a young woman with blue hair who was studded with piercings and inked with tattoos. She told Tilly and Rina that her name was Sarah and she'd be back with water and pita bread.

When she left, Tilly said, "She has such a pretty face. Why would she want to walk around with pins in her like a voodoo doll? And the tattoos? Do you understand tattoos?"

"Kids get them to be unique. But when I see them, I immediately think of my parents, who were Holocaust survivors with tattooed numbers. What are you going to have?"

"What are you going to have?"

"I was thinking about the tofu curry or the vegan burger deluxe."

"Get the curry. I'll get stir-fry. I like soba noodles."

Ten minutes later, Sarah came over to take the order. They made small talk until the food came. Then Tilly put her napkin on her lap.

"So what's this about finding a body at Bogat Trail?"

"They found bones. Actually, I found bones." Rina brought her up to speed. "Of course, the immediate thought was that it might be one of the missing girls from the colleges. Since you've been there for a while—"

"Don't remind me."

Rina pulled out a small pad. "What can you tell me about them?"

"I remember Delilah better than Yvette because Delilah was more recent. It was very sad. She was coming home from a party about three years ago and never made it to her dorm at Clarion. Her disappearance caused this whole brouhaha about lax campus security especially at night. The colleges agreed to post more guards. The board also instituted this walk-home policy that if anyone—male or female—felt the need to be accompanied anywhere on the campus at any time, day or night, there would be someone available to them."

"Is the service used?"

"All the time. It was said that Delilah had to be the sacrificial lamb before the colleges wised up that sometimes campuses can be unsafe places."

"I agree. But it seems like they'd have to hire an awful lot of guards to keep up with the demand."

"No, no, no. It's like Uber. We have a huge list of

students from all the colleges who are willing to walk other students to and fro for pocket change. A person calls the office and we check around to see who is available at that time. We usually have at least forty to fifty students on call."

"And how well are the students vetted?"

Tilly looked perturbed. "Honestly, they probably aren't vetted. But the security office does have a list of the students from the call logs. If there's a problem, someone knows who was called out."

"Have there been problems?"

"I haven't heard, but if there were, I'm sure they're not publicized." Tilly dug into her stir-fry. "Hmmm . . . good."

"Yeah, the food's really good. I can't get my husband interested in vegetarian food."

"That's just men," Tilly said. "You know, your husband could probably talk to the colleges about the Delilah Occum disappearance."

"I'm sure he will." Rina smiled. "What do you remember about Yvette Jones?"

"She also disappeared at night. I don't remember the circumstances, Rina. Just that she never made it back to her dorm room."

"I heard she was coming back from a lecture."

"A lecture?"

"Something about socially conscious investing?"

"Ah . . . that sounds like Hank Carter. He gives free lectures bimonthly. They're usually packed."

"This happened over seven years ago. He was giving lectures back then?"

"He's been at Morse McKinley for years. I've gone to a few of his talks. He's a great speaker."

Rina wrote down the name. "When you say packed, like how many people?"

"They're at Murphy Hall, which holds at least three hundred students. He's not the only one who gives free talks, but socially conscious investing is his topic. He's been mining that pipeline for years."

There was a lull in the conversation as Rina scribbled a few notes.

Tilly said, "Bogat Trail. That isn't far from town."

"About fifteen minutes," Rina looked up. "The hike isn't exactly strenuous, either. It's around two miles before you hit a fork. Then there's a switchback or you can go farther, and I think that one trail is a four-mile loop. I've never taken that road. It's too deep in the woods for my taste."

"I think you're fearless just walking out there by yourself."

"I had a gun in my purse when I found the bones, but to tell you the truth I forgot about it."

"You carry a *gun*?"

"It's for protection, Tilly. The woods have critters. Haven't you ever read Stephen King?"

Tilly smiled. "You actually know how to shoot a gun?"

"I do."

"You could actually shoot another human being?"

"I've never been tested so I don't know. I probably should go to the range, though. Hone my skills."

"I can't believe you own a gun."

"My husband is a police officer."

"Yes, he is. I shouldn't be surprised. It's just you're . . . we're Jewish. What do we know from guns?"

"Israel does have an army. And women are drafted. It's where I first learned how to shoot. My pedigree goes long and deep."

The bones were assembled on the metal table, disarticulated but arranged as a human skeleton. Decker and McAdams were standing in a small room that was used for hospital autopsies, very different from the multiple-roomed L.A. morgue. What was persistent and all too familiar was the smell—decayed, cloyingly sweet, and medicinal. It was an odor that stayed in the nostrils long after the visit.

Most bodies in hospitals died from natural causes. Decker wondered how many actual murder victims Jerome Donner had dealt with in his career. Not that it mattered that much. It was clear how the victim had died.

Decker said, "The skull is caved in."

"Blunt force trauma," Donner told him. "By how severe the skull is depressed, it was more than one blow."

"Any idea of what type of instrument could have done this?"

"It's irregular in shape, but repeated strikes could do that. My guess is a rock or a stone maybe. Or even the butt of a gun."

"So she died of blunt force trauma?" McAdams said.

"That's the cause of death, yes. The she part? Not so fast."

"You're kidding." McAdams said.

"Look at the pelvis, Detectives. We've got a small

pelvic outlet, a forward-tilting sacrum, and the anterior view shows an angle of less than ninety degrees. We've got a dude."

A moment of silence, then Decker said, "Well, that certainly changes a few things. What else can you tell us?"

"According to my calculations based on the femur length, I'd say he was easily six feet."

"To bash someone who tops six feet, it would have to be a tall person," McAdams said.

Decker said, "Or our victim could have been on his knees."

"That, too," McAdams said.

"The trauma was at the lower end of the parietal right above the occiput. More like a swing to the back rather than on top of the head."

"He was ambushed from behind."

"Probably. By the way, our victim had thin bones and long fingers . . . piano fingers."

"Lanky guy?"

"More lanky than stocky."

"The skull also has a full set of straight teeth," Decker said. "Any dental work?"

"Yes, you are lucky because very few kids have cavities anymore with all the sealants. There are two small class-one amalgams. If you have dental records, you can probably do a match with them as well as the roots of the teeth."

"Okay. Do you have an approximate age?"

"Early twenties to midtwenties by the skull sutures and the teeth. See, we have two erupted third molars and these two in the mandible. Those puppies are impacted. And you're right. The teeth are aligned, indicating good genetics or good dental care."

"Race?"

"Spatulate teeth . . . no flaring of the nostrils. European. Better known as Caucasian."

"A white male with long, thick hair." Decker raised a finger. "Could be why we only found a single earring—a small, silver hoop. I looked for the mate, but when I didn't find it, I figured it was lost during a struggle."

"He could have been gay," McAdams said.

Donner said, "Maybe. Look at the nails on the fingers and toes. There's some keratin left on the digits."

Decker and McAdams leaned over. The tips had a purple glow to them.

"Nail polish," Decker said. "Any idea how long he's been in the ground?"

"It's really hard to date once the bones have been stripped of the meat. But since there's still a lot of hair and a little nail polish, I'd say probably less than ten years. If you get some possibilities, we can match the dental records."

Decker looked at his list. Identifying the body was the first order of business.

Most of the missing people were female between the ages of eighteen and forty-five. But there were a few Caucasian males in the proper age range. Two had been students at the colleges. If none of those fit the description; he'd have to fan out the search. The young man could have been from anywhere and dumped in the woods. Worst-case scenario, if they didn't get an ID, it was possible to do a forensic re-

construction of the face based on the bony land-
marks.

But he wasn't complaining too much, because he
had something to work with. The height, the age,
the long hair, the earring, and the purple nail polish
were a pretty distinctive combination. Not too
many edgy young people lived in town. The colleges were a car ride away. It was as good a place as
any to start.

❧ 4

Fourteen years ago, Byron Henderson, a twenty-one-year-old member of the wrestling team, disappeared from Duxbury College. He went riding on his bike and never came back. He had been five ten with a stocky build and short curly hair, and since he didn't match the physical description, Decker ruled him out.

Kneed Loft student Kirk Landry had been nineteen when he disappeared after attending a party eleven years ago. He'd been very drunk and it was theorized that he might have fallen through the ice in one of the many numerous ponds and lakes in the Greenbury woodlands. When springtime came and there was still no sign of the boy, people gave up the search. He had been short with thinning hair: not Decker's current set of bones.

"What's the next step?" McAdams said.

"I should get dental records of the two boys just to make certain it's not one of them." Decker shook his head. "I hate that. It panics the family and then if it's not him, they crash. I'll put something over the wire, also. This isn't going to be a quick resolve.

You're back in school soon. You don't have to concern yourself with this."

McAdams thought a moment. "You know—with the long, long hair and the nail polish—I can call up the LGBT Center in the colleges. I'm not saying our John Doe is gay, but we've got to start somewhere."

"He doesn't fit the description of any of our missing boys." Decker stood up. "What the hey. It's a ten-minute walk to the colleges. The weather is beautiful. Your idea is worth a shot."

After Labor Day, Greenbury started gearing up for the cold weather. No more picnics, parades, or lazy days listening to impromptu acts playing in the park's bandstand. Instead of swimsuits and shorts, the boutiques' window displays featured the latest styles in sweaters, parkas, and skiwear. Although autumn was still weeks away, all the local coffee shops and supermarkets featured anything with pumpkin.

Walking the grounds of the Five Colleges of Upstate, it seemed to Decker that more students were sprawled out on the lawns than learning in the classrooms. The consortium sat on a sizable swath of acreage featuring manicured lawns and wooded land, all of it walking distance from the town of Greenbury. Each institution had its own dean, its own professors, its own campus and dorms, and its own identity. Duxbury was the oldest, a top-tier liberal arts college akin to Amherst or Williams with architecture that would blend into any Ivy League university. Clarion Women's College was built in the 1920s with scaled-down brick federalist buildings adorned with hints of art deco. Morse McKinley was the government/economics college built after World War II. Students were taught in functional classrooms that sat in functional structures. The residence halls looked more like dingbat apartment buildings than college dorms. Kneed Loft was the smallest and most bunker-like of the five colleges. It specialized in math and sciences and engineering. Littleton, built in the '60s, was the art and theater college. In its hallowed halls and environs, students grew their own kale, squeezed their own apple cider from the college orchard, and raised sheep for wool.

The clubs, associations, and student centers were more storefronts than actual buildings, and all of them were located within a mile from one another. Most of them were considered Five C organizations, which meant that anyone from any of the colleges could join. There were dozens of places to find affiliation and camaraderie, and the LGBT Center was just one among many. The sign had been up for ages and someone had added a Q in bold, black marker after the T.

As they walked into the room, a tiny bell rang. It was stuffy inside because it was still warm outside, and the place didn't have air-conditioning. Several fans in the corner were blowing tepid air. The space held a large dining room table topped with dozens upon dozens of pamphlets dealing with everything from sexual identity—Was it even necessary to have one?—to safe sex that will rock your world. A moment later, a petite girl wearing shorts and a T-shirt strolled into the area from a back room. She had blue eyes and a pixie haircut. She stuck out a manicured hand, nails coated with pink polish.

"Arianna Root." She shook McAdams's hand first and then Decker's. "How nice of you to bring your son into the center. It shows a real willingness to be accepting. And I want you both to know that the Five Colleges are among the most liberal and tolerant colleges in the states. You won't have any problems here, I assure you. How can I help you specifically?"

Decker looked at McAdams, who said, "He's not my father, and I'm not gay. But don't be embarrassed. It isn't the first time that someone has made either of those mistakes." He pulled out his identification.

Arianna's expression went from cheerful to suspicious in a nanosecond. "You're the *police*?"

"I am," McAdams answered. "We both are. I'm Detective McAdams. This is Detective Decker—"

"Wait here a second." Arianna disappeared and came out with reinforcements. His name was Quentin Lewis. He looked to be around twenty with short hair, brown eyes, and dozens of pieces of ear jewelry—rings, studs, and cuffs. He was slight of build and also wore pink nail polish.

After introductions were made again, Decker got down to business. "Do either of you know what's happening up on Bogat Trail?"

"I'm not even aware of a Bogat Trail," Quentin said. "I'm not much of a hiker."

McAdams explained the situation. "We have no idea if the guy was gay or not but because he had very long hair and an earring and nail polish, we thought we'd talk to someone at the center first. We're not biased. We don't need to be woke. But we have to start somewhere."

"What was the color of the polish again?" Arianna asked.

"The nails had a purplish hue that has probably worn off over time."

"So it was dark when it was first applied?"

"Probably."

"Our signature color is bubblegum pink so if he wanted to be identified with the center, his nails wouldn't have been dark. Deep purple nail polish was all the rage about five years ago. It sounds like Vex or Vampire. How old is the body?"

"To be determined," McAdams said. "But it could be five years old."

"Obviously, I wasn't here five years ago."

Decker said, "Is there anyone who was here five years ago?"

"No, this is a student-run center," Lewis said.

"What about faculty members?"

"The center is for the students," Arianna said. "We do have LGBT faculty who are supportive and come to our events as a show of solidarity. But we run the show."

"But you might have faculty involved with the center for a long time?"

Quentin nodded. "Sure."

Decker said, "Could you supply us with some names?"

"I don't know . . . privacy and all that." Quentin turned to Arianna. "What do you think?"

"I think *we* should contact the professors and ask if they want to help. This is not our decision to make. Sorry."

At that moment, a fortyish man with salt-and-pepper hair walked into the center. He looked at Decker and McAdams and then at Quentin and Arianna. "Is everything okay?"

"We're from Greenbury Police Department." Decker showed the man his badge. "And you are?"

"Jason Kramer. I'm a professor of psychology at Duxbury. Why are you here?"

"We found the bony remains of a young man yesterday afternoon near Bogat Trail. We're trying to identify him. His physical description doesn't jibe with any of the young men who disappeared from the colleges in the last fifteen years, but he could have been a former college student. We're at the very early stages of our identification. We're asking for help."

"Is there something that makes you think the man was gay?"

"Long hair, earrings, nail polish. It's just one avenue we're exploring."

"If he wasn't a student at the colleges, why would he be associated with the center?"

"Students come and go. They transfer to other colleges, some transfer to here. And they graduate and revisit their old haunts." McAdams smiled. "Like Detective Decker said, we're at the very early stages and we're trying to work with whatever information that we have available."

Kramer pursed his lips. "Describe him to me again?"

Decker said, "Long, thick brown hair, one silver earring. He wore purple nail polish on his fingers and toes."

Arianna said, "You mean you have just bones, nails, and *hair*?"

"Flesh goes, hair and nails often remain long after."

Kramer said, "And how old are the remains?"

"I don't know. We suspect within the last ten years, maybe. Or do you mean the age of the person who died?"

"Both, I guess."

"The bones are of a man in his early twenties: a tall young man, six one or two. The coroner said he had long fingers. He called them piano fingers." Decker could see a light behind the man's eyes. "He sounds familiar to you, Dr. Kramer?"

"Jason is fine." He sighed. "There was a student here around six or seven years ago. Lawrence Pettigrew. Brilliant guy. He went to Morse McKinley—PEG major."

"What's that?"

"Political science, economics, and government," Quentin answered. "You have to apply to be in the major. Seven years ago was before my time."

Kramer said, "He played a concert at the Christopher Street Gay Pride Fete while he was here."

"I was a junior in high school," Arianna said.

The professor said, "Lawrence was always on. He was exuberant—the proverbial life of the party. He had long, long hair, but it was blond when I knew him. He dressed in costumes rather than clothes: long silk scarves, crazy hats, patterned pants and shirts that purposely clashed. He wore lots of jewelry—rings, earrings, necklaces. I don't recall the nail polish."

Decker wrote down the information on his pad. "Would you know where I could find him? Just to rule him out?"

"No, but the administration might know."

"And would you know where I could get a picture of him?"

"No idea."

"Do you remember anything else about his face? Eye color, the shape of the face? Beard or mustache? Moles? Tattoos?"

"I didn't pay much attention because his clothing was so outrageous." He blew out air. "Long face, but no facial hair. I want to say he had brown eyes, but I'm not sure. I don't remember tattoos."

"Okay. And did anyone ever report him missing?"

"He didn't go missing here, Detective. He dropped out at the end of his junior year, which was a real shame. The last I saw of Lawrence, he was alive and well."

"And when would that be?"

"Like I said. Around seven years ago."

"Any idea why he dropped out?"

"I believe he dropped out with the intention of getting hormonal therapy. He told anyone who was listening that he was planning on having a sex reassignment operation."

❧5

Decker switched his cell phone to his other ear. He and McAdams were walking to the Morse McKinley administration building. "I don't know that he's missing, Kev, just see if you can find an address for him . . . Lawrence Pettigrew. Do you want me to spell the name?"

McAdams was on his iPhone. "No listing of him in the immediate area."

"Yes, he went to Morse McKinley . . . hold on." Decker turned to McAdams. "What did you say?"

"No listing in the immediate area."

Back to the cell, Decker said, "Pettigrew supposedly dropped out to have a sex change operation. I'm on my way to see if I can't access his school file. I'll try to get a home address and phone number. Anything you can find on him would be helpful, starting with a photograph. . . . Okay . . . thanks, Kevin. Bye."

McAdams said, "You know, if he had undergone a sex change operation, he could be listed missing under a woman's name."

"True, but he probably kept his last name. Check the women on our missing persons list and see if any of them match Pettigrew's physical description."

McAdams said, "The tallest missing woman we have is five nine.. Caroline McGee. Blond hair, blue eyes. She's from the greater Boston area." He did an image search and then showed it to Decker.

She was a plain-looking woman in a drab uniform with shoulder-length brown hair. She was older—around thirty-five. Decker shook his head. "The hair can be grown out, but the age doesn't match."

"This is an aside, but what should we call the remains? He, she, or it?"

"Let's go with he until we find out that he was officially a she."

"Right. We didn't find tons of jewelry with him. If he was wearing a lot of flashy stuff when he was murdered, it seems reasonable that whoever buried him might have taken the stuff off his body. The earring was small. He might not have noticed it."

"Agreed." Decker sighed. "Why would Pettigrew even be here if he had dropped out of the colleges?"

"Like I said, maybe he was visiting friends." McAdams paused. "Assuming that he came just to say hi to old buddies, what could he have done to get himself murdered and buried?"

"First thing that comes to mind is a hate crime."

"Someone from the colleges or someone local?"

"Don't know, of course. The colleges make a big show of being supertolerant, but that doesn't mean individual students don't have their prejudices. It also could have been a townie."

"Greenbury's filled with retirees."

"True, but Hamilton, which is only ten miles

away, is strictly blue collar and has a high unemployment rate since the Elwood air-conditioning plant closed down."

Decker thought a moment.

"I've been here through two winters. I don't see many kids from Hamilton drink in Greenbury. They would stick out. Then again, I only get called in to the college watering holes if there's a problem. And despite what happened last weekend, that's really not too often."

"Yeah, you're right. It's not often. I do remember getting called down to the College Grill to break up a drunken brawl right when I came here. No weapons but a lot of punches were thrown. There were lots of bloody faces. The college boys claim the townies came in to cause problems. The townies claim they were just passing through and the college kids started the whole thing. We told them to walk it off and go home, no official arrests."

"So you wouldn't have names of the participants."

"Nope. Mostly it was Kevin and Ben who handled everything. I was new—inexperienced and very obnoxious—so no one talked to me much."

"Some things never change."

"Har-de-har-har."

"You came on three years ago, right?"

"About."

"Do you remember . . . hold on." Decker consulted his notes. "Delilah Occum's disappearance?"

"It was about six months before I arrived. Besides, we're not looking for Occum, we're looking for a dude. I'm just saying that it is possible that a bunch of drunk kids did a number on Pettigrew and after they realized what they did, they all got shovels and dug the hole."

"Maybe. First we have to find out if Pettigrew is even missing. For all we know, he may be alive and well and living happily as a woman."

"That assumes that women are happy."

Decker laughed. "Lots and lots of women are very happy, Tyler."

"True enough, boss. Maybe women are just not happy with me."

It took them awhile to muck through the red-tape bureaucracy, but eventually they found a person willing to talk to them, and even he was making their life difficult. Leo Riggins was about thirty-five, clean cut, wore wire-rimmed glasses, and had a small nose and big ears. He had been working for Morse McKinley for ten years.

"I don't see why I should divulge this information if the former student hasn't even been reported missing."

Decker said, "If the bones are his, he probably has been reported missing. We just don't know where the report was filed. That's why we'd like to know where he's from. If we can rule him out, we can move on."

"I will not give out his number without his permission."

McAdams said, "Well, if you get his permission, then we won't need the number."

Decker said, "If his cell number is listed in his files, just call him up and talk to him. It won't violate his privacy and it'll confirm to Greenbury Police that we should concentrate our efforts elsewhere."

"By the way, he could be a she by now," McAdams said. "Apparently he left school to undergo sex reassignment surgery. So if a woman answers, ask him if he was the *former* Lawrence Pettigrew."

"I probably should go to my boss about this."

"It's a phone call, Mr. Riggins," Decker said. "Please?"

"Hold on. Let me see first if I can find him in the files."

"Thank you."

"You really should bring in proper warrants or whatever you people need to search through files."

"If Pettigrew turns out to be our bones in the woods, we'll do just that."

Riggins licked his lips. "How awful! I've hiked Bogat Trail before. That's really creepy. It makes you wonder what else is out there. Did you find any other sinister things?"

"Not so far," Decker said. "You say you've worked here for around ten years?"

"Yes."

"And you don't remember Lawrence Pettigrew?" Decker said. "From what we've gathered, he was an out-there kind of guy, dressed in lots of colors and played piano all the time."

"I don't deal with students directly. If something is amiss in the files, I shoot them an e-mail and ask them to rectify the problem. It usually involves updating their personal information. Everything is done electronically."

"Not a lot of face-to-face contact," Decker said.

"Exactly." Riggins blew out small puffs of air as he scrolled through the files on his computer. "Okay, here we go. He does list a cell phone." He muttered some numbers to himself. After he punched in the numbers on the desk phone, Decker took the handset from him.

Riggins furrowed his brow. "Excuse me?"

"This is a homicide. It's better if I handle it." The phone rang and then disconnected. "Hmm . . ." Decker said. "That's not good. Does he list a number for his parents?"

"You know, he does." After putting in the numbers, Riggins gave the handset to Decker.

"Thank you."

"If this guy is missing or dead, I'm definitely not talking to his parents."

"Good thinking."

The phone machine kicked in.

Hello, you've reached the Pettigrews. Please leave a name and number and we'll call you back as soon as we can.

Beep.

Decker left his name, rank, and serial number without specifying the reason for a phone call from the police. If Lawrence Pettigrew was alive, there was no sense in alarming anyone. And if he had been missing, the parents would know exactly why he had made contact.

As they left the colleges, Decker heard a small voice calling out, "Detectives!" They both turned around to find a winded Arianna Root trying to catch up with them. She waved. They waved back. When she finally reached the two of them, she held out her hand asking silently for a minute to catch her breath.

"Take your time," Decker said.

"Is there . . ." Pant, pant, pant. "Is there a place where we could talk privately?"

McAdams said, "We have a few private rooms at the police station."

She waved the suggestion off. "I was thinking like a café."

Decker looked at his watch. It was almost twelve. "How about Bagelmania? It's just a block or two from where we are."

"That's fine." She held her side as she walked. "Do you know for sure that you found Lawrence Pettigrew?"

"No idea," Decker said, looking at the girl. "You knew him."

"Yes. I didn't want to say anything in front of Jason and Quentin."

"Fair enough," Decker said. They reached the café and everyone sat down. McAdams took their order while Decker pulled out a notepad.

"When was the last time you saw Lawrence?"

"Around five years ago."

"Was Pettigrew a he or a she?"

"He was dressing like a woman and he was taking hormones. Whether he actually went through with the surgery?" She shrugged. "I just ran into him. He recognized me before I recognized him. He told me he was glad that I decided to come here. He said he hoped that I was happy. I told him I was."

"How was his affect?"

"He's always friendly. He did seem preoccupied, though. I asked him if he wanted to get coffee and chat, but he said he was in a rush. We left it at that."

"Can you back it up a little? How did you meet him?"

"At the Christopher Street Gay Pride Fete seven years ago when I was doing my college tour. I wanted to experience the different LGBTQ centers. I wasn't out yet, but I knew what I was."

McAdams came back with the bagels and coffee. He passed the food and cutlery around and then sat down.

Decker said, "She originally met Pettigrew at the gay pride fete seven years ago, but she also saw him about five years ago. She ran into him. He was taking hormones and dressing like a woman, but he hadn't undergone sex reassignment." He turned to Arianna. "Did I get that right?"

"Perfect."

"Was Lawrence still calling himself Lawrence?" McAdams asked.

"He introduced himself as the former Lawrence Pettigrew. He was now calling himself Lorraine Pettigrew."

Decker said, "Is the name Lorraine Pettigrew on the list?"

"Let me check."

"I'll send something out over the wire using both names." Decker turned to Arianna. "Tell me about this Christopher Street fete where you met him. Obviously Lawrence made an impression on you."

"He was dressed in drag, but that was no big deal.

A lot of the guys were in drag. The costumes are outrageous: chaps with no underwear, feather head-dresses, angel's wings, leather thongs with leather masks and whips."

"Sounds like Halloween in the Village," McAdams said.

"Kinda, yeah. The party isn't sanctioned by the administration, but as long as we mind our manners, they turn a blind eye. Lawrence came up to me and introduced himself. He was very nice—really funny and warm. I told him I was interested in Morse McKinley and he talked to me for about twenty minutes. He was articulate and smart. Actually it was because of him that I made the decision to go here."

Decker said, "And when you ran into him about five years ago, you talked for about five minutes and that was that?"

"About. You see, by the time I came here, he wasn't in school anymore. So when I ran into him, I wanted to find out why he dropped out. I wanted to know if people were giving him a hard time about his change from male to female."

"Ah," Decker sipped coffee. "What did he say?"

"He said his dropping out had nothing to do with the attitude of the colleges. They were very accepting. He dropped out for personal reasons—his sex reassignment. And that's when he said that he was glad I decided to come to Morse McKinley. And that was the end of it because he was in a hurry."

McAdams said, "And he didn't give any hint as to why he had come back to Morse McKinley?"

"No. Nothing."

"Do you know if he was close to any particular faculty member?" Decker said. "Was there someone he might have wanted to visit?"

"What about Jason Kramer?" McAdams asked.

"Jason has been there awhile but by the way he was talking about Lawrence, they didn't seem close. Lawrence was more than just a gay man. He was brilliant."

"But you don't know who he was close to."

"No idea. But Morse McKinley is a small school. Besides, you don't even know if it's him."

"You're right."

McAdams said, "Not to seem lurid, but a description of him as a woman might be helpful."

Arianna sighed. "A tall girl with makeup and big boobs. He still had long hair, but it was brown. He wore tight jeans, a sweater, and boots."

"Good memory," Decker said.

"Lawrence made a big impression on me, obviously."

"And you haven't seen him since that time."

"No."

"And you didn't keep in phone contact or anything like that?"

"No. You know how it is. I was more interested in my own life than his."

"Of course."

She stood up. "I have to go catch a class. It's an important one."

"Where can I contact you if I need to talk to you again?"

"Why would you need to talk to me again?"

Decker said, "You never know. What's your cell?" After Arianna recited the numbers, he gave her his card. McAdams followed suit.

She turned the cards over in her hand then stashed them in her satchel. Then she picked it up and left without saying good-bye.

McAdams said, "What do you make of her?"

"Seems like a good kid. She volunteered the information."

"Maybe to lead us off-track."

Decker stood up and smiled. "You have a very suspicious mind."

"That's a good thing for a detective." McAdams raised his eyebrows. "It's even a better thing for a lawyer. In my meager dealings with both professions, I've found that clients lie a hell of a lot more than the suspects I've encountered."

"It's a close call." Decker's cell rang. He fished it from his pocket. "Not our area code." He depressed the button. "Decker."

The woman on the other end didn't bother to introduce herself. "He's dead."

It took a moment to register who it could possibly be. "Mrs. Pettigrew?"

Silence. Then she said, "Yes, I'm returning your call."

"Thank you very much for calling back. Where are you calling from?"

"New York City. Staten Island. I assume you're calling about my son, Lawrence. You found his body?"

"Since you're being direct, I will be direct as well.

I'm from Greenbury Police. We found a body in the woods near a popular hiking trail. We're trying to identify it."

"So you're not sure it's Lawrence."

"No, we're not. Did you report your son missing, Mrs. Pettigrew?"

"Five years ago."

"Do you remember the exact date?"

"December ninth."

"Okay." So the timing certainly fit. "Where did you report him missing? What police department?"

"We live on Staten Island. But Lawrence wasn't living with us at the time. But I didn't know who else to call, so I called the local police."

"Okay, I'll certainly contact them if I need to." Decker paused.

"Do you think it's him? You must have some idea. Otherwise you wouldn't call me."

Decker sidestepped. "I hate to ask you this, but do you have dental records?"

"So he's been in the ground for a long time, right?"

"You're a very astute woman."

"How much do you know about my son?"

"Mrs. Pettigrew, I think any further conversation would be best in person. I'm about three hours away from you. I could be down at around . . ." Decker checked his watch. "Around six or seven in the evening depending on traffic."

"That would work." She gave Decker her address. "I suppose you'll want me to pick up his dental records?"

"That would be very helpful to my case."

"It's a murder case, then?"

"Yes."

"That was Lawrence, Detective. Wherever he went, trouble followed."

6

Over the phone line, Rina said, "But I want to come with you."

"I'm not staying overnight. I'm talking to the poor woman, then turning around and heading back up to Greenbury with the X-rays."

"Just drop me off and I'll get to Brooklyn. Why waste an opportunity to see the kids?"

"Lily will probably be asleep by the time you get there."

"Maybe they'll keep her up long enough for me to read her a bedtime story. And don't you want to hear what I found out about Yvette Jones and Delilah Occum?"

"They're not my remains, Rina."

"This guy disappeared between the times the two women disappeared. You're not the least bit curious?"

"I'm always curious about a missing person, but I can't see how Delilah Occum or Yvette Jones would have anything to do with my guy."

"Who was in the process of becoming a woman when he disappeared, no?"

Decker paused. "Are you suggesting a serial killer?"

"I'm just saying until you know who you're dealing with, doesn't it pay to consider all possibilities?"

"Fair enough. I'm leaving the station house in ten minutes. Be ready and I'll pick you up."

"I'm ready right now. But while I'm waiting for you, I'll pack us dinner. That way you won't have to stop for food."

Ten minutes later, Rina slid shotgun into the car with a big brown bag. She turned around. "You okay back there, Tyler? I took your *kisay hakoved*."

"Which means?"

"Your place of honor."

"I'm fine in the back. This way you can deal with his crankiness."

"Ah, c'mon," Decker said. "I'm not even out of the driveway."

Rina placed the bag in the unoccupied backseat and turned down the AC. "How about if I tell you my conversation with Tilly Goldstein."

McAdams took out his iPad. "I'm ready whenever you are."

It didn't take too long. Afterward Decker said, "Two things come to mind. Who is Hank Carter? And more important, why didn't the colleges institute the walking-home policy after Yvette disappeared?"

"Can't help you with the second question," McAdams said. "I can look up Hank Carter when I get some Wi-Fi. Unless you want me to use my phone, but it's always pretty slow when we leave Greenbury. It gets very rural."

"Indeed." Rina gazed out the window at the open road. It was all green and leafy but within a month or two, it would catch fire with the brilliance of autumn. City folk poured into the area to leaf watch.

From the backseat, McAdams said, "Interesting theory about a serial killer, Rina. All of them in the wrong place at the wrong time."

Decker said, "What did you do with the original list of missing women in the area?"

"It's on my iPad."

"Can you pull it up?"

"I think it's in my e-mail, so no. As soon as I get connected, I'll give it to you."

Rina said, "Are you looking for other remains near where you found Pettigrew?"

"Not *actively*, no."

"Maybe you should."

"Not a bad idea," McAdams said. "We should at least look around before the ground gets frozen over."

It was a good point. Decker said, "Maybe I'll ask Radar about bringing in a cadaver dog, but first let's identify the body. If it's Pettigrew, I'd be interested in knowing who he was meeting up with in Greenbury."

"And you think the parents would know?"

"Perhaps his mother might. Usually, kids talk more to their mothers than their fathers."

McAdams said, "It's kind of a toss-up with me. My mother is nice, but she really isn't listening to what I'm saying. My dad is listening. That's the problem."

Rina smiled. "If this Pettigrew was undergoing hormonal therapy, how could you keep that from your parents?"

"You could if you were estranged from them," McAdams said.

"I suppose, although if he was that in your face when he went off to college, the parents would suspect something, right?"

Decker said, "They probably knew something but maybe they didn't know everything. And I'd just like to point out that we're getting a little fixated on Pettigrew's sex change. The murder could have nothing to do with Pettigrew, the woman. It's better if we first find out about Pettigrew, the person."

After dropping off Rina at their son and daughter-in-law's apartment, Decker wended his way through the neighborhoods of lower Brooklyn, relying on navigation because he sure as hell wasn't familiar with the area. Within ten minutes, he hit the on-ramp to the Verrazano-Narrows Bridge, better known to natives as the VZ, crossing over the bay until he exited into Staten Island. The Pettigrews lived five minutes from the VZ in a compact, one-story brick house on a block of one-story brick houses. Daylight was almost gone, but there was enough to see the sidewalks lined with old oaks and yellow-tinged leaves although the weather was still hot and muggy. Eastern summers were one of those things that Decker had forgotten about after living in L.A. all those years. Southern California was hot but for the most part dry, and even when people complained it was muggy, it usually wasn't all that bad.

After parking curbside, he and McAdams got out,

their faces hit by a wave of wet heat as they walked to the front entrance. Someone must have been watching because the door opened before either of them knocked.

They came face-to-face with a woman in her midfifties: five nine, average build, short brown hair, dark eyes, thin lips, roman nose set into a long face. She wore a long-sleeved black T-shirt, and baggy jeans a tad too short for her height. There were slippers on her feet.

"Joanne Pettigrew," she said. "Please come in."

Decker and McAdams followed her into a tidy living room—couch, chairs, tables, and a baby grand piano that couldn't be played because the lid was weighted down with framed pictures of family adventures. Plenty of photos of a long-haired teen-ager, but as he grew older, the pictures disappeared. Before Decker sat down, he introduced himself and McAdams. Both of them gave the woman their cards. She pointed to the couch. The men sat, but she didn't. Instead she walked out of the room and came back holding a manila envelope.

"I had plenty of time to pick up the dental records." She handed the envelope to Decker. "If they don't match, could you please get them back to me?"

"Of course," Decker said. "Thank you so much. I know this must be hard for you."

She let out an exhale. "The local police have a copy so if they come across unknown bones or whatever you call them—remains, I guess—they automatically plug them into their system." She dropped down into a chair and dry-washed her face. "What makes you think it's Lawrence?"

Decker said, "The description we got of your son roughly matches the dimensions of the body that we found."

"There are a lot of men who could match my son's dimensions, Detective."

"Of course."

"So . . ." She held up her hands in a shrug. "You must be going on something else."

Decker said, "The body had long, dark hair. The coroner also described him as having piano fingers. There were remnants of nail polish on his fingers and toes. We also found an earring. We asked around the colleges and found someone who told us the description might match Lawrence. We don't have a whole lot to go on and we may be completely wrong. And if we are, I'm sorry to put you through all this. But I'm following the meager leads we have."

Joanne nodded. "So you know that Lawrence went to Morse McKinley."

"Yes," Decker said. "He dropped out after his junior year."

"Do you know why?"

"I heard he dropped out to get hormonal treatments."

"So you know." She rolled her eyes. "He went around calling himself Lorraine. The boy always had a flair for the dramatic."

"Tell me about him."

"I have three children. The first two were just . . ." She threw up her hands. "Like normal people. Lawrence was the youngest and he was always different. Don't get me wrong. I loved my son. I won't exactly say I was supportive of his choices, but I accepted who he was. There are men who are gay. And then there are gay men. Lawrence fit the gay men category. Everything he did revolved around showing the world his sexual identity. And if you didn't like it, he was right there in your face. I stopped counting how many times I got a call from high school: 'Don't worry. No one was hurt, but Lawrence got into an altercation.'"

"It can get wearisome."

"You've got that right. Lawrence kept claiming he was being bullied and that he had to defend himself. That was probably true. There were a lot of, you know, regular kids who went to his high school. We have a lot of cops and firemen and just normal guys in the community. I'm sure the school wasn't big on sensitivity training."

"Do you think he was bullied?" McAdams asked.

"I don't know. But he certainly didn't act like a bullied teenager. He wasn't the least bit withdrawn. He did really well in school. And he had friends, Detectives. Lots of friends. Lawrence could rein in the act if he had to. For instance, he never got into fights with the neighborhood boys. They liked him even though they knew what he was."

"The people in college who knew him described Lawrence as very bright and very friendly."

"All true." She looked down. "Lawrence changed drastically after puberty. He became so overt. It was embarrassing at first, but eventually my husband and I got used to it. And, yes, Lawrence was very smart. Everyone knew that. His teachers knew that. They recommended Morse McKinley to him. He was always interested in government and economics."

"Morse McKinley would be a good fit then," McAdams said.

"We thought it would be a terrific fit. And we hoped that maybe he'd settle down in college with more expected of him. Of course, he just went even more extreme without any family constraints." A shrug. "I may not have understood my son—he could be challenging—but I loved him."

"Of course you did," Decker said. "When did you find out he was undergoing hormonal therapy?"

"He told us right away. He announced: 'I'm dropping out of school to become a woman.' You know what my husband said?"

"What?"

"He said, 'There aren't women in college?'" Joanne shook her head. "I think it deflated the shock value that he hoped he'd get. Like I said, I loved my son. I would have loved him as a daughter." Tears moistened her eyes. "Male or female." The tears escaped and fell down her cheek. "When he started taking hormones . . . it seemed to me that he was starting to find peace. He took the test for his stock brokerage license and got a job with a small firm as a woman. He started dressing like a conventional woman—clothes, makeup, the whole bit. So maybe he did find his true self."

She wiped her eyes with the back of her hand.

"He didn't come around the house anymore—that was probably for our sake—but he did call. And we had normal conversations. He talked about work instead of his gender. It was refreshing. When he hadn't called us in over two weeks, I got concerned."

"Where was he living, Mrs. Pettigrew?"

"Joanne. He was living in the city, but I didn't know where at first. Later on, after he went missing, I found out he was living in the East Village in a very nice studio apartment in a doorman building. So he must have been making money."

"You were at his apartment?"

"Yes. When he stopped calling and wouldn't answer his cell, I began to get very worried. I called up his work. I didn't have the number, but I knew the name of the firm. After a couple of tries, I found the right branch. It's when they told me he hadn't been at work for the last two weeks. I became . . . that awful feeling of dread. Like his life on the fringes finally caught up with him."

"His life on the fringes?" McAdams asked.

"Parties, alcohol, drugs, and lots of weirdos."

"You think it was someone from his fringy life?"

"I don't know. Maybe."

"Do you have any names?" Decker asked.

"Not a one." She waved it off. "Anyway, I finally got his city address from his work files and I went over to the apartment. At first, the super wouldn't let me in. But I pleaded, and he finally opened the door."

She stared off into space.

"His apartment was very large—superneat—he was always a neat person. There was no sign of him."

"What about things in the apartment?" Decker asked.

"His clothes and personal items were still there."

"Did you happen to check the refrigerator?"

"A few items—mostly water, beer, and club soda. I think Lawrence ate out a lot. I guess he could afford it. His clothes were nice—custom made to fit his body."

"And that was the only time you ever visited his place?"

"No, there was another time afterward. The management called me to say he hadn't paid his rent. At that point, I knew something was wrong. I told the police something was wrong. But they kept insisting that without anything to go on, they couldn't do much. Lawrence could have disappeared on his own accord. When they found out he was undergoing a sex reassignment, they really stopped paying attention. They thought that if something terrible happened, it was because of his lifestyle. Which may be true. But that doesn't mean you don't investigate."

Decker said, "You must have been frustrated."

"Beyond frustrated. No one was listening to us."

"What happened with his apartment?" McAdams said.

"I paid his unpaid bill for the month, but I told the apartment management I wasn't paying anything else. I didn't cosign the lease. I wasn't obliged to pay them anything. After I explained the situation, the building supervisor let us in there to clean up. I boxed up Lawrence's things . . ." She lowered her head. "My husband and I went through everything we could find. Every bill, every piece of correspondence, every scrap of paper. We didn't find his phone or laptop or iPad. And the service providers wouldn't give me access to his information because they didn't know if Lawrence was alive or dead. He was a grown man—or grown woman. For all we knew, he could have been put in witness protection."

"Why would you think that?" Decker said.

"Like I said, he knew a lot of counterculture people. Not that Lawrence seemed to be the type of guy to become an informant, but I really didn't know a whole lot about his life, did I?"

"Right."

"Besides, Lawrence bucked authority wherever, whenever. Anyway, when it was plain that he wasn't going to suddenly show up, we hired a private eye."

"And?"

"He talked to people—Lawrence's old friends, his new friends, his friends on Facebook. The investigator talked to people Lawrence worked with, talked to old college friends and faculty. He charged us a lot of money. He got nowhere."

"Did he give you the files, Mrs. Pettigrew?"

"He gave us a report. You can have it if you want. But if the body isn't Lawrence, I'd want that back as well."

"Of course," McAdams said. "Could we have the PI's name? He probably has an entire file on Lawrence—more than he included in the report."

"His name is James Breck. He was a former New York police detective. He came highly recommended. My opinion is he was just churning up hours. But of course, I wasn't thinking charitably about anyone at that point."

"We'll check him out," Decker said. "Where is his office?"

"Somewhere in Queens. I have an address, but I don't know if it's current."

"Anything you can give us will help," McAdams said.

Decker said, "In the report, did he list the people he talked to?"

"I don't remember. I haven't looked at the report in a while. I did have a list of people that I thought he *should* talk to. If you hold on, I'll get you the report and see what I still have in the file."

"That would be great," Decker said.

As soon as she left, McAdams said, "Breck is in Astoria." He took out his cell and called him up. He reached a human voice. Surprise, surprise. "Hello, this is Detective Tyler McAdams from Greenbury Police Department in Upstate New York. I'm trying to get hold of James Breck . . . okay, do you have any idea how often he calls in for messages?" Tyler paused as he listened. "Could you please have him give us a call as soon as possible? It's important. . . . yes, thank you." McAdams spelled his name and left both his and Decker's cell numbers. He hung up.

"Answering service?" Decker asked.

"Yes. It's strange to actually talk to someone. Here's the address." McAdams looked at his watch. It was seven in the evening. "I don't think he'll be in, but we could swing by and leave cards to show we're serious."

"Let me call Rina after we're done here . . ." Decker stopped talking as Joanne Pettigrew came back into the room.

She said, "Yes, I suppose we did give James a list of all Lawrence's friends." She handed it to Decker along with a folder. "Tell me if you find anything interesting."

"I'll keep you posted."

"Although I suppose you won't want to be wasting your time if it's not Lawrence."

"I'll be happy to look it over regardless." Decker smiled. "Anything you'd like to ask me?"

She sighed again. "Not at the moment. Maybe I'll think of something later on."

"You have my number. Feel free to use it."

"Thank you."

There was a moment of awkward silence. Then Decker stood up and said, "Thank you for your time and for the dental X-rays. If we have something, I'll let you know right away."

He extended his hand and Joanne took it with the slightest of touches. No energy in the gesture. She had used up her reserves for the evening.

7

McAdams looked over Lawrence Pettigrew's PI report as Decker drove back toward Brooklyn. Just as they wended their way over the bridge and into Flatbush, the Bluetooth kicked in. It was a number Decker didn't recognize. He accepted the call.

"Decker."

"This is James Breck."

"Mr. Breck. Thank you so much for calling me back. I'm here with my partner, Detective McAdams."

"What is this in regards to?"

"Lawrence Pettigrew."

"Ah, so you found him . . . or her, I guess."

"We don't know. We're in Brooklyn right now. You have a listed address in Queens. We can come to you."

"I'm at home. I don't have his folder on me. It's in the office."

McAdams said, "Is it possible to meet you at the office?"

"Let me think . . . maybe around nine."

"Nine is fine. Thank you."

Breck said, "Being that you don't know if you

61

found Lawrence or not, I'm assuming you found a body."

"We did."

"In an advanced state of decomposition."

"Yes."

"I have a copy of his dental records."

"We got a set from Mrs. Pettigrew."

"She has the originals so they're probably better. I'll see you later."

"Thank you," Decker said.

McAdams looked at his watch. "That's an hour from now."

"We're ten minutes away from my son and daughter-in-law's house. I'd like to stop in and say hello."

"Sure." McAdams paused. "Do you ever discuss your cases with your kids?"

"Not really, no, especially now that Sammy has a child. Parenthood is like the first stage of mortality. Once you have children, you realize you're no longer invincible."

After an interlude of coffee and cake with Rina, Sammy, and Rachel, the two detectives were off to Queens.

McAdams was unusually quiet.

"Tired?" Decker asked.

"No, I'm fine." He paused. "It's weird. This is probably the most I've ever seen of the other four boroughs. Well, three actually. We haven't made it to the Bronx yet. To us Knickerbockers, the only city is Manhattan."

"You're an original Knickerbocker?"

"Not at all, but I have enough money to buy the title."

The car's navigation told Decker to turn right in one hundred feet.

"I really am sheltered," McAdams said. "I only know Queens as an exit on the highway going to Kennedy. I really have to get out more."

It took another ten minutes until the navigation informed them that they had reached their destination. It was a three-story '60s-style office building—read it as no style—located in a strip mall. Breck's office was above a fast-food sandwich shop, now closed, and next door to a Pilates studio, also shuttered. There was some illumination coming from behind the closed blinds. The door was locked: Decker rang the bell. Several footsteps could be heard before the door opened.

Breck was in his fifties: short and slight, white hair that held hints of blond. Pale blue eyes were focused behind spectacles and a flared nose sat on a round face. His smile was white and broad. He immediately asked for ID. Decker showed him his badge, and he and McAdams went inside a one-room office. Furnishings included three desks, each with a computer, a printer, and a landline phone, two walls of file cabinets, a copy machine and a fax machine, a small kitchen bar with a coffeepot, a water cooler and a fridge, and a very big cardboard box that held a junk pile of laptops, phones, and electronic tablets.

Breck saw McAdams staring at the electronics. "It's confiscated stuff. After a certain period of time, we can erase the drives and reuse them or just donate them to the local schools. Sit wherever you'd like. I've already pulled the file and made each of you a copy. So you found the body in Greenbury?"

"In a hiking area called Bogat," Decker answered.

"I always wondered if Pettigrew had gone back to Greenbury. From what I gathered, he seemed attached to the school."

McAdams pulled up a folding chair. "In what way?"

"Everyone I interviewed said he seemed happy there. It was at Morse McKinley where he really figured out who he was. Or who she was. It's all in the file."

"How many people did you interview?" Decker asked.

"The list is pretty long because he had acquaintances from a lot of different groups—his friends in high school, his college buddies, and people from the gay and transgender community. He had a lot of alternative friends. You've got to be comfortable talking to those guys. If not, you'll never get anything out of them."

"It's not a problem," Decker said.

Breck faced McAdams. "You'd probably have better luck. No offense, but you're less threatening than your partner."

"No problem for me," McAdams said. "I had two gay roommates in my suite. I was always running interference between them. They tolerated me, but they hated each other."

Breck managed a small smile. "Exactly. They are as different as you and me. I do a lot of PI work for the LGBT community. When Lawrence Pettigrew became a missing person, Fred from Staten Island

PD recommended me to the family. From the start, I had a feeling it wasn't going to end well."

"Why's that?" Decker said.

"Lawrence . . . Lorraine . . . from what I gathered seemed well adjusted to her new persona. For one thing, she had a husband."

"She was married?" Decker took out a notebook.

McAdams said, "Was it even legal for gay people to be married when he disappeared?"

"Definitely, but it wouldn't have affected them anyway. Pettigrew was married as a man to a woman who was in the process of sexual reassignment; he was named Karl—née Karen. The last name was Osterfeld. But I think Lorraine and Karl kept their own surnames."

"Okay," Decker said. "So they were married as a man and a woman, but they were both in the process of getting surgery."

"It's not as uncommon as you might imagine. It's all in the file."

"What about Lawrence's mate as a suspect?"

"I don't think Karl had anything to do with it. He was very broken up by Pettigrew's disappearance."

Decker was paging through the file. "The address is in Manhattan."

"Chelsea."

Decker looked up. "Does he still live there?"

"Last I checked he did. Short, chubby guy. Pettigrew was tall and lanky. Odd couple. But then again who am I to talk. My wife is three inches taller than me. No great feat, but there you have it."

"If it isn't Pettigrew, I don't want to put the spouse through emotional trauma." Decker checked his watch. "But if the remains are Pettigrew's, I'll have to come back." He looked at Breck. "You have Lawrence's dental records on your computer?"

"I do."

"Could you please forward them to my police department captain? He can take them over to the morgue first thing tomorrow, and if he gets an initial match, we'll confirm with the original X-rays when I get back upstate."

McAdams said, "You want to stay in town for the night."

Decker said, "If that's okay with you."

"It's fine with me. You want to bunk out at Nina's house?"

McAdams's step-grandmother. She owned a huge co-op on Park. "I think Rina would rather stay with the kids even though it means sleeping on a pull-out couch or, even worse, an air mattress. She'd probably like to be there when Lily wakes up." He turned to Breck. "Our granddaughter."

"Don't have any of those. Don't even have any married children although that doesn't stop people from having kids these days. If there's nothing else, give me the e-mail of your station house computer and I'll send in the X-rays on file."

"I'd really appreciate it." Decker gave him Captain Mike Radar's e-mail address and then his card. "If you should think of anything else, please call."

Breck gave Decker his card. "Likewise."

"Thanks for your time. You've been very helpful, Mr. Breck."

"Jimmy."

"Pete," Decker said, pointing to himself.

"I'm Tyler." McAdams handed him his card. "But people don't usually call me Tyler."

"What do they usually call you?"

McAdams smiled. "People call me lots of things. Most of the names aren't fit for polite company."

"Helpful guy." Decker started up the motor.

McAdams shuffled through the pages. "Big file. My nighttime reading. Where are we going?"

"Let me give Rina a call."

"Do you want me to drive while you talk?"

"No, just hang on a sec. It'll be a quick conversation. Do you mind staying overnight?"

"I've got my toothbrush and jammies in Nina's co-op. What's the plan?"

"Interviewing in the city tomorrow. I'd like to get it done as long as we're here." Sammy picked up the phone. "Hey, son."

"Hi. How are you?"

"Fine. You sound tired."

"Not too bad. At least I'm not working as late as you are. Are you picking up Eema, now?"

"Actually I'd like to stay the night if that's possible."

"Of course it's possible. It's great. Eema will be happy. I'll pull out the couch. I've got an extra air mattress, too. You should be okay although your feet might stick out."

"I'm sure I'll be fine. Is Eema there?"

"Of course."

Rina got on the phone. "So we're spending the night?"

"Okay with you?"

"Do I really have to answer that? Where's Tyler staying?"

"At his grandmother's apartment in Manhattan."

"Nice place."

"It is. I might be there very late, Rina. I want to do some reading and it's easier for us to spread out at the co-op."

"Why don't you just spend the night there? A sofa mattress won't do your back any good."

"My back is fine. Besides, I want to see Lily."

"Peter, it isn't a social visit. You can see Lily when you come to pick me up tomorrow. Go get some rest. A sofa bed is fine for me. It's even fine for you if I'm not there. It's not good for the both of us."

"Are you sure it's okay?"

"Positive. This is the rule: you can sleep wherever you want, just not with whomever you want. You stick to that and we'll both be fine."

❧8

The next morning at nine, just as Decker got off his cell phone, McAdams walked into his step-grandmother Nina's eat-in kitchen—a caterer's space that held the most up-to-date appliances, rare wood cabinets, and countertops of concrete and stainless steel. Nina didn't cook but there was a housekeeper who made morning coffee and had set out china, silverware, and linen napkins. The table had fresh-squeezed juice, iced water, toast, croissants, pastries, and jam and butter.

"I see Esther has put out the spread."

"A lovely woman," Decker said.

"Nina only gets the best." McAdams poured himself coffee and nabbed a piece of wheat toast from the basket. He took a nibble on the dry bread. "What's up?"

"That was Mike Radar. We've got a tentative match."

"Really?"

"You sound surprised."

"Yeah, a little. We pull out this random set of bones from the ground. And by asking a few questions to the right people, we identify the remains. It just seemed like a long shot."

"It's called being a detective."

"Well, I can't argue with success. Poor Lawrence . . . Lorraine. Are we going back to Staten Island?"

"We'll tell Joanne Pettigrew today, but if Pettigrew was legally married, our first obligation is to the spouse."

"Who is usually the primary suspect."

"Yes. Keep that in mind."

"Are we sure they were legally married?"

"I thought of that as well. I'll check with records. Even if Pettigrew wasn't legally married to Osterfeld, I'll want to talk to her. See what she can tell me about the day Lawrence disappeared."

"Actually, Lawrence is the she and Osterfeld is the he."

"Yes. Right."

"Do we tell Osterfeld about the match?"

"We only have a preliminary match. I'd hate to tell Osterfeld and be wrong. I'll have to think about how I want to handle this. The most recent address I have is in Queens. Astoria. Not far from James Breck." Decker sipped his coffee. "Ready when you are."

"Just let me wolf down some breakfast."

"Take your time."

"Thanks." Tyler buttered his toast. "How many people on the list that Breck gave us?"

"About forty."

"How many will we need to reinterview?"

"We'll prioritize. First the closest to Pettigrew and then we'll fan out. Work with the usual questions, McAdams. Who has motive and opportunity? Who stands to gain by Pettigrew's death?"

"I'll check insurance." A pause. "If Pettigrew was

reported missing, there wouldn't be a payout right away. Don't you have to wait like seven years?"

"Yes. But there are other things to look at besides insurance payouts. For instance, did Pettigrew and Osterfeld have any joint accounts? Did they own any real estate? Were they in business together? Did they make investments that went south? Was either having an affair? Was there abuse?"

"Got it."

"I hope we find a suspect. If not, it's called a random killing and those stink. But it'll be my problem, not yours. You'll be back in law school."

"How likely is it that Pettigrew was a victim of a serial killer?"

"Why are you asking?"

"If the death was due to an altercation between friends or even a one-off hate crime because Lawrence was gay or transgender, do you bother to lug a body deep into the woods and bury it? Seems like the kind of thing that you might do if you've done it before."

"I see what you're saying. But right now we only have one body. Let's take it one measly step at a time. Otherwise, we'll both trip and fall."

It took a while to locate Karl née Karen Osterfeld's two-bedroom apartment. It was a few blocks past the Queensboro Bridge, on the seventh floor of a ten-story unadorned redbrick building. There was a small, slow, hot elevator that emptied them into a narrow, stuffy, but well-lit hallway. The unit was the last one on the right. Through the door, children could be heard running around.

Decker knocked and a feminine voice asked who it was, and after they identified themselves as the police, the door swung open. The woman was petite with short dark hair, green eyes, and delicate features. Her hands were tiny and kneading each other as she read their police badges. "What's going on?"

"I'm looking for Karl Osterfeld?"

"It's Karen Osterfeld. She's not here."

"Okay." There were noises in the background. Decker said, "Do you have a contact number for her?"

"And you want to talk to her because . . ."

"Can we come in?" Decker asked. "It's odd talking out here."

The woman hesitated, but then relented. Once they were in the apartment, she decided to be hospitable. "Would you like some coffee?"

"Water would be great," McAdams said.

"Times two." Decker's eyes followed a boy of around four and a toddler who wore nothing but a diaper as they ran constant circles around the couch. The boy didn't stop moving, but the toddler finally did. The little thing had short, curly blond hair. She stuck fingers in her mouth. Decker bent down—as close to eye to eye as he could get—and decided the toddler was most definitely a little girl. "Hey there. Aren't you very pretty?"

She stared, then gave him a drool-laced smile.

The woman came back in and Decker stood up. "What is she? Around eighteen months?"

"Right on the money." She handed him the water. "What's her name?"

"Birgitta. Say hello, Birgy."

The girl remained mute and rooted to her spot.

The woman gave McAdams a glass. "And this handsome guy is Aesop. I'm Jordeen Crayton." She looked at the kids. "Hey guys, let's do some quiet time. I'll put on a video."

"Power Rangers," Aesop said.

"How about Mickey Mouse?" Jordeen said.

Birgitta smiled and said, "Moss . . ."

"No, that's stupid!" the boy protested.

"Aesop, we don't talk like that. Let's go."

The two little kids disappeared with Jordeen, who returned five minutes later. "I have to get them a snack. Please." She pointed to the sofa and the men sat. "I'll be right back."

When she disappeared, McAdams whispered, "Karen to Karl to Karen?"

Decker shrugged.

McAdams said, "Maybe we're working with a love triangle?"

"It's as good a theory as any."

Jordeen came back into the living room and sat down. "Why are you looking for Karen?"

McAdams said, "We were told that she became Karl."

"She's been Karen for over two years. Is this in regard to Lorraine Pettigrew? I mean, why else would you be here and asking for Karen as Karl. Did you find her? Lorraine?"

"First, I'd like to ask you something, Jordeen," Decker said. "Were Karen as Karl and Lorraine ever legally married?"

"Not legally, no. They were going to get married,

but then Lorraine disappeared. But if it concerns Lorraine, it concerns Karen, and if it concerns Karen, it concerns me. We *are* legally married."

"Okay. As a woman to a woman."

"Yes, of course. Do you think I'm transgender?"

"No, ma'am," Decker said. "We were wondering about Karen. I heard she was planning to undergo sex reassignment surgery."

"Well, she didn't, and there you have it. Karen hasn't been Karl for over two years."

"How'd you two meet?" McAdams asked.

"Why does it matter?" She waited but no one said anything. "I was hired as a babysitter for Aesop. One thing led to another. We were married two years ago. It was love at first sight for me. It took a while for Karen. She was still mourning Lorraine."

Decker said, "Karen was Karl when you met her?"

Jordeen was peeved. "What does it matter?"

"I was wondering why she went back to being a woman if she was intent on marrying Lorraine as a man."

"You'd have to ask Karen."

"I will," Decker said. "But I'd like your opinion. We're all on the same side."

"Are we? You haven't even told me what side you're on."

"We all want to know what happened to Lorraine Pettigrew."

"You found her body, right?"

"We found remains, yes, ma'am."

She sighed. "Oh God. I've been dreading this day. Karen will be devastated. She loved Lorraine." Tears started falling. "Lorraine loved her. Aesop is his . . . hers . . . Lorraine's. Whatever. Karen got pregnant from him. Both of them had started transitioning when they met, but neither had completed it where it counts. And then they fell in love and wanted a baby together before it was impossible. They both stopped taking the hormones, of course. Luckily the pregnancy happened quickly. After it did, Lorraine went back on her hormones, but Karen didn't. She couldn't. Not while she was pregnant."

"Of course."

Jordeen said, "No one would call Karen feminine. But I think after the baby, she became comfortable in her biological skin. And then I came along. Of course, I knew she was gay because I was referred from a nanny organization that deals with gay, lesbian, and transgender people."

McAdams looked confused. "I don't mean to sound like an out-of-touch geek but there's a specific organization for gay nannies?"

"You don't know how much prejudice gay people face when raising children, even in New York City. It was just business at first. We were all about Aesop's well-being. But then we became emotionally close. Karen had confided in me that she was in the middle of transitioning. But then she decided she was more comfortable as a lesbian than as a man. Frankly, I didn't care what gender she was. Birgitta is my biological daughter. One of each. We thought that was fair. Karen's the primary breadwinner and I'm the primary caretaker."

"What does Karen do?" McAdams asked.

"She's in law school." McAdams rolled his eyes

and Jordeen caught it. "You have something against lawyers?"

"Me and a trillion other people." He smiled. "Relax. I'm also in law school."

"Oh. Do you go to night school?"

"Yes," McAdams lied.

"Do you like it?"

"Not really. But I don't hate it."

"That sums up Karen's opinion of the profession. She has to learn all these things she doesn't care about. She wants to work as an advocate for children of LGBTQ people."

Decker said, "Do Pettigrew's parents know they have a grandson?"

Jordeen sighed. "Karen didn't talk much about Joanne. After Lorraine disappeared, I believe Karen's main goal was moving forward. I don't know if she ever got around to telling her about Aesop."

McAdams said, "You don't *know* if Karen told her?"

"She hasn't told her," Jordeen admitted. "Karen wanted to hold off just in case Lorraine came back. And then time passed and then it became awkward, I guess." Jordeen lowered her head. "I'll talk to her . . . to Karen about it."

"We need to talk to her, Jordeen," Decker said.

"She won't be home until seven."

"We can catch her at school," Decker said. "I think she'd like to know about the latest developments."

"Of course she would. She goes to CUNY School of Law."

"Can I have her cell number so I can make arrangements to meet with her?"

"It might be best if I phone her. If she sees it's from me, she'll be more likely to answer."

"Go ahead and call her, but please let me talk."

Jordeen punched in the numbers and gave Decker the phone. The conversation was two minutes during which Decker told Karen about the remains. Afterward, he said to Jordeen, "We're meeting in a half hour. I think that's about it for the moment. I know this must be overwhelming for both of you. Thanks for your help."

"Did I help you?"

"You were honest and forthright so the answer is yes."

Jordeen gave them a small smile that didn't last long. "About Aesop. Do you think the Pettigrews would want to know about him?"

"As a grandparent, I would really want to know about the grandchild of my deceased son or daughter. It's the moral thing to do, Jordeen."

"I agree." Again tears moistened her eyes. "How can Karen advocate for children if we deny grandparents the right to see their grandchild?" She stood up. "I'll walk you out." She opened the door and paused. "I'm not trying to be selfish but I am concerned about Joanne Pettigrew causing trouble: saying that we're not fit to raise our son and things like that."

"I can't guarantee anything, Jordeen," Decker said. "But when I spoke to her last night, I thought she was a very reasonable woman. I'm sure she'd work with you. Besides, I think whatever fight she had possessed left her a long time ago."

❧9

By the time they reached CUNY, it was almost noon and the day had become warm and humid. Decker was suffering in a suit and tie. Karen had asked to meet them at a nearby sandwich café that lacked air-conditioning and depended on a giant fan to make the inside tolerable. The place was overflowing with people. Besides a long line at the counter, all the tables were taken. Beyond ordering, there was very little conversation going on. The patrons, interchangeable in their shorts and T-shirts, were either reading or glued to electronic devices.

McAdams looked around. "That person in the corner table is guarding those two empty chairs like they hold the secret of the ancients. She has a short haircut, no makeup, and no jewelry except for a wedding ring. I think we've found our woman."

Decker loosened his tie. "Let's go."

"Why do you dress like that when it's boiling outside?"

"Like what? You're wearing a jacket."

"With a black T-shirt underneath. Not a long-sleeved shirt and a tie."

"This is my professional uniform. People talk to

me easier if I'm in a suit. That's what they see on TV and that's what they've learned to expect. Shall we go? The woman at the table is eyeing me, probably because I'm old and dressed in a suit and tie."

"Yeah, you don't exactly blend in."

"Astute of you to notice." He walked up to the table. "Karen Osterfeld?"

She nodded and the men sat down. Karen's expression was somber: intense dark eyes capped by thick brows. There were wisps of facial hair over her lip, but her complexion was smooth. She was dressed in a white T-shirt and red board shorts showing considerable downy arm and leg hair. Her feet were shod in sandals.

"I'm Detective Decker, and this is Detective McAdams. Thank you for speaking to us."

"You found remains."

Decker nodded gravely. "The bones have been tentatively identified as Lawrence or Lorraine Pettigrew."

"Call her whatever you want. I knew her as Lawrence as well as Lorraine. I've been expecting this day for a while. Where did you find the bones?"

"They were off a hiking trail north of Greenbury."

"Which one?"

"Bogat Trail."

"I don't know it, and I knew most of the trails up there."

Decker said, "You went to Morse McKinley?"

"Clarion. I was a year ahead of Lorraine in school. Back then we weren't romantically involved. We met again down here—same circle of friends."

"Bogat was put in after you graduated," Decker said. "Karen, was Lorraine a hiker?"

"Not that I knew." A beat. "I remember that once I asked him—he was him back then—if he wanted to go hiking with me. I remember it was an easy trail and it was a beautiful autumn day. He gave me a resolute no. I can't imagine why he'd be in the woods voluntarily."

"When Lorraine disappeared, did you two still have friends in the area?"

"Not so much for me. When she vanished, I'd been out of school for a while. I knew maybe a couple of teachers. No one close."

"What about Lorraine?"

"She had some connection up there. The day she left to go up north, she told me she was visiting some friends. And that was the only thing she told me."

"No names?"

"No, and I didn't ask. As showy as she was, Lorraine could be very private. I didn't want to intrude into her personal space."

"By asking her who she was visiting?"

"If she had wanted me to know, she would have told me." Karen winced. "You've got to remember that I was pregnant. It was a rough first trimester. I was happy to be alone and I thought that Lorraine just needed some time to herself."

"How was her mood?" Decker asked.

"Like, did I detect something wrong?" Her eyes moistened. "Nothing that I saw. I certainly didn't expect her to vanish."

"Of course not," Decker said. "And you have no idea who her old friends were?"

"I knew she was still in contact with a few of her old professors via e-mail. She contacted them once she started working in finance."

"So she might have been visiting them?"

"Possibly." Karen blinked a couple of times. "After she disappeared, I combed through her e-mails to see if I could figure out where she went and who she was seeing. I know Joanne hired a private detective. I'm sure the PI talked to dozens of people. I know I did. You don't know how panicked I was. I was alone, I was pregnant, and I was very, very confused."

She looked at the tabletop as she spoke.

"When she didn't come back Sunday night *and* I couldn't contact her by phone, I started calling people that we knew in common. No one even knew she was going up to the colleges."

Tears started falling down her face.

"At the time, I thought she might have lied to me. That she was having second thoughts about the baby. That she was having second thoughts about me. That she found someone else. I was half mad at her as well as half panicked. When I called her work on Monday and she hadn't shown up, I was beside myself."

"What did you do when you couldn't locate her?"

"I frankly don't remember too much because I was in such a state. I did call the Greenbury Police. They wouldn't take a report right away. Since no one remembered seeing Lorraine, they claimed it was doubtful that she made it up north. They were claiming that she probably disappeared in the city. After a while, I began to believe that she really did cut bait and run."

"Did you contact Pettigrew's parents?"

Karen sighed. "No. Lorraine didn't want her parents to know about the pregnancy. She wanted to wait until after the baby was born."

"Whose idea was the pregnancy?" McAdams asked.

"It was hers. That's why I couldn't figure out why she disappeared. She wanted a baby way more than I did. But I loved Lorraine, and she wanted to be a mom of her own biological child. So we decided to do it before we finished off our sex reassignment surgeries. I'd already had top surgery, so I knew I couldn't nurse, but that was fine with Lorraine. She wanted to be the primary caretaker."

There was a long pause.

"I never transitioned completely. After I had the baby, it didn't seem important. Gender is fluid, and I am who I am. I don't need gonads to tie me down."

Decker nodded. "Karen, you said you called people when Lorraine didn't come home."

"Yes."

"Do you still have any record of who you called?"

"Of course. I made a list. I have a whole file on her."

McAdams asked, "Who's in the file?"

"People *I* called. As much as I could, I tried to get hold of her phone records or her e-mail because without a body, she still could be alive. I just couldn't believe that Lorraine would take off on me. I kept thinking there had to be a reason. I didn't want to think bad of her."

"We'll subpoena the records. In the meantime, could I take a look at the file?"

"Sure. It's at home." Karen put her head down. "You might also want to talk to Joanne Pettigrew . . . like that never crossed your mind. I suppose you already talked to her."

"Yesterday," McAdams said. "Before we got tentative confirmation of the remains. We're going to her house after we've finished talking to you."

"Joanne still doesn't know about Aesop."

"We know. Jordeen mentioned that you never told her about her grandson."

Karen sighed.

"At first, I didn't tell Joanne because I felt I was sort of honoring Lorraine's last wishes. And I was dealing with so much. I really didn't want to have a pity party with Joanne. I know that sounds callous, but there was only so much grief I could take." A long silence. "You can tell her."

"It might be better coming from you," Decker said.

"I was afraid you'd say that." A sigh. "Yeah, you're right. I'll man up and call her."

"Wait a few minutes until we call and tell her that the remains have been identified."

"When are you going to do that?"

"Right now." Decker stood up. "I'll be back in a moment. You can talk to Detective McAdams."

"About what?" Karen asked. But Decker had left the café. "Strange one, your boss."

McAdams thought: *Pot . . . kettle.* "How did you and Lorraine fall in love?"

"When I came back from top surgery, Lawrence—he was still a he back then—he told me he admired my commitment to who I was. We started talking about sex reassignment, what it would mean to us, to our families and friends. We had long, long talks about it. When we met again in New York City, he told me that I had inspired him to take the plunge and undergo sex reassignment surgery. We talked some more and we fell in love. We made love. You know, just because you identify as the other gender doesn't mean that your biological gonads don't function. He was dressed as a woman and I was the man with my top surgery, but we were still technically boy and girl. What a world, huh?"

McAdams nodded, but remained silent.

"We were both going to get surgery that summer. But then Lorraine got it in her head to have a baby. What could I do?"

Decker came back. "I told Joanne that we'd be there in an hour." Silence. To Karen: "This might be as good a time as any to make contact with her."

Karen looked at her watch. "I've got class in ten minutes." When Decker didn't answer, she said, "I suppose I should get it over with. I named my son Aesop because those were Lorraine's favorite stories. Believe it or not, she loved morality pieces. They provided absolutes in our ambiguous world. Are we done here?"

"Yes," Decker said. "When can I get your Pettigrew file?"

"Come to my place around eight. By then the kids are asleep and if we need to talk at greater length, I can concentrate on you instead of the children." She looked at her watch again and stood up. "I gotta get this call over with. I'll see you tonight."

After she left, Decker said, "What did you two talk about?"

"How they fell in love and wanted to marry: she as a boy and he as a girl. I know that none of this is relevant, but even she admitted it was a strange world."

"It is a strange world. But as a detective I don't care about those things. All I care about is who put Pettigrew in the ground."

It had been an emotional day with tears coming in all directions. There was one positive upshot. As he and McAdams were talking to Joanne, Karen and Jordeen dropped by with Aesop and Birgitta. That's when the waterworks became unstoppable. It was a good time to make an exit and leave the newly formed family in peace.

After dealing with Joanne, they went back to Manhattan. Decker went to the local Staples and made two copies of Karen's files, which she had brought to Joanne's. By the time he was done, it was close to six in the evening. He walked back to the Park Avenue apartment. The door was open when he knocked.

McAdams was stretched out on a rose-colored silk brocade sofa in his pajamas. He had his nose in a book. "Wassup?"

"Good book?"

"A course book." He put it down. "One year down, two to go." He shrugged. "What's our next step?"

"I'm going to Brooklyn for dinner."

"Have fun."

"You're not coming?"

"I didn't know I was invited."

"Don't be ridiculous. Of course, you're invited. I'd like to make it to Brooklyn within the hour so you might want to change."

"Funny ha-ha. Where are we going for dinner?"

"Does it matter?"

"How should I dress, Old Man?"

"In street clothes would be a start. Rina made supper so we're eating in. Dress lightly. Sammy and Rachel have very poor AC."

"So why don't we go out?"

"They couldn't find a babysitter."

"So why not just take the kid?"

"I don't make the decisions, Tyler, I just follow orders. When you've been married as long as I have, you just show up and smile. Rina invited you. Do you want to come or not?"

"Yes, I'll come. Jeez."

"By the way . . ." Decker plopped down a box onto the floor. "Your copy of the files. We can go over them tonight after dinner."

"Where? Here?"

"I'd like to stay here for one more day. There are people on the list who live in New York. Might as well question them while I'm here. And I have to return all the original files to Breck and to Karen now that we have copies."

"What about the Staten Island police? Do you think we should talk to them since Joanne filed a report with them?"

"We should give them a courtesy call and help

them clear their missing persons file. But since Pettigrew was murdered in Greenbury, they don't have anything to do with the case."

McAdams stood up and hefted the box. "We've got a lot of reading to do."

"And it's only going to grow once we get the e-mails and the phone records. Get dressed already."

"Patience, man. I know you're starved, but I'm not the cause of your low blood sugar."

"I know you're not the problem. But, at present, you're the only scapegoat I have. Put some clothes on and let's get out of here."

Tyler had retired an hour ago, but at two in the morning, Decker was wide awake. By three, he finally crawled under soft down covers. It had been a good night. Gathering all the files and cross-referencing proved to be beneficial. He had put almost all the names listed into four categories: Pettigrew's relatives, his closest friends, his work people, and his old friends from his Greenbury days, this last category being the smallest but the most important because Pettigrew was murdered there. As for the others, he had narrowed the New York City field down to four people he still wanted to interview:

1. Harold Cantrell: Pettigrew's boss for two years at a place called the McGregor Fund.
2. Marta Kerr, aged thirty: described by PI James Breck and Karen Osterfeld as a close friend of Pettigrew. He had even stayed with her for a couple of months. Her address was

in Chelsea and there was an associated phone number.

3. Darwin Davis, aged twenty-five: a friend of Pettigrew from his Morse McKinley days. They reconnected once Davis graduated and moved to the city.

4. Dr. Elwood Marshall (aged, well, who really cares?): Pettigrew's surgeon and doctor, who specialized in sex reassignment surgery. He had been working with Pettigrew since he was twenty up until his disappearance five years ago.

Decker would make the calls first thing in the morning. He was thinking about how he'd arrange his day when he drifted off and lost himself in a world he wouldn't remember in the morning.

❧10

The medical practice was in the East Village, near Washington Square and in a maisonette that fronted a six-story residential brick building. Dr. Elwood Marshall specialized in cosmetic and reconstruction surgery, and judging by the amount of people in the waiting room, he did well. All the couches and chairs were taken, and there was a small line at the reception window. Decker waited his turn and it took almost eight minutes before he faced a heavily made-up receptionist wearing a brunette wig of long waves. A pretty woman in that extreme way, except the voice told another story. It was beyond throaty: it was deep as in a well-developed Adam's apple. The name tag said Eloise.

"Can I help you?"

Decker discreetly took out his official ID. "We have an appointment with Dr. Marshall."

"We?"

Decker looked around until he spotted McAdams leafing through the magazine entitled *Gay Today*. If he could have beaned the kid from across the room, he would have done it. He looked back at Eloise, the receptionist. "My detective seems to have found some interesting reading material."

"People have all sorts of interesting facets to their personality." Her smile was a smirk. "I'll tell the doctor you're here. It may take a few minutes. We're swamped today."

Decker thanked her and the glass partition slid closed in front of him. He walked over to McAdams and elbowed him hard. He whispered, "Learning something?"

"There are some real hot-looking dudes in this magazine." He put it down on the table. "If I were gay, I wouldn't stand a chance. Lucky for me that women just aren't that picky."

Decker stifled a laugh. "Try to concentrate on the investigation, Tyler. It's what you're being paid to do."

"You mean that paltry sum that's handed to me twice a month?"

"You were the one who turned down those cushy, well-paid internships." Decker heard someone call his name. "That's us. C'mon, Harvard. Let's go find some answers."

They were escorted into an office that looked out on a small back garden. The sun had ducked behind clouds, leaving the foliage to grow in gray, sooty light. The air-conditioning was running full blast. The nurse was tall with long thin hands. He said, "The doctor will be with you as soon as he can. Have a seat."

There were two wooden chairs and one plush leather desk chair separated by a large, rosewood desk holding one pile of paperwork, a bamboo file

organizer, a cup of pens, a stapler, and a large phone
that had many blinking lines. The walls were covered with diplomas and certifications. Ten minutes
after the detectives were seated, a white-coated man
in his mid to late fifties flew in like a rogue gust of
wind. He was medium in stature with a paunch that
lay over a Gucci belt. He had a long face with wiry,
silver hair and eyes somewhere between tawny and
brown. He sat down at his desk chair and extended
his hand to both detectives. "How can I help?"

"As I told your receptionist over the phone, it has
to do with a case we're working on involving one of
your former patients."

"And I suppose you know that even if we're dealing with former patients, there is confidentiality.
Who are we talking about? My receptionist didn't
say."

Decker said, "We found some remains up north
in Greenbury near the Five Colleges of Upstate.
We have a tentative match to Lawrence Pettigrew.
Lorraine Pettigrew."

Marshall sat back in his chair, a pained look on
his face. "That's awful." He regarded Decker. "Because the police are involved . . . was it murder?"

"Yes."

"How?"

"The developments are recent, but the murder
was not. He has been dead for quite some time. Anything you can tell me about him would be helpful."

"Like what?"

"Did he confide in you on personal matters, for
instance?"

"They all confide in me on personal matters.

When people come to me, they are very confused and very emotional. I'm just as much therapist as I am surgeon."

"What about Pettigrew?"

"He was no exception."

"Anything specific that you can tell me?"

Marshall picked up the phone. "Donnie, can you get me Lawrence/Lorraine Pettigrew's file, please?" After he hung up the receiver, he said, "It's been a while. From what I recall, he was very gung-ho on having surgery. When I first see them, they usually are. I always go slowly. Any change, be it a nose job or breast implants, takes getting used to. Let alone something as drastic as sex reassignment surgery. I start with the face. We did some skin sanding, some hair removal. He did well with those procedures, so we took the next step."

"Which was?"

"Hormonal therapy." A moment later, Donnie came in with the file and then left. Marshall began to skim through it.

"Yes, I put him on a low dose of the appropriate hormones needed to override the androgens. That's when the problems started. He didn't like how it made him feel. He said . . . this is what I wrote down . . . it made him feel on edge and moody."

"PMS," McAdams said.

"Yes, it does mimic some symptoms in some people. But with time, most transgender people adjust to it. Lawrence not only disliked how it made him feel, he also didn't like the changes in his body."

"Meaning?"

"He liked losing his body hair, but he didn't like having actual breasts although he had been dressing with prosthetics for two years. He loved the way he looked in women's clothing. But he didn't like looking at his naked body." Marshall looked at the chart. "He said he didn't feel beautiful as a man or a woman, just some kind of weird chimera. Now, adjustment can take months. But he didn't seem to want to adjust. So we began to talk about alternatives."

"Which are?"

"His problem was not that unusual. There are many men who feel as he did. They consider themselves women in men's bodies. They are attracted to men. But they don't want to do the last, fateful step because they can't adjust to their bodies as women."

"Okay," Decker said. "I talked to a few of Pettigrew's friends. Karen Osterfeld and her current partner, Jordeen Crayton. I believe that Pettigrew intended to marry Karen Osterfeld, who was Karl Osterfeld back then."

Marshall said nothing.

"Do you know anything about that?"

"If I did, I wouldn't say. Karen Osterfeld is still very much alive."

"And she's your patient?"

"You know I can't say anything."

"How about if she gave you permission to talk to me?"

Marshall said, "Has she?"

"I haven't asked her."

"So then there's nothing to talk about." Marshall

stood up. "I hope I've been helpful. I have examination rooms filled with patients. I really must get on with them."

Decker said. "I have one more question. Since Lawrence didn't adjust to his womanly body, I assume that sex reassignment surgery was off the table."

"Yes, of course. It was not appropriate for him. He kept on with hormones but at an even lower dose. And he wanted to continue with cosmetic dermabrasion and laser hair removal. I didn't have a problem with that."

"Did he do those procedures here?"

"Yes."

"And he was still your patient up until he disappeared?"

"Yes. As I recall, we found out about his disappearance because he didn't show to one of his appointments. Pettigrew was usually reliable."

"His disappearance must have come as a shock to you."

"It was disturbing, yes. But your news is not just disturbing, it's awful." Marshall was silent for a moment. "My patients are often not socially acceptable to their families. The rejection causes them to seek other means of support—a community that understands them in the best of all worlds. But sometimes they seek solace in bad habits—crazy partying, alcohol, drugs, and promiscuous sex. That kind of edgy lifestyle often gets them into deep trouble."

Getting a caffeine fix in the city was as easy as walking down the block. Small cafés, stores, and take-out markets abounded. The detectives had a little over an hour before their appointment with Harold Cantrell, Pettigrew's manager at McGregor in Midtown near the UN Plaza.

McAdams sipped iced tea. "We've got two Pettigrews: the conventional Lorraine and the in-your-face Lawrence."

"But both of them were very smart."

"I'm not denying the intelligence. I'm thinking maybe the conventional Lorraine went up to Morse McKinley to have one last fling as Lawrence. He certainly wasn't forthcoming to Karen about what he was doing up there."

"True."

"If the murder happened up there, shouldn't we be concentrating on his last days in Greenbury?"

"We're down here now. We might as well get whatever background we can before we go back up. It's not like the usual case where time matters. We can be deliberate."

McAdams said, "What do you think of Pettigrew's rejection of sex reassignment surgery?"

"In terms of what?"

"Karen, who was Karl back then, thought she was marrying a woman. Maybe she was angry that Pettigrew refused to go through with the surgery?"

"But she herself didn't go through with the surgery. They obviously came to some kind of understanding. They were having a baby together." Decker finished his iced coffee. "I mean, what are you thinking? That Karen and Pettigrew got into an altercation and she killed him, dragging his body back up to Greenbury?"

"Maybe she tailed him to Greenbury and caught him in a compromising position. The coroner thinks that Pettigrew was hit from behind by someone shorter than him. Karen is definitely shorter than Pettigrew."

"I don't see a pregnant woman lugging around a six-foot-plus body and burying it deep in the woods."

"Maybe she had help. Maybe Jordeen isn't as innocent as she makes herself out to be. Isn't it you who told me to look at the spouse first?"

Decker didn't answer right away. "Sure. It could be Karen. Maybe they did fight. Accidents happen."

"Especially if Pettigrew was living a double life."

"Sure, why not?"

"I hate when you're noncommittal."

"Tyler, I'm not being deliberately vague. I just don't know what's going on. But keep the hypotheses coming. It gets my senile brain working." Decker checked his watch. It was half past noon and their appointment was at one-fifteen. He put a twenty on the table. "If we leave now, we can walk it easily. Let's go."

"Want to Uber? It's like ninety degrees outside."

"I'm the one in the suit."

"All the more reason why we shouldn't walk. You're going to sweat and then go into an air-conditioned office and you'll catch a cold."

"I'll take my jacket off when I walk. That way, when I put my jacket back on, I'll be comfortable in an air-conditioned building. C'mon. I need some exercise."

"Don't blame me if you collapse from heat prostration."

"I won't. Besides, you know CPR." When McAdams didn't answer, Decker said, "You did finally take the course, right?"

"I signed up."

Decker exhaled and walked out of the café. McAdams had to hotfoot it to keep up with him. "Honest Abe, I really meant to do it. The time got away from me."

"What's the matter with you, McAdams? I understand taking shortcuts but not when lives depend on it."

"Mea culpa. I am truly humbled. I promise I'll take a course once I get settled in school."

"Not good enough. There's a life-size doll at the firehouse in Greenbury. As soon as we get back, I'm giving you a few lessons. It won't be official. You'll still have to be certified. But it'll give you a jump start."

"Are you kidding me?" McAdams protested. "Do you know how many germs have settled in that orifice? C'mon!"

"No excuses, McAdams. End of discussion."

"Fine." McAdams rolled his eyes. "Anything else?"

"That's sir to you."

"Anything else, *sir*?"

"Yes, there is, McAdams. Because you were derelict in your duties as a sworn officer of the law, you can carry my jacket."

UN Plaza was a gleaming skyscraper set in blocks of open space. It was fronted with hedges and concrete barrels and poles with flapping banners depicting its member countries. From Harold Cantrell's office at the McGregor Fund, Decker could see people gathering in orderly queues, waiting for a tour.

The only chair in the office was behind the desk. Five minutes later, a kid—probably an intern—came in with two folding seats. It seems that Mr. Cantrell was called away to an emergency meeting but should be back shortly.

Shortly was almost a half hour. Cantrell was a slight, thin man in his thirties with a cue-ball head and algae-green eyes. He sat down and shook his head.

"I'm sorry about Lorraine." He took out a handkerchief and wiped his sweaty forehead. "I've been having a bad day, but I suppose a death puts things in perspective. You're from Greenbury so I'm assuming she was found there."

"She was."

"Was she murdered?"

"Unofficially, yes."

"So what are you doing here?"

"Talking to people who knew her. Trying to recreate her life just before it happened."

"When did it happen?"

"Probably right after she disappeared."

"So around five years ago."

"Yes. I'd like to ask you what you remember about her disappearance."

"Wow. It was a while ago but you don't forget things like that. From my standpoint, I didn't even know she was missing until she didn't show up on Monday. When she didn't call in sick, I called her, but it went straight to voice mail. About an hour later, her boyfriend called asking if Lorraine was at work. That's when we both knew something had happened. I continued to call her boyfriend after that, just to see if there was anything new. After a while . . ."

He threw up his hands.

"Life goes on." Cantrell shook his head again.

McAdams said, "You were her boss?"

"Yes. Lorraine was hired as a junior analyst. She was on probation as any new employee would be. She was doing a good job. She had potential. It was really sad."

"Did you hire her?"

"I was one of the people who interviewed her. She had several rounds of interviews. Everyone was keen on her. She was a smart person and a hard worker. It's just a shame."

Decker said, "Did she have any problems with any of her coworkers?"

His nostrils flared. "Why would she have *problems* with coworkers?"

"It's what you ask when you're dealing with murder victims."

"Oh. Not that I know of."

"She was transgender," Decker said. "Anyone have problems with that?"

Cantrell suppressed a laugh. "I can see you don't know much about McGregor."

"Enlighten me, Mr. Cantrell."

"Our investments are socially conscious. We make it a point to be diverse, and as a result, the company appeals to a lot of people who live alternative lifestyles."

"Just because two people are gay doesn't mean

they get along," Decker said. "How did she get along with her coworkers?"

"As far as I know, she fit in fine. I don't know anyone who had a problem with her. She didn't work here all that long. And she wasn't in publicity or human resources. She mostly sat at her desk and analyzed stocks."

"Did she have a specialty?" McAdams asked.

"Not a sector, no. We hired her to work with institutional endowments. A lot of schools have considerable funds but they're not big enough to hire their own full-time analysts. We have a number of institutions as clients. That's what attracted Lorraine to our company. She loved working with schools and colleges."

Decker was writing furiously in his notebook. "Lorraine went to Morse McKinley up north in Greenbury."

"Yes, I know. She didn't finish because she was supposed to undergo sex reassignment surgery. She told us everything."

"She told her partner that she was going up to Morse McKinley the weekend she disappeared," Decker said. "We know she made it up there, but we don't know why she went in the first place. By any chance, would it have something to do with the firm?"

"No." Cantrell was puzzled. "Why would it have something to do with us?"

"Perhaps someone sent her up there to raise awareness of your investment strategy?"

"I was her boss and I certainly didn't do that. Her job was analysis, not finding new clients."

"But if she knew someone up north, maybe she

went there with the specific goal to recruit new clients."

"I would never ask her to do something like that. And I couldn't imagine anyone else asking her to do it."

"Maybe she was trying to show initiative," McAdams said.

"This is all speculation on something that happened years ago."

"I realize that," Decker said. "But because it happened so long ago, speculation is a part of the investigation."

"I can appreciate your position, but unfortunately, I have nothing to add." Cantrell checked his watch. "Anything else?"

Decker stood up and closed his notebook. "Thank you for your time. If I have anything else to ask you, where can I reach you easily?"

"Here's my card." Cantrell scribbled on it. "My cell is on the back. It's terrible what happened to her. I hope you find out who did it."

McAdams took the card. "Thank you."

Decker gave Cantrell his card. "And please let me know if you hear of anything."

"Why would I hear of anything?"

"This has turned into a murder investigation, Mr. Cantrell. Like the police, people speculate. And sometimes they even know what they're talking about."

It was a little past two when they left. Clouds that looked like balls of Brillo pads had materialized, blocking out the sun but keeping in the heat,

making the city swelter. Decker felt like a walking
water balloon.

McAdams pulled out his phone and pressed the
Uber app. "Two-minute ETA. You can come or
not, but I'm not walking."

"This time you win. It's hot."

They both stood under a dry cleaner's awning.
McAdams said, "I remember going back to school
when I was very little dressed in a jacket and tie.
When I finally went to boarding school, I was happy
about the fact that New Hampshire was quite a bit
cooler than New York in September. Of course,
once the winter hit, I would have killed to get back
into the city. Even if Manhattan was just as cold as
New Hampshire—which it rarely was—you see a
great deal more of the sun." He looked at the over-
cast sky. "Believe it or not."

A car pulled up.

"Our ride, boss."

The men hopped in the air-conditioned car and
sped off to Park Avenue. An hour later, both men
had showered, changed, and were ravenous. Neither
had had much beyond coffee, and it was after three.
Decker picked up his cell and there were three
missed calls from the station house within twenty
minutes.

McAdams came in the room rubbing a towel over
his curly, wet hair.

Decker said, "Did you get missed calls from
Greenbury?"

The kid checked his phone. "Two. Want me to
see what's up?"

"I'll call. If they're calling both of us, it's important." He connected to the police line. "This is Detective Decker."

"Oh, hi, Detective, hold on." Immediately the line went into idle mode.

"What's going on?" Tyler asked.

Decker shrugged. Captain Mike Radar came on the line. "Are you still in New York?"

"Yes."

"Is the kid with you?"

"The kid is with me."

"Put your phone on speaker."

"This doesn't sound good." Decker pressed the speakerphone button. "What's up?"

"We found another grave. Same area as Pettigrew—guesstimate is around a hundred to two hundred yards away."

Decker raked his fingers through his wet hair. "When did this happen?"

"The murder? I have no idea."

"When did you find the remains?"

"Oh, right. About an hour ago. I think you're right. We'll need the dogs."

"We'll pack up and leave as soon as possible." He checked his watch. "We'll try to make it back before seven. We should still have some daylight."

"Enough for you to see the remains."

"By remains, do you mean another skeleton?"

"Yes."

"Male or female?"

"We haven't gotten to the pelvic area yet, just the human skull. We've got some hair but far less and it looks to be shorter than Pettigrew's hair."

"What color?"

"Brown. We also found a watch and more than one earring this time. We found seven. Mostly studs and cuffs."

"Multiple ear piercings. What about nose or tongue piercings?"

"There's no soft tissue. Maybe there's a little cartilage so there could be a pierce through it. No tongue, but there might be a stud inside the jaws. The coroner just got here. It would be good to have you here before we dig up any more graves."

"Good Lord, I hope not."

"Decker, we've got two bodies interred close to each other. I'm no big-city expert, but what are the odds that this is a coincidence?"

"It's no coincidence."

"Any thoughts?"

"A lot but they're a little jumbled right now."

"Well, unjumble them. It's not like I can go on Amazon and pick up a copy of *Serial Killers for Dummies*."

"I'll keep that in mind, Mike." Decker cut the line.

"That would make for interesting reading," McAdams said. "What can you tell me about serial killers in . . ." The kid checked his watch. "In ten minutes."

Decker was about to brush him off, but the question made him think.

"They're rare, and despite what you've been told by TV and movies, they don't fall into neat categories. Some are smart—or organized as the FBI likes to say. Some are dumb and disorganized. Some are organized sometimes, and disorganized at other times. There are those who kill within race, but others don't give a damn about the color of the skin. Some have a definite type, for others any type will do. Some stalk, but some don't. Some are loners, but others have families—wives and kids.

"Almost all of them are opportunistic. If it's easy and convenient and they're in the mood, they'll hit. Most of them—if they have a car—spend lots of time driving around at night, looking for prey. Some have long-distance driving jobs that make looking for prey easy—like truckers or house movers. Some have transient jobs like short-order cooks and work temporary construction crews. But others hold down regular day jobs and prowl around after the wife and kids go to sleep. They clock lots of miles on their cars. It's not only their transportation, it's their place of operation.

"That's the who and the how. As to the why? Your guess is as good as mine. They kill for sexual satisfaction, they kill because it gives them a physical charge that's exciting, they kill because they're warped, they kill because they get their jollies playing cat and mouse with the police, the press, and the public. In other words, they kill because they can."

McAdams said, "That's the last time I ask you a question."

Decker checked his watch. "I still have six minutes to go."

"Is there anything else you'd like to add?"

"Yes, there is as a matter of fact. Maybe it is a serial killer—but right now, let's not get fixated on that idea. It could be just what you said before: that

Karen went up north and found Pettigrew and the Doe we just unearthed were involved in a tryst."

"A love triangle."

"Possibly. It also could be that Pettigrew and Doe were murdered at the same time—not sequentially."

"Okay. Sure. Fair enough. And what if we find other bodies?"

"You're really into this being a serial killer."

"I'm just asking a question, Old Man."

"If we find other bodies, then I'll revise my thinking accordingly."

❦11

After dropping off Rina, Decker and McAdams headed for the crime scene. They arrived at Bogat just as the sun was sinking behind the horizon. It was cooler in the forest than in town, even cooler than a couple of days ago when they had discovered Pettigrew's body. The foliage was starting to turn— small peeks of gold and rust. The sky had burst into purples and pinks, and a cricket or two started in song as twilight emerged. Nightfall would hit soon and the woods would become lines and shadows.

Under the tent was a whirl of activity with police and coroner officials. There was a picnic table covered in white cloth. Atop were unearthed bones, tufts of hair, clothing fragments, and a few personal effects—jewelry and something that looked like leather—maybe a purse or a wallet. Two arc lamps attached to battery packs provided high-intensity illumination. Ben Roiters was watching the action from ringside. The man still had a head of hair— most of it dark—even though he had passed the six-zero mark a few years ago. He was stoop shouldered with a paunch and alert, dark eyes. He had been a seasoned detective in his heyday but had worked for

Greenbury for the last ten years. Decker motioned him outside the tent.

Roiters said, "This is unbelievable. What're the odds that you have two bodies in such close proximity that are not related?"

Decker shook his head. "Zero."

"So what is it? A gang fight in the woods gone wrong? A satanic ritual? A serial killer?"

"My vote is on C," McAdams said.

Decker turned to him. "Okay, Tyler. Defend your choice."

McAdams shrugged. "I don't know who the other body is, but there are no indications that Pettigrew was a hard-core gangbanger."

"What about a satanic ritual?" Decker asked.

"Pettigrew was smacked in the head. If it was satanic, I'd expect to see more knife action in a ritual sacrifice: cut marks on his bones and things like that."

Roiters said, "I agree with the kid, Pete. As soon as we found a second body, I thought of a serial killer."

"Could be a one-off where the killer whacked two people at the same time," Decker said.

"Coroner thinks the bodies weren't buried at the same time. So a serial killing makes more sense."

Decker said, "Then it's someone who kills men and women."

McAdams said, "Pettigrew had been consistently dressing as a woman when he came back to Greenbury."

"Yeah, I know," Decker turned to Roiters. "When was the Bogat hiking trail put in?"

"I don't have a clue. I'm the quintessential couch potato."

McAdams was already on his iPhone. "I can't get reception. What are you thinking? That it doesn't make sense to bury two bodies so close to a public trail?"

"Yep. I'm thinking the bodies were interred before the trail went public. Karen Osterfeld doesn't remember Bogat when she was here around seven years ago. And it had just opened up when I came on the scene, after Delilah Occum's disappearance."

"Do you think there are more bodies out there?" McAdams stowed his phone.

"Possibly." Decker blew out air. "Radar's getting some dogs so we can cover a much bigger area." He raised his eyebrows. "When are you going back to school?"

"Classes start in a week. But that doesn't mean I have to show up right away."

"Let's see what we accomplish in a week." He turned to Roiters. "You can direct the digging out here?"

"Not a problem. What kind of radius are we talking about?"

"Let's draw a five-hundred-yard radius. Even before the dogs, we can hunt visually for unnatural depressions in the ground."

"I'll mark it off in the morning," Roiters told him.

"That's fine. Whoever is out there will keep." Decker returned his attention to the activities inside the tent. He went inside where the coroner was shaping the remains into skeleton precision. To

Decker, he said, "These bones are in worse shape than Pettigrew's."

"Male or female?"

"Female and young judging by the teeth."

"How young?"

"Molars are barely in. Once I X-ray the jaw, I'll get a better idea."

"Young as in young girl or young adult woman."

"Not a child . . . probably late teens. Are you looking for anyone specific?"

"Two females disappeared within a few years of Pettigrew. Delilah Occum went missing about a little more than three years ago. She was a Clarion student. Then there's Yvette Jones who vanished seven years ago. She went to school at Morse McKinley, which happens to be the same school that Lawrence Pettigrew attended."

"Is that the sum total of your missing persons list?"

"No, there are a few women within a hundred-mile radius. Not as young as late teens, though. I've got people hunting down those dental records while I do Occum and Jones. If we could exclude either from our list, it may rule out a school connection."

The coroner nodded. "Bring in as many radiographs as you can. Once I have those, science can do the rest."

Eliminating Occum and Jones meant getting dental X-rays from their parents, dashing the faded remnants of hope and bringing back the horror all over again. Decker rubbed his temples and called out to McAdams who was talking to Roiters. "Hey, Harvard. Where is the list of missing persons that we compiled before we identified Pettigrew?"

McAdams walked over to Decker while Roiters went back into the tent. "It's on my iPad, boss."

"Which you can't use because you have no Wi-Fi here."

"Actually I can bring it up because it's in a Word file, which doesn't require Wi-Fi. The problem is that my iPad is out of juice."

"I have an Apple charger in the glove compartment that's compatible with my car's cigarette lighter. You can charge your iPad there."

"You actually have a charger in your car?"

"When I came out to Greenbury, I thought I might need it. Long trips back and forth to New York to see the kids."

McAdams looked incredulous. "Why are you first telling me about it *now*?"

"Because you didn't need to use it until *now*." When the kid stalked off, Decker shouted after him. "Hold on a second."

McAdams turned around. "*What?*"

"Do you want to just juice up your iPad or do you actually want to know what I'm looking for?"

The kid made a point of sighing when he walked back to Decker. "What specifically do you want to know . . . sir?"

"The hometowns of Delilah Occum and Yvette Jones. We'll need dental records."

McAdams nodded. "Are we doing the notification by phone?"

"What do you think?"

"Of course, you're going to do it in person because how fun is it to actually *look* into the parents' eyes and see all that agony and pain."

"I can do it myself, Harvard. You have school as an excuse."

"I don't make excuses."

"Come or don't come. It's up to you."

"I'll come with you. Can't let you one-up me. I've just got too much ego for that."

Delilah Occum lived in Akron, Ohio, around forty minutes away from Cleveland—land of King LeBron James and the Rock and Roll Hall of Fame. Decker wasn't familiar with the area, but it was in the Eastern time zone: upon arrival, he wouldn't have to change his watch.

Yvette Jones had come from Lower Merion, a wealthy suburb of Philadelphia. Decker was somewhat familiar with the area because his daughter was part of the Philly PD. His son-in-law, Koby, was now in his third year of medical school at Drexel, having transferred from Mount Sinai to be closer to Cindy's job. They were renting an apartment near Rittenhouse Square, which had to be one of the liveliest places on earth on a Saturday night. The added benefit was that his grandsons, being mixed race, fit in with the city's population. The boys were already being scouted for basketball at several prep schools even though they were only seven. But talent is talent and the boys were fast on their feet, coordinated beyond their years, and off the charts in height. Decker liked to think that he played a genetic role in the tall factor.

Both cities were within a day's driving distance

from Greenbury. The plan was to first go to Akron—along the north—then go south to Lower Merion. Decker made calls to the families as soon as he arrived home at ten in the evening.

The conversation with each set of parents was almost identical: yes, there were some new developments in the Greenbury area but these new findings may or may not have anything to do with your daughters, and yes, he would certainly tell them more about it when he came out to visit them in person.

At ten-thirty, he hung up the phone after talking to the Occums. Both families were gracious enough to talk to him as well as acquire the necessary original dental X-rays for him. He was beat from a long day and mental exhaustion.

Rina was wearing a robe over lightweight pajamas. "At least the murders didn't happen on your watch."

He sat down at the kitchen table. "I haven't worked a cold case in a while. This one is particularly difficult because any kind of DNA transfer has been degraded by the water in the ground. An archeologist would probably have better luck."

"That's your stomach talking. You must be hungry."

"Famished, but I want to shower first."

There was a knock on the door. Rina said, "Go shower. I'll take care of Tyler."

"How do you know it's Tyler?"

"If you're hungry, so is he." She went to the front entrance and opened the door. "Dinner's heating up. It'll be ready in about ten minutes."

She let McAdams in. His hair was wet and he was

holding two bottles of kosher wine: a Herzog zin reserve and a Covenant Landsman zin. He said, "Are you coming with us tomorrow?"

"To Philadelphia? I hope so. I'd love to visit the boys."

"I think the plan is to go to Akron, then go to Philly."

"That's fine. I can make myself scarce while you do the interview." She relieved him of the wine. "I'm thinking that we'll arrive early enough to have dinner with Cindy and Koby. You're welcome to join us. Your picture is up on the piano. That means you're officially family now."

"The pain-in-the-ass kind of family."

"Tyler, stop fishing for compliments. Just say thank you."

"Thank you."

"Have a seat." Rina set down the bottles of wine. "Are we staying overnight in Philadelphia?"

"I think so. We'll probably interview Yvette Jones's parents the following day. There's a Marriott nearby where I'll sleep. I'm assuming you two will bunk down at Cindy's?"

"Yes, they have a spare bedroom."

McAdams pulled up a chair at the dining room table. "What are you going to do while we do business?"

"There are always museums and shopping. I like being by myself. It's a skill I've developed being married to Peter all these years."

"Yeah, I'm sure L.A. detectives don't work nine to five."

"It's not L.A. detectives, it's most Homicide detectives. Especially Peter. But that's fine. I love him for who he is. He's really distressed about this case. He thinks it might be a serial killer. He thinks there could be more bodies. It's frightening."

"It happened a while ago. Maybe whoever did the work has moved on. I looked up when the Bogat Trail was first opened to the public. It was just like Pete said, about three years ago—six months *after* Delilah Occum disappeared. That has been the Old Man's theory all along. That the bodies were buried before the trail opened."

"It's so sad." Rina picked up a corkscrew. With a few twists, she expertly opened the Covenant wine and poured him a glass of red. "Good?"

"Very. It's got some peppery notes in it."

"Then it should go well with the tacos. I'll be right back."

McAdams sipped wine and a moment later, Decker came into the living room. He filled his own glass and said nothing. The silence made Tyler nervous. He said, "Rina invited me to dinner with your family . . . Koby and Cindy." No response. "If that's okay with you."

"Sure." He sounded more annoyed than reassuring.

"You okay, boss?"

"Just thinking ahead. If we identify the bones as Occum or Jones, the colleges are a common link between them and Pettigrew. If it's not those girls, I suppose we'll start by looking up cases that deal with multiple bodies buried in remote areas." He took another sip and looked up. "I'm getting ahead of myself. When do you start law school again?"

"In a week. I'm still all yours until then."

"Thanks, Tyler. I may need it."

Rina came in, holding a plate of tacos over rice with oven mitts. "They're hot. I'll serve." Peter didn't answer her. "Are you okay?"

"Sure. Looks good." He gave a forced smile. "I'll take as many as you want to give me."

She gave him four, she gave Tyler three, and she gave herself two. After twenty minutes of eating in silence, she cleared the plates and brought out a fruit salad. "The watermelon is a little mealy. The season has passed." When no one answered, she said, "Or you gentlemen can skip dessert and go directly to bed. We've got an early morning tomorrow and you both look worn out."

Wordlessly, the men got up.

She didn't have to say it twice.

✥12

Akron, Ohio, was once known as the rubber capital of the country, hosting Firestone, Goodrich, and Goodyear, which was the only company still headquartered in the region. Rubber had diminished in importance for the area. Instead there were now over four hundred companies specializing in polymers. Akron's other (dubious) moniker was the meth capital of the country. There had been some progress in cleaning up the drug trade, as well as talk of urban renewal: of green spaces and community centers donated by pro athletes and civic businesses. The trappings were great as long as there were jobs for the populace.

The Occums lived in the Montrose-Ghent area in a two-story brick Tudor resting on rolling green lawns, and surrounded by dozens of leafy trees. In Beverly Hills, the price of a lot like this would be upwards of twenty million. In this area of the country, it was high six figures if the economy was great. Dr. Richard Occum was an internist; his wife, Natalie, was a high school math teacher. There were two remaining children, both younger than Delilah and both attending college in New York. It was to

117

the family's credit that they loosened the apron strings after their daughter had disappeared.

"We couldn't hold them back," Natalie whispered. She was small and thin with a withered face and sunken dark eyes. She had on a white blouse under an oversize black cardigan and jeans. Her feet were housed in espadrilles.

Decker and McAdams were sitting in a parlor at the front of the house. It was filled with light and contemporary furniture—all sleek lines and monotones—but softened by vases of flowers and a greenbelt view out the window.

"Did they already go back to school?" The gray couch that Decker was sitting on had zero give.

"They never come home for more than a few days in the summer. Internships are more abundant in the big city." A weak smile. "It's no doubt more pleasant for them away from here. I can't seem to move on. In a way, it's easier without them. I don't have to hide my emotions . . . which I don't do well. I don't fool anyone."

She scratched her neck with long, red nails.

"I do my best. I'm involved with other parents in the same situation, but I've tried to expand a little. I started going back to church . . . visiting with old friends. I just got tired of excluding everyone because they didn't understand. Anyway, I'll get you the X-rays so you can be on your way."

Decker said, "If you wouldn't mind, I'd like to hear a bit about Delilah."

She paused. "Like what?"

"Just tell me what she's like."

"Using the present tense."

"She's missing. That's all I know."

"It's been over three years. What are the chances that she's still alive?"

"I know what you're saying."

Tears fell from her eyes. "Delilah was fun, energetic, enthusiastic. She was smart, but she was more a people person than a book person. I know she was last seen leaving a party. And from what I've been told, she might have been a little tipsy. But she wasn't promiscuous, she didn't have a drinking problem, and she was, by and large, a good girl. She was a college student, having fun and enjoying the freedom of living away from home. What in the world is wrong with that?"

"Nothing."

"She was obviously in the wrong place at the wrong time." Natalie wiped a tear from her eye. "I know that some people think that she somehow brought this on herself, but honestly, she wasn't that type of girl."

Decker said, "If anyone made you feel that way, they're idiots. I'm just trying to get a feel for Delilah. Were the two of you close?"

Natalie took a tissue and blew her nose. "She could be secretive."

"About what?" McAdams said.

"If I knew that, I wouldn't have said she was secretive."

Decker smiled. "What do *you* think she was secretive about?"

"Anything she didn't want to talk about, which upon reflection was probably a long list. I had no idea what she did at college. Once she hit adolescence, she didn't share a lot. And that was okay with me. She was entitled to her privacy. I didn't want to pry. When I tried, it just caused conflict."

Decker paused. "Did you have a lot of conflict with her?"

"Do you have children, Detective?"

"Yes. Teenagers are very trying. My kids are all grown, but we still have our moments."

She sighed. "Some play the child-parent game better than others. Some kids actually like talking to their parents." She looked at McAdams. "Right?"

"Right," he answered.

"How do you get along with . . . ?" Natalie stopped herself. "Never mind."

"I have a tortured relationship with my parents," McAdams said. "And I know it's not all them. Sometimes it's me, as much as I hate to admit it. But even if you two were very close, there was nothing you could have done or said to prevent this. Bad stuff happens."

No one spoke. Then Natalie said, "As a parent, you think . . . I should have asked more questions, I should have demanded more answers, I should have insisted she check in with me, I should have kept a tighter rein, I should have sent her to a different college. I should have kept her closer to home. You drive yourself crazy because you want to turn back the clock and you can't."

Decker said, "What happened had absolutely nothing to do with you."

"Do you think it's her?"

"We don't know." Decker debated how much to

tell her. "Clarion did the initial notification that she was missing, right?"

"Yes."

"And then you filed with Greenbury police?"

"Yes. They got involved—such as it was—as soon as we went up to the college. I think both departments kept on shunting responsibility back to each other. But Greenbury did do some investigating. They talked to her friends . . . her teachers . . . things like that."

"What do you know about her college friends?"

"Not much, as I told you. I do know Emily Crowler because I know the family. Emily's father, Bud, and Richard are both physicians in orthopedics. The Crowlers live in Cleveland." Natalie wiped her eyes with a new tissue. "After it happened and the police weren't getting anywhere, I went to the college and tried to resurrect Delilah's life. I found out she had a boyfriend. Cameron Snowe."

Decker was leafing through a summary folder on Delilah Occum's disappearance. "I see that Emily was interviewed, but not the boyfriend. Is Snow spelled S-N-O-W?"

"S-N-O-W-E. I didn't like him at all. I think he had something to do with her disappearance. And when I told the police, they said they'd check him out. Whether or not they did, I don't know."

"Oh, here we go. I'm looking in the wrong place. Snowe was interviewed along with several other young men. The kids alibied one another." He read the file. "It doesn't say anything about him being a boyfriend."

"He probably denied it. And friends lie, you know."

"Friends lie all the time. Was he at the same party as Delilah the night she disappeared?"

"Yes. It was a Morse McKinley party and he went to Morse McKinley. I heard that the two of them had a fight and she stalked off. She left, but supposedly he didn't. Who's to say he didn't sneak out and follow her and do something nasty to her?"

"Is that what you believe happened?"

She sighed. "I'm just saying it's plausible. But once he was alibied, the police took him off the list." She leaned forward and crumpled, deflating like slack sails in a becalmed sea. "Do you think it's Delilah? In the woods?"

"I don't know. But if it is her, I will do whatever I humanly can do to bring down whoever is responsible." Decker paused. "When nothing happened with the police, did you try your luck with a private investigator?"

"I see you've talked to parents like me before." She blew out air. "We hired *two* private investigators. The first one only cared about money—Daniel Brewer. The second one was more responsive but equally unsuccessful. Her name is Ashley Corrigan. I have both sets of files and reports. Would you like me to retrieve them for you?"

"That would be very helpful, thank you very much."

When she left, McAdams raised his eyebrows. He whispered, "How did you do this stuff for so long? It's so fucking draining."

"Most of the time, the people turn up in one piece. Often they're runaway teens or children kidnapped in custody disputes. Missing person cases have a fair amount of successes. What we're working with are basically homicides but without bodies. And, yes, they are fucking draining."

Natalie returned holding several manila envelopes. "The files are here." She handed him a third envelope. "These are her X-rays. I'd like everything back if it isn't her."

"Absolutely."

"I suppose I should thank you for taking the time to come out."

"Of course. We'll keep you updated, Mrs. Occum."

"At this point, I don't expect anything—from you or anyone else."

Decker stood and placed a hand on her shoulder. "I'm so sorry for all you've gone through. I promise you this. Even if it isn't Delilah, I'll take another look at her file. It's been three years. Sometimes a fresh perspective helps."

She looked him squarely in the eye. "I'll keep you to your word."

Decker took a card from his wallet. "My office number and I'll write my cell number on the back." When he was done, he handed it to her. "Call me anytime."

"That's what they all say."

"He means it," McAdams said.

She turned to him. "Do you have a card?"

"He's full-time in law school," Decker said. "I'm your contact man. And I'm sincere. I was a detective lieutenant in the Los Angeles Police Department. I've worked a lot of cases. I can't promise you anything, but I'll do my best."

"What will you do that hasn't been done?"

"Yes, it's all been done, but sometimes, by rereading the files, there's a lead that we missed first time around. Sometimes the guilty party has been questioned and the name is right there in black and white."

"So why the hell didn't they get the person in the first place?"

"Because files are thick and have a lot of extraneous information. It's not that we're incompetent, although sometimes we are. But it's like a data-processing thing. Sorting all the junk from the useful information. If you didn't like Cameron Snowe, he's worth another look. Mothers have good instincts."

"For some odd reason, I believe you're taking me seriously."

"I am taking you seriously."

"Too much to hope for." She shook her head. "It's okay . . . whatever."

Spoken like a woman who had given up on life.

Heading southeast toward Philadelphia, Decker drove while munching on a breakfast bar, listening to a Jane Monheit CD that Rina had bought him. After walking around all day, she was worn out and had fallen asleep ten minutes into the ride, her head resting against the car door. The sky was black and cloudless, the night was mild: not nearly as hot and muggy as the evenings had been just a week ago.

They still had a few hours of driving left before they reached the City of Brotherly Love. McAdams had closed his eyes.

He said, "Who listens to CDs anymore?"

Decker startled at the sound of his voice. He had thought that the kid had fallen asleep. "Obviously I do."

"What you need is an auxiliary feed on your media system. Then you can listen to everything you like on your phone instead of listening to the same twelve tracks over and over and over."

"I don't like to fool around with music while I'm driving. That's the problem these days. Everybody is on the phone or texting or fiddling with music or setting navigation."

"Or eating."

Decker ignored the gibe. "They're doing everything except paying attention to the road."

"Spoken like a true codger."

"Nonsense," Decker said. "I'm very au courant. I've got Pandora at home, fyi."

"I like that fyi. If you'd like me to drive, I will do so. I can actually multitask."

"No such thing. Your brain isn't doing two things at once. It's constantly shifting from one task to another in microseconds, which means you're not really giving anything your full attention. No wonder all you youngsters have ADD."

"You're just jealous because it takes you forever to switch gears."

"I do prefer a symphony to a jingle. Besides, what is wrong with hearing twelve songs by Jane Monheit?"

"I'm not commenting on your taste, just your delivery system."

"Okay, McAdams, I can see you're bored. Tell me your thoughts on the case."

"This is what I'm thinking." He sat up and cleared his throat. "Even if Jane Doe isn't Delilah or Yvette, we still can't rule out that Pettigrew and Jane Doe are connected. But if Doe is Delilah or Yvette, they have the added college connection."

Decker said, "Both Yvette and Delilah were murdered two years apart from Pettigrew. Was there any overlap in school with Pettigrew and the girls?"

"There's probably no overlap with the two girls. But it's possible that Pettigrew overlapped with both of them."

"That would put at least two of them in the same time frame."

"Yvette vanished first," McAdams said. "Maybe Pettigrew knew something about her disappearance. Maybe that was the real reason why Pettigrew dropped out of school."

"If so, why would he come back to Greenbury a few years later?"

"To confront the murderer. Pettigrew was a different person from the one who had left school. Maybe after finding his true self, he finally felt the need to do the right thing."

"Then why not just go to the police?" Decker said.

"Maybe he wasn't sure. Maybe he wanted to feel the situation out."

"If Pettigrew came back to talk to the killer,

who'd come out with the short end of the stick in that one-on-one?"

"Maybe Pettigrew felt he could handle himself. He was a tall guy. Maybe he didn't think whoever he confronted would dare to kill again."

Decker said, "If he thought that, he was not only naive, he never watched a true crime show in his life."

McAdams gave a half smile. "If Jane Doe is Occum, then you'd have to reverse it since Pettigrew disappeared first."

"That Occum saw Pettigrew being murdered?"

"Exactly."

"Then why wouldn't the killer murder Occum and Pettigrew at the same time?"

"Maybe the killer didn't know Occum had witnessed the murder until much later."

Decker said, "And Occum—after witnessing a murder—would stick around in school a full year and a half after it happened and act like it was nothing?"

The car went silent. Then McAdams said, "Maybe she was part of it?"

"Occum had a part in Pettigrew's murder?"

"He was hit from behind by someone smaller."

"Okay, I'm open to anything. Let's find out if Occum was even in the colleges when Pettigrew disappeared."

"Or if they knew someone in common."

"That's more likely," Decker said.

The kid punched a button on the sound system and the CD popped out. "That's the third time we went through the disc. Enough."

"Put on whatever music you like. Or not. I don't mind the silence."

No one talked for a few moments.

Suddenly McAdams announced, "We spend a summer bored shitless and just when we start to deal with something interesting, I've got to leave."

"You can come down on the weekends."

"My sublease is up in a week." McAdams brightened. "I could stay with you . . . just until you get a solve—which won't take long with your expertise and competence."

"Thanks for the compliment."

Silence.

Then more silence.

"Of course, if it would be an imposition for me to stay with you, I could rent something."

"Why don't we see what plays out in the week you're here?"

"Sure." McAdams looked glum.

Decker tapped the steering wheel. "And if I'm floundering with the case—and that looks likely—I will be happy to have your help and your input. And of course you can stay with us. But I don't get it. Tyler, you're a very rich young man. Why don't you just rent a place here for the year? The price is like pocket change for you."

"My own place would mean stocking my own fridge, doing my own laundry, and cleaning my own floors. If I stay with you, I get free room and board."

"So you're a mooch."

"I bring you flowers and wine for dinner."

"You're a classy mooch."

"Decker, you're the one that always says that I'm one of your honorary kids."

"You are."

"If I'm an honorary kid, then I, like your other kids, should have mooching privileges."

Decker laughed. "That's fine with me, Harvard, just as long as I don't have to pay your tuition."

13

 Rittenhouse Square was near downtown Philly. The area overflowed with people and apartment buildings, restaurants, cafés, boutiques, and clubs, all within walking distance from the city's elite universities. In the daytime, traffic was bad: at night, the roadways were wall-to-wall cars, most of them looking for nonexistent parking spaces. Koby could walk to work, but Cindy wasn't as lucky. She regularly battled traffic, but at least parking wasn't the problem. Her building came with a space and she had left it open for Decker's car.

He, Rina, and Tyler arrived just as the sitter was putting the boys in pajamas. Nana and Grandpa's appearance was a cause for celebration and the delaying of bedtime. The boys were tall and strong and talked over each other. When things started getting wild, the sitter announced that it was ten minutes until lights out; if they cooperated, Nana and Grandpa would read them two books and tuck them in.

Just as the door closed to the boys' room, Koby came home. Decker's son-in-law was tall and lean, made even leaner by the demanding hours of medical school coupled with his advance to middle age. He was dressed in scrubs. After he excused the sitter, he said, "I'll just go kiss them good night."

Cindy arrived five minutes later via cab. She'd left her car at the station house so parking wouldn't be a problem for Decker. She was also tall and had lost the kind of weight that comes with fatigue rather than exercise. She looked the professional in black slacks, a white blouse, and black blazer with black flats on her feet. She had crossed the threshold into her forties and was beginning to show signs of wear and tear: white in her red hair and wrinkles around her bright, brown eyes, which instantly lit up when she saw her father.

Gigantic hugs ensued. "Oh my God, it's *great* to see you guys."

"Same here." Decker regarded his daughter at arm's length. "Detective Sergeant Kutiel. I don't know if I like you outranking me."

"In name only." She kissed his cheek and gave Rina a hug, then McAdams. "Hello, Tyler. Is he still picking on you?"

"Yes."

"Well, better you than me. Are the boys asleep?"

Rina said, "Koby's with them right now."

Cindy checked her watch. "They're still up?"

"I think we're to blame for that."

"Can't fault them for being excited. I'll just be a minute. Dinner's ready by the way. I just have to heat everything up."

"I can do it," Rina said. "I'll set the table as well."

"Great. It's the shredded beef and vegetables. There's also a baguette in the freezer. Just stick it in the oven with the meat. And open a bottle of wine. We're celebrating!"

Cindy retreated to the boys' bedroom. Decker and Tyler sat on a brown corduroy couch, the color not quite masking the multiple stains. Decker said, "What I should do is help Rina out. But what I want to do is just sit here. My conscience and my aching bones are embroiled in this internal debate."

Rina came into the dining area with a stack of dishes. "What debate?"

"Should I help you or not?"

"This is the deal. First of all, I slept on the ride here. Second, I'm already standing so I'll do the work. When you get up, your goose is cooked."

"So as long as I sit, I'm exempt?"

"Yes. How was your day?"

"Long," Decker said. "Most of it was driving. Why does driving make you so tired? It's not as if you're exerting any energy."

"Being bored is tiring," Rina said. "Did you learn anything about Delilah Occum?"

Cindy and Koby emerged from the boys' room. She said, "Yeah, I want to hear about that."

Rina said, "Why don't you two shower and by then everything will be ready."

"I'd love to, but don't start without me."

Koby said, "Are you sure you don't want help, Rina?"

"I'm fine."

The couple retreated to their bedroom. Tyler stood up and stretched. "I need to be upright. What do you need, Rina?"

"You're making me look bad," Decker said.

"You don't need me for that."

"Whoa," Rina said. "Snap."

Decker laughed but didn't move. With Tyler setting the table and Rina in the kitchen, he was irrelevant anyway. McAdams came back to the couch with two old-fashioned glasses of whiskey. He plunked one down in front of Peter. "At Rina's behest. You don't deserve her."

"It's impossible to compete with an angel, so I don't even try." Decker kicked off his shoes and put his socked feet up on an ottoman. Then he picked up the glass of booze and this morning's unread *Inquirer*, and put on his reading glasses.

Old age did have its compensations.

The household started early—to be expected with a med student, a cop, and two young boys. It was therefore convenient that Decker's own workday also started at dawn.

Radar was on the phone. "We got a situation up here. We found another body."

It shouldn't have been a shock, but it was. Maybe because Decker was still in his pajamas. "When?"

"We found a depression in the ground right before sunset. The bones were discovered about twenty minutes ago. Ben Roiters and Kevin Butterfield are up there now. Coroner should be here in an hour. What X-rays do you have?"

"I have Delilah Occum's and I'm talking to Serena Jones in about five hours. Her daughter is Yvette Jones."

"She has her daughter's X-rays?"

"I don't know if she has them at six-thirty in the

morning. But she did say she'll give them to me
when we speak."

"When's the appointment?"

"Eleven."

"Can you bump it up?"

"I'll call her at eight and see if she can meet as
soon as possible. In the meantime, I'll start packing
up. I don't suppose you know anything about the
bones?"

"Not yet. As soon as we knew we found a body,
we stopped to wait for the coroner. If you're back by
noon, we should know more."

"We need to expand the search area, Mike. At
least another half mile out in all directions."

"Agreed," Radar answered. "I'm putting up posts
for volunteers over the Internet and in the local
paper. We've got a lot of retirees who've helped us
out before. We should have a cadaver dog by this
afternoon. What a PR nightmare. You want to
handle it?"

"Ask Karen to do it. She's pretty slick."

"Okay. I'll keep you updated."

Radar cut the line. Decker stood, put on a robe,
and shuffled into the kitchen. Rina had already
showered and was helping Cindy with breakfast for
the boys. She took one look at him and escorted
him into the living room, away from young ears.

"Bad news?"

"Another body."

She brought her hand to her mouth. "Good heav-
ens."

"Three cold cases with very little forensic evidence. I come to Greenbury for semiretirement and I'm saddled with a serial killer."

Cindy walked out, drying her hand on a dish towel. "Another set of bones?"

"Yes," Decker said.

Cindy said, "How extensive is your missing persons list?"

"I'm winnowing it down."

"If you need a bigger data bank, I'm here for you."

"I might take you up on the offer." Decker kissed her forehead. "Thank you, sweetheart."

They heard one of the twins scream out "Mommy!"

"My exit line." Cindy went back into the kitchen.

To Rina, Decker said, "We've extended the search area. At this rate, the whole area will be dug up by Halloween. Talk about ghosts . . . more like zombies rising from the graves."

"I can't think of a more competent detective to have on a case of this magnitude."

"Thank you for the endorsement." He smiled. "I'd better wake up McAdams. At best, he's not a morning person. I'm hardly awake myself. I really need coffee."

"There's a fresh pot in the kitchen, as well as your grandsons. It's time to put on your game face and greet your loved ones."

Decker was already smiling. "How are they?"

"Go in and find out."

Dr. Michael and Serena Jones lived in a plush, up-scale neighborhood a few blocks away from the old

Barnes Museum. Decker and Rina had visited the world-class art collection years ago on their historic vacation through Boston and Philadelphia. The collection was now housed in the culture corridor of downtown Philadelphia. What was lost was the charm of seeing the paintings in a mansion in Lower Merion, where the houses were roomy and cushy and the acreage was green and sylvan.

The Joneses' address put the two detectives in front of a sizable brick house with a pitched roof on a lot with mature trees. Around the house and up the stone walkway were multihued mums—a blast of color and texture throughout the yard. Decker picked up a brass knocker in the shape of a lion's head and gently rapped it against a polished walnut door. The woman who answered appeared to be in her sixties with brown eyes set in a round face and framed by blond bouffant hair. Her makeup was expertly applied: rosy cheeks, rosy lips, and matching rose nails. She was average height and carried a few extra pounds around her middle. She wore a white sleeveless blouse—her wrists sparkling with jeweled bangles—and cuffed denim jeans. Flesh-colored, studded sandals highlighted rose-painted toenails. She led them into a front parlor that held a love seat and two chairs upholstered in chintz. A baby grand was tucked into the corner. Muted light was streaming through the front mullioned window.

"Please have a seat," she said. "My husband would have been here, but he got called out on an emergency."

Decker sat down on a chair and McAdams took the love seat. "What kind of a doctor is he?"

"Psychiatrist. Most of his patients are in facilities and are medicated, but when one goes haywire, it affects the entire place." A brief smile. "Coffee? Tea?"

"Unfortunately . . . we're in a big rush. We have to leave for Greenbury as soon as possible."

"Oh?" A beat. "Dare I ask why?"

Decker raised an eyebrow. "You know that we've been scouring a wooded area around the Five Colleges of Upstate."

"Of course. Where you found . . . bones," Serena said.

"Yes. Our department, in their search of the area, found another set of remains." The woman didn't speak. "We could really use those dental X-rays, Mrs. Jones."

Serena wiped a tear from her eye before it could smudge her mascara. "I'll get them for you right now."

"Thank you." It didn't take more than a minute before she handed him an envelope with the films inside. He said, "I would like to ask you a few questions, though, before we head off."

"Certainly." She hesitated but sat down in the unused, matching chair. She waited for Decker to speak.

"The school—Morse McKinley—has the particulars of your daughter's disappearance. So does the police station. I'm traveling with a very abbreviated file. Could you tell me what you know about your daughter's disappearance?"

Serena spoke quietly. "The last time anyone saw Yvette was around eight in the evening. She had attended a lecture and never made it back to her dorm."

"Do you know if she was walking alone back to her room?"

"No, I have no idea where she went. And no one claimed to see her after the lecture. But you know how it is. No one wants to get involved."

"That is a problem. By any chance did you hire a private detective?"

"After the police failed, yes."

"Do you have anything from him or her that might be useful to me?"

"I have a file."

"I'd like to take it with me so I can read it carefully. Would you mind?"

"As long as I get it back."

"I'll copy it and send it back. I promise."

"It might take me a few minutes to dig it up. I have so many notes and files."

"Could I have your entire files?"

She stared at him. "It's a lot of notes."

"The more I know, the better."

"You actually intend to *do* something?"

"To the best of my ability. And even if the remains are not a match to your daughter, I'll reopen the case and do my best to figure out what happened."

Tears welled up in her eyes. "I'm going to remember your words, Detective."

"That's fine. Briefly, could you tell me a little bit about Yvette? What would you like her legacy to be?"

"Wow . . ." She looked down. "Yvette . . . she was a good girl—strong willed, opinionated, outspoken. She was always advocating for the underdog. She was very idealistic. Lots of kids go through that stage."

McAdams said, "You thought it was a stage?"

"How do I put this so I don't sound judgmental?" Serena sighed. "At the time of her disappearance, I felt she was very confused."

"In what way?" Decker asked.

"In *every* way. What she wanted to be . . . *who* she wanted to be. She came home at Christmas during her freshman year and announced she was gay. Then she came home for spring break and announced she had a boyfriend."

"Who?"

"She didn't say. He must have been short-lived, because when she came home after her first year, she told us she was dropping out to join an ashram in India. We quickly disabused her of that idea. By the time she went back to Morse McKinley in her sophomore year, she had forgotten about it. But some time later, she called me and decided she was bisexual although she didn't want to be labeled. Gender was a concept not a reality, she announced. I thought she was nuts. Either you're male or female regardless of whom you have sex with."

"Sounds like she gave you a run for your money," McAdams said.

"If there was some kind of issue to be had, she would have it." She gritted her teeth. Even in memory, the girl had gotten a rise out of her. "She didn't call me that often. So I didn't think anything of it when she hadn't called in three, four days. It wasn't until *we* got a phone call that we realized something was wrong."

"Did you suspect anyone at the colleges?" Decker asked.

"So far as I know, everyone was cleared. But someone must have known what happened. You just don't disappear off the face of the earth and no one knows anything."

Decker nodded, although sometimes that was exactly what happened. The disappearance was seven years ago. Everyone had graduated or moved on. "Thank you very much, Mrs. Jones. I was hoping I could speak to you at greater length, but I really need to get back."

"That's fine. Thank you for coming out personally."

"Of course. Could you get me your daughter's files?"

"Oh, right. Hold on. It'll take me a minute."

After she left the room, McAdams whispered, "Noticing a pattern? Disaffected kids with strained relationships with their parents?"

"Makes them vulnerable." Decker was thinking out loud. "More susceptible to bad people."

"Especially charming psychopaths."

"Yeah. College kids have underdeveloped radars for danger."

"That wasn't me." McAdams smiled. "I was always a suspicious guy. Traits that make you steer clear of bad people, but don't do much for making you popular."

"Yeah, you pretty much steer clear of everyone."

"I have an almost girlfriend. Mallon adores me."

"Mallon is three thousand miles away."

"Hence the qualifier almost."

Serena came back into the room carrying a box. "There's a lot of material in here."

"I'll take good care of it." Decker relieved her of the files. "Even if we haven't found your daughter, I'll still take a look at the case. Fresh pair of eyes."

"Well, the bar certainly wasn't set very high by your police department." She sighed. "I'm sorry if I offended you. I know you're trying to help."

"You're angry at the lack of progress. I'd be angry too."

A tear leaked from her eye. "I waver between grief and anger." She looked up. "You want to know the truth? I also have a tremendous amount of guilt. Not because of what happened. There was nothing I could have done to prevent what happened. I wasn't there."

A pause.

"Yvette caused a lot of drama. With her gone, it's so . . . quiet. And sometimes, that's a relief." She wiped her wet eyes. "Do you think I'm terrible?"

"Not at all. I know you loved your daughter. What you've gone through . . . what you're still *going* through is completely overwhelming and you're certainly entitled to your emotions."

"That's nice of you to say." She took a Kleenex and wiped her eyes. "It would really help if I *knew* something. And it would be nice if I could bury my little girl!"

"I promise I'll do my best." Decker stood up with the file box and the envelope with the X-rays. He handed her his card. "Feel free to call me anytime."

"Thank you." She escorted them to the door and managed a smile when she said good-bye.

On the way to the car, Decker handed McAdams the box and the envelope. "When we get back, take the dental X-rays over to the pathologist and see if we get a match. After you do that, get me a list of sex offenders in the Greenbury area. If we are working with a serial killer, he might have done something lesser and worked his way up to murder."

"Right away, boss."

"Also, call up Karen at the station house and see if she can talk to . . . the friend of Delilah Occum."

"Emily Crowler."

"Yeah, her. If she's still in Clarion, tell Karen to go by and have a chat. I'll talk to the boyfriend, Cameron Snowe."

"Who may not be a boyfriend."

"Right."

McAdams said, "Do you think they will have unearthed the remains?"

"Hope so. We've got about three hours of travel time. After you've taken in the X-rays, start going through the material we have on Delilah and Yvette. See if you can tell me what was or wasn't done."

"You may be stepping on toes. Radar was here when these girls went missing."

"Let me worry about the bruised egos, you just organize the files."

They got to the car. Decker took the driver's seat.

McAdams sat shotgun. "I'll move to the back when we get Rina."

"That's right. I have to pick up Rina."

"You forgot about your wife?"

Decker smiled. "I would have remembered eventually."

"I'll let her know that." When Decker threw him a sneer, McAdams said, "Just kidding." He rubbed his hands together. "Their murders happened years apart—Delilah and Yvette. And then there's Pettigrew. What do you think? They were killed by someone they all knew or they were murdered by someone living in the area that chose them randomly?"

Decker thought a moment. "Same burial ground, so it's the same killer. And he didn't kill all of them at the same time. Yvette and Delilah are too far apart. Were there any other university students who went missing?"

"Not from the Five Colleges—unless you want me to go back more than twenty years."

"Do you have a list that goes back twenty years of people who went missing?"

"In the trunk of the car."

Decker thought a moment. "What about that girl who went missing four years ago? Didn't she work in Greenbury?"

"I think she worked in Meridian. I've got the details in my backpack along with the names of other missing girls that we haven't looked at. It's all in the trunk of the car."

Decker pulled the car over to a street curb. "Go get the list."

"Yes, sir." McAdams got out, rummaged in the trunk for the list, came back, and closed the car door. They took off. "The girl worked in Greenbury at a convenience store that bordered Meridian: the Circle M Mart."

"The one right off the highway."

"Correct. She disappeared around four years ago. Erin Young. And she wasn't a girl. She was thirty."

"Okay. Who else should I be looking at?"

"Twelve years ago: Margo Marino. She went to Hamilton Community College. She was nineteen when she disappeared. Thirteen years ago: Jaclyn Ungero. She vanished from Pace in the middle of her sophomore year."

"Pace?"

"It's a tiny liberal arts college about forty miles southwest of Greenbury. The next college student I have after Jaclyn was . . . this was seventeen years ago—Rhonda Burns. She grew up about fifty miles north of Greenbury. She went missing from SUNY Purchase. How far back do you want to go, boss?"

"Couldn't tell you right now, Harvard. It depends on how many bodies we find."

🍂14

They started out at one in the afternoon for the three-hour drive back to Greenbury. Ordinarily, because it was Friday, they would have spent the weekend with Cindy, Koby, and the boys. That meant Rina hadn't prepared for the Sabbath. But there was food in the freezer and with any luck, she'd be able to warm it up and set a nice table before it was time to light candles. Peter seemed to sense her thoughts.

Decker said, "We're making good time. We should be there at least a couple of hours before sunset."

"I'm fine. Worst comes to worst, I'll open up a can of tuna and a bag of potato chips and we can all pretend we're in grade school again."

"I, for one, like canned tuna," McAdams said. "It's one of those much maligned food products that's actually pretty good."

"Simplicity is your middle name," Decker said.

"Someone is grumpy."

"Someone is right here. And yes, I'm a little preoccupied. Three sets of bones and counting. Of course, I'm upset."

"And to think that Bogat Trail used to be one of my favorite walking spots." Rina took out a can of soda water. "It's so violating. I don't think I'll feel safe on any trail for a while."

"Get a dog," McAdams said.

"Talk to the boss," Rina said. "I've been trying for a year and he has yet to budge."

Decker said, "Are you really keen about getting up in zero-degree weather for a walk?"

"And to that I answer, we can always lay down a patch of sod in the sunroom."

"No, we're not going to do that. It smells after a while."

"We can change it out," Rina answered.

"Where do you get sod in the dead of winter on the East Coast?"

"You import it from places that grow sod. It's not a hard thing. And by the way, I spoke to the insulation guy. He can do the entire job including adding a freestanding radiator and new double-hung windows for about ten grand. I think it's worth it—sod or no sod."

"Probably," Decker concurred. "But no sod."

"Spoilsport."

"I thought you didn't want any more pets."

"Sometimes a gal gets lonely."

"I'm home most of the time by five and you work. What are we going to do with the dog while you're working?"

McAdams said, "Greenbury Police Department is pet friendly. Karen brings her poodle to work all the time."

"You're not helping."

"Yes, I am. It's just that I'm on her side."

"If you don't want a dog, Peter, we won't get a dog," Rina said.

Decker didn't answer right away. Then he said, "Okay, Rina. What kind of a dog?"

"I thought we decided that if we'd ever get a dog, we'd get a Bouvier. It's nonallergenic for one thing. It's also a great guard dog and great for walking trails."

"What about the grandchildren? You really think Rachel will be okay with bringing Lily up to visit when we have a huge dog?"

"They're not huge and are known for their intelligence. Besides, we mostly go visit them."

"And the few times they come up here like on Thanksgiving?"

"I'll take the dog," McAdams said.

"You live in Boston."

"So send the dog up with Uber. Just give me a few days' notice."

"Last year you came down here for Thanksgiving," Decker reminded him.

"Peter, if you don't want a dog, I understand," Rina said. "There are two people in this marriage. I get it. But please stop manufacturing problems."

"Fine." Decker made a big show of sighing. "We'll get a dog. But it'll be your dog. I don't want anything to do with him."

"Her. I want a girl dog." Rina turned to McAdams. "We had a dog when we first got married. An Irish setter named Ginger. Dumb as a brick, but we loved her. It knocked him out for six months after she died."

"Basket case," Decker admitted. "I cried like a baby. I can't go through that again."

"He's a sensitive soul deep down." Rina patted his back. "What can I say, darling. Love hurts."

Two hours and twenty-six minutes later, Decker pulled the car into the driveway. McAdams sat in the car, waiting to be dropped off at the station house while Rina dashed into the house, turned on the oven, and put a frozen cooked chicken sitting on a bed of frozen rice pilaf into the heat. She'd make a salad later. As Decker walked in, Rina said, "Can you turn on the lights in the living room while I set up candles?"

"Sure. I'll also turn down the bed."

"You're a doll." Rina adjusted the temperature so the oven was on low. It would take at least an hour to thaw everything out, but she wasn't in a hurry. She took out two frozen challahs. Thank God for modern refrigeration. Out loud she said, "I'll wait to eat until you come back."

Decker came out of the bedroom and looked at his watch. "I'll do a turnaround as soon as I can. They don't need me for the dig, but I'd like to stick around and see if we get a match with Delilah Occum or Yvette Jones. I'll want to give the parents updates as soon as I get them."

"Of course." She kissed his cheek. "Hurry home."

"I'll probably have McAdams with me."

"What else is new? There's plenty of food once it's defrosted."

"I'll direct him elsewhere if you want to be alone."

"It's okay, Peter. I know you two will have a lot to discuss."

"I don't have to burden you with that."

"It's no burden; I'm actually interested. I was the one who found the first grave, remember?" She checked her watch. "Go. See you later."

"And you're sure you don't mind having Tyler?"

"Not at all. He's like a grandchild. A lot of fun, a lot of work, and you can send him home at the end of the day."

At ten, the pair arrived at the house and they, along with Rina, ate a hot but rather joyless Shabbat dinner. The meal was short and everyone retired early, including Tyler who chose to sleep over rather than take the extra five minutes needed to drive to his apartment and sleep in his own bed. He went home the next morning when Decker and Rina went to synagogue, but he was back again at one for lunch. He wore a brown polo under a light tan sweater and black cords with loafers on his feet. The mornings were beginning to cool down but still lacked the nip of fall.

"I don't have anything to eat in my fridge. I'm clearing out food because I'm leaving in a week. Besides, I thought the boss might need me."

"Need you for what?" Decker was sitting on the couch, reading the morning newspaper, his rimless reading glasses perched midway on his nose. He looked up. "Is there something new going on?"

"Nothing new at Bogat, if that's what you're asking. I made you a copy of the list."

"What list?"

"Sex offenders in the area?"

"Oh, that's right. Anything?"

"Nothing that smacks me in the face. I'll go over it again more carefully."

"I'll get someone to help you." Decker went back to his newspaper. He had changed from a jacket and slacks to sweats and had slippers on his feet.

Rina served a plate of nuts and dried fruit. "Have a nosh. I'll be back in a jif."

"What's for lunch?" McAdams asked.

"We're having dairy. Lox, smoked trout, whitefish, cream cheese and bagels, deviled eggs and fruit salad. As a matter of fact, Tyler, while I change, you can cut up tomatoes, cucumbers, and onions and organize everything on a servable plate."

"Why him and not me?" Decker asked.

"Because he knows my kitchen better than you do."

Decker looked up. "Was I just maligned?"

"No, dear." Rina patted his shoulder. "Just saving you some KP."

Decker threw his head back and sighed.

Rina said, "Was that a tired sigh or a discouraged sigh?"

"Sometimes they're one and the same." He smiled. "Just been having a few long days after a very quiet summer. Go get comfortable."

By the time she came back down, the entire table had been set. Rina had on a loose denim jumper that fell midcalf over a white long-sleeved T-shirt. Her hair was tucked into a white beret. Decker made the blessing over the wine, and then they ritually washed their hands and broke bread. Rina passed around the fish plate. "I love this kind of stuff. Although my parents were Hungarian, my mother's family was originally Russian stock."

"Actually the Ukraine if you want to be specific," Decker said. "Although the way Putin is going, that is Russia."

"Odessa," Rina said. "You tell Russians that you're originally from Odessa and they say, oh, you must be Jewish. I heard it's a lovely beach city."

"Don't know," McAdams said. "Never been there. But I do like caviar."

"Which reminds me." Rina got up and brought back a small jar of salmon roe. "It's even got kosher certification. I like it on my deviled eggs."

"Lay it on me, girl," Tyler said.

Decker had already finished half of his lox sandwich when the phone rang. All three of them looked up. McAdams stood. "I'll get it."

Radar's voice came over the speakerphone. "We've got a match for the second set of bones. Yvette Jones."

"It's Tyler, Captain. Do you want us to come down to the dig site?"

"No need. We're in the process of cleaning the skull of body number three."

"Do you know if it's male or female?" Decker said out loud.

"Small skull. Probably female. We'll know better once we send it all to be X-rayed."

Decker said, "I'll notify the Joneses. I don't think Mrs. Jones will be surprised, but that doesn't mean she'll be okay with it. I'll tell her we're officially working on the case again."

"Sure," Radar said. "What's the link here, Pete? The school? The other missing people? Did she and Pettigrew know each other?"

"All good questions. Tyler has a list of local sex offenders who have registered."

"And?"

"Just did a preliminary check. Some are still here, others are gone. No one matched for murder. Were you here in Greenbury, Mike, when Yvette initially went missing?"

"I came about six months after. I was here when Occum went missing. I never heard about Pettigrew, which makes sense because no one knew he disappeared in Greenbury. Don't be nervous if you step on some toes."

"I'll try to be nice about it. Just let me know if you discover any new graves."

"We're still digging around with the dog. Anyone else missing from around here?"

"No one from the Five Colleges."

McAdams broke in and told him about the local cashier at the gas station mart—Erin Young. "As far as we could tell, she had nothing to do with Pettigrew or the colleges."

"A one-off?" Radar asked.

"A one-off of what?" Decker asked.

"I suppose that's the question on all our minds." Radar hung up.

"The captain certainly isn't proprietary." McAdams sat back down and took a deviled egg.

Decker said, "After lunch, could you pull everything we have on Yvette Jones and bring it from the station to my house?"

"Sure. I might as well pull Delilah Occum and Erin Young while I'm at it." McAdams helped himself to a generous dollop of salmon roe. "You still have the Pettigrew files, right?"

"Right."

"Find anything?"

"I read them, but I didn't know what I was looking for. I still don't. But with Jones being identified, we can see if the two of them had anything in common."

"Besides being troublemakers."

"They were troublemakers?" Rina asked.

"Yvette's mother described her as confused," McAdams said. "She was constantly trying out different identities."

"Who isn't confused at that age? Even kids who look like they have it together are often searching for something."

"Maybe that's what Pettigrew and Yvette had in common," McAdams said. "They were both searching for something with the wrong people."

"What would constitute the wrong crowd at the colleges?" Rina said. "Everyone is experimenting with different identities. Almost all have been passed-out drunk at one time or another. Probably a large percentage light up as well. Risky behavior is more accepted than being well behaved."

"Which brings up a point," Decker said. "You get into all sorts of problems when you're drunk or loaded. Did these students have a rep for regularly taking drugs or drinking?"

McAdams said, "According to Pettigrew's doctor, Lawrence had a very alternative lifestyle."

"He didn't exactly say that," Decker said. "But let's find out if the three of them had things in common, including bad habits. We need to concentrate on friends, faculty, fields of study, college clubs, favorite bars and restaurants, athletic teams . . . anything that would put them in contact with one another." Decker gave out another large sigh. "I've got to make a notification call to Yvette's parents. I'll do it in the library."

"Are you done eating?" Rina asked.

"Save my sandwich in the fridge. I'm sure I'll want it later."

"Will you be in the mood for dessert?"

"Yeah, sure. I'm fine." He left the table.

McAdams said, "Greenbury is utter boredom all summer and then we're digging up bodies faster than we can process them."

"It's scary, Tyler. Whoever put the bodies near Bogat stopped burying people when the hiking trail went in. But that doesn't mean the killer stopped killing."

"There's another graveyard somewhere?"

"It's a possibility."

"Yes, it is. I'd look except I have to leave for Boston. God, that pisses me off."

"I'm sure you'll be needed for input even when you're back up north."

"Nice of you to say."

"On a more mundane subject, I have some pecan bars that you made a while back. I also have some chocolate chip cookies. They're probably defrosted by now."

"You know coffee goes real good with pecan bars and chocolate chip cookies."

"It's Shabbos, Tyler. I can't make coffee."

"But there's nothing stopping me from picking up a to-go container from one of the local shops."

"It's up to you."

"I'll stop by the station house and pick up the files. I'll be back in about an hour."

Decker came out ten minutes later, his hair disheveled. Whenever he talked on the phone about something upsetting, he mussed his hair. "Where's the kid?"

"He went to pick up the files and a to-go container of coffee."

"You asked him for coffee?"

"I didn't ask him for anything. He just said he's picking up coffee. We'll wait until he gets back for dessert."

"What's for dessert?"

"Pecan bars and chocolate chip cookies."

"Coffee does go well with that."

"For the more diet conscious, I also have some grapes."

"I think I could use a shot of sugar." Decker checked his watch. "When's he coming back?"

"He said about an hour."

"What do we do in the meantime?"

Rina smiled. "If you have to ask, I'm not going to tell you."

"Just trying to be a sensitive guy."

"Don't bother." Rina took his hand. "Sensitivity is for chumps."

*   *   *

Along with the coffee, McAdams brought in several loads of boxes, which he plopped on the dining room table. Rina brought out paper coffee cups and a plate of the cookies and pecan bars. Decker passed out a stack of Post-its. To Rina, he said, "Would you mind reading Pettigrew's file? I'll take Occum, and McAdams will take Jones."

"Happy to help. What do you want me to sticker?"

"Sticker names and anything else that catches your interest. When we're all done, we'll make a list and McAdams will write them down."

They worked in silence for hours until the sun set and the stars began to peek out of a twilight sky. When it was dark, Rina got up and prepared for Havdalah, taking out a beeswax braided candle, a container of spices, and a cup of wine, things necessary for the ritual blessing that ended Shabbat and welcomed the new week. Traditionally the words in the prayer delineated the sacred from the profane, but in this case, the entire afternoon had been devoted to profound depravity. Nonetheless, the blessing was made, and then the three of them went back to reading and marking the files.

Usually Decker put off any kind of unnecessary work until Shabbat was over. But until the murderer was known and behind bars, every second that passed presented an opportunity to kill. And with all the activity going on in Bogat Trail, if the murderer was still around, he had to know it was only a matter of time before the police would start full-scale hunting.

They were already at a disadvantage. The devil never slept. That gave Satan a seven-hour head start each and every day.

⌘15

By ten o'clock that evening, they had multiple lists: people who showed up in just one file, names appearing in two out of the three files, and individuals who intersected all three, consisting of town employees, college professors, and college administrators who were around from Jones to Occum—a four-year span.

It was harder to weave Erin Young into the mix. She disappeared between Pettigrew and Occum and she didn't seem to have much in common with the students. It was plausible that all four had shopped at the same markets and frequented the same cafés or restaurants. But since Decker couldn't find anything definitive, he put her file aside until he could figure out a way for her to fit in.

"We'll work the cases individually as well as together," Decker told McAdams. "I know you have school in a week. Unless something falls in our laps, we're not going to solve anything by then. Do what you can and I'll give your files to Kevin or Ben."

"Sure. Where do you want to start?"

"We'll start by interviewing the names that intersect all three victims. Delilah Occum is the most recent gone girl. There may be some people in Clarion who remember her and her disappearance."

"But we don't know if she's part of the bone yard," McAdams said. "Don't you want to wait until the remains are identified?"

"Even if she isn't there, I promised her family I'd take a look at the case. I need to talk to Ben Roiters, who was the original investigator on the case. Then I want to talk to the boyfriend, Cameron Snowe. The mother didn't like him."

"Do parents ever like boyfriends?" Rina asked.

"Probably not. But boyfriends with missing girl-friends are especially interesting. Tyler, find out if Snowe is still in school, and if he is, set up an appointment with him for tomorrow."

"Which college did he attend?"

"Morse McKinley. Did you call Delilah's best friend, Emily Crowler?"

"You said to have Karen do it."

"Yeah, I did say that. I'll call Karen, then." He turned to his wife. "Rina, could you do me a favor? It's busywork."

"What do you need?"

"Make some calls. Find out how many of those intersected names are still associated with the college and who has moved out of town. It would give Tyler and me a starting point."

"I can tell you right now that Hank Carter made the Pettigrew list. Lawrence took one of his classes. And we know Yvette Jones was last seen attending one of his lectures. He's still in town."

"Yvette also took one of Carter's classes," McAdams said.

"He made Occum's list as well. He's definitely worth checking out." Decker stood up from the dining room table. "I'm going to give Ben Roiters a call and let him know what I'm doing. See if he can fill in some of my blanks since Occum was his case to begin with. Geez. Three dead bodies and counting."

"Peter, if you need me, I'm here," McAdams said. "I can always take a leave of absence."

"Not necessary, but thanks for the offer."

"It's no biggie. People go in and out of law school all the time."

"Taking a leave of absence from law school would make your dad very unhappy."

"Yes, I know. It's what makes the idea all the more appealing."

The station house had ceased running the air-conditioning since the first of September, a cost-cutting measure. That meant that the interview room the next day was warm bordering on uncom-fortable. Okay for Decker as he watched Cameron Snowe squirm on the other side of the one-way mirror. The space was taken up by four chairs and a table with a pitcher of water and paper cups. The kid was over six feet, high waisted with long legs and good-size shoulders. He had sandy hair and amber eyes and a strong chin. Tan complexioned, he resembled a lion. He wore a gray T-shirt over loose jeans and high-tops. It was Sunday afternoon at one P.M.

Roiters came into the room first. Snowe had talked to Roiters before, but he was still clearly uncomfort-able. He wiped sweat off his forehead. A moment later, Decker and McAdams introduced themselves and that made three against one. Even the kid remarked on it. "I thought you worked in pairs." When no one responded, he said, "Whatever."

It had taken all morning to track the kid down and once he finally did call back, he wasn't happy about coming down to the station house.

Decker said, "Been in a fight?"

"Huh?" The kid looked confused.

"You've got bruising on your face," Decker said. "A cut on your forehead."

Snowe waved it away. "Just some horsing around that got a little rowdy."

"More than rowdy. You look like you walked into a pole."

"I fell facedown on the floor. So what?"

"No need to get defensive." Roiters wore a white short-sleeved shirt that showed off hard muscle. "Been a hard couple of days for you, Cameron?"

"It's been a hard couple of years. I should have been done with college by now. I took a year off after it happened."

"Why's that?" Decker asked.

"Why do you think? Everyone was looking at me like I did something even though I clearly did not. I was with about six other guys that night. I don't even know why I'm here."

"You've been following the local news at all, Cameron?" Roiters said.

"The bodies at Bogat Trail." He looked down. "So you found her. God, it's gonna happen all over again."

"What is?" McAdams said.

"Everyone suspecting me of something." He shook his head. "Shit! I *knew* I shouldn't have come back here."

"Why did you?"

"Credits. I didn't want to start all over again someplace else, especially because I didn't do anything. I don't even know why I'm here."

Second time he said that. Decker looked at the boy. "We're giving the Occum case another hard look. You're here because you were involved with the victim. That shouldn't surprise you."

"But I didn't do anything."

"No one said you did. We're just asking questions. And we're asking for help. Maybe you can help us."

"I don't know how. I've told you everything I know." Snowe was looking at Roiters, who said nothing. The kid drummed his fingers on the tabletop. "I bet if I squeeze in a couple more econ classes in this term, I can graduate a semester early. I just can't go through all that shit again."

Roiters said, "You want to go through that night again for Detective Decker?"

"It was over three years ago. I've tried to blank it from my mind! Jesus!" He exhaled. "God, I didn't have anything to do with it! How many times do I have to say it?"

Decker said, "What was she like?"

"What?" Cameron lowered his voice. "You mean Delilah?"

"Yes, I mean Delilah. Who else would I be talking about? What was she like?"

"What difference does it make?"

Decker kept his voice even. "She's a ghost, Cameron. I want to find her humanity. What was she like?"

He looked chastened. "She was fun . . ." He looked down. "A lot of fun." He looked back up. "It was nothing serious. Just a college thing . . . for both of us."

"So what did you two like to do together?"

Snowe looked at McAdams. "Can you help me out here?"

"I think Detective Decker is asking about attraction other than sex," McAdams said.

"If I had to quantify it, I'd say ninety percent was sex. The other ten percent was the stuff leading up to the sex. Drinking, partying . . . having fun. She was a party girl. She was good in bed. She was my consistent booty call." He shook his head. "I know that sounds rough but like I said, it wasn't serious."

Decker said, "If it wasn't serious, what did you two fight about that night?"

"I don't even remember."

"That's not true," Decker said. "I've been doing this for a while, Cameron. Memories get hazy, but you wouldn't forget the harsh words exchanged right before she disappeared."

The young man looked at the ceiling. Then he poured himself a glass of water and drank it. He plopped the paper cup down. "I just know that we fought about something. I don't remember too well because I was drunk at the time."

"I'm waiting, son," Decker said. "I've got all the time in the world."

A long pause. Snowe said. "You cannot judge me, all right?"

"Fair enough," Decker said.

"I suggested a threesome. It pissed her off."

McAdams held up a hand as he rooted through his notes. "You were with a bunch of guys all night, it says here."

"Exactly."

McAdams looked him in the eye. "So how did you decide who the other guy was?"

Snowe blushed and looked away. "I don't know what you mean."

"What I mean is a party girl may not balk at a threesome. But she might balk at a gangbang."

No one spoke. Finally Snowe said, "Whatever."

"No, not whatever," Decker said. "He's bringing up a pertinent point. Maybe one of your buddies got excited and didn't want to take no for an answer."

"Look, Detective, all I know is that she left and I wasn't about to go chasing after her. In retrospect, I wish I had. None of this would have happened if I had been there."

"Maybe one of your buddies went after her."

"Anything's possible, but I don't remember. I told you I was piss drunk."

"If you had to guess which one it would be, who would you name?"

Snowe shook his head. "No clue." When no one spoke, he looked down. "What a fucking nightmare!"

"Tell me how you spent the rest of your night," Decker asked.

"It's all there in the files."

"I make my own notes, son. What did you do the rest of the night?"

"God . . . I . . . The group of us took the party back to Casey's dorm."

"That would be Casey Halpern?" Decker said.

"So you read the file. What do you need me for?"

"Go on."

"It was just the usual college shit. We were drinking in Casey's room . . . his roommate, Marcus, was there."

"Marcus Craven," Roiters said.

"Yeah, Marcus Craven," Snowe said. "It started out pretty crowded, but eventually it just wore itself out. People began pairing off. I was with Eloise Braggen until like five in the morning. She graduated, but she vouched for me then and she'll vouch for me now. Can I go? No. Let me rephrase this. I have things to do. I'm gonna go now." He stood up but didn't move. "Really, this is a waste of—"

"Sit down, Cameron," Decker told him. "Bear with us. You owe Delilah that much." Snowe remained rooted. "What did you think when you found out Delilah was missing?"

"I dunno." He was still standing, but the question caused him to wilt. He sat down. "I thought maybe she just had enough."

"Enough of what?" McAdams asked.

Snowe looked at Tyler. "You know."

"No, I don't know."

There was a pause as Snowe tried to find the right words. "College is hard for some people."

"Did she tell you it was hard for her?"

"Yes, she did, and more than one time. Deep down, she was a lonely girl. She missed home. When she disappeared, I thought she just wanted to get away. I felt guilty that I may have pushed her over."

He shook his head.

"I know it sounds self-centered, but I was traumatized. I took a year off because I couldn't concentrate. I kept thinking . . . like, how could this happen?"

"Did you come up with any answers?" Roiters asked.

"None then, none now." Snowe was pensive. "But it affected me. I really got my shit together after it happened. I went home and started a business. Then I sold my share for fifteen grand and came back with an entirely different perspective toward my life. I'm not the same man who started college three years ago."

"What kind of business?" McAdams asked.

"Huh?" He shrugged. "Oh. We started an emergency day-care service. I had a list of licensed day-care centers all over greater Atlanta and mothers would call me up in a panic. I'd call my sources and find a day-care center in their area that was willing to take the baby for the day."

"That's a good idea," McAdams said.

"Yeah, I do have a brain."

"No one implied you didn't have a brain," Decker said. "Who was your partner in this homespun business?"

"You're really nosy."

Roiters said, "Just answer the question, Cameron."

Snowe's smile was fleeting, but it was definitely

there. "Her name is Priscilla Hardy. She's a house-wife with three kids. She lives on my parents' block. We got to talking one day and a business was born."

Got to talking one day. Horny boy meets frustrated housewife? Decker would give her a call. Maybe the kid let something slip in pillow talk. Snowe was still bragging and whining.

". . . saying that I came back to Morse McKinley with goals. Something I was lacking when I first started. The whole mess really put everything in focus. I'm applying to Wharton and Harvard for an MBA. I don't know if I'll get in, but with all my experience, including my life experiences, I think I have something. I'd like to put this whole mess behind me so I can concentrate on the future."

Roiters said, "I would think the best way to put the mess behind you is to find out what happened to Delilah."

Snowe pinkened. "Yes, of course. But that's your job, not mine. I have to live my own life. I have to push forward." He checked his watch and drummed his fingers again. "I really do have a couple of tests to study for. So if we're done . . ."

Decker looked at Roiters, who said, "We've got some leads with this new development. We'll be in touch, Cameron. Don't go anywhere without letting us know."

"I'm not going anywhere." The boy wiped sweat off his face. "You're totally wrong if you think I'm involved. I had nothing to do with it. Just ask Eloise Braggen."

"I'll do that." Decker gave the boy his card. "If you do think of anything, give me a call."

Snowe flipped it over between his fingers. "Can I go?"

Roiters gave him a nod and the boy left. A moment later, Decker turned to McAdams. "Go follow him."

"Now?"

"Of course now. I want to see what he's up to."

"What makes you think he's up to anything?"

"A group of buddies who are as drunk as you are isn't an alibi. Go."

McAdams got up and left the room.

Roiters said, "I always felt that the kid had blood on his hands."

"I hear you. But the thing is, Cameron wasn't around when Yvette Jones went to Morse McKinley. If Delilah is victim number three, we can't have three independent murders with all the bodies buried in the same location."

"Your guess is as good as mine," Roiters said. "We should wait until the newest bones are IDed. We might get surprised."

"Right."

"How many people do you have that were around when all three murders took place?"

"Twenty, I believe. The list includes not only teachers at the colleges, but people who worked in the bookstore or at the local bar or in administration."

"So it's not twenty students."

"No, no. Rina made some phone calls this morning. I'm going to talk today to an econ teacher named Hank Carter. He was on your list of Delilah's teachers. You checked him off so he must have had an alibi."

Roiters paused. "I don't remember him or his alibi."

"Delilah took his Intro to Econ class. So did Pettigrew. And Yvette Jones had attended his lecture the night she disappeared. Plus she had him for a teacher. After him, I have a potential interview with a guy named Jason Kramer. I talked to him initially regarding Pettigrew. He's involved with the LGBT Center and he taught Intro to Psych. Both Delilah and Yvette had his class as well."

"And Pettigrew?"

"No, but he knew Pettigrew, so that's enough to put him on the all-three list. He was also checked off your list for Delilah."

"Sorry. I suppose I should have put the alibi next to each name but there were like what . . . a hundred names?"

"I know. You want to be as concise as possible because the file becomes very long. You questioned them. I'm sure they remember you."

"I'm glad we're looking into this again." Roiters stood up. "You're looking into it . . . a fresh set of eyes."

"Having identified bodies makes a huge difference."

"Yeah, it does. Look, Deck, I'm going to say this out loud. Don't be concerned about stepping on my toes. If I fucked up, that's my bad, not yours."

"I didn't see anything missing in the file, Ben. We've all had open cases."

"Just do what you have to do, Deck. I'm not about the ego. I'm all about the solve."

16

"So what can I do for you?" Hank Carter's face registered concern. His light eyes narrowed, and his forehead became a series of lines like windswept sand. He was in his fifties and lanky with thick gray hair. "I'm assuming it's about Bogat Trail."

"It is," Roiters said. "We're asking for help."

"Please sit."

"Thank you," Decker said. He gave a once-over to his surroundings. Carter had tenure and seniority and as a result, he had a decent-size office. The space was ample enough to hold a large desk, a couch, and scattered chairs. They were on the fourth floor of Barrett Hall, which held most of the econ/poli-sci/government classes. The window overlooked the Morse McKinley quad, students spread out on the lawn, basking in the last glows of summer. It was in the low seventies with a lemon sun in a perfect blue sky. It was three o'clock in the afternoon.

"So how can I help?" Carter asked.

Roiters said, "I was the primary investigator on the Delilah Occum case."

"Yes, that's right." Carter nodded. "I remember you."

"We're just going over all missing person cases in the area for the last ten years. Delilah Occum is the most recent. We're reviewing every name in her file."

"Why am I in her file in the first place?"

"Delilah took your Intro to Economics class."

"That's probably the largest class in the school. I usually have around three hundred fifty students each term. I don't recall her at all."

Decker said, "But you remember when she disappeared."

"Of course. How many times do students just disappear?"

"Do you remember where you were the night she disappeared? We're asking everyone we interviewed three years ago the same question."

"No, I don't remember. I can check my calendar. It's all online, and I'm sure it goes back that far."

"Please." Roiters gave him the date.

Carter swiveled his desk chair toward his computer, clicking the keys as he stared at the monitor, giving Decker a chance to check over his wall's worth of diplomas. Penn (Wharton) undergrad, Yale grad with an LLD and an MBA in economics and business. He was a member of lots of professional societies. He had been given lots of professional awards.

"Okay. I taught in the morning. I don't know what I did between twelve and two. Maybe lunch. I had scheduled appointments at two P.M. and three P.M. . . . open door for students four to six. Then I had cocktails with one of my colleagues at five. Unfortunately, she is no longer with the colleges but her name is Nancy Halloran." He looked up and swiveled toward them. "I probably went home after that and stayed in all evening because I don't have anything else on my schedule."

Decker was writing as Carter spoke. "As long as you have your calendar, can you look up this date for me? It's around five years ago."

"Why?" Suspicion in his voice.

Decker said, "Another Morse McKinley student disappeared, although he wasn't a student at the time. He came up from New York City for a visit to the colleges and that was the last that anyone had heard from him."

"Who was this?"

"Lawrence Pettigrew."

"And you're asking me about him because . . ."

"He took your Government and Ethics course."

"Okay." Carter was quiet. "So you must not have identified anyone specific at Bogat Trail." He paused. "But surely you know if it's a man or a woman."

Decker said, "Could you look at your calendar, please?"

"I thought you needed help."

"We'll get to that soon enough. Can you bring up the date?"

Carter moved like a reluctant man. But he cooperated, checking with his computer once again. "Yes, I do have my appointments for that date as well. I taught in the morning . . . student hours in the afternoon. Nothing scheduled for the evening, but that doesn't mean that my wife and I didn't go out for dinner or to the movies."

"How many students are in your Government and Ethics course?"

"Around one hundred. I don't remember Lawrence Pettigrew."

"He was distinctive," Decker told him. "He was very tall and very thin and very dramatic. Long blond hair, loud jackets that didn't match his loud pants. He also dressed with lots of scarves."

"Of course." Carter hit his head. "He was a very smart guy. Despite the getup, he knew the material and asked very intelligent questions. If you hold on, I'll see if I still have the roster for that class . . . no, sorry." He looked up. "My rosters don't go back that far. But you can check with the administration. I believe I gave him an A. Like I told you, he was bright."

"You never saw him again after the class?"

"I'd see him walking around campus."

"One more person I'd like you to look up," Decker said. "Yvette Jones."

"Wow. I haven't heard that name in a while. When did she disappear?"

"About seven years ago."

Carter said. "Don't tell me. She was in one of my classes as well."

Roiters said, "Also Intro to Economics."

"She was last seen attending one of your lectures," Decker said. "Investment for the Socially Conscious."

"That would be me," Carter said. "Obviously, then, you know where I was when she disappeared. I was at my talk." He laughed. "Look, gentlemen. After my talks, I am always deluged with people. It usually takes me at least a half hour to clear the auditorium."

"She could have waited around for you," Roiters said.

"It's just for process of elimination, Dr. Carter," Decker said. "I'm sorry to bother you."

"Detective, I wouldn't know Yvette Jones if I met her face-to-face." A pause. "By your questions, you obviously think that all three cases are related."

"We're exploring all the possibilities."

Carter tented his hands. "Am I the only one on your list who had all three students in their classes?"

"No, not at all," Decker said. "There are others, but we have to start somewhere."

"Why all the questions now? Why not when Delia disappeared?"

"Delilah," Decker corrected. "We found evidence to reexamine all three cases."

"So you found more than one body at Bogat." A pause . . . almost an afterthought. "Terrible business you're involved in."

"Someone has to do it," Roiters said.

"Well, I hope you get somewhere this time. It must be frustrating for you to have open cases that go nowhere." Decker felt the dig, but Carter was just winding up. "Furthermore, it must be hell on the parents . . . not knowing about their children. You must get blamed for things beyond your control."

Decker said, "Most people recognize that we're doing all we can."

"Too bad that sometimes it's not enough."

"You're right," Decker said evenly. "It sucks to fail."

The statement took Carter by surprise. He switched gears and shook his head somberly. "Is there something else I can do for you? As I said, I don't remember the girls, but I do remember the young man."

"That's why we're here, talking to you. Trying to jog your memory."

"Wish I could help, but . . ."

The man had tuned out. Decker gave him his card and Roiters followed suit. "If you think of anything at all, no matter how trivial, give us a call."

"I will." Carter laid the cards on his desk. "I wish you luck."

"Thank you."

The two men walked out of the office and through Barrett Hall, thin with students because it was Sunday. The boys they spotted were tall and patrician. Morse McKinley was noted for having a good-looking male population. They aspired to be future bankers, venture capitalists, and hedge-fund directors. A few of them would end up as fraudsters and felons. Whenever big money is involved, the two things go hand in hand.

"What did you think?" Roiters asked Decker.

"I think the cards will end up in the trash. I didn't like his little gibes at me or police work. Plus, he didn't seem nervous."

"Maybe there's no reason for him to be nervous. On the surface, it doesn't look like he had much contact with them."

"He called Delilah 'Delia.'"

"I noticed," Roiters said. "A simple mistake?"

"Doubt it. I mentioned her name at least twice."

"I think it was three times."

"Why use the wrong name unless you want to distance yourself from the victim?" Decker exhaled. "Not many suspects, Ben. I'm not saying that Carter is up there with Snowe, but his smugness has put him on my radar."

McAdams said, "Snowe has been in his dorm for over an hour. Do you want me to sit here all night?"

Decker spoke into his cell. "Where are you?"

"I'm under an outside gazebo on my third cup of tea trying to look busy. But I'm the only one out here."

"Where did Cameron go when he left the station house?"

"Hold on . . . lemme . . . okay. First he went to the dining hall to grab dinner. He joined a table of four guys. They had lunch together and he seemed to be doing most of the talking, or rather ranting— probably the prick police and the interview. But I wasn't close enough to hear."

"Do you know who the guys were?"

"No, but I took pictures. I had to sneak in there, you know. I guess I looked like I belonged. Anyway, an hour later, three of the four guys left, and it was just Snowe and another dude. I took more pictures. They talked for about twenty minutes, and then I followed Snowe to his dorm, which has three entrances. I parked myself to guard the main one, but so far nothing. I can't guarantee you that my eyes have been glued to the door the past two hours. I left for the facilities and to rewarm my tea. Now you're up to date."

"Okay, Harvard, call it a day."

"Where are you?"

"At the station house writing up the interview with Hank Carter."

"Anything?"

"He doesn't remember the girls, but he did remember Pettigrew once I described him. Other than that, he didn't add much. I have a feeling that it's going to be that way with all our interviews. It's been a while. Innocent people forget, guilty people don't talk."

"Is Carter crossed off the list?"

"Not yet. I didn't like him—he seemed shifty, but that isn't indictable. Go home."

"Thanks. Should I come to the station house or to your house?"

"Don't you have your own apartment, kid?"

"I shipped my clothing to Cambridge and my fridge is empty. I'm living out of my suitcase."

"Pick up dinner. It's the least you can do."

"What is wrong with you? Did you miss your nap?"

Decker laughed. "Go to Pita Delight and get some falafel, Israeli salad, tabbouleh salad, and spiced carrots. And also get hummus, tahini, and baba ganoush."

"Can you repeat the order now that I have a pencil and paper?"

Decker did. He added, "Also, get some slaw. Rina likes the slaw. We have some leftover chicken. Between all that, we should have enough for dinner."

"For anyone else except Jews, it's enough for a party."

"Now, now," Decker said. "I can say that. You can't."

"Of course I can. I'm your honorary son. And that makes me an honorary Jew."

"Are you sure you want that?"

"Listen, Old Man. I've been alienated all my life. I might as well have an excuse for it."

17

"We got the report back from the forensic odontologist." Radar was talking over the phone. "It's Occum. Expected—although it could have been that clerk at the gas mart."

"Erin Young." Decker had papers spread out at the dining room table. He picked up one of the folders from her file box. "She disappeared about a year after Pettigrew. I can't seem to work her into the puzzle."

"Maybe she's not part of it. She wasn't a student, correct?"

"Correct. She was a local and she was older."

"We'll keep digging for a few more days before we pull back. Last thing I want is to miss something. If you want, I'll make Occum's notification. I'm going to call her parents anyway."

"No, I'll do the notification," Decker said. "I just got off the phone with Karen. She interviewed Occum's best friend, Emily Crowler, who wasn't at the party. She wasn't even in town. She had gone home because she had a massive allergic reaction to an insect bite. Didn't show up until the following Monday. I've crossed her off the list."

"Anything else I should be aware of?"

"No, not so far," Decker said. "Mike, regardless of what you find out there, I want to reopen Erin Young's file. If her parents see us working the other three cases and not hers, they're going to be rightfully upset. Even though we haven't found her body, I don't want anyone who lives here to think that college students are more important than the locals."

"There was just a single mother. Her name was Corrine. Erin didn't live with her, but there was contact between them. Jerry Plains was the detective on the case. He retired to Florida about two and a half years ago. Did you ever meet him?"

"No, because I replaced him."

"Yeah. Right. I believe Erin went missing four years ago. For all I know, Erin could have made contact with her mother and the old woman forgot to tell us."

"If Erin hasn't contacted her, do you think Corrine might have hired a private investigator?"

"That's what they usually do when we crap out. But in this case, Corrine had a drug problem and not a lot of disposable income. I don't see how she could have afforded one. Do you have the coroner's report for Yvette Jones?"

"Not yet. It'll probably be in tomorrow."

"What about Occum?"

"Nothing yet. I also expect that soon. If we don't make some headway on this, I'm going to have to fan out to other police departments. It's possible our killer moved on after Bogat was opened as a public trail."

Radar paused. "I'll contact Boston and New York.

They both have a lot of colleges and universities. They both also have a lot more crime and missing person cases compared to our little department."

"You're right about that," Decker said. "This thing is like a tsunami. Rarely comes, but when it does, it just drowns out everything."

Decker, Rina, and McAdams spent early Sunday evening going through the roster of the names that intersected all three students. A handful of people on the list had died; others had moved away. The updated list included two who worked administration for Morse McKinley, including Leo Riggins, whom Decker met a few days ago while trying to track down Lawrence Pettigrew. There were three students who started as freshmen when Yvette went missing and were now finishing up MBAs in the MM graduate school. On the list were also five teachers, including Hank Carter and Jason Kramer, the psychology professor associated with the LGBT Center who routed them to Lawrence Pettigrew. Others included a clerk who manned the MM bookstore, an MM librarian, and two dining hall servers, two bartenders who worked at places off-campus, and Henry King, who was close to ninety and owned the local Army Surplus and More retail outlet next to the Burger Haven.

Decker hung up the phone. "That was Priscilla Hardy."

"Who?" Rina asked.

"Cameron Snowe's former partner. They started a business when he took a leave of absence from school."

"What'd she say?" McAdams asked.

"That he was a nice kid, that he was haunted by Delilah's death." Decker made a face. "Did he seem haunted to you?"

"No, but college boys hide their emotions—except anger and horniness." McAdams was looking at his list of names. "Ricardo Diaz is a bartender at the College Grill, the gastro pub on Yale. He was in town when Pettigrew, Erin Young, and Delilah Occum disappeared."

"What about Yvette Jones?"

"I don't know. We should ask him. Do you think he might still be on tonight?"

"Go for it," Decker said.

McAdams picked up the phone and was met with success. "The place closes early on Sunday. Diaz is off at nine."

Rina said, "You've got over an hour. Why don't you go down and buy a beer from him. It may make him more amenable to talking."

"Good idea." Decker turned to his wife. "You want to come? With you there, it'll look super-casual."

"Sure, I'll be your decoy. I'll get my jacket."

McAdams said, "If I order booze, can I have the department pay?"

"What did you have in mind?"

"I won't go overboard. Macallan 12 is fine."

"Do they even have Macallan 12?"

"Yes, they do."

"So you've been there?"

"Throughout my time in this town, I have frequented a bar or two on more than my share of lonely nights. The food at the grill is mediocre, but the whisky is plentiful and often nice."

"The twelve is a little rich for the department. How about if I buy you a good-luck-in-your-second-year-of-law-school drink?"

"If you're buying, I'll jack it up to Macallan 18."

The bar was twenty stools separated from the grill's restaurant by a half wall. It was dimly lit and smelled of wood polish and cooking oil, probably because the kitchen was behind mirrored shelves that held dozens of liquor bottles. Not a whiff of tobacco since the county had outlawed indoor smoking in public places.

There was thirty minutes left until closing time and last call had just been announced by the bartender. He was in his midthirties with straw-colored dyed hair and very dark brown eyes. Medium height with large shoulders, he wore black pants and a black long-sleeved shirt rolled up to expose tattooed arms.

The three of them took stools in the corner. Decker signaled the bartender, who nodded as he set out drinks for three college-aged girls who were talking too loud and laughing too much. One of them was perched precariously on the stool, fingertips hanging on to the bar top for balance.

After serving the ladies, the man came over and put down three round paper doilies with scalloped edges. "Last one of the night, folks. Make it a good one."

McAdams said, "Macallan 18 . . . neat."

Decker said, "Times two."

Rina said, "A Diet Coke."

The bartender smiled at her. "Sure. On the house."

"You can put my drink on the house," McAdams said.

"Save your parents some money, eh?"

"They're not my parents . . . not my biological parents." He presented his badge.

The bartender frowned. "You're early. I'm not off for another forty-five minutes."

"I know, Mr. Diaz," Decker said. "But there's nothing wrong with us enjoying the evening, right?"

"I'll get those drinks for you." He turned and started pulling down glasses and an amber-colored bottle. A minute later, he returned, drinks in hand. "Here you are. Did you want ice, ma'am?"

"I'm fine," Rina said. "Lively crowd here. Is it always this busy on Sunday?"

"Are you a detective as well?" Diaz said.

"Just married to one."

The trio of girls let out a huge peal of laughter. Everyone turned around. Diaz shook his head. "Yeah, it's busy over the weekends. Even on Sundays. Especially on Sundays." He cocked his head in the direction of the girls. "They're getting in their last licks."

"Regulars?" Decker asked.

Diaz shrugged. "I've seen them before." He took out a rag and started to wipe down the bar top. "When this place gets jammed, it's hard to distinguish one from another unless they fall over dead drunk and make a spectacle of themselves. Even then, they'd have to do it several times before I'd take notice."

Decker said, "Telling me in a not-so-subtle way that you can't remember yesterday's customers let alone someone from four years ago."

"Maybe." Diaz smiled. "But lemme see the pictures anyway. Sometimes I zero in on a face." He pointed to Rina. "Like you. I'd remember you. You're older, no offense, and dressed differently than the average female student. You're also pretty."

"That's my wife you're talking to," Decker said.

"Facts is facts."

Decker smiled and took a sip of his whisky. It was smooth and warm. McAdams laid two pictures on the bar top: Delilah Occum and Yvette Jones, respectively. Diaz mulled them over. "I've never seen this one."

He slid Yvette's photograph over the bar top back to Decker.

"But I do remember her. I had moved here around two years before she disappeared. I remember thinking that crime can happen even in a small town. But then I came to understand the way college towns work. The colleges are contained entities that have nothing to do with the town. They are all about placating the rich kids. That's not to say we don't card. Of course we do. And if the ID is obviously fake, we'll call them on it. But lemme tell you. There are lots of good fakes out there. It isn't up to me to pore over every detail of every state driver's license."

Decker said, "We're not interested in fake IDs, Mr. Diaz."

"This is all about the Bogat thing."

"Yes."

"Okay. Gotcha." Diaz looked at the photograph of Delilah Occum. "This is the girl who went missing about three years ago. I don't remember if I knew her from the bar or if I just remember seeing her face on flyers. They were plastered all over town."

There were several copies of the flyer in the case files: a full-face colored snapshot with the caption: HAVE YOU SEEN THIS GIRL? Underneath the caption was the contact information. Decker said, "Can you recall anything about her?"

"Just that she went missing. Some kids are always disappearing for a day or two, but usually they come back."

McAdams had downed half his whisky. "Tell me about those kids."

"Just that I overhear talk. Something along the lines of 'Where the hell did Ashley go over the weekend?' Then you find out Ashley had a bender and was drying out in some frat house after drinking herself blind and getting banged by guys she didn't even know."

"Poor Ashley," Rina said.

He turned to her and blushed. "Pardon my language."

"Was that the case with Delilah Occum?" Decker asked.

"I don't remember the details of her disappearance. How old was she?"

"Nineteen."

"Yeah, she looks it. I definitely would have carded

her and given her driver's license a good once-over. So I must've remembered her from the flyers. What happened to her?"

"She had a fight with her boyfriend at a party and walked out. That was the last anyone saw of her."

"Typical," Diaz said. "I see it here all the time at the bar. The guy gets drunk and the girl gets disgusted and stomps out. I tell the guy: 'Don't let her walk alone. It's dark outside. It's late.' The guys are almost always tossed themselves."

"Do you like what you do, Mr. Diaz?" McAdams said.

"Yeah, actually I do. Rich kids give good tips and you meet some interesting people. Like you. Never would've taken you for a cop."

"What does he look like?" Decker pointed to McAdams.

"A grad student. A rich grad student. The coat is the giveaway. We get our fair share of rich people. This is an acceptable bar, and the kids bring in their parents to show them off to me. I make a point of being nice. Not just for the big tips, but I've dropped hints about wanting to open my own place in a bigger city."

"New York?" McAdams said.

"New York or Boston. In the meantime, I'm still here. Maybe one day." He looked at Decker. "Anything else?"

"Yes, actually." Decker showed him the photo of Erin Young—the cashier who went missing between Yvette and Pettigrew—and laid it on the table.

"That's Erin. She worked here for a year. I was stunned when I saw her flyers."

"Erin worked with you here at the College Grill?" Decker asked.

"Not as a bartender, as a waitress."

"We were told she worked as a cashier for a local convenience mart."

"After she left here, yeah."

"Why did she leave her job?" Decker asked. "Surely it paid better than working as a cashier for Circle M."

"I don't like to speak ill of the dead—if she's even dead. Anyway, she was caught with her hands in the till. I noticed that the register wasn't matching the receipts, and I pressed her on it. Eventually she fessed up. She begged me not to report her. She had fallen on hard times and jobs were scarce. I told her I wouldn't say anything, but she had to leave. When she got a job as a cashier, I debated telling the owner of the Circle M, but then she disappeared and I thought . . . what was the point?"

Decker was annoyed. "I've read her files. You never contacted the police after she went missing."

"What for? She hadn't worked here for a while. I'm sure she knew dozens of people who didn't contact the police."

"Yes, but those people didn't catch her stealing. You did. What if she was stealing from her current boss and he wasn't as nice about it as you were."

"Meaning?"

"She's missing, isn't she?"

"You think Derek Kinny had something to do

with it?" He made a face. "He might have fired her, but c'mon. He's been around here for years. Does Erin have something to do with Bogat?"

"Everything is still being investigated."

"Well, then maybe you want to talk to Derek Kinny."

"Crossed my mind, Diaz," Decker said. "Take a look at this guy." Out came a photo of Lawrence Pettigrew.

"Him, I remember," Diaz said. "The cross-dresser. Really bright guy. He was underage. I never served him anything stronger than espresso coffee. We talked politics all the time." He looked at Decker. "I didn't know he disappeared. Never saw any flyers."

"He dropped out of college and moved to Manhattan," McAdams said. "One day, he came up to visit the colleges and that was the last anyone has ever seen of him."

"Wow, that's freaky! When was this?"

"Five years ago. Before Erin Young disappeared," Decker said. "Tell me about him."

"I told you. Bright, crazy gay guy. Real flamboyant."

"But smart," Rina added.

"Real smart and a good tipper. Lots of gay people are big tippers. The order of generosity is gay men, straight men, lesbians, and straight women. Especially straight women who get pissed with friends." He cocked his head in the direction of the three young women at the end of the bar who were in the process of trying to exit with dignity. The two of the less-drunk girls were supporting the third. Diaz said, "Good night, ladies."

They grunted something in return. Diaz scurried to the end of the bar and picked up seventy-five dollars in cash. "To prove my point, their total bill was seventy-two, forty. I get two dollars and sixty cents for serving them for the last three hours."

Rina took Decker's wallet from her purse and pulled out a fifty. She laid it on the bar top. "Keep the change."

Diaz said, "You don't even know what your bill is."

"I know it's a lot less than fifty dollars," Rina said. "Not all women are misers. And we're not all spendthrifts, either. Like guys, we run the gamut."

Decker said, "Notice how she proves a point by taking my money out of my wallet."

"Excuse me, it's *our* money."

Decker laughed. "Of course, dear. I was just joking."

"The way I figure, half of it is morally mine as your wife, and the other half is actually mine since we were married in California, which has community property. So two halves make a whole. That means that in reality our money is all mine."

Decker scrunched up his face. "But I could say the same thing."

"But you didn't and I did. First come, first serve." She pushed the money at Diaz. "Enjoy."

"You snookered me," Decker said to Rina.

"That's what you get for marrying a math major."

❧ 18

Driving home, Decker said, "I'll drop you off at home. I'm going back to the station house."

"Why?" Rina said. "What's up?"

"I'm thinking about Erin Young. I've been assuming she had nothing to do with the others since she wasn't a college student. But maybe she's connected."

"You think she's buried at Bogat Trail?" McAdams said.

"I don't know, but even if we don't find her body, I think she may be involved. She worked in a place where college students hang. Maybe our killer noticed her. I need to reread her files."

"Can I make a copy for myself?" McAdams said.

"Why?"

"I can review her file when I get back to school; that way you can concentrate on the bodies we do have."

"No, no. It's one thing to take them to my house. It's another to take them out of Greenbury. What if they're stolen?"

"Unlikely, but I do have a safe in my apartment."

Decker relented. "Call up Kevin and see if he can

pull them out of the cage. See how many boxes there are."

McAdams took out the phone. "Sure."

Rina said, "It's out of the way to take me home. Besides, I can make copies while you two read." She smiled. "As a matter of fact, I can read through them myself and let you know what I think."

Decker shrugged. "Okay."

Rina was shocked. "*Okay?*"

"Sure. This isn't LAPD. I could use the help."

McAdams hung up. "Kevin's not at the station house right now. He said he'd be glad to come back and pull them from the cage in a half hour after he's finished watching *Roman Gladiator*. It's smack in the middle of the fight scene between Flavius and the lion."

"No spoilers, please," Rina said. "I'm streaming the show."

"I couldn't spoil it because I don't know how it turns out. I have no idea where I am in the series."

"Where are you at?"

"Nero has just caught Flavius and is demanding the return of Octavia Portia, but Flavius has a plan for escape."

"You're at least three episodes behind."

"So I guess if Flavius is fighting in the lion's den, he doesn't escape."

"You'll have to watch it and find out," Rina said. "I would have never guessed you as a *Roman Gladiator* fan."

"I got hooked on it last year at school."

"Tell this guy how good it is," Rina said. "He still won't watch it with me."

"I just don't want to come in the middle of a series," Decker said. "With real bodies piling up, I don't have a lot of time to watch a stupid TV show."

"It's not stupid." Rina crossed her arms. "Well, it is sort of stupid, but it's very addictive. Maybe you could use something to take your mind off reality for an hour."

"Thank you for your concern, but that's why I tinker with my car. At least when I change the oil, I feel I've *done* something."

"Besides get the garage floor dirty?"

"That's what garage floors are for. They aren't supposed to be white and shiny. They're supposed to look like someone has done something besides passively watch a bunch of overpaid actors with coiffed hair pretend to be Roman warriors."

"Well, aren't you just above the fray!"

"You know what? Maybe I should drop you off at home."

"Fine. Suit yourself."

The car went silent.

McAdams said, "Are you guys *really* in a fight?" When neither Decker nor Rina answered, he said, "I mean, seriously? Over a TV show?"

He was met with more silence.

"Peter, you just passed the station house. Let's get the boxes and start copying the files. There's no sense wasting time taking Rina home when we can use her help. Turn the car around and let's go back to plan A, all right?"

Wordlessly, Decker made a U-turn and headed for the station house parking lot.

Shaking his head, McAdams said, "It's a sad state of affairs when I have to be the adult around here."

As Rina worked at the copy machine, Decker took the warm duplicate pages from the tray and began to scour through Erin Young's file. McAdams was updating the list of intersecting people he had originally taken from the files of Pettigrew, Yvette Jones, and Delilah Occum. They worked in a precise but cold harmony, attentive to the job and civil to one another.

Decker's cell rang. Sheila Nome introduced herself as the medical examiner who performed the autopsies on the bones of Yvette Jones and Delilah Occum. She said, "There is only so much you can do once the soft tissue is gone."

"Anything will be helpful."

"That's the problem. I can't tell you anything. With Pettigrew, there was a big dent in his skull. With the girls, unfortunately, there isn't anything definitive. If these were bones from two hundred years ago on a family burial plot, you'd assume natural death. But given the context, we know something went very wrong. There's nothing in the bones to suggest that the victims died from gunshot or blunt force trauma. And there were no cut marks in the bone—either in green bone perimortem or white bone postmortem. Now they could have been stabbed in the neck or the leg—caught the carotid or femoral artery and bled out—but there weren't any cut marks in any of the bones I examined."

"What about the hyoid?" Decker asked.

"They were broken in all three bodies. The girls could have died from strangulation. So could have Pettigrew. But you have to remember that it's a thin bone and there were other broken bones in the body—fingers, toes, the orbits, and the septum. It could be regular erosion of the bone or maybe the body was dragged. We don't know because the eyes have disintegrated. It also could have been suffocation. Or poison. We can test the bones and the hair for arsenic and heavy metals. But if it was an OD, it's unlikely that we'll find traces in hair or bones. I'd like to tell you more. I'm sure you'd like to have more. What can we do?"

"It's fine. Thanks for the information. When can you deliver the report?"

"You can either pick up a copy at my office or I can mail it to you with the photographs tomorrow, which will take God only knows how long. I can also e-mail you the text now and send you the photographs in snail mail."

"The photos don't reproduce."

"Not well, no."

"Then I'll pick up the report tomorrow, but if you could e-mail me the text tonight, that would be helpful."

"Are you working on the cases now?"

"I am."

"On Sunday?"

"Crime doesn't take the weekend off."

"Dedicated or bored?"

"Truthfully? Maybe a bit of both."

Decker hung up the phone and went back to his reading.

Erin Young had been working for the Circle M twenty-four-hour market, and the night she disappeared was completely unremarkable. It was a warm spring evening bordering on hot and humid. The change of shift was eleven-thirty at night. She had left the market wearing jeans, a white wifebeater tank top, and sandals—appropriate dress considering the AC in the mart was malfunctioning. There was no indication that she was going anywhere other than home—an apartment she shared with a friend.

Since then no one had heard boo from her.

Decker sorted through her photographs. They presented a living, breathing human being: round face, short blond hair, small freckled nose, and blue eyes. She might have been described as pixieish had she been a little younger and less tired-looking. There were blue and black shadows under her eyes—the mark of hard living. He leaned back and let out a sigh. "We're going about this half-assed."

McAdams looked up from the desktop, a highlighter in his hand. Rina stopped photocopying. She said, "What do you suggest?"

"We start from the very beginning. I want to interview each victim's immediate circle and then start moving outward. In each case, since family wasn't around when they disappeared, I want to talk to those who were closest to them in school—friends, boyfriends, roommates, classmates, and teachers."

"You said you thought that all three cases were related because all three were in the same burial site," McAdams said. "Did you change your mind about that?"

"No."

"So why would you want to interview roommates and boyfriends of Yvette Jones, for instance, when they weren't even in town when Delilah Occum went missing?"

"Because I want to know each victim individually."

"I understand your need to be thorough, but why don't we interview the people on the list first and then go back and interview everyone else?"

"Depending on how many people Radar can spare, we can do it simultaneously," Decker answered. "I'll start with Yvette Jones because she's the oldest case. I'll also do Erin Young because she's an outlier. You're starting school soon. Once you leave, I'll put Kevin on Lawrence Pettigrew and Ben on Delilah Occum."

"I can probably come down weekends and help you out."

"Only if it's convenient."

"I've been thinking about Erin Young," Rina said. "Is it possible that she was the lucky one who made it out alive?"

Decker said, "Tell me why you think she's still alive?"

"I'm just thinking that if Erin was attacked—she was walking home late at night—what if she managed to escape and decided to disappear rather than go to the police? From what Diaz said, she was a thief. Could be she was hesitant about contacting them. Plus, she didn't seem to have anything tying her to the community."

"Her mother still lives here," Decker said.

"Yes, and that brings us to another point. If Erin is still alive, maybe she has been in contact with her mother."

"The other bodies aren't going anywhere." Decker shrugged. "I'll set something up with Erin's mother for tomorrow."

McAdams said, "I'll come with you."

"That'll work." Decker looked at Rina. "So you think she's tied in with Bogat?"

"Just a gut feeling I have."

"For what it's worth, I agree with your gut."

"It's worth a lot. Thank you for not dismissing me out of hand."

"I wouldn't do that, no matter how mad I was."

"Are you mad?"

"No, I'm not. Are you mad?"

"No."

McAdams said, "So you two are okay?"

"Of course, we're okay." Rina was offended. "We're not children. We're not even college students who can't handle microaggressions without falling apart."

Decker laughed. "Even so, I'm sorry if I was microaggressive-ish. I want you to feel safe in your environment."

"Duly noted."

"You know, I really work hard not to make a mess on the garage floor."

"I know. But you are gone a lot. So when you have some free time, it wouldn't hurt for you to watch a half hour of TV with me before you go off on your own thing."

"We watch TV together all the time. Just going

through *Midsomer Murders* is going to take another decade."

"Sometimes I'd like to watch something other than sports or a cop show."

"I thought you liked cop shows."

"I do like cop shows. And I like sports. But I also like *Roman Gladiator* and you should watch it with me because I don't ask much of you."

"Duly noted." Decker managed a brief smile. "Sorry."

"Sorry, too."

"Aw, you're all made up," McAdams said. "How sweet!"

"You know, McAdams," Decker said, "I can turn my aggression toward you on a moment's notice, and believe me, there will be nothing at all *micro* about it."

19

The bungalow was on a rutted lane surrounded by woods. With shorter days and cooler nights, the forest was on the cusp of fall, the leaves turning gold, crimson, plum, and russet. The drivable pathway ended about a hundred yards from the house. There was a twenty-year-old black Ford pickup off to the side and Decker parked next to it. He and McAdams got out and walked the remaining distance to the small, one-story structure that, up close, was more boards nailed to a frame than actual house. The steps to the front door were pockmarked and the windows were panes of soot. At eight in the morning, it was chilly and dank and a thoroughly gloomy place—like an evil cottage in a Grimm's fairy tale.

Decker knocked on the front door—a piece of splintering board—and the woman who answered was in a brown housecoat. She appeared to be in her sixties with a tired face, damaged bleached blond hair, dark eyes rimmed with dark circles, and a frown for a mouth.

"Corrine Young?" Decker asked.

"Who else?" She stared at them as she lit a cigarette, the source of her husky voice. "Come in."

The living room was spare and tidy. No couches, just a few mismatched chairs next to a couple of mismatched end tables. No overhead lighting but plenty of lamps, which was good because the interior was dark. She motioned them to a dinette table surrounded by four folding chairs. She looked around. "You want some coffee? I'm making a fresh pot."

"Thanks, sure."

"What about you?" She was looking at McAdams.

"Coffee would be great, Mrs. Young."

There was a dazed expression on her face. "You can call me Corrine, by the way."

"Thank you." Decker surveyed the room after Corrine left. There was a paper bag behind the front door that held three empty bottles of vodka. To McAdams, he mimed a person drinking with his hands. Then they both sat at the dinette table and waited for Corrine to bring in the coffee. The mugs looked clean and the milk was fresh. She sat down with a steaming cup in her hand. She placed it on the tabletop and then rubbed her covered arms.

"You have news for me?"

"As I told you over the phone, we found some human bones at Bogat Trail. The three bodies have been identified and they're not your daughter, Erin. But with the discovery, we are delving into all the reported disappearances from the area within the last ten years."

Corrine picked up the coffee mug and let the steam run over her face. She remained silent.

Decker said, "Have you heard from your daughter at all?"

"If I did, I woulda told you over the phone."

"I had to ask. Corrine, it would be helpful for me if you could take me back to the day when your daughter disappeared."

"I didn't even know she disappeared until about a week later." Corrine put the mug down without drinking. "Erin didn't live here with me. She moved out when she turned sixteen. Don't blame her. My ex was a brute. He never touched her—I would have killed him if he did—but that don't mean she never saw us fight." She paused. "Real bad fights. He was a mean drunk."

"What is his name?"

"His name was Richard Pellegrino. He died ten years ago. Erin didn't go to the funeral."

"So he was out of the picture before Erin disappeared."

"Unless you believe in reincarnation, that would be the truth." She said, "Drink your coffee before it gets cold."

Decker took a sip. "Good coffee."

"My own blend of beans. I get them at the local farmers' market, although where they get coffee beans is beyond my ken. I thought coffee grew in the tropics."

"It does," McAdams said.

"So how do they get beans at farmers' markets?"

"Beats me." Decker knew that Corrine was skirting around the issue. So he waited for her to settle back down. "Were there any other brutes in your life after Richard died?"

"You have men in your life, you have some brutes."

"Could they have had something to do with Erin's disappearance?"

Corrine shook her head. "Nope."

"You're sure about that?"

"Yep. You can go down that road, but you'll hit dead ends."

"Why are you so sure?"

"Because once she left the house, she didn't look back."

"You were estranged from her?"

Corrine took a drag on her cigarette. "No, we'd talk on the phone mebbe once a week. That's why I didn't know she was gone until about a week later."

"How often did you *see* her?"

"Not often. When she was in between jobs, she would stay here for a month or two to cut down on rent."

"So she could have met your boyfriends."

"No, she wouldn't come here if I had someone staying with me. There wasn't enough room for one thing."

McAdams said, "What happened once you found out that Erin had disappeared?"

Slowly Corrine turned her eyes from Decker to the kid. "I talked to the police. Pretty much like I'm talking to you." She sipped coffee. "When Erin didn't call me back after a week, I knew something wasn't right. It's all in the report that I gave the first policeman."

"I know. But I'd like to hear it from you."

"Not much to hear. She wasn't answering her phone so I went to her apartment. No one was in. I got the manager to open up. Everything looked okay, messy, but not like a burglary or anything.

Her clothes were still in her closet, and her jewelry was still in her dresser drawer."

Jewelry was pronounced with three syllables. Decker said, "Did you talk to her roommate?"

"Caroline Agassi. Yeah, I talked to her. Once you start talking to her, you can't shut her up. She didn't seem to know a lot about Erin."

"Did she mention any boyfriends?" McAdams asked.

Again her eyes turned from Decker to Tyler. "If Erin had a man, I didn't know about it. The only thing Caroline talked about was how she was freaked out, not a word about my daughter who was the one missing." She looked down at her lap. "I don't have anything to add from the first time."

Decker said. "So you don't know about boyfriends."

"I just told you no."

"What about girlfriends?"

"Ask Caroline. She probably knows more than I do, and she'll love talking to you."

"Did Erin ever disappear before?"

"For four years without contacting me? No."

Decker said, "I'm not making myself clear. Did she ever go away from here for an extended period of time?"

"I suppose she went away from time to time. She never told me one way or the other. She was thirty when she vanished." Her eyes watered and she looked down. "I didn't keep tabs on her."

"Do you think if she relocated, she would have contacted you?"

She wiped a tear away. "Probably."

"But you haven't had any contact with her, right?"

"You already asked that and the answer is still no! Think I would be wasting your time if she had called me? I haven't seen her since she vanished!"

She was very vehement.

"Besides, why would she leave without her clothes and jewelry and all her things?"

Decker said, "Sometimes, if people are in trouble, they leave without a trace and try to start life over under a new identity."

Corrine shrugged.

"You know she was fired from the College Grill for stealing."

"I didn't know, but it doesn't surprise me."

"Why not?"

"She's had sticky fingers. I took to hiding my purse when she was around."

"Okay. If she stole something big this time, would she take off without contacting anyone?"

"Mebbe." Corrine looked down again.

"But usually . . . eventually . . . even if people take off, they try to contact loved ones."

This time, Corrine didn't protest. She said, "Detective, if she started over, I have no idea where she is."

"If she was starting over, where do you think she might have gone?"

"Why are you asking me all these questions like she's alive?"

"Do you believe she's alive?"

"How would I know? It's been years!" Her voice had gone up an octave. "You didn't answer my question. Why do you think she's alive?"

"Until I know differently, that's what I assume. Where would she have gone if she wanted to start over?"

"For the last time, I don't *know*."

"Let me phrase the question another way. Did she ever talk about a town or a place she wanted to visit?" When Corrine didn't respond, Decker said, "No special place where she wanted to visit or live?"

Corrine said nothing at first. Then she whispered, "California."

"She wanted to live in California?"

"She talked about it."

"Did she say what she liked about California?"

"Sunshine . . . the beach . . . movie stars. What girl wouldn't wanna go there?"

"So when you say California, do you mean the city of Los Angeles?"

"She talked about Hollywood." A pause. "Is that part of Los Angeles?"

"Yes, it's part of the city."

"You've been there before, Detective?"

"I have."

"Did you live there?"

"Yes, I did."

"Really, now." Corrine sat back in her chair. "So what are you doing out here in the middle of no-where?"

"Working for Greenbury PD."

"Obviously. Why'd you move here?"

"I wanted to live somewhere a little smaller and a little quieter."

She turned to McAdams. "Where are you from?"

"New York City."

"I suppose you wanted something smaller and quieter, too." Corrine's eyes went from Decker to McAdams. "Are you guys bored? Is that why you're digging up old cases like Erin's?"

"It has more to do with finding the bodies on Bogat Trail," Decker answered. "I'm wondering where your daughter fits in."

Corrine nodded. "What makes you think she fits in anywhere?"

"She may not." Decker was looking at her eyes. "I'm sure we'd both like to know one way or the other."

"I do miss her." The woman's eyes watered again. "So what are you gonna do if you don't find Erin's bones?"

"I'm going to look for her, Corrine. I'm going to try to find out what happened to her."

"Well, good luck with that."

"Did you ever hire a private detective?"

"Yeah, with all my extra money." Corrine laughed. Then she got serious. "I don't mean to appear cold, but she was thirty. If she wanted to disappear, I wasn't going to stop her."

"Do you think she wanted to disappear?"

"I already told you. I don't know." She stared at Decker. "You don't believe me. I can live with that. Cops usually don't believe me."

"Corrine, I believe that you're doing the best you can, okay? I'm not here to challenge you, just to get to the truth. That's what I'm paid for."

"Then go out and find the truth, Mr. Detective."

Decker smiled. "I'll do my best."

"No offense, but I think you're crazy to move from L.A. to here."

"None taken."

She looked down. "If you think she took off and doesn't want to be found, why are you wasting time looking for her? If she's trying to start a new identity, why stick your nose into it? She's an adult. She can do what she wants."

"Once I find out that she's alive, I'll back off. But until I know otherwise, it's my job to ask questions. I'm sure you can understand that."

She shrugged. "Are you done?"

"We are for right now. I know this is difficult and I appreciate your cooperation."

Corrine paused. "I'm sorry if I seem rude. I'm a little tired. Change of seasons and all."

"No problem, Corrine." Decker stood up and so did McAdams. "Thanks for the coffee and thanks for your time."

"If you need to ask more questions, you can come back again. I won't tell you anything different. Still, I have plenty of coffee and way too much time."

After they left and were in the car, McAdams said, "She's lying."

"I think so."

"She knows where her daughter is."

"I hope that's what she's holding back. That means Erin is alive and well."

"Do you think she knows where Erin is?"

"I don't know. It's possible that Erin made contact with her. If Erin calls her again, Mom will tell her that we're reopening the case. But . . . it could be that Erin is dead."

"Yeah, maybe we're just engaging in wishful thinking because we have three bodies and no clues."

"Could be. I still know plenty of people in L.A. I'll make contact and see if they can come up with anything."

"How do they weed out a missing person in a city of millions?"

"They've got a system, but it's not going to happen overnight."

"If she ran away, there has to be a reason."

"Maybe she stole money again. Maybe this time she got caught by a boss who wasn't as sympathetic as Diaz." Decker paused. "Any police reports in her file?"

"Not that I've come across. We should talk to her former boss at the Circle M. Want to do that now?"

Decker checked his watch. It was a little after nine. "Sure. Give him a call."

McAdams picked up his cell. "No signal."

"We'll get one soon. Let's get out of here."

They walked in silence to the car. Decker started the engine to let it warm up.

McAdams rubbed his hands together. "Or perhaps like Rina said, Erin escaped the clutches of a serial killer and took off to get a new identity."

"It's a theory."

"If it is a serial killer, he doesn't kill that often," McAdams remarked. "Once every couple of years."

"Yeah, I thought of that," Decker said. "It could be that the urge gets overwhelming. Or it could be he's an opportunist and the situation just presents itself."

"Like Erin walking home alone at night."

"Exactly. The only thing I can say is he has to be associated with Greenbury because all three victims were here when they died. And they all died when the colleges were in session."

"So why do you want to explore the cases individually instead of looking at points of intersection?"

"I keep going back and forth." Decker put the car in drive. "What do a thirty-year-old cashier, a transgender person who didn't totally make the plunge, a lost girl with a fluid sexual identity, and a party girl have in common?"

"I give up. Tell me."

"No, you tell me because I don't know the answer." Decker turned the car around and slowly drove over the dirt pathway. "Maybe it's like a common social cause."

"If it's a common social cause, it lasted through eight years."

"Yes, social causes do wax and wane in popularity." Decker finally reached a paved road. "But there is always a cadre of professors to take up the mantle even if the cause changes."

"Hank Carter and his socially conscious investing?"

"Maybe." He stopped the car. "I don't like him, but his charisma is interesting. Let's learn about the most popular professors in the Five Colleges. Because where you find a charismatic leader, you find acolytes—devotees who play follow-the-leader right off the cliff."

❧ 20

Decker said, "I'm going to make it decaf if it's okay with you."

"Sure." Rina was on the couch, making a list of what she would need for the upcoming high holy days of Rosh Hashanah and Yom Kippur. "Nice of you to stop by during your workday."

"I rushed out this morning. Thought a ten o'clock coffee break was in order. I'll set some fruit out for us as well. Be back in a minute."

While Decker was in the kitchen, McAdams sat next to Rina on the couch.

"What holiday are you planning for?"

"The Jewish New Year is in a couple of weeks."

"That's right. Is your family coming in?"

"No, they usually come up around a month later for the holiday Sukkoth. But I'm doing something for Hillel. I'm having a huge buffet for the students who are stuck at the colleges during the holiday."

"How huge is huge?"

"Around a hundred people more or less . . . or maybe just more."

McAdams smiled. "Does the old man know about it?"

"No need to worry him about things that are a little ways off."

"So that would be a no."

She smiled at Tyler. "You can keep the secret, right?"

He made a zipper sign over his lips. Decker walked in with a tray of coffee. "Derek Kinny called back. He can meet with us in an hour."

"Who's Derek Kinny?" Rina asked.

"Erin Young's boss at the Circle M," McAdams said.

"Ah. Are you making any progress?"

"Nothing to be excited about," Decker said.

"After talking to the mother, the boss thinks she might be alive," McAdams said.

"Really?" Rina said. "Why?"

"We both think Mom is holding back. But that's a gut feeling."

"Follow your gut."

"My gut is saying my blood sugar could use a jolt." Decker handed out the coffee cups. "Can I sit next to my wife, please?"

"Sure." McAdams scooted down until they were three in a row on the sofa.

Decker picked up a piece of apple. "Are you busy right now?"

"What do you mean?" Rina snapped back.

"I mean, are you busy right now. What is confusing about the sentence?" Decker regarded his wife. "What's going on?"

"Nothing."

Rather than argue the ridiculous point, Decker remained quiet. Rina looked at McAdams who said, "Don't blame me. I've been here the entire time."

She turned to Decker. "I'm planning an open house buffet for Rosh Hashanah."

McAdams said, "I for one think it's a great and charitable idea. Students could use a home-cooked meal. You're doing a service for every parent who has ever sent a kid to college."

"Thank you, Tyler," Rina said.

"Nice of you to check in with me beforehand," Decker said.

"I was going to tell you tonight."

"Tell me?"

"Ask you. If you don't want me to do it, I haven't formally sent out any e-vites."

"And then I look like an ogre."

"You are the ogre."

"You're pushing it, kiddo." He exhaled. "How many people?"

"Around fifty."

"That's not so bad."

"Maybe more."

"I already doubled the amount of people in my head." Decker sipped coffee. "It's a nice thing to do, Rina. I'm just not a nice guy. But go ahead and send out the e-vites. It'll be fine."

This time it was Rina who stared at him with a knitted brow. "You want me to do something for you, don't you?"

"I won't even pretend innocence. I'd like you to talk to some of the Hillel students. Find out who the popular professors are."

"And?"

"That's it."

"Okay. You know I deal with students from all five colleges. Do you want me to zero in on Morse McKinley College?"

"Not necessarily. I'd like to know the professors who are always at the forefront of social activism. I already interviewed Hank Carter. I didn't like him, but as of right now, I have no reason to suspect him. If you could find out about others, that would be helpful."

"You may be talking about two different groups of people: popular teachers and socially active teachers."

"I need those who overlap."

"And why are you looking at socially responsible, popular professors?"

"I'm really looking for socially responsible, popular professors who have a very bad dark side."

Rina was taken aback. "You suspect a professor is your serial killer?"

"I'm looking for someone who has been around for the last eight years. It could be a townie, but since we have three bodies who were students, I'm thinking it's someone employed by the five colleges."

"So it doesn't have to be a professor."

"No," Decker said. "Who else did you have in mind?"

"The clergy deals with all five colleges."

"Are you insinuating something about Rabbi Melanie?"

Rina laughed. "Just saying. And I'm sure you know that there are alternative clubs that traverse all five colleges."

"I don't know. Tell me."

"Well, without thinking about it, I've heard of a tattoo club, a piercing club, a liars club for both guys and gals, a B and D club à la *Fifty Shades of Grey*—"

McAdams said, "How do you *know* all this?"

"I hang around students all the time."

"And they just walk up to you and say, 'Hey, Mrs. Decker, did you hear about the *Fifty Shades of Grey* Club?'"

"The gossip happens when we're doing stuff like baking challah or packing weekend meals for the poor: when there are crowds of kids working in a small room. I overhear them talking. Most of the gossip is second- or thirdhand, but that doesn't mean it isn't accurate."

Decker said, "Just see what you can find out, okay? I'll do the same."

"Do I get paid for this?"

Decker smiled. "You get paid by me being in a good mood." When Rina rolled her eyes, he said. "I'll make it up to you. I promise."

McAdams said, "There isn't by any chance a serial killer club?"

"Not that I know of, but who knows what lurks in the shadows." She turned to her husband, "In return for my intel, I want you to do something for me."

"I've already said it's okay to host Rosh Hashanah here. That's quid pro quo."

"I have something else in mind." Rina made a face.

"You want to also host a break-the-fast meal after Yom Kippur."

"Uh, no, but that would be a very nice thing to do as well."

"Okay. *What?*"

"I wanted to host a Sukkoth party during the week. But if you can only tolerate one more social event, I think a break-the-fast buffet would be better. Hillel will give me a stipend for the food, by the way."

"You know, Old Man, parties are a good way to hear student gossip," McAdams said.

Rina gave Tyler a thumbs-up.

"You two are always conspiring against me." Decker laughed. "Do whatever you want, Rina. Actually I like the big parties better than the small ones. When it's big, the kids speak to one another and I don't feel the need to make small talk."

He turned to McAdams.

"You can come down if you want. This year, most of the holidays are over the weekend. Being a student yourself, you'd fit in nicely. You can be my mole."

"I thought I was your mole," Rina said.

"A good detective has more than one source of info."

"As long as I'm your main mole. Anyway, Tyler probably won't make it out on Yom Kippur this year. It's on a Monday and there's no reason to miss school."

"It's not a problem, Rina," McAdams said. "As shocked as you may be by hearing this, the law school usually empties out on Yom Kippur. Because who the hell has ever heard of a Jewish lawyer?"

* * *

The Circle M was interchangeable with any of the hundreds of twenty-four-hour convenience stores across the nation. The cashier sat in a lozenge-shaped area that contained a register, a locked glass cabinet of razor blades and batteries, a popcorn machine, a hot dog roller roaster, a microwave, a glass shelf of dough-nuts and pastries, three coffee thermoses, a napkin holder, paper cups with lids, plastic utensils, coffee accoutrements, and condiment dispensers of ketchup, mustard, and relish. The ICEE section—cherry, blue raspberry, and lemonade—was self-serve just outside the contained area. There were shelves holding jars, cans, and bags; a refrigerated area for beer, soft drinks, orange juice, and milk; and a small separate freezer unit that held ice cream and Popsicles.

Derek Kinny manned his post behind the regis-ter. He was in his late sixties, a doughy bald man with thick arms and stumpy legs. He had brown eyes, a ruddy complexion, and a bulbous veined nose from too much imbibing. He wiped down the countertop as he spoke to Decker and McAdams.

"I knew what Erin had done before I hired her."

"How?" Decker asked.

"It's a small town. Word gets around. I never asked her about it—I guess I was waiting for her to tell me. But she didn't, so I watched her. Far as I could tell, she wasn't stealing. I checked the receipts. Everything squared with the register."

"You took an awfully big risk."

"She was desperate. I believe that everyone de-serves a second chance."

"That's nice of you."

"Turns out I was right. She was a hard worker." Kinny shrugged and put the dishrag under the counter. "I was real sorry when she went missing."

"Tell me how you found out."

"She didn't show up at work and she didn't answer her phone. That was unusual. She was dependable for the most part."

"Did you go over to her apartment?"

"I did. Knocked on the door and no answer. I just thought she had enough."

"Enough of what?" McAdams asked.

"The town. She used to tell whoever would listen that she had dreams of better things."

"What were her dreams?" Decker asked.

"She wanted to go to beauty school in Hollywood and work with the stars." A small smile. "Problem was, she didn't have money. And she wasn't saving much, judging by how often I saw her at the local hangouts. She was kind of what we used to call a barfly in movies."

"She was older than most of the college students," Decker pointed out.

"Not *that* much older. And you know college boys. They'll screw anything that isn't nailed down."

"She hung out with college students?" McAdams said.

"Students, teachers, locals . . . anyone who'd buy her a beer and wanted a good time. She used to talk to me about it. I used to tell her if she really wanted to get away, she shouldn't be spending her cash drinking and getting tattoos."

"And what did she say to that?" Decker asked.

He smiled. "You know. 'Ah, Derek, a girl's gotta

have a little fun now and then.' We'd run into each other sometimes. Me and my wife. By the end of the evening, Erin was usually wobbly on her feet. We took her home several times as a matter of fact."

"So she'd drive home drunk?"

"She didn't have a car. She had a bike. The few times we took her home, we put her and her bike in the bed of our truck."

"Can we go back to the night that Erin disappeared?"

"If you want. Don't have much to tell— Damn. Excuse me."

A male transient with unwashed hair and dirty clothes had wandered into the store. Decker knew most of the small homeless population. There was a shelter, but when the weather was decent, most of them preferred the streets.

Kinny said, "Whadaya need, Jackson?"

"Just looking, Mr. Kinny." He looked at Decker with hooded eyes.

"Hey, Jackson, what's up?" Decker said.

"Don't suppose you could spare some change, Mr. Officer."

McAdams started to reach in his pocket, but then Kinny shook his head. "It's warm outside, Jay Jay. Move it."

"You got anything for me, Mr. Kinny?"

Kinny kept his eyes glued to the man's hands. He slipped his own underneath the counter and took out a big paper bag and pulled out a seed bagel. "It's old but not so bad if you dunk it in coffee. You can have a cup of coffee this time. But don't be expecting it every time."

"No, sir." Jackson grabbed the bagel and the coffee and went outside to eat his impromptu feast on one of the parking cement blocks.

Kinny said, "One second." He rushed outside and pointed Jackson in the direction of the road. The homeless man got up and left. When Derek returned, he said, "It's the deal I have with these guys. I give them a little food if they don't hang around my store. I'm right off the highway. We get a lot of fall leaf watchers who want a quick cup of coffee and a little somethin'. When they hang around here, it drives the tourists away."

A pause.

"Answer me something," Kinny said. "Why do they live on the streets if they can get a bed and a decent meal at the shelter in town?"

"They have mental problems. The shelters have rules. They don't like rules, and they especially don't like taking medication. But winter is the great equalizer. They'll be out of your hair soon enough." Decker smiled. "You were going to tell me about the night that Erin Young disappeared."

"The day after, she didn't show up for night shift."

"What did you do?"

"Locked up the store, went over to her apartment, and banged on the door. No one answered."

"She lived with a roommate," McAdams said.

"Well, her roommate must have been out. When she didn't show up the next day, I figured she finally left for Hollywood."

"When did you think something was wrong?"

"When she was reported missing about a week later by her mama. The papers said she still had her belongings in her apartment. I thought to myself, that isn't good." He paused. "The police came and talked to me. Then they talked to Lindsey Terrehaute who was the last one to see her before she disappeared. Lindsey didn't suspect anything bad. She said that Erin seemed in good spirits."

"The report said she was walking home the night she went missing."

"She often walked when the weather was mild. She didn't live more than a half mile from here."

"And when the weather was bad?"

"If she couldn't get a ride or she couldn't ride her bike 'cause of the snow, she'd bundle up and walk. Lots of people around here are retirees and don't have cars. It's not unusual to see people walking even in winter."

Decker nodded.

"I was retired when I bought this place." Kinny thought a moment. "Might have bit off more than I can chew. Some days when it's real cold, I just don't want to get out of bed. But the store is warm and it keeps me busy even if it's busywork. Fact is, everyone needs a place to go when they wake up in the morning."

Back in the car, Decker said, "When the police did a search of Erin's apartment, did anyone make note of a bicycle?"

"I don't remember a bicycle in the file, but I'll check it again."

"Even if it's there, she couldn't have gotten to L.A. on a bicycle."

"She could have pedaled far enough to catch a bus or even a train."

"Taken her bicycle with her?"

"There are racks on buses for bikes. I'll do a little probing."

"Good." Decker's cell went off and connected immediately to Bluetooth. Radar's voice said, "Where are you?"

"Tyler and I just left after interviewing Derek Kinny."

"Who the hell is he?"

"He owns the Circle M where Erin Young worked."

Radar paused. "Get a hinky feeling about him?"

"Not really," Decker said. "What about you, Harvard?"

"Seemed straightforward."

"Why?" Decker asked. "Don't tell me you found another body?"

"No new bodies. As a matter of fact we have the opposite: a student who vanished three days ago from Morse McKinley. The college just called. The parents are with the administration right now, and they finally figured that *maybe* someone should call the police. Idiots."

"What can you tell me about it?"

"Her name is Dana Berinson. She was last seen leaving a party at Morse McKinley at around eleven at night. She said she was going back to her dorm. Her roommate said she never returned. She's not answering her phone. Friends haven't seen her. Her boyfriend hasn't seen her. Get over there and find out what's going on."

"On it, Mike."

Radar said, "McAdams, when are you leaving?"

"Next week."

"Great. You can go with him."

"Not a problem."

"Tyler, just be sure to write up a summary of your assignments this summer so when I hand them over to replacements, they'll know what's going on."

"Already done."

"Good. Just keep me in the loop." Radar disconnected the line.

Decker turned the call to off. "Could you call Lindsey Terrehaute tomorrow? Ask her about Erin?"

"Sure. I'll also call the loquacious roommate, Caroline Agassi, and see what she has to say."

"Great. Have you really written up your summary?"

"Yep. Just have to log it into the computer. I'm nothing if not diligent." A pause. "Another missing girl?"

"Let's not assume anything."

"Even the obvious?"

Decker said. "With this new development, I think I'm going to be tied up for a while."

"I'm here for you, Old Man. Just let me know what you need."

"I need help. I need your help."

"Wow." McAdams paused. "Did I just hear you right?"

"I said, you're getting on my nerves and I'd like to see you gone ASAP."

McAdams smiled. "That's what I thought you said."

21

Flipping through several pictures of Dana Berinson, Decker saw a long-haired brunette with brown eyes, a long face, thin lips, and a prominent forehead. In the close-ups, she stared at the camera straight-on with a defiant look. When he asked about her height and weight, her mother, Jamie, told him she was five four and tipped the scales at 125 pounds. Mom was also a brown-eyed brunette with short hair. She was dressed in black slacks and a wheat-colored sweater that emphasized her wan complexion. Larry Berinson, Dana's father, was average height. His hair was white and his eyes were blue. He had on a dark suit, white shirt, no tie. He did most of the talking.

"Explain to me how a girl—a child really—goes missing for three days and no one does a damn thing about it?" His remarks were addressed to the president of Morse McKinley, Benedict Veldt, a slight man with sunken, pockmarked cheeks and blow-dried hair. "You explain to me how the hell this happens!"

"I assure you we'll get to the bottom of this."

"I'm not interested in your assurances. I'm interested in finding my daughter!"

"Mr. Berinson, I'd be frantic, too. But I promise you that *most* of the time, these things resolve with positive results."

Decker had never dealt with Veldt before. The president's voice was calm, but his actions belied him. He kept clasping and unclasping his hands. He turned to Decker and said, "Has that been your experience?"

"Most missing persons return after a few days, yes," Decker said. "But we're not going to wait around. I'll need a list of her classes, a list of her friends, and a list of all the students in her dorm." To her mother: "Any names you can provide me will be a start."

"I'm drawing blanks."

"Well, think, Jamie!" Berinson bellowed. "It's important!"

"Stop pressuring me!"

Decker held up a hand. "If you think of something, Mrs. Berinson, let me know."

"The only person I can think of offhand is her roommate, Allison. She hated her."

"Oh?" Decker said. "Do you know Allison's last name?"

"I'm blanking again."

Veldt got on the intercom. "Georgia, can you tell me who Dana Berinson's current roommate is?"

"You don't know?" Dad was once again outraged.

The intercom buzzed. "Allison Park."

"Thank you." Veldt turned to Mr. Berinson. "Students switch all the time. I wanted to be sure."

"Why didn't she like Allison Park, Mrs. Berinson?" Decker asked.

"I don't know specifics, just that Dana complained about her. Personality conflict."

McAdams said, "What about a boyfriend?"

"Mitch . . . Law or Lowe."

"Mitchell Law," Veldt said. "He's a junior here."

Decker said, "Could you get him down here now?"

Jamie said, "I'm not sure if it was serious."

"I'd still like to talk to him."

Veldt picked up the phone. He asked his assistant to find Law and send him over.

Decker turned to Veldt. "When was the last time her dorm card was swiped to get into the building?"

The president pinkened. "I'll find out for you."

"Do you have CCTV at the door of the dorm?"

"Certainly. I'll get that for you as well."

"I see you've come prepared!" Berinson snarled.

"We're all on the same side, Mr. Berinson," Decker said. "Has she done this before? Gone away for a few days without telling you?"

"Not three days!" Jamie answered. "Besides, I can usually reach her by phone or text. My calls are going straight to voice mail. And now her mailbox is full. I'm . . ." Her eyes teared up. "Something's wrong!"

"I'd like to get her phone records." Decker turned to Dad. "Do you pay for her phone?"

"Of course."

"Can I have permission to access her phone records if I need to?"

"What do you mean, if you need to?" Jamie snapped.

"It takes a day or two to get the records once I've

submitted a request. She may have shown up by then."

"Oh." Jamie looked away.

"Anything you need," Larry Berinson said. "Just tell me where to sign."

"I'll get you the papers," Decker said. "Does she text or e-mail you as well?"

Dad said, "She mostly corresponds with her mother. She only phones me when she wants money."

"Larry!"

"It's true. Why hide the obvious? According to Dana, we have *issues*. Her term, not mine. She's difficult. But that doesn't mean I'm not concerned."

"I know you are, Mr. Berinson. Children can be trying, but of course you love them." He turned to Dana's mother. "How often would you say you speak to Dana?"

"Like I said, it isn't daily. But she does text and she does e-mail me when she has something on her mind."

"Like what?"

The woman sighed. "Some injustice."

"Real or imaginary," Dad added.

"Larry, please!"

"Sorry." Larry held up his hand. "Sorry."

"Many college kids find injustices in the world," McAdams said. "It's part of the curriculum. How to protest against authority. And I'm not being facetious."

"You can say that again," Dad muttered. "All this tuition for her to tell me how my views are antiquated and immoral. It seems I haven't had an original thought in my head since she's reached adolescence."

"It's part of growing up, Larry. We weren't exactly angels when we were young."

"I would never talk to my parents the way she talks to us."

"What difference does that make now?"

"I'm just praying she didn't piss off the wrong person, Jamie."

"Excuse me," Decker interrupted. "Mrs. Berinson, could you please give me your phone?"

"Why?"

"I'd like to copy her texts and e-mails to you."

"If it will help, of course." With shaking hands, she unlocked her phone and handed it to Decker.

Decker scrolled down the list. "Is Dana.Katherine. Berinson@gmail.com her e-mail address?"

"Yes. Her personal e-mail. She also has one at school."

"dberinson2020@morsemckinley.org."

"Yes."

"Can I have your permission to access her e-mails from her various accounts as well?"

"Don't you need Dana's permission?" Larry asked.

"Under these circumstances, the service providers are usually cooperative if the parents contact the police and give us permission."

"Then of course."

Decker gave McAdams the phone. "Detective McAdams is more tech savvy than I am." To Tyler: "Send the correspondence to my phone and to the station house as well."

"Okay."

"Do you need somewhere quiet to work?"

"No, I'm fine here, thanks."

As McAdams started scrolling down the phone, Decker said, "Mrs. Berinson, I need you to be truthful with me. Does Dana have any bad habits?"

"I'm sure she's not perfect, but she's never been to rehab if that's what you're asking." Jamie was huffy.

"Tell me about the times she disappeared in the past?"

"She didn't *disappear*!" Jamie was insistent. "She wasn't always diligent about telling me where she went."

Decker nodded and waited.

"It was mostly over the weekends," Jamie told him. "From Friday night until sometime on Monday—I often wouldn't hear from her. She always laughed, told me, 'Ma, I'm fine. It's college. Leave me alone.'"

"Where do you think she went over the weekends?"

"I have no idea and she never told me. But she's never gone off like this without me being able to contact her!"

At that moment, President Veldt's phone buzzed. He picked up the receiver. "Mitchell Law is here."

"Thank you. Do you have a quiet place where Detective McAdams and I can talk to him privately?"

"Why not talk to him right here?" Larry demanded. "If there's something funny going on, I want to know about it!"

"I'll find out more one-on-one, Mr. Berinson. I'll tell you everything I know afterward."

Veldt spoke into the phone. "Put him in the comptroller's office, Georgia."

Decker said, "I'm still going to need that list of her friends and her dorm mates, Dr. Veldt."

"Of course. And I'll get you the CCTV tape as well as her card swipe. Let me tend to Mitchell first and I'll get what you need while you're talking to him."

"Don't tell him what's going on yet," Decker said.

"I won't." Veldt turned to the parents. "Feel free to call me. I'm here for you."

Mr. Berinson snorted. Jamie said, "What do we do in the meantime?"

"If you could give me a list of any of her friends— old or new—that would be a starting point." Decker gave her a piece of paper from his notebook and a pencil. "After that, just hang tight. Where did you two travel in from?"

"The Boston area," Dad said.

"Are you staying here overnight?"

"We're staying here until we get some answers!"

"I understand. Are you staying at the Inn of the Five Colleges?"

"Yes."

"Then I suggest you go back to the hotel. There's nothing further for you to do right now except make out that list. I promise to give you updates. And you can call me anytime you want. Hopefully this will be resolved positively and very soon."

Again, tears leaked from Jamie's eyes. "That

would be nice." A pause. "When do I get my phone back?"

"I'll bring it over personally when we're done with it." Decker tapped McAdams's shoulder. The kid had been deep in e-mail concentration. "Mitchell Law is here."

McAdams looked up. "Okay. Stay here and do this or . . ."

Decker said, "No, come with me."

Veldt came back in. "My secretary will show you where he is."

"Thank you." Decker shook hands with the parents. "I'll be in touch."

Waiting in the receptionist's office, they stood and watched Georgia speak in hushed tones over the phone. She gave them a two-minute sign with her fingers.

"Anything?" Decker whispered to McAdams.

"Mom's last communication with her daughter was a text the day before she allegedly went missing. It said . . . ah, here it is. *Can't come this weekend, Mom. Other plans.*" He looked up. "Is the 'other plans' sitting in the comptroller's office?"

"Who knows? I'm sure he'll make a point of telling us it wasn't serious. That's usually what they do when a girlfriend is missing."

"Let me take the lead on this one, boss. It's to your advantage to have a young guy go toe-to-toe with Mr. Boyfriend."

"Sure, go ahead. I'll feel free to jump in as needed."

"A jump is acceptable. Just don't pole-vault over me. I do have an ego, but then again, don't we all."

❦22

In college surveys, Morse McKinley always places within the top three spots for the best-looking undergraduate guys, and Mitchell Law was probably one of the reasons for the five-star rating. He was tall, well built, with regular features, thick dark hair, and eyebrows arching over probing blue eyes. He wore a brown cable-knit sweater over a blue-and-white plaid sports shirt and faded jeans. His knapsack rested at the side of his chair. He looked up from his phone when Decker and McAdams came in, but quickly returned his attention back to his cell. Without asking, McAdams took it from his hands and placed it in his pocket.

"Hey." Law frowned. "You can't do that."

"I just did." McAdams pulled up a chair and sat opposite, so close that their knees almost touched. "I'll give it back. I just want your undivided attention for a few minutes. We're the police by the way. The city police, not the school police."

"If you call this a city."

"Yeah, we are pretty nonessential except once in a blue moon. Today the moon is azure, my friend. A girl is missing: your girlfriend to be exact."

Law took his time before speaking. "I need to correct a couple of misconceptions."

"Please."

"One, I don't know anything about a missing girl. And two, I don't have a girlfriend. I have steady hookups . . . as in plural. Who are you referring to?"

"Dana Berinson."

Mitchell's face became a question mark. "She's missing?"

"No one has seen or heard from her in way too many days."

"Since like . . ."

"When was the last time you saw her?" When Law glanced at Decker, McAdams said, "Don't look at him, Mitch, look at me. Tell me what's going on."

"I don't know what's going on."

"When was the last time you saw Dana Berinson?"

"I think it was at a party."

"When was the party?"

"Last Thursday night."

"Where?"

"Morse McKinley."

"Please don't make me pull teeth. Where at Morse McKinley?"

"Beecher Hall—third-floor common room. It was the usual Thursday-night thing. I didn't even come with her."

"Who'd you come with?"

"I didn't bring a girl. Why limit your options?"

"So you went stag?"

"I knew just about everyone there. After a few years here, that's not unusual. It's a small college."

"I'm going to need names, Mitch."

"Of who saw me there?"

"Yes."

"How many do you want?"

"I'll take as many as you want to give me."

"Sure. Can I have my phone back?"

"Eventually. Did you talk to Dana at the party?"

"Yeah, sure. Of course."

"What'd you talk about?"

"Nothing much."

"What constitutes nothing much?" When Law wasn't forthcoming, McAdams said, "Mitch, if you're honest, it'll go a long way."

He shrugged. "As the party started winding down, we were both a little hammered. I asked her if she wanted to come back to my dorm and continue the party there."

"And she said?"

"She said no." He looked down. "I was surprised, actually. She rarely said no to me."

"So then what did you do?"

"What do you mean? I didn't give a shit. There were plenty of fish in the sea."

"You just said the party was winding down," Decker said.

"Still enough girls to reel in a big one." A smirk. "It didn't take long."

"We'll need a name," McAdams said.

"No problem. Babette Froiden."

"Dana's mother was under the impression that you two were an item."

"I dunno what Dana told her mom, but I'm not an item with anyone."

"And that was the last time you saw her?" McAdams said.

"That I can remember, yes." He grew serious. "Has something bad happened and you're not telling me?"

"Everything is under investigation," Decker said. "Did Dana have any worrisome habits?"

"She was up for whatever, you know."

"No, I don't know. Tell me."

"The usual."

"Which is?" McAdams asked.

Law exhaled. "She smoked a lot of weed, but that isn't exactly crises calling, right? I've seen her do pills . . . coke . . . molly."

"How often?"

"Often enough."

McAdams said, "Who'd she buy from?"

"Usually she brought her own stash."

"She had her own stash?"

"Yep, and she usually brought enough for sharing. It made her very popular." A pause. "Do you think she ODed somewhere?"

"Is that what you think?" Decker asked.

"I dunno. You're the professionals."

McAdams said, "Where'd she get her goodies, Mitch?"

"I told you I don't know."

"What if I were to tell you that I don't believe you."

"I don't care if you believe me or not, the answer is still the same. I don't know where she got her shit."

"If she wasn't missing, I wouldn't care," McAdams said. "But she is. Any information would be helpful."

Law just shrugged.

Decker said, "Are we going at this the wrong way, Mitch?"

The young man looked up. "What do you mean?"

"Was she the supplier who sold the shit?"

"Maybe . . . on occasion."

"Well, that's not good for long-term survival," Decker said.

McAdams said, "You have to start naming names, Mitchell."

"I don't know any names." He started squirming.

"I know you don't want to rat anyone out. I respect that. But you are talking to the police. People are going to assume stuff, so you might as well be honest with us."

"I don't know where Dana bought her shit." He shook his head. "That's God's honest truth." Another pause. "It probably wasn't local."

"Why do you say that?"

"Last year, she was always disappearing over the weekend. When she came back, she had a pharmacy with her. It made her very popular, like I said."

"It also makes you a target," Decker said.

"Maybe. But it's not hard to find shit. If one source doesn't have it, there's always someone else."

"You said Dana disappeared over the weekend. Any idea where?"

"Nope."

"Do better than that, Mitchell," McAdams said. "At least make a show of *thinking* about the question."

"I don't know where she went. Like I said, we weren't an item."

"And she did this every weekend?"

"Usually. But she always was back on Monday with her bag of stuff."

"So it wasn't unusual for her to go off for the weekend."

"Nope."

McAdams looked at Decker who said, "Again where do you think she went?"

"You can keeping asking, you'll get the same answer. I don't know."

"Take a guess." McAdams took out the kid's phone but held it firmly. "We need some help, Mitchell. Would I find it on your phone?"

"You know it's against the law to go through my phone without my permission. I could get you in big trouble."

"You don't think I thought about that before I took your phone?" Luckily the cell was still unlocked. McAdams began to scroll down his most recent calls. "I'm in Harvard Law. There are a lot of loopholes in search and seizure, did you know that?" He kept scrolling. "Christ, you do get a lot of action."

"Look, I'd help you if I could, but I don't know anything."

"Where do you think Dana Berinson went over the weekend?" McAdams tossed him back his phone. "Think, kiddo. It's why your parents are paying 60K in tuition at this vaunted institution."

Law pocketed the phone. "This is just a guess, okay."

"Got it."

"If she didn't get her shit locally, she had to go elsewhere to buy. So I would assume that she went either north or south to get her stuff."

"North or south as in . . ."

"The big cities. Boston or New York. Since she was from Boston, I'm thinking that if I was you, I might wanna look there first."

As they were walking back from the president's office, McAdams said, "What do you think?"

"Great interview."

"Thanks. What do you think about Law?"

"I believe him."

"Suppose theoretically I really did scroll down his phone."

"As long as it's theoretical."

"Suppose, theoretically, there were no phone calls or texts between Dana and him over the weekend. That would support your conclusion. On the other hand, it could mean that he knew she was already dead. If that was the case, he'd delete everything between them."

"I don't know, Harvard. She didn't swipe her card on Thursday night. Now, it could be that someone let her in. If that's the case, we should pick it up on CCTV. Or it could be she didn't go with Law because she had somewhere else to go. Maybe her roommate can help us out with a time frame."

"The roommate that she didn't like."

"She could still tell us if she went to sleep in her bed." Decker fingered the list given to him by President Veldt. "We know people in the Boston and

New York areas. I can certainly give them a call to find out if any bodies have been discovered. Beyond that, there isn't a lot we can do in the big cities."

"Maybe we should talk to Dana's old high school friends. They may know more about her habits than Law does."

"I agree with you. Start contacting them and see what you can find out."

"Will do. I suppose the elephant in the room is Bogat," McAdams said. "Do you think Dana is a fourth victim?"

"I don't know enough to answer that. What are you thinking? That digging up all those bodies reminded the killer that it was time to do it again?"

"The thought crossed my mind. Obviously, it crossed yours as well."

"Hope for the best, prepare for the worst." Decker checked his watch. It was a little after three. "I'm going to go check out Dana's room and talk to some of the kids in the dorm. You want to come?"

"Of course." McAdams rubbed his arms and looked across campus. The skies were deep blue as the sun burned off the clouds. The lawns were fading and the trees were starting to turn. "My favorite time of year. It gives me a certain transient energy. The days feel very fleeting, like you have to hurry up and finish whatever you've started. Autumn is this anteroom before you step into a cold, dark space."

"You dread going back to school?"

"No, I just don't like winter." He laughed. "Probably has something to do with being shot in the last two consecutive seasons."

Decker raised his eyebrows. "Don't come back until the snow starts melting."

"Oh, I'll be back." McAdams laughed again. "Third time's the charm, you know."

Decker smiled. He hoped it wasn't tinged with anxiety.

"Are you going to tell Dana's parents that their daughter is a dealer?"

"No need to stick it in their faces right now. But even if it comes to that, I'm thinking that the parents won't be shocked about the revelation. First, let's see how today goes."

"Want me to call up the people we know in Boston and New York?"

"Please. Do you have numbers?"

"I have Chris Mulrooney's number in Summer Village."

"Go for it." Decker stuck his hands in his suit jacket. "You might want to wait until we're indoors. You'll hear the call better."

"Sure." He put the phone away. "It really is fortuitous that Rina discovered the grave when she did. In another month or two, the ground will be completely frozen over."

"If it's the Bogat killer and he's found another place in the woods, we're toast if we don't find Dana before winter hits. When are you going back to school?" A pause. "I've asked you that question several times, haven't I?"

"I forgive your senility, Old Man. Or maybe you don't want to see me go?"

"That could be it, Harvard."

McAdams smiled. "School officially starts in a

week. I'd like to be there by the weekend unless you need me to search or something like that."

"If it comes to a search, I'll need you, yes." A beat. "Is next weekend Rosh Hashanah?"

"No, Rosh Hashanah is the weekend after this one. If Dana is still missing by then, I can come down over the weekend. You won't work, but I can."

"We're probably getting ahead of ourselves. I'm still hoping she'll turn up, none the worse for wear."

"Weird," McAdams said. "I've never known you to be an optimist."

"I'm closeted, Harvard. Deeply, deeply closeted."

23

Not more than a few minutes into the search of Dana's belongings, her roommate showed up. She was around five feet and not more than a hundred pounds, a pixie of a thing. Her face as well as her last name suggested Korean ancestry. She had long straight hair and dark eyes. She wore jeans, a green T-shirt, and a black hoodie.

"Excuse me?" Her voice was angry outrage. Mc-Adams looked up from the drawer he was rifling through and took out his badge. She examined it carefully. "If you're looking for her stash, I can tell you where she usually hides it."

Decker said, "Sure, show us where it is. She might have other things hidden there."

McAdams said, "And you are . . ."

"Allison Park. I knew this would catch up with her eventually."

"What would catch up with her?" Decker said.

"You don't have to play coy cop, okay? Everybody and their brothers knew she was dealing."

Coy cop? Where was the respect? If not for the position, at least for the fact that he was an old guy. "So we've heard."

Allison went to the closet and using a chair as a step stool, she looked on the highest shelf. "Here we go . . ." She brought down a knapsack and gave it to McAdams. "I have some studying to do now so if you wouldn't mind . . ."

Decker closed a desk drawer. "Your roommate has been reported missing." When the girl shrugged, he said, "You don't seem concerned."

"She'll show up."

"Does she go missing a lot?"

She shrugged.

"When was the last time you saw her?"

"We try to avoid each other. We're roommates, not friends." Allison plopped down on her bed, opened her backpack, and took out a laptop.

"That's not what I asked." No response. Decker walked over and closed her laptop. "I asked you a question."

"Hey. You can't do that."

"Allison, would you like to continue this conversation at the station house or can we keep it civil?"

"You can't take me in. I didn't do anything."

"You've got sacks of drugs here," McAdams said.

"That is so unfair! You know they aren't mine!"

"Well, someone's a serious dealer," McAdams said. "There are a lot of pills and a lot of powder in here."

"Allison, your roommate is missing," Decker told her. "People are worried about her. Just answer a few questions—politely—and then we're out of here. When was the last time you saw Dana Berinson?"

The girl looked down. "I dunno. Sometime last week."

"Last week has seven days. Can you get more specific?"

"Wednesday maybe." She scratched her nose. "Maybe Thursday."

"The last time she used her card swipe was Thursday afternoon. I heard she went to a party in the evening."

"That sounds like Dana."

"Did you see her leave for the party?"

"Thursday night I was in the library studying. Some students do that, you know."

"Okay. You didn't go to the party. Do you remember if she slept in her bed Thursday night?"

"Let me think. I came home around one . . . she wasn't there. I went to sleep." She looked up at Decker. "She wasn't there when I woke up the next morning."

"Did her bed look slept in?"

"She always tosses the top duvet over her mattress when she leaves, so I wouldn't be able to tell." Allison bit her lip. "Why do you think she's missing?"

"No one has heard from her since Thursday." Decker regarded the young woman. "Why don't you think she's missing?"

"Hey, that's *my* dresser," Allison told McAdams, who was still opening drawers.

"Maybe Dana hid something there," McAdams said. "I'll be careful."

"What you're doing *has* to be illegal."

Decker picked up Dana's mattress. "You really don't like her, do you?"

"No, I don't."

"Then why are you rooming with her? I thought as sophomores you have choices who you live with."

"I'm a transfer to Morse McKinley from Clarion. And from what I heard, no one wanted to room with Dana when they chose suites. So I got stuck with her. I've already requested a transfer, but the college is booked and I don't feel like going back to the PMS palace at Clarion, which is the only place that has room."

McAdams said, "School just started. You've been living with her for what? Three weeks?"

"You don't understand. It's like a zoo in here. People come in at all hours wanting to buy shit." Her eyes started to tear up. "I can't do any work, I can't get any sleep. So no, I'm not concerned about her. Why should I be? She's a pain in the ass."

Decker stood up from checking out Dana's bed. "Does she often disappear on the weekends?"

"I've only just started living with her, but she is gone a lot."

"Does she have a boyfriend?"

"She gets around from what I've heard."

"Can I take a look at your phone?"

"What for?"

"Yes or no."

"What difference does it make if I say no? You'll just grab it from me."

When Decker didn't answer, she unlocked it and handed it over. He scrolled down through the phone numbers and texts. There was nothing to imply that Allison had contact with Dana. He gave it back to her. "Thank you."

The girl's eyes spilled over with tears. "I don't know why people say this is the best time of your life. I hate college. I hate everyone!" She looked down. "I'm homesick! I'm such a stupid *baby*."

Decker sat next to her. "What's your major, Allison?"

"Economics/poli-sci." She wiped her eyes. "I want to be a lawyer. My father's a lawyer. We're real close."

"It's wonderful to be close to your dad. Give him a call. I'm sure he'd love to hear your voice. When my kids called from college, I was always happy to hear what was going on."

"I bet your kids didn't call you all the time like I do. God, I'm stupid."

"You're obviously not stupid. It's good that you stay away from Dana. She sounds . . . problematic. To answer your question, my kids are all grown now with families of their own. But even as old as they are, they still call me and my wife whenever something's on their minds. That never changes and I'm happy about that."

She nodded. "I'm sorry I was such an asshole. I'm really not that way. It's just everyone here is so tough. I need to buck up if I'm ever gonna be successful."

"Having a thick skin is helpful." McAdams closed a drawer. "But what is even more useful is sticking your nose in your studies and not getting distracted by bullshit." To Decker he said, "I don't see anything, boss. And I think I'd find something if it was there. This is one of the neatest college dorms I've ever seen."

"I'm compulsive," Allison said. "Dana's neat. I'll give her that much."

Decker said, "Can we talk about Dana for a moment?"

"I really don't know where she is. I hope she's okay. I just would be happier if she wasn't in my life."

"Who does she hang out with, Allison? I need to talk to some of her friends."

"Let me think." She wiped her eyes with her hoodie sleeve. "Charlie Wetzel. He's a big druggie, but you didn't hear that from me. He lives one floor up. Jennifer Adler . . . and maybe Katie Dentner. I've seen them both here a few times. They live in Clarion."

"Friends of yours."

"Not hardly, but I know who they are and I've seen them around Dana. Oh, also Mitch Law."

"Right," Decker said. "I've heard he's her boy-friend."

"Mitch hooks up with anything that's alive. Sheep and dogs beware."

Decker smiled. "So Dana and Mitch weren't exclusive."

"No one is exclusive at Morse McKinley. The guys here are good-looking and a bunch of ass-holes."

"So why did you transfer to Morse McKinley?" McAdams asked.

"It's a great college."

"You can take classes here even if you're enrolled in Clarion," McAdams said.

"Yeah, but I want to take the majority of my classes here, and it looks more prestigious to graduate from here than from Clarion. Plus, they have some outstanding profs here."

"Like?" Decker asked.

"Well, Hank Carter, of course." When Decker nodded, she said, "So you know him."

"I've heard the name. Tell me about him."

"He just won the Maybrown Award. That was a real coup."

"I don't know what that is."

"It's for social consciousness in finance. That's his specialty: socially relevant capitalism. I've signed up three times for his Intro to Social Government, but it's always full. And for a full tenured professor, he's a great lecturer. Always so interesting."

"So if you didn't take his class, how did you hear his lectures?"

"He gives a lot of free seminars. They're always full, too, but if you get there early enough, you can find a seat. He's been at Morse McKinley for a long time, and he's still as popular as ever."

"Any other favorite professors?" McAdams asked.

"I just enrolled in Dr. Kramer's class. So far, so good."

"That would be Jason Kramer?"

"Yes. How do you know him?"

Decker said, "We've been talking to people at the colleges regarding what's going on at Bogat Trail. He was one of many."

"Oh yeah, that." She bit her lip again. "Creepy. But I heard the bodies were, like, old."

"The bodies were buried years ago."

The lightbulb went off. Allison made a face. "You don't think that Dana . . . you know?"

"No theories, Ms. Park. All we want is for Dana to be found alive and well." Decker stood up. "Thanks for your help. We may call you again, if that's all right."

"Of course. I wouldn't want Dana . . . I do want to help. And I'm sorry for the attitude."

"Not a problem. And call your dad."

"Yeah, thanks." Allison's phone was already at her ear.

As they left, Decker heard her say, "Hi, Daddy."

"I'm going upstairs to talk to druggie Charlie Wetzel," Decker told McAdams. "Could you do me a favor?"

"You want me to find out everything I can about Hank Carter and Jason Kramer."

"You're getting good at mind reading. I know Hank Carter has been here for a while. Jason Kramer knew Pettigrew."

"He was also on our list of intersections of all three," McAdams said. "The girls had taken his classes."

"Do you know his specialty?"

"Psychology, but that's a broad field. I'll look up his field of interest. Isn't Rina working on charismatic teachers?"

"She is."

"I wonder if Kramer's name will come up."

"She should be home. I'll call her."

McAdams said, "You know, it would really be

helpful if I could take copies of the files and study them in my free time. I have a safe in Cambridge. I'll take full responsibility if something happens."

"We've had the conversation. Ask Radar."

"He'll say to ask you."

"If it's okay with Mike, it's okay with me. Just be careful. We're looking for a murderer who's responsible for three bodies. Don't underestimate what he's capable of doing."

"I have a gun—two guns. Don't worry. I'm into self-preservation."

"Okay, if it's okay with Mike, take the files with you back to school."

"You know, Rina invited me down for Rosh Hashanah. It's worth coming back just for her cooking."

"I can't believe the holidays are almost here. The year went fast." He turned to McAdams. "It was a really good summer."

"But nothing happened."

"That's exactly what I mean."

✌24

Charlie Wetzel was fuming. "Who told you about me? Her bitch of a roommate?"

Decker stared at the young man—six feet, well built, dark eyes, dark curly hair, and a nice-looking face except for the thin-lipped sneer. He wore a red sweatshirt emblazoned with MORSE MCKINLEY in gold letters, ripped jeans, and slippers on his feet. "Can I come into your room or do you want the entire floor to hear me?"

Reluctantly, Wetzel stepped aside and Decker went into the dorm room. It was messy and smelled like a gym locker. There were clothes on the floor, on the bed, on the desk, and even a few in the closets. Food wrappers and Styrofoam cartons of takeout overflowed from several garbage cans. Rows of beer cans took up an entire bookshelf. Decker elected to stand rather than figure out where to sit. "I'm not interested in your bad habits, Chuck. Dana Berinson is missing and your name came up as someone who knows her."

"And?"

"And I was wondering if you had any ideas about what happened to her."

"How would I know?"

"I'm not saying you do. I'm asking for help. Where do you think she could be and what do you think happened to her?"

"Oh." Wetzel sat next to a pile of clothes on an unmade bed. "You know she's like . . . a dealer here."

"I know. Any idea where she gets her stuff?"

He was quiet. Then he said, "I don't think it's local. She's from the Boston area. I have a feeling she dealt in high school and just continued on in college."

"She told you she dealt in high school?"

Wetzel nodded. "The stupidity of it all is she doesn't need to deal, you know. Her parents always give her whatever she asks for. They gave her a car on her seventeenth birthday—a Mercedes. She cracked it up two months later."

"You know her well?"

"Well enough for her to tell me some things. She thought it was hysterically funny. It's not that I'm self-righteous. I take things for granted. But that kind of spoiled behavior is an anathema to me." The kid scratched his cheek. "My opinion? Dealing makes her popular . . . gives her access to parties that she might not be invited to if she didn't bring some goods with her."

"She gave the stuff away or . . . what?"

"No, she charged, but not much. I don't think it's a commercial venture for her. Like I said, her parents give her plenty of money."

"How often does she go up to Boston to get the stuff?"

"This is judging from last year . . . which is when I met her."

"Go on."

"At least twice a month."

"How long was she usually gone?"

"I don't keep track of her business." The kid bit his lip. "Just logically, I think she'd be back on Mondays for school. But I really don't know. We're not close. It's a . . . business relationship."

"I heard she gets around."

A beat. "Maybe."

"Are you speaking from experience?"

"Does it matter?"

"It shows how well you knew her."

"When guys get drunk, they'll do anyone who happens to be around. And she was around a lot. But that doesn't change anything. I don't know where she is, Detective. I really don't know."

"Fair enough. Do you know who she's close to?"

"She does like guys. Mitchell Law. You should talk to him."

"What about girlfriends?"

He thought about it for a minute. "I saw her at several parties with Katie Something who goes to Clarion. I don't know her last name."

Decker looked at his notes. "Katie Dentner?"

"Yeah, that's it. She's kind of a stoner."

"Anyone else?"

"Not off the top of my head."

"When was the last time *you* saw Dana?"

"Last week . . . Tuesday or Wednesday." He thought a moment. "You know, she told me she was running low on shit. Maybe she went up north to buy more. But that's just a guess."

"And you think she bought her drugs in the Boston area."

"I don't know, but that's where she's from. If she got waylaid anywhere, I would think it would be up there rather than down here."

"You don't think it's possible that something bad happened to her in Greenbury?"

"Nothing happens in Greenbury—good or bad."

"Except for the bodies at Bogat Trail."

The boy looked blank, then wide-eyed. "I thought those bodies were real old. That they were put there years ago."

"How many years are there in years ago?"

"Why are you asking me about that? Isn't that your domain?"

"Rumors are my domain as well."

"I dunno specifics. Just that I thought I heard someone say it was like twenty years ago." Again he looked at Decker. "Not true?"

"Not true. Eventually it will be in the papers. We'll be asking for help following the coroner's reports on the bodies."

"Geez . . . so it's not like twenty years ago?"

"No."

"I hope it's not too recent." When Decker didn't answer, Wetzel said, "That would be creepy, like there's someone still out there killing people."

Decker remained silent.

The kid said, "Oh shit. You *do* think there's a killer on the loose, right?"

"No one has ever been charged for the murders, Charlie. You can draw your own conclusions."

* * *

It was past eight in the evening by the time Decker made it home. The place was serene and quiet. Rina walked out of the kitchen.

"You're home." She stood on her toes and kissed him. "I didn't hear you come in. Must be the dishwasher. I think there's something wrong with it. It groans like an old man."

"Hey, hey, hey."

"No reference to you, darling. You want dinner or do you want to wash up first?"

"I haven't been trekking through the steppes. I'll take dinner first. Did you eat?"

"No, I waited for you. I don't like to eat alone."

She went into the kitchen and Decker followed. "What'd you make?"

"Steak, salad, and if it's okay with you, let's crack open the Champagne."

"Why the celebration?"

"We're alone, for one thing. Tyler vacated his apartment but decided to check into a motel instead of staying here. I said he didn't have to, but he insisted."

"How was your day?" Decker asked.

"I was at Hillel making arrangements for the holidays. Sure you don't want to wash up first?"

"Do I stink or something?"

She hit him gently on the shoulder. When he returned—clean and in comfortable clothes—she was setting the steaks on the table along with a wooden bowl of salad.

"Smells wonderful."

"Probably won't be able to use the grill much

longer. Fall is coming on." She sat down and took a steak. "If you wouldn't mind opening the Champagne, please?"

Decker took a towel, wrapped it around the plastic cork, and popped it open. "Pink. Lovely." He poured them each a glass in a cut-crystal flute. Then he sat and took a steak. It had char marks on the outside and was medium rare on the inside. He was practically drooling over it even before he managed to get a piece into his mouth. It tasted as good as it looked. "Fantastic."

"Thanks. How was your day? Any luck with finding the missing girl?"

"Dana Berinson." Decker wiped his mouth. "I talked to her parents, I spoke to several guys she hung with, a few of her girlfriends at the colleges." He shook his head. "The picture isn't nice. She dealt drugs. And from what others told me, she's been dealing drugs for a while."

"Yikes. Do the parents know?"

"They claimed they had no idea. On the other hand, they didn't protest my assertions with any real venom. They're worried, Rina. When I suggested that she could have been in Boston over the weekend and that may be where she disappeared from, they became even more frantic. A big city is a scary place to be missing. Cities are good at keeping secrets."

"Poor girl." A pause. "Poor parents. It's only Monday. Is it possible she went on a bender and might suddenly show up?"

"That would be the best-case scenario." Decker took another bite of steak, savoring each chew. "If she did go traveling, road accidents are another possibility. I'm going to start checking hospitals when we're done." He took another bite. "What about you? How are the arrangements for the holidays going? How many people are you up to?"

"One fifty."

"Uh, I hate to sound cheap, but how much is this costing me?"

"It's officially a Hillel event so whatever I put out, they'll reimburse."

"Sure they will. After like a year or whatever."

"I'll put in the receipts right after the holiday. I do have a little news for you."

"For me?"

"Didn't you ask about charismatic professors?"

"Yes, I did, indeed. Let me get my pad." He came back and said, "Lay it on me."

"From Morse McKinley we have Calvin Greek in the Black Studies Department, Hank Carter in Economics/Poli-Sci, and Lydia Urbana in Women's Studies. In Duxbury . . ."

"Hold on a sec. Lydia with a Y?"

"Yes. Everything is how it sounds."

"Go on."

"Duxbury, I have Jason Kramer in Psychology and James Hopshoff in Poli-Sci."

"I've met Kramer. He was the one who pointed us in the direction of Lawrence Pettigrew when we found the first body."

"Where did you meet him?"

"He was helping some students out at the LGBT Center."

"So he's gay?"

"I never asked him. Whether that's relevant or not, I don't know. Is there more?"

"There is. In Littleton, we have Hortensia Ballask, who specializes in contemporary automotive design. Apparently she is very attractive. Every year, she has a waiting list for her course."

"That's six."

"Our final candidate is Michael Pallek from Clarion—Psych Department. His specialty is bias and prejudice in standardized testing. His Intro to Psych course is always overbooked. These are winnowed down because all of them have been at the colleges for at least eight years, which would put them in town with your oldest body at Bogat."

She handed Decker her list.

"I also found out where they studied: they're all Ivy Leaguers except for Hortensia Ballask, who has an engineering degree from USC, an MA in design from Otis, and worked for GM for ten years before she came out here. I figured you're going to do your own research so I didn't go into any great depth."

"This is terrific. Thank you." Decker looked up. "How did you get the names?"

"I asked my students at Hillel. The association serves all five colleges so I was able to get a good cross section. But of course, there may be others that fit your criteria."

"This is an excellent start. Thank you very much." Decker paused. "Do you mind if I call Tyler?"

"Why don't you invite him over for dessert, Peter? That way you can finish your steak."

"I've stripped it pretty good. Unless you want me to eat the bone."

"I'll save it for the dog."

"As of yet, Rina, we don't have a dog."

"Not so fast."

"You got a dog?"

"No need to panic yet." Rina smiled. "Jacob called me. He and Ilana are coming in for the *chagim*."

"That's nice . . . wait. How many dogs are they up to?"

"Three pugs." When Decker didn't answer, she said, "At least they're small." Another pause. "The house will be a free-for-all anyway. It'll be fun."

"If you say so."

"You love Jacob and Ilana."

"Especially Ilana."

"Hey! That's my son you're talking about."

Decker laughed. "He's my son as well. Jacob's a wonderful kid. He's just a little . . . restless."

"He's odd, but we love him. At least his start-up is no longer losing money. Maybe eventually we'll even get our money back."

"Better to give it to him while we're still alive." Decker stood up. "Let me call Tyler. Don't clean up. I'll do it."

"I don't mind."

"No, no. I'll do it. My watch keeps beeping me that it's time for me to stand up anyway." He laughed. "It's funny. My wife never nags, but my watch is a bitch and a half."

❧25

When the cell rang, it was still dark and Decker had been sleeping deeply, dreaming about racing with either a car or a horse or maybe it was some kind of mongrel, robotic hybrid. He groped for the phone on the nightstand and grabbed it as quickly as he could, but not before Rina murmured out a "What is it?"

"Tyler." Decker was already up and putting on a robe. Into the phone he said, "You okay?"

"Yeah, I'm fine," McAdams answered. "I've been looking over the names we talked about and this is what I came up with. Do you have a pencil?"

Decker went out of the bedroom and into the living room. He turned on a lamp and looked at the time on his cell. "It's four-thirty in the morning."

"Yeah, I couldn't sleep. Too much coffee. Are you ready?"

"No, I'm not ready." Walking into the kitchen, he turned on the cooktop and put on a kettle of water. "Do you know that even if *you* can't sleep, most other people *are* sleeping at four-thirty in the morning?"

"Not if you work at a bakery. Listen, Old Man, if

259

you want an apology, mea culpa. But you know that you're not going to fall back asleep, so just hear me out. Do you have a pen? Yes or no?"

"I'll call you back in five minutes." Decker hung up and exhaled audibly. He turned off the kettle and decided to go full on with brewed caffeinated coffee.

Entitled little bastard.

He took out the coffee can and hunted around for the scoop.

Rina came trudging out. "I can do that."

"Go back to sleep." He turned and knocked over the coffee can. Grounds spilled everywhere. "Shit!" Another exhale. "What the hell is wrong with him?"

"No sense being mad. He's just enthusiastic."

"No, he's inconsiderate. But I gave him a lot of work yesterday and he came through."

"Everyone has their good points. I'll take care of the coffee, Peter. As a matter of fact . . ." She checked the clock. "The first batch of fresh bagels usually comes in around five. I'll clean up the mess, make the coffee, and then fetch the bagels. You find out what he has to say, and we can have a very leisurely breakfast before we both go to work."

"How can you be so chipper after being woken up at four-thirty in the morning?"

"It's the calm before the storm. Once the holidays hit in a couple of weeks, I'll be a monster."

"You're never a monster—at least not to the guests."

"What does *that* mean? Never mind. Don't ask the question if you don't want to hear the answer."

She pushed him out of the kitchen. "Go make your call."

Instead of calling right away, Decker took the opportunity to put on sweats and slippers. He made the bed, albeit with lumps, and then took out his pad and pencil. As he was phoning McAdams, he smelled the distinct aroma of a fresh brew of java. "What?" he barked into the phone.

"You have a pencil—"

"Yes, I do. *What?*"

"I'm going to ignore your piqued tone of voice and cut right to the chase. Let's talk about Jason Kramer. He's not only involved in the LGBT Center, he's also deputy chairman of the Psych Department at Duxbury *and* at Clarion."

"He's got an appointment at both colleges?"

"He does. And get this. He's also one of the liaison faculty members for the incoming freshman classes at Clarion. Delilah Occum was a psych major. She took his Intro to Psych class her freshman year at Duxbury, which is usually SRO, and it's only open to Duxbury students because psych is a popular major. When Kramer is listed as the prof, it's got a waiting list a mile long. Delilah must have pulled strings to get into the class. And Kramer's got a lot of fans judging by the Duxbury rate-a-prof survey."

"What is that?"

"All the colleges have them: yearly surveys of how the students feel about classes and teachers. It's the first website I went on once you gave me the list of names. Usually the only people who have access to the Five Colleges rate-a-prof website are students. But I use Mallon's address. Even though she graduated, her e-mail is still active. Colleges usually keep them active for a while before they pull the plug."

"Does she know you're using her school address to access files?"

"Yes, Dad, I asked permission. It's mallon.j.euler@ kneedloft.edu in case you're interested. Anyway, Kramer gets high marks for content as well as teaching. Plus, he identified Pettigrew when we first met him, so there's our link between him and Lawrence. We also know that Yvette Jones was active in the LGBT Center during her freshman year. It's certainly possible that she and Kramer crossed paths. So I would rate him a keeper on our potential killer list."

"What about Erin Young?"

"She was working as a waitress when he was an assistant prof. Beyond that, I haven't found a link. You could probably ask around and find out if Kramer drinks at the College Grill."

"Okay. Done. What else?"

"Hank Carter, of course. He's definitely up there in the charisma category. He was voted number one teacher at Morse McKinley for the last five years running. In addition to being a prof—and this may or may not be relevant—for the last five years, he has been developing a nonprofit mutual fund of socially conscious investing. Every penny that the fund makes at the end of the year is disbursed to charity."

"Is there something fishy about it?"

"Nothing came up when I did a prior lawsuit search. But usually saints are too good to be true."

"I would agree." Rina brought Decker in a fresh cup of coffee. "Thank you."

"You're welcome," McAdams said.

"I wasn't thanking you. I was thanking Rina for making me fresh coffee."

"Rina's up at four-thirty in the morning?"

"This may come as a revelation, but she and I share a bedroom."

"Tell her I'm sorry for waking her up."

Rina shouted so McAdams could hear. "Apology accepted—this time." To Decker, she said, "I'm off to get bagels. Finish this up by the time I get back."

"Do my best." He kissed his wife. To McAdams, he said, "What else?"

"Hold on to your mustache, Old Man, I'm getting to the interesting part. About two other popular teachers: Lydia Urbana, who teaches women's studies at Morse McKinley, and Michael Pallek, who is a full professor in the Clarion Psych Department with an adjunct appointment in Littleton and Morse McKinley."

"Links to our victims?"

"Yvette took some women's studies courses at Morse McKinley. She could have easily crossed paths with Lydia. And Delilah, like I told you, was a psych major at Clarion so she could have theoretically crossed paths with Pallek. Not sure where Pettigrew fits in. I'm still looking."

"Good. Is that it?"

"One more thing that I found interesting. Hank Carter's wife's name is Christine. Her maiden name is Urbana."

"She's Lydia's sister?"

"She is. Hank Carter is Lydia's brother-in-law. And if that's not enough for you, Michael Pallek is *married* to Lydia Urbana. He is also Hank Carter's brother-in-law. I've heard of husband and wife serial killers. I know about fraternal and sororal serial killers. Yes, FYI, sororal is the proper adjective. Anyway, I looked up family serial killers. There have been a few in history—the Benders of Kansas in the late 1800s, the Sawney Bean clan on which the movie *The Hills Have Eyes* is based."

"Interesting," Decker said. "It's not just biology that determines a homicidal family, Harvard. Think Manson."

"Yeah, of course."

"What about the other teachers on the list?"

"Nothing to report so far. I can't find connections between them and our victims except that they were all teaching at the colleges when the girls went missing. But I'll keep looking." A pause. "That's it for now."

"Good start, McAdams, but it could have waited until seven in the morning."

"Whatever. What do you think about a murderous family hypothesis?"

"Anything's possible."

"C'mon. What do you think? Honestly."

"The connections are interesting, but we're talking about a bunch of educated—highly educated—people."

"Intelligence is orthogonal to evil. You know that. And if you know anything about academics, you might even say there is a correlation between the two."

"I'll do a little digging. You go make those phone calls."

"Yeah, yeah. They're on my to-do list." McAdams paused. "You know, I could really use a cup of coffee."

"Lucky for you there's a café on almost every corner of town."

"They don't open until six. I guess it's off to my favorite twenty-four-hour truck stop, Paul's. Don't blame me if I smell like bacon and sweat. It's not me, it's the company I keep."

The profiles of serial killers over the centuries ran the gamut of race, religion, socioeconomic status, intelligence. Most killers were from disturbing backgrounds that included sexual and physical abuse, but some were spawned from intact families with nothing to suggest a bad seed in the making.

Pairs who killed—siblings, friends, and couples—usually came from highly dysfunctional and sadistic backgrounds, like Rosemary and Fred West. But there were exceptions. Karla Homolka for instance was an attractive, middle-class, popular teen. When she hooked up with Paul Bernardo, she became monstrous, arranging the rape and murder of her younger sister, Tammy, as a Christmas present for her psychopathic husband.

Serial-killing blood-related families—there weren't a slew to draw from—tended to be poor and uneducated, usually living in isolated rural areas. Within the family, strict rules were enforced, and frequently parents carried out acts of sadism and incest with their children. Away from the prying eyes found in cities and towns, the clans committed barbaric acts, including torture, dismemberment, and cannibalism.

By the time Decker closed the computer, it was eight in the morning. He had spent sunrise reading synopses of some of the most notorious depraved human beings in history. He sat back in his desk chair at the station house and exhaled in a whoosh, trying to rid his body of all the poison he had just ingested.

Three bodies were buried up at Bogat Trail and every possibility of how they got there was up for consideration. Although professors were sometimes petty and backbiting, especially in pursuit of tenure, a family of sexual serial killer academics seemed a little far-fetched. Besides, Carter, Urbana, and Pallek all had tenure. As interesting as the theory was, the workday had started and Dana Berinson was still missing.

It was the living before the dead.

All morning Decker and McAdams did a block-by-block canvass, showing people her picture, trying to get a toehold on Dana's whereabouts. When luck proved to be elusive, Decker spent the afternoon calling up police stations, jails, hospitals, and morgues from Greenbury to Boston. Three hours into the search, a morgue near Boston reported an unidentified beaten female body brought in two days ago. The age and race fit and Decker asked for a photo. Twenty minutes later, he was e-mailed a bloated, lacerated, and bruised face. The features were hard to distinguish, but eye color doesn't change. Dana's were brown; the body had eyes with blue irises.

At four in the afternoon, after another three hours of phone calls, he finally found another possibility. After being placed on hold numerous times, he was put through to the ICU at St. Beatrice, a small hospital seventy-five miles north of Greenbury in the tiny New England burg of Marrison in Massachusetts.

"One-person car accident," the nurse told him. Her name was Edie Aarons. "The car went down a steep embankment and caught fire, but somehow the driver got out and crawled to safety. She was brought in Sunday afternoon and she was unconscious. I don't know how long she'd been out there."

Decker's eyes narrowed. "The car caught fire?"

"That's what I was told."

No matter how many times it happened in movies, it was rare for cars to explode on impact. The fuel was there—that is, gasoline—but conflagrations usually required a heat source to get the fire going. Something like matches or even better a torch. The nurse was still talking.

". . . the accident *could* have happened any time over the weekend. Regardless of when it happened, she was brought in Sunday afternoon."

"And she's still unconscious."

"She's in a deep sedation to reduce the swelling on the brain."

"Is she going to make it?"

"Touch and go."

"And she didn't have any ID on her."

"Like I said, the car burned—probably along with her ID."

"But she managed to escape and crawl to safety."

"Miracles do happen."

"I'm sure. So if she was unconscious, who called it in?"

"I don't know. But I do know that Traffic is looking into it."

"Who in that area does the collision report?"

"That would probably be the Massachusetts State Police. But I'd start with the Marrison Sheriff's Department first. Less bureaucracy. They usually coordinate with MSP. We get a fair number of crashes along that stretch of road because it's dark and can be slippery in winter. Of course, it wasn't winter. Anyway, try them. You need a phone number?"

"I have Massachusetts State Police. I can look up the Marrison Sheriff's Department. Thank you, though. Could you text or e-mail me some description of your victim? Eye color, hair color . . . things like that?"

"Sure."

"Also, is there a way you can send a picture? I have a set of very concerned parents."

"It isn't pretty."

"I was a homicide detective for thirty years. I can handle it."

"You wouldn't want to show it to the parents."

"And I won't." At that moment, McAdams walked in. Decker waved. "I'm not bad at facial recognition. If it's close, the parents will want to drive up and see for themselves. Actually, they shouldn't be driving. I'll arrange a car."

"Do you have a picture of what she looks like normally?"

"I do. I'll e-mail it to you." After they exchanged cell numbers and e-mail addresses, Decker said, "Before I tell the parents anything, let's compare pictures and have another conversation."

"Sure. And I hope this is your girl."

"Thank you, I hope so, too. But whoever she is, I hope she recovers soon." Decker hung up.

"You found Dana Berinson?" McAdams asked.

"Possibly. Where were you?"

"Talking to Lindsey Terrehaute and Caroline Agassi."

"Erin Young. Learn anything?"

"Nope. Caroline does talk a lot, but both of them seemed honest. They don't know what happened. What's going on with Dana?"

Decker gave him a recap. "You know, Harvard, maybe you should go up north and start preparing for school. I may need you up there."

"Trying to get rid of me. I'm *sorry* I called you early, okay?"

Decker laughed. "No, Tyler, I'm being honest. I may need your help as a liaison up north."

"Actually, I was thinking about settling in over the weekend."

"Good. It would serve both of our needs if you did."

"Sure you're not trying to get rid of me?"

"Not this time, amigo. Not this time."

* * *

"It was a 2014 Honda Accord sedan. There was enough framework still left to determine make and model. Light gray paint on the exterior and black leather in the interior."

Over the phone, Decker was talking to Byrd Hissops—the Massachusetts detective assigned to the car accident. "That matches my missing person's vehicle."

"We've towed the car to the lab and we put a team on it."

"Is something off-kilter?"

"Why do you ask?"

"Because you towed the car to the lab—unless that's your usual procedure."

"It's not."

Decker said, "I thought it sounded off when I first heard about the accident. Even going over an embankment, cars usually don't catch fire. Interiors burn—they have soft material that's flammable—but it takes a very high temperature to burn metal."

"Well, since you asked, I'll tell you what we found," Hissops told him. "But first I'll tell you what we didn't find. A license plate. We found a frame, but no license plate."

"That's not good."

"No, it's not. Plus, Traffic didn't find any skid marks. There were tire tracks going over the embankment so it's possible that she fell asleep at the wheel. No sudden move, no skid marks. But the treads on the tracks look like the tires were rotating very slowly, not moving at high speeds."

"Someone pushed it over."

"It's one scenario, especially if the burn turns out to be arson. State has towed the car from the scene and put investigators on it. Whatever happened, it's a miracle that the girl is alive." A pause. "She is still alive, right?"

"Yes, but she's in critical condition." Decker was writing as he talked. "So you think you're dealing with the collision as an attempted murder?"

"Nothing is definite until we get all the reports back, but that's what it looks like to me."

"Could you find a VIN number anywhere? It would be confirmation."

"We're working on it," Hissops said. "Want to tell me about the girl?"

"Her name is Dana Berinson. She's a student at Morse McKinley."

"That's one of the colleges in Greenbury."

"Yes."

"We get lots of students driving that road. It's more direct but often it isn't any faster because it's two lanes and very dark. I keep asking the state for more road lights, but bureaucracy is slow to the point of slothful. Anyway, that's not important in this case because I don't think this was an accident. What's your interest in this case?"

"The colleges asked Greenbury Police to help find the girl. There are things I need to tell you about this girl that will probably be relevant to your case. She has a reputation as a dealer." Decker recapped what he knew about Dana Berinson.

"And she dealt up north?"

"That's what several people told me. Whether it's true or not . . ."

"I'll check it out."

"There's one more thing."

"I'm listening."

"You must know that Greenbury is working on a series of unsolved murders."

"I thought those bodies were old."

"They are not recent murders, no. But the victims were all students at the colleges, and the buried bodies were discovered in the same area—Bogat Trail. We're probably looking at serial killings. We don't have any suspects, but our thinking is that it's someone local and someone associated with the colleges."

"So how does she fit into this?"

"I don't know that she does. We haven't a clue to the killer's identity, so he may still be active in the area. I'm just thinking that since Bogat is now off-limits, maybe the killer is trying something new."

"Makes more sense if he just buries the bodies elsewhere."

"Of course that would be logical. There are acres of virgin woods out here. But now all eyes are on activities in the woods. And Dana is a college student who—like the others—seemed to vanish into thin air. I'd be interested in any forensics you pull up regardless of how large or small."

"I'll make a note of it. Are you going to notify the parents?"

"Yes. I've already booked a car to take them to the hospital. Thanks for your help."

"Good luck," Hissops said.

"Regardless of the outcome, I'll keep in touch." Decker said good-bye, hung up, and blew out air.

He grabbed his coat and went over to the Inn of the Five Colleges.

It wasn't as bad as a death notification, but it was painful. After the expected moans, groans, and cascades of tears, Decker managed to convince Larry Berinson to take the provided car service rather than drive the seventy-five miles to the hospital.

Afterward, Decker went back to the station house, called Morse McKinley, and updated the college. Then he filed a mountain of paperwork. Home by ten, he was tired, grumpy, and famished. An hour later, he was in bed, showered and fed, with a book about the Founding Fathers of America in his hand. He was reading words but not comprehending anything because his mind had wandered from Dana Berinson's "accident" to the Bogat bodies to the teachers that McAdams had singled out.

Rina got into bed and crawled under the covers. "Sleepy?"

"A little."

"We got up at four-thirty in the morning. How could you not be zonked?"

"My brain won't turn off."

"I could talk to you about *my* day. That usually puts you to sleep."

"C'mon now." He put the book on his nightstand. "Play nice."

"At least one of your cases was solved."

"Yes, it looks like we found Dana Berinson. But we're far off from solving the case." Decker gave her an update.

Rina was wide-eyed when he was done. "You really think it's related to Bogat?"

"I don't know, Rina. Superficially no, but right now I'm not about to rule anything out."

"Is Dana Berinson's accident even your case?"

"The crime is not in my jurisdiction. It isn't even in the state of New York. But she was my case to begin with, so I'm sure they'll extend me a courtesy. The dude on the phone sounded reasonable."

"Will she even make it?"

"I certainly hope so. I'm working with so many unknowns. Like Erin Young. I don't know if she's alive or dead."

"They haven't found any more bodies in Bogat?"

"No."

"So maybe she is alive."

"If she is alive, she left without taking anything. Meaning she was scared to death."

"Like we said, maybe she was the lucky one." Rina's voice was hushed. "You'll solve it."

"You think?"

"Yes, I think. And you think too much. Try to get some sleep."

"I suppose I should." He kissed her good night and turned off the lights, his mind slowly drifting off with images of bloated faces, mangled metal, boxed graves filled with bones and bodies, all of it ripped out of his current and former case files.

❦26

Calling for an appointment didn't mean getting an appointment. Decker knew from his last murder case that college professors could be very elusive. He left messages with Michael Pallek at his office at Clarion, for Lydia Urbana at Morse McKinley College, and for Jason Kramer at Duxbury. With that done, he regarded the boxes that held files from the disappearances of Pettigrew, Occum, and Jones. He also took out the newly minted murder books for each of the three victims. Often it helped to compare old and new.

The first time that Decker had read the missing person files, he had started with Occum and worked backward. This time, he decided to start with Jones and work forward. He had previously filled the pages with Post-its and it annoyed him that he was still asking the same questions. He hadn't learned anything new or spotted a different avenue of detection. Even after he talked to the professors, he doubted that he'd come away with something meaningful.

Cold cases were the worst. But when you got a solve, they became the best.

By ten-thirty in the morning, he was prematurely tired and hungry and still in the dark. He took out his tuna sandwich from the station house fridge, filled his coffee cup, and opened up Erin Young's missing person file. As usual, he ate too fast. He looked up from the pages and saw Kevin Butterfield hanging up from a phone call. He was tall and bald and had been with Greenbury PD for over twelve years. "Kev?"

"Yo."

"Are you familiar with someone named Quentin Newhouse?"

"Quentin Newhouse?"

"He's in Erin Young's files."

"Oh yeah, him. We call him QVC."

"The homeless guy who sells junk at the underpass to the highway?"

"Hence the name QVC. What do you want with him?"

"Why was he interviewed in connection with Erin Young?"

"Let me see the pages." Decker handed them to Kevin, who said, "Yeah, now I remember. He was selling a pair of sandals that looked like the ones Erin's roommate described her as owning."

"Were they the same sandals?"

"Nothing to say yes or no." He paused. "We have Erin's DNA on file, but we didn't test the sandals at that time. She was a grown woman with not a lot of ties to Greenbury. She could have left of her own accord."

"She didn't take anything with her."

"Rumor said she lifted money from her previous

job. If she took money from her new boss, that could explain her sudden departure."

"Absolutely."

Kevin thought a moment. "The sandals are still in evidence. We could have them tested."

"Yeah, let's do that." Decker's eyes reread the interview. "He said he found them in a Dumpster. And you went back and checked the Dumpster."

"Yes, I remember that very clearly. We didn't find anything else that clued us in to Erin's disappearance. But I'll tell you what I did do. I took a lot of the paper from the Dumpster. Not the garbage, but the shit that people usually throw away—useless mail, old receipts, things like that. It's all in the evidence room if you want to take a look. If you pull out the sandals, I'll get them tested."

"Maybe. Thanks." Decker paused. "Do you think if I go see Q, he might be able to remember anything about the case?"

"He's usually pickled. That was the problem we had with him. But be my guest. Sometimes you catch him on a good day and he's pretty lucid."

"I'm not getting anywhere and I have nothing better to do." Decker stood up and took his jacket from the back of the chair. "Besides, you never know what wares the guy has from Dumpster diving."

It was the first gray day outside, but the September air was still mild. As a native Floridian and transplant Angelino for the last sixty-plus years, Decker was still acclimating to the changes of seasons. Most normal people gravitate toward hot climates as they age. He and Rina went in the opposite direction, but he didn't mind. In fact, he liked the cold. There was nothing better than curling up in front of a fire with a good whiskey and reading a great book. It was a luxury of his dotage: no small, runny-nosed, noisy children underfoot who needed to be dressed and undressed every time they went outside to play.

During the summer months, there was a small homeless camp at the underpass. When the days got shorter and the temperature dropped, some of them moved into the homeless shelter that provided a comfortable bed and three squares a day. But there were rules: no booze, no illegal drugs. The tenants were required to make up their beds, shower, and take their meds. Some capitulated; others evaporated only to materialize at the underpass in the following year's thaw. Gray days like this one were arrows pointing the population to warmer places with a tolerant police presence.

The area was empty except for a man sitting on the dirt with a blanket spread out in front of him. On top of the cloth was junk that he apparently felt was valuable. Q could have been anywhere from thirty to sixty, so Decker split the difference and placed him around forty-five. The homeless man had a straggly gray beard, a lined face, and hair that was partially combed and partially matted. He had red-rimmed blue eyes and thin lips and repeatedly jerked his head to the left as if beckoning someone to come hear a secret.

"Hey, Q."

"Hey, mister."

"Where is everyone?"

Q shrugged. He gave Decker a smile with a

mouthful of yellow teeth and jerked his head to the side. He pointed to his junk with a loving gesture. "Need something?"

"Whatcha got?"

"Take a look."

Decker tried to find something that wasn't too dirty or too broken. The closest he came was the head of a hammer without the handle. He could turn it into something useful. He bent down and picked up the head. "What about this?"

"It's a good one."

"How much?"

"For you, five dollars."

"I'll give you a dollar and that's nice of me." When Q waved him off, Decker said, "I'm not paying five dollars."

"Four."

"Two."

"Three."

"Two."

"All right, all right." Another jerk of the head.

Decker pocketed the hammerhead and gave the man two bucks.

Q took the bills with dirty hands. "So what do you really want, mister?"

The man was a homeless alcoholic and probably mentally ill, but some native intuitiveness was still there. "I'm a cop."

"Yeah, I know you're a cop. You're looking right at me. Most people look away. Whadaya want?"

"Do you remember a missing woman named Erin Young? She disappeared from here about four years ago."

Q jerked his head. "I never hurt no one."

"I believe you. Do you remember Erin?"

"Don't think so."

His eyes shifted downward. Decker knew he was lying. He said, "She worked as a cashier for the Circle M Mart. Her mother lives about three miles away from here in the woods. Corrine Young. I'm sure you know Corrine." Decker paused. "She gives you some food and a little nip now and then, right?"

"Yeah, so what's the harm?"

"No harm. So now that you remember Corrine, do you remember Erin?" A pause. "Erin was Corrine's daughter."

Q nodded his head. "She was nice. She worked at the mart, yeah."

"Right. Did she also give you things?"

"Sometimes."

"Food?" When Q nodded, Decker asked. "What else?"

"Once she gave me a pack of batteries. Said they were expired and weren't no good. Even so, I put them in my flashlight. It worked. So there you have it."

"Good deal."

"Mama didn't raise a fool."

Decker smiled. "So you must remember when she went missing."

Q jerked and nodded. "Now I do, yeah."

"The police talked to you about it."

"I didn't hurt her. I didn't hurt no one."

"I know. But you do remember that the police talked to you."

"Yeah, I remember. I'm not retarded, you know."

But you are cagey, Decker thought. "What'd they talk to you about?"

"They talked to me about the shoes."

Decker stared at him. "Right. The sandals. Do you remember where you found them?"

"Where I find everything. In the Dumpsters."

"Do you remember which Dumpster?"

Q shook his head. "Don't think so."

"How many Dumpsters do you have?"

Q shrugged. "More than one."

"Five?" No answer. "Ten?"

"Between five and ten," Q answered. "I 'member showing the police where I found the shoes. So go ask them 'bout it, Mr. Cop. Your own guys took them from me and they didn't even pay. That's stealin'."

"They thought they were Erin's sandals."

"It's still stealin'. And like I told you, I didn't hurt her."

There was nowhere for Decker to go with the questioning because what Q said was true. He had taken them to the Dumpster and the police had combed through the garbage. Unless he was deliberately lying about the specific Dumpster he pointed out. Still, it felt like the man was holding back.

Decker thought for a moment. "Q, in the Dumpster where you found the sandals . . . did you find anything else?"

The homeless man narrowed his eyes. "I didn't hurt her."

"I believe you. What else did you find?" When Q didn't answer, Decker said, "I'm not going to arrest you. I'll even pay you for the sandals, but I need your help. Please answer me. Did you find anything else?"

Slowly Q stood up and went over to one of his three trash bags and began to search it. After about five minutes, he pulled out a baggie. He gave it to Decker.

Inside was a half-inch silver heart on a broken silver chain.

"You got this out of the same Dumpster you found the sandals?"

Q sidestepped the question. "I thought this was pretty." He looked at Decker. "Is it hers?"

"I don't know."

"I kept it all this time. In a baggie. Just like you see it."

"And you never tried to sell it?"

"No. I thought it might be hers and she'd want it back."

"You never thought about showing it to the police?"

"I did, but then I didn't 'cause I was mad. They didn't pay me for the shoes."

"I need it, Q. It might be important." The man was quiet. Decker said, "Did you find the necklace with the sandals?"

"It was right on top of everythin'. It winked at me in the moonlight. Am I in trouble?"

"No, you're not in trouble." Decker handed him a ten-dollar bill. "That's for the necklace and for the sandals."

"Very nice of you, Mr. Cop."

"I might talk to you again. Stick around."

"I'm not goin' anywhere."

"Where do you go when it gets cold?"

"Around."

"You know, there is a shelter in town. It's warm there. There's also food and a bed and a shower."

"But they tell me what to do and I don't like that."

"I understand, but you can't live out here in the winter."

"I got my ways, Mr. Cop. Don't waste your time worryin' about me."

Staring at the necklace in the baggie on his desktop, Radar said, "It's Erin's?"

"I showed it to the mother," Decker said. "She told me that Erin wore something very similar to it. But silver hearts on silver chains are common. When I was looking to identify it, I found at least a dozen companies that manufacture this type of jewelry. I couldn't distinguish between them just by looking at pictures."

"And Q had this stashed away?"

"That's what he told me."

"You think he killed her?"

"I can't rule it out. But no."

"Why?"

"He doesn't look like he has a lot of physical strength for starters. But more to the point, why would he give me the necklace if he did it?"

"Throw you off the scent."

"He's not that calculating." Decker sat opposite the captain on the other side of his desk. "The fact that it's broken is interesting."

"Someone pulled it off her neck?"

"Possibly."

"So why didn't he keep it as a trophy?"

"If she got away, why would the killer want to relive his failure? Maybe the killer took the sandals and necklace initially, and then he threw them away because the items didn't give him any sexual charge."

"That's a leap."

"Of course it is. But it's still a plausible explanation. The upshot is I'm thinking that Erin Young may still be alive. Her mother suggested that if she'd run anywhere, it would be to Los Angeles. I'm sure she's using a false name, but it's possible that she's still using her own birthdate and her own Social Security number, for instance, if she applied for a job. If I can get hold of a tax return that uses the birthdate and the SSN, then I'm home free. I can get her new name, her address, phone number, where she works, the whole bit."

"If she pays taxes."

"If she's not a street walker or working as a domestic and taking cash under the table, you're right. But if she has a normal job, someone is filing a W-2 form, which means she's paying taxes. We should be able to get some kind of court order that will allow us to see if there's anyone paying taxes with her Social Security number."

"Maybe," Radar said. "But I've never done it before."

"It would help."

"I'll look into it if you really think she's still alive."

"It could be wishful thinking, but why not try? I'll do all the paperwork if you'll file."

"Okay. It'd be good to know whether she's alive or dead even if it isn't related to Bogat. How are you doing with Bogat? Making any progress with what you have?"

"It's still early, but we're thinking that the killer is connected to Greenbury and the colleges since all three victims were students. As of now, I've had McAdams look at professors who have been teaching there for at least seven years, when Yvette Jones initially disappeared. We're also searching for someone local who might be connected to the students. I don't have any good candidates in the town department right now. In the gown department, I'm looking into charismatic professors who could have lured the victims by dint of their charm. I've got a list of a half-dozen well-liked professors who have likely crossed paths with all three students."

"So let's run with that until we've exhausted the possibilities. I'll need that list of names."

"No problem. And I'll give you my reports as soon as I interview them. I'll make a copy of the entire file for you, if you want it."

"Don't bother. Why waste trees? When you have something to tell me, just make sure you tell me. I'll see what I can do about getting a tax file with Erin's Social Security number. That's going to take time."

"I know."

"I'll talk to a lawyer and find out what rights we have." Radar gave Decker back the necklace. "What do you want to do with this?"

"If it's Erin's, it might have DNA on it."

"Q lives outside. The bag's been exposed to the elements. Even if there was DNA, I'm sure it's degraded by now. Not going to waste money on that until you have more information."

"Okay. I'll book it into the evidence room. I've got an interview in fifteen minutes, so that's it for now."

"No prob, Deck, keep at it. Lucky for us there's no time limit on murder."

27

Two morning callbacks resulted in two appointments. Decker was pleased. It was about as good as it gets with academics.

At ten to two in the afternoon, Decker headed for Duxbury. It was the oldest of the Five Colleges, founded as a liberal arts school in the early nineteenth century. It had been ranked consistently among the top schools in its class and had always been noted for its excellence in the classics, history, and the social sciences. The students there were among the brightest in the consortium and often more than a little full of themselves. There were a lot of protests about issues the previous year on campus and mostly from the Duxbury students: everything from serving inauthentic cultural food in the cafeteria—bánh mì sandwiches on soft rolls instead of sourdough—to solidarity with whatever aggrieved group was in the spotlight. Most of the professors now kept a low profile—heads down and teaching their subjects in as neutral and as boring a way as possible.

Jason Kramer's space was on the top floor of the Psychology and Sociology Building, a wood-paneled office with a nice view. Joining his impressive credentials—undergrad Yale, Ph.D. in clinical psychology from the University of Washington—were certificates and special awards that plastered the walls. From the dates, Kramer was in his forties. He wore a white dress shirt tucked into jeans with loafers on his feet and stood when Decker walked across the threshold. The man looked worn—droopy blue eyes and a pasty complexion. He offered Decker a chair opposite his desk.

"It's been a long couple of days." A weak smile. "For both of us, I suppose. You've been very busy up there at Bogat."

"We have."

"What's going on? I've heard the police have unearthed Yvette Jones and Delilah Occum."

"It takes a while to get an official-official confirmation."

"*Two* officials. So you must have some preliminary confirmation."

"We do." A pause. "Thanks for seeing me on such short notice. You were very helpful in pointing us in the right direction with Lawrence Pettigrew. I was wondering if there is anything else you can tell me about him."

"Like what?"

"We think he came back up to the colleges to meet someone here and soon afterward he was murdered. Any ideas?"

"None whatsoever. He didn't contact me if that's what you're asking. I knew Lawrence but not well."

"What can you tell me about him?"

"Just what I told you before."

"Refresh my memory."

"Lawrence was an extrovert. From what I remember, he was very smart and in your face."

"Do you know of any people he offended?"

"I'm sure he irritated some, but I don't know anyone specifically. He was a showman. He loved to play the piano and sing and get the crowd going. He reminded me of the Emcee in *Cabaret*."

"Do you know who he was friendly with?"

"No, I'm sorry, I don't."

"Any faculty member perhaps?"

"Detective, I'm not holding back. If I knew something, I'd tell you. Being that he was a Morse McKinley student rather than a Duxbury student, I didn't have the eyes and ears of the college."

"One of the women at the LGBT Center told me he was very helpful to her when she did her high school tour of colleges. Arianna Root."

"Ah, yes. She was there when you first popped in."

"You have a good memory."

"It was just a week and a half ago. I'm glad Lawrence was helpful to Arianna. Did she know him well?"

"Not well, no. But she did see him at Morse McKinley on the day he disappeared. Beyond that we can't get a timeline."

"Exactly when did Lawrence disappear?"

"Five years ago—a couple of years after he left school. But we know that he came back to Five Colleges. He was a woman when he returned to Greenbury and went by Lorraine Pettigrew. Why do you think he came back to Morse McKinley?"

"No idea. My dealings with Lawrence had been

pleasant but superficial." A canned smile. "Anything else?"

"As you mentioned, we have been busy at Bogat. Whatever you can tell me about the two other girls would be useful."

Kramer fiddled with a button on his shirt. "I don't remember much about Yvette other than that she disappeared. I was younger and more self-absorbed. Delilah was more recent. We looked for her, you know. The entire consortium did several grid searches of the immediate acreage and the surrounding wilderness. We scoured the area for a full week. I was there every day. We found nothing, but obviously that's irrelevant in light of your discovery. I just wished it would have happened sooner—the discovery. All that forensic evidence that's lost . . ."

Decker nodded.

"Anyway, I'm sure you're acutely aware of that. What do you have?"

"Forensically?"

"Stupid question. You can't tell me."

"No, I can't tell you specifically. It's less than ideal but more than you think. In your grid search, did anyone find clues?"

"I didn't find anything. If someone did, I'm sure the police would know and it would be in her files."

"I'm not asking about anything official. Just things that you remember about the case."

"I know that she disappeared from a party. Mix alcohol with anything and it's a potentially lethal combination. It used to be that the school gave freshmen lectures about safety. Minimal material: walk home with a buddy, don't drink alone, don't go with strangers . . . that sort of thing. But some of the women here said that the lectures put the onus of responsibility on them and not on the male students. They accused the school of being patriarchal. So we stopped about two years ago. Not that it mattered much. I'm sure the lectures went in one ear and out the other."

"You seem to get along well with the kids at the LGBT Center."

Kramer smiled. "They're good kids—very, very serious, but it's a group to which I can relate. Being gay and alone, I was very grateful to Yale's LGBT Center in my freshman year. It gave me a place to go to when I felt abandoned."

"So you're giving back."

"Giving to whoever wants the benefit of my experience."

"I would think that's a natural by-product of your profession."

"Psychology? You'd be surprised, Detective. Most academic appointments, even clinical psychology appointments, are research oriented. I do very little therapy—well, I take that back. I do very little paid therapy. I do a great deal of listening at the LGBT Center."

"You're a good listener?"

"I try to be."

"So what did you hear about Delilah Occum?"

"So we're back there." Kramer shrugged. "There were a few rumors that she ran away with someone she met over the Internet. When she wasn't located within a week, most of us thought the obvious."

"That she had been murdered."

"Yes."

"Any candidates for whodunit?"

Kramer shifted uncomfortably. "I think that's your department."

"If you have some names, I'm also a good listener."

"No names. The rumors were that she liked to party. And she liked boys. At her age, what girls don't like boys? Kids get drunk. Kids use drugs. There's always a possibility of something accidental happening. At least that was the theory."

"Okay. What did you think about Cameron Snowe?"

"I don't know her."

"It's a him. He was Delilah's part-time boyfriend."

"I don't know him. Was he a Duxbury student?"

"Morse McKinley."

"That's probably why I don't know him."

"Had you ever crossed paths with Delilah?"

"I know she had been enrolled in my Intro to Psych class because I was notified when she went missing. But I don't recall ever talking to her. I didn't even know what she looked like until I saw her picture in the paper."

"How many people are usually enrolled in that class?"

"It's one of the largest in the consortium. I think Deerfield Hall holds seven hundred students and the class has a waiting list. I only teach once a week, and the seminars are run by my TAs. You can see why I don't know every individual student, although I do try to reach out as much as I can. I have student hours twice a week although I'm only required to hold them once a week."

"Yes, I meant to ask you about that. It's a Duxbury class and Delilah was a Clarion student. How did she make it into a Duxbury class when you had a waiting list of Duxbury students?"

"I have an appointment in both colleges."

"I know that. But there is an Intro to Psych class at Clarion."

"There's no favoritism, Detective. I'll tell you how it works, okay?"

"Fill me in."

"Clarion is considered the sister school to Duxbury. If Delilah was a psychology major, even if she went to Clarion she'd have priority over a nonpsych major at Duxbury."

"But you don't remember her."

"Seven hundred people? No, I don't remember her. I just remember when it happened. It was a very intense experience. The police helped the school organize the search. You should talk to your colleagues. They'd probably have way more to tell you than I do."

"I've talked to my colleagues and read the files. There are a lot of names. But I wasn't around here when it happened and you were. It always helps to get a direct account."

"Of what? I don't know anything."

"But you know college students better than I do." Kramer sighed. "Is there anything else?"

"Professor, I'm just trying to get Delilah some justice. There are always some bad apples in the barrel, and the faculty usually know who they are."

"Are you talking about students?"

"Students . . . faculty . . . employees."

"I don't know anyone." He paused. "But as you said, there are always bad apples everywhere and in my opinion—my *nonprofessional* opinion—the women are *always* at a disadvantage. Despite all this female empowerment, if something bad happens to them, they either blame themselves or tell themselves it really wasn't rape when it was. In a school like Morse McKinley, the boys take pride in their aggression. The saying is: no means yes, and yes means anal. I would have thought it was a male student who went too far with Delilah. *But* the fact that you found three bodies up there would point to something more than an *accidental* murder."

"Unless it was a bad apple who continually had accidents. And since we are dealing with three students, it's likely that there's an association with the colleges."

"Are you saying we have a serial killer *here*?"

"I'm not saying anything. I'm asking for your help. You probably know nasty pieces of work who have been around the colleges for the last eight years."

"I know more than a few nasty people who have been here for eight years, but I don't think any of them are murderers. And I would never name names."

"Even if it meant catching a person who potentially has murdered three times?"

"Bring me evidence. I'm not telling you names based on what I feel." Kramer looked at his watch. "I have a meeting to catch. Anything else?"

Decker handed Kramer his card. "If you change your mind about naming names, there are several sets of parents that would be very grateful."

"That's a low blow."

"You tell me to do my job, Professor. Low blows are an integral part of it."

The rest of the afternoon limped along: bits and pieces surfaced that might be relevant in the future, but had no meaning in the immediate. Since he had an interview with Michael Pallek scheduled at six in the evening, Decker took off early and was home by four. Rina had just started to prepare dinner. The sound of her voice was soothing to his nerves.

"Are you going to have time to eat before your interview?"

"Probably not." Decker sighed. "Just keep it warm for me."

"Will do," Rina said. "Jacob and Ilana and the dogs are coming in on the Friday just before Yom Tov."

"Is that a problem for you? All those dogs?"

"No. The dogs are fun. They never talk back." She laughed. "Honestly, I'm more concerned about feeding all those people. I really think I took on too much this time."

"You always say that and you always come through like a pro. I'll help you with the lunches, darlin'. Just tell me what to do. God knows you've always come through for me."

He was down. Rina said, "If anyone can find out what happened at Bogat, it's you."

"You know how these cold cases work. For every year that has passed, it takes that much time to solve it. I'm looking at seven years from the disappearance of Yvette Jones."

"I'm sure it won't take you seven years."

"You're right. It could take me longer."

"How's Dana Berinson?"

"Ah, the one positive note. It looks like she has a fighting chance. They're going to bring her out of her induced coma. It has to be done in stages."

"That's great. What happened? Did she fall asleep at the wheel?"

Decker debated how much to tell her. He always found it easier to be truthful. "It wasn't an accident, Rina. It was attempted murder."

"Oh . . ." She brought her hand to her mouth. "Oh my, that's horrible."

"Yes, it is." He explained the circumstances.

"Wow. Someone put in a lot of effort to hide the crime." She paused. "Drug dealers."

"Most likely."

"Will she be in a state to be interviewed later?"

"I don't know. I sent McAdams up north to prepare for school. If she wakes up, he can go to the hospital and I'll meet him up there. I have to eliminate her from the Bogat murders."

"Why would you think this is related to Bogat?"

"I don't know that it is, but I haven't totally ruled it out. Most likely, her bad habits caught up with her."

Rina managed a strained smile. "How did the interview go with Kramer?"

"All right. Nothing explosive. I don't think I'm going to find out much from Pallek, either. It was so long ago. And profs tend to be a little arrogant."

"Are you thinking of anyone in particular?"

"Hank Carter comes to mind, although I have nothing on him. He's slick. I'd love to interview him again."

"So why don't you just show up and do it?"

"I need a reason, Rina. Otherwise, I'm just harassing the guy."

"Why did he make your list in the first place?"

"Yvette Jones was last seen leaving his lecture."

"That's right."

"Dana Berinson's roommate was rhapsodizing about him. His classes are so popular that they're impossible to get into. He does give these free lectures in the evening about once a month. Even those are SRO."

Rina thought a moment. "I've got a lamebrain idea."

"No, you're not going to talk to him."

"Of course not. What would I ask him? Are you a serial killer?" Decker laughed and she said, "But I could go hear one of his public lectures . . . let you know what I think."

Decker didn't answer. He took out his phone and began to play with the search engine. "And as it happens, he's giving one *tonight* at eight. What's today? Wednesday?"

"Yes, today is Wednesday. Come with me."

"I don't know about that. Harassment and all that." He exhaled. "Look, darlin', I'm your biggest fan. No one is as sharp and perceptive as you. But if he is guilty of something, I have to think twice about putting you near him."

"It's a public place. If the lecture is as crowded as people say, why would he notice me?"

"You're noticeable. I don't feel comfortable sending you there alone."

"Peter, there will be hundreds of other people. Forget about dinner. Pick me up afterward and we'll talk and grab some coffee and even maybe something to eat. What's he lecturing on by the way?"

Decker looked down at the search engine. "Uh, the talk is called 'Societal Dynamics of Wealth Inequality.' What does that even mean?"

"Let me go and I'll find out. You can meet me outside the hall when it's done. Then we'll go out afterward. A perfectly nice evening."

Decker was reluctant. "Okay, go. I'll pick you up after it's over. Do *not* walk home by yourself even if I'm late. Wait for me."

"Deal."

"Thanks." Decker smiled. "I will be curious about what you think. People who talk about Carter keep using the word *charismatic*. Don't fall under his spell."

Rina shrugged. "I'm not one for prognosticators and prophets. I'm usually not taken in by charisma."

"Obviously." Decker leaned over and kissed her. "You married me."

❧28

Over the phone, McAdams asked, "How did the interview with Kramer go?" After Decker gave him the synopsis, the kid said, "You're not liking him as a serial killer?"

"No. When does law school start?"

"Monday. What about the other two, Michael Pallek and Lydia Urbana?"

"I'm meeting with Pallek in an hour at the Coffee Encounter on campus. I don't know why he chose a public place rather than his office."

"Maybe he doesn't feel comfortable with the police."

"I don't think he feels comfortable with anything. I got a weird vibe from him."

"Care to elaborate?"

"Kramer's a psych prof but he's got normal affect. With Pallek, there were a lot of awkward pauses, like he was shrinking me in his head."

"That could be the baloney afraid of the slicer."

"Or he could be weird."

"That, too."

"The final autopsy report came back on Delilah Occum. Her cranium looks intact, no gunshot wounds or stab marks on the bones. Her hyoid is broken, but it's a small bone that breaks easily. She could have been strangled, drowned, or poisoned."

"Wouldn't poison show up in her hair?"

"Her hair was checked for arsenic and thallium. Nothing. If she overdosed, it wouldn't show up in what was left of her. We're still waiting on the final report on Yvette Jones. Her bones are also intact except for the hyoid. I'm sure her death will also be ruled inconclusive."

"But we know that Pettigrew was definitely murdered."

"Yes. He was bashed on the head. We've been scouring the area for additional bodies and a possible murder weapon for Pettigrew. Everything happened so long ago. It's hard to piece things together. I talked to Radar yesterday. He's trying to get a court order to see if anyone with Erin Young's Social Security number has filed taxes in the last four years."

"So you still think she's alive."

"We haven't found her at Bogat. I'm clinging to whatever I have. That's pretty much it, Harvard. I'm starting to pore over the material that we found in or around the graves, see if anything's worth testing."

"What do you have?"

"Bits of fiber and fabric in the graves, but a wealth of things around the graves: old articles of clothing, a few errant sneakers, and tons of trash—mostly discarded food containers or wrappers. Litterbugs are alive and well. That's it for now. Go back to your study group or whatever you Ivy Leaguers do."

"It's five in the evening. This Ivy Leaguer is eating a sandwich."

"How's your sandwich?"

"Not as good as the ones Rina makes. What's going on with Dana Berinson? Is she still alive?"

"Ah, yes. I called earlier in the afternoon. She's defying the odds every hour she breathes. The swelling on the brain is going down. It looks like she's going to pull through, but even if she does, there's a good chance that she won't remember what happened to her. Traumatic amnesia."

"She could also have some recollection later on."

"We can hope. The local police have a guard stationed outside her hospital room. No one is coming in to finish off the job. Not that she's ever left alone. One parent is always with her."

"Poor kid."

"Indeed. How's the second-year curriculum looking, Harvard?"

"I'm at a real disadvantage not having taken an internship in corporate law. On the other hand, criminal law is going to be a breeze. It's interesting for me to examine cases from the defense side."

"Are you thinking of switching sides, Benedict?"

"You have to *know* the other side to know the weaknesses. Call me after you've spoken to Michael Pallek."

"Sure."

"You said you'd call me after Jason Kramer, yet here I am calling you. Why do I feel like I'm getting stood up?"

"I'll call you after the conversation," Decker said. "It might be late, though. Rina and I are going to meet for coffee and then we have to watch *Roman Gladiator*."

"You're watching *Roman Gladiator*?"

"Yes, I am. It's something that Rina and I have decided to do together."

"So, you can teach an old man new tricks."

"I'm hanging up now."

"Seriously, it's nice that you guys have a good marriage."

"It's all about the compromise, Harvard. She scratches my back: I give her a shiatsu massage."

At six feet, four inches—maybe minus a half inch for older age—Decker was used to looking down at faces. Even so, Michael Pallek was short: in shoes, maybe two inches taller than Rina, who stood five five in her stocking feet. What he lacked in height, he made up for in hair—a thick brown mop that sprouted on him like a mushroom. He had pond-colored eyes, a straight nose, high cheekbones, and a white smile. He was lanky and might be considered boyish and cute rather than masculine and handsome. He wore a polo shirt and jeans with Vans on his feet. He was thirty-nine, but could have passed for ten years younger.

The Coffee Encounter was filled with tables and chairs occupied by dozens of coeds, and the entry of two older men made most of the women look up from their laptops, tablets, or phones. Everybody was dressed casually—shorts or jeans and T-shirts with the occasional hoodie. Being as it was packed with no AC running, the room was hot. Decker had ordered an iced coffee, but it turned out to be lukewarm with tiny flecks of ice floating in a sea of black. He loosened his tie and took off his jacket, hanging it on the back of a wooden chair.

Immediately, Pallek checked his watch. The meeting was scheduled for 6:30. It was now 6:32. Decker said, "In a hurry?"

"I have a seminar in an hour. How long do you think this will take?" His voice was newscaster mellow, but he was anything but. He kept shifting in his seat. He took a sip of what looked to be iced tea. "I don't know why I'm even here. Well, I take that back. I think it has something to do with Bogat. I know you've talked to others about it. I don't know how I can help you. I don't know any more than anyone else."

He certainly said a lot without prompting. Decker said, "What do you know about Bogat?"

"Nothing. I mean, I know you found bodies up there. They're the missing girls, right? I heard you also found a young man who was a former student at Morse McKinley. Lawrence Pettigrew."

"So you know quite a bit."

"Everyone knows that. Everybody is talking about it. I mean, how many students go missing from the colleges? Just the few, right?"

"What can you tell me about the disappearances?"

"Nothing."

"You must remember when the women disappeared."

"Of course. The first one was a student at Morse McKinley. It was very upsetting for us. I mean, for everyone, but especially Morse McKinley."

"Did you know her?"

"Yvette Jones? No, I didn't know her. I didn't even remember her name until I looked it up before I met with you."

"It was upsetting for you, but you didn't remember her name?"

"A lot of students have come and gone since then, Detective."

"She was a psych major," Decker pointed out.

"As far as I can tell, she never took any of my classes at Clarion. And that makes sense because my classes are small and specialized. I did teach an Intro to Psych class way back when, but not since I received tenure eight years ago. So we never crossed paths."

"What about Lawrence Pettigrew? He was a Morse McKinley student. I know you teach there as well."

"I do remember Pettigrew from Morse McKinley. He's a hard one to forget. I had no idea he was missing. I heard he just dropped out of school."

"He did."

"So why would he be up at Bogat? Was he thinking of returning to college?"

"I don't know, Dr. Pallek. But since he was buried in Bogat, he obviously did come back to Greenbury for some reason. Did you happen to see him while he was in town five years ago?"

"No. Like I said, I thought he dropped out."

"Do you know why he dropped out?"

"Everybody knew, Detective. He was planning to undergo sex reassignment surgery."

"So you knew him pretty well."

"No, I didn't. Lawrence was a colorful character. He'd tell anyone—whether they were interested or not—that he wanted to be a woman." A pause. "Did he do it? Become a woman?"

"He had become Lorraine. He was a she in all but the final cut. So you have no idea why Pettigrew would have come back to Greenbury."

"Maybe he—or she—was thinking about returning to college."

"Everyone I talked to said Lorraine was happy with her job and with her life."

"Sorry. I can't tell you what I don't know."

"Was Pettigrew in any of your classes?"

"As a matter of fact, he—I'll call him he because I knew him as a he—Pettigrew was in my psych class. My specialty is bias and prejudice in interviews and standardized testing. I suppose Lawrence, as a transgender woman, might have encountered bias. My class, by the way, is usually reserved for upper-division students and of course for Clarion women. I made an exception with Lawrence. He was very bright. He seemed quite keen on pursuing the subject. I was surprised when he dropped out of school entirely. He could have come back as Lorraine and continued his studies. No one would have cared. He would have fit in at Clarion, certainly."

"And he never contacted you after he dropped out? By text or e-mail, say."

Pallek folded his hands and brought them to his mouth in contemplation. "If he did, I certainly don't remember. It was years ago. Maybe your memory is that good, but mine is not. What would it matter, anyway? It wouldn't bear on why he was killed and buried up at Bogat."

"I don't know, Professor. Sometimes little things help. Would you mind checking your records?"

"Sure, but it may take me a while. Anything else?"

"What do you remember about Yvette Jones's disappearance?"

"She was a student at Morse McKinley. The faculty was shaken up when she went missing. I don't recall anything about her. She wasn't in any of my classes. I wouldn't know her if she walked into the room right now."

"How do you know she wasn't in your classes?"

"I looked her up. I looked all three of them up. I know you've been talking to others about Bogat so I did my homework. Why waste your time?"

"I appreciate that. I've only started interviewing some of the faculty. I'm curious. Who have you talked to?"

"Let's just say word gets around."

"You are Hank Carter's brother-in-law, correct?"

"I see that I'm not the only one who does homework." Pallek appeared annoyed. "Hank talked to me, yes. He wasn't happy after he talked to you. He said some of your questions seemed pointed."

"Really?" Decker made a face. "That's surprising. I started with him only because Yvette Jones disappeared after attending one of his lectures. I certainly didn't ask him anything pointed."

"So you say. Cops have a way of twisting things."

Decker didn't speak. Pallek was uneasy with the silence. "That's just my opinion."

"Maybe we play a little loose when interviewing a suspect, but not when we're trying to get help. And that's why I'm talking to all of you. I'm asking for help—from Dr. Carter, from Dr. Kramer, from you, from the community. Three people were murdered and buried in the same spot. I'd think the colleges would want this cleared up as soon as possible."

"Of course. And I wish I could help. But I don't know anything." Pallek started to talk, but thought again. "Anything else?"

"What about Delilah Occum? What do you remember about her?"

"I remember the case because it was more recent. The community looked all over for around four days. I don't know how we missed Bogat. It's such a popular hiking trail."

"Bogat wasn't a trail back then. Just woodlands."

"Ah, that makes sense. Well, we searched plenty of woodlands, but you can't search everything." He shook his head. "I didn't know Delilah personally, but I knew she was a Clarion student." He checked his watch again. "Anything else?"

"You still have a half hour before your seminar."

"I have some calls to make and some business to take care of." A pause. "If you have anything else specific, I'm happy to answer but I really can't help more than I have."

"No, nothing specific. Thanks for your time." They both stood. Decker gave him his card. "Just in case you find something in your e-mails about Pettigrew, Jones, or Occum."

"Sure." Pallek stuck it in his jeans pocket. He gave a nervous smile and left.

This time, it was Decker who checked his watch. Carter's free lecture was starting in about an hour. Allowing an hour for the lecture and questions, Decker had a considerable amount of time to kill before he was picking Rina up.

He could nurse his tepid iced coffee and play with his phone like everyone else in the room. Or he could take a short drive to the station house where there was always an infinite amount of paperwork on his desk; he'd perhaps reread the files and call the kid like he promised.

Option B, hands down, won out.

❧29

The talk started at seven-thirty rather than eight—the time change announced in the *McKinley Crier*. Rina was late by fifteen minutes and had to stand at the back with the others. She still managed to catch most of the lecture. Carter was an engaging speaker and struck the right combination of layman and professional with occasional humor thrown in for good measure. The lecture ended by nine-fifteen, so rather than wait for Peter to arrive, she decided to walk home because it was a lovely night. Eventually, she called Peter just to let him know where she was.

"I just passed town. I'll be home in ten minutes."

"Rina, go back there and wait for me at Bagelmania. This wasn't what we planned."

"I'll be fine."

"Darling, I'm not going to lose my temper, but if you don't listen to me, I will. It's very dark outside and I'm interviewing people about a serial killer. Don't be an id— Just please listen to me."

"An idiot?" Rina had to laugh. "I'm turning around now. You're right. It is dark. I'll see you at Bagelmania."

"Thank you."

She hung up and turned around, almost bumping into a body. She hadn't realized that someone had been behind her. She certainly hadn't heard anything. Her heart started racing. "Excuse me." Then she realized who it was, and her heart really took off. She took a deep breath. "Professor Carter. I just heard your lecture. It was fabulous."

"Thank you very much." A wide smile. "You work at Hillel, don't you?"

"I do." It was Rina's turn to smile, although it took great effort. "Rina Decker. How do you know I work at Hillel?"

"I make it my business to know a lot of things."

"Then you're much more with it than I am." She was a minute from town. She tried not to walk too quickly. "Is there something I can help you with?"

"I'm wondering what prompted you to hear me speak. It's not often I get . . . older women at my talks."

"Older women?"

"Older but beautiful."

"Good save, Professor. It's not often that I get young whippersnappers following me home."

"I live this way. And I've noticed you've changed directions."

They were on the border of the business district. People were out. She felt her heartbeat start to slow. "I'm meeting my husband at Bagelmania. Last-minute change of plans." When he didn't answer, she said, "I came because students talk about what a

great lecturer you are. It's a week before the Jewish
New Year, the time when you take stock of your
failings. I know nothing about economics—socially
conscious or otherwise—and decided to get better
educated."

"Very admirable. What did you think? Besides it
being *fabulous*."

"Well, it was also very . . . entertaining." She saw
his eyes cloud over. A moment later, she saw Peter
parking their car in front of Bagelmania. As soon as
he got out, she called out. He looked up and started
walking over. "My husband," she told Carter.

"Ah. I didn't think you randomly called out to
men on the street."

She rolled her eyes. As soon as Decker arrived, he
spoke calmly. Rina was sure it belied how he felt.
"You're out early."

"The lecture started early. This is Dr. Carter, the
professor who spoke tonight."

"We've met," Carter said. "He came to my office
to talk to me about the terrible goings-on at Bogat
Trail." He turned to Decker. "Anything new?"

"The investigation continues."

"I'll take that as a no."

Decker smiled but said nothing. Rina could tell he
was seething. She said, "You'll excuse us, Dr. Carter.
The detective has been very busy with unfortunate
police business and I guard our time together
fiercely." She took Decker's arm and nodded to the
professor. "It was nice meeting you."

"Are you coming to my next talk? I promise you
it'll be equally as *entertaining*."

"I'd love to hear it. Maybe I can even get this guy to go with me. Good night."

"Good night to the both of you." Carter disappeared back into the shadows of the residential area.

When he was out of earshot, Rina said, "Don't say it . . . just don't!"

"Don't say that I told you so and this is precisely why I didn't want you out alone?"

"Thank you, Peter, because of course it makes total sense that he'd sneak up behind me and follow me after he just gave a lecture to over two hundred people. My heart is still going a mile a minute so could you wait a moment? Or better yet, say something like are you all right?"

Decker exhaled. "He must have scared the wits out of you. Are you okay?"

"I'm fine." She snuggled close to his body. "Better now that I'm with you. My hero."

"God, that was creepy," Decker said.

"Creepy, stalkery, upsetting, scary . . . take your pick of adjectives."

"Do you want to go home?"

"No, no, no. Let's go to Bagelmania as planned. He still could be watching us, and I don't want him to think he got to me."

"Good point."

"I think it's pretty obvious that he knows where we live."

"I know where he lives so we're even. My only question is how badly I beat him up."

"Peter, why would he *do* that?"

"I talked to his brother-in-law about an hour ago. He told me that Carter thought my questions to him were pointed. The simple answer is he doesn't like me. The more complex answer is he has something to hide and he's doing a mind f-u-c-k on me. He probably thinks I'm a yokel and enjoys seeing me sweat." He realized he was speaking too loud and lowered his voice. "I've got to think about what's going on with the dude. My thoughts are muddled right now because I'm angry. I need to calm down."

"Was I his veiled threat to you to stop what you're doing?"

"Maybe, but if so, it's clumsy. It's downright stupid."

"Want to know what I think?"

"Of course."

"I think he's trying to make you mad, trying to get you to snap so you'll be removed from the case. Because I'm sure he looked you up and knows you're the most experienced Homicide cop on the force."

Decker nodded. "Someone is thinking logically."

"I've got a confession to make." When Decker looked at her, she said, "I'm packing. Three bodies, no suspects, going alone to a lecture, and you're asking questions about local murders. Despite what you think at times, I'm not an idiot."

"You're the smartest person I know." Decker kissed her hand. "I'm glad you're thinking defensively, but you still shouldn't be walking home alone at night. And you shouldn't be overly sanguine even with a weapon. There are always attacks from behind."

"I know. I did *not* hear him." She arched her neck

and kissed his cheek. "Believe me, I'm on the watch now."

"We're all on the watch now." He opened the door to Bagelmania. "After you."

"Thank you."

"What can I get you?"

"Valium?" She smiled. "A latte and an onion bagel with cream cheese."

"Got it." Ten minutes later, Decker brought the order over to their table. He smiled at her and took a bite.

"What?" Rina asked. "You have something on your mind."

"My brain is buzzing with thoughts. We'll talk when we get home. Other than that, how was the play, Mrs. Lincoln?"

"The lecture was good. He asked my opinion about it. I told him it was entertaining."

"Ooh, dis."

"Exactly. I can sling mud with the rest of them. He is a very charismatic speaker."

"That's how you reel in unsuspecting people."

"I'll have you know that I think I handled myself very well with him."

"You're always quick on your feet. I don't doubt it for a moment."

"Jackass . . . scaring me like that. I want to clobber him myself." She kept her voice very low. "He's waiting for you to slip up. You have to mind your manners. You can't stalk him. He'll slap you with police harassment. He'll get the entire college behind him. It doesn't take much these days to rile up the kids."

"You're right. I've got to think. And I can't think clearly if I'm worried about you." He looked up. "How do you feel about an escort?"

"How's that going to look to Herr Doctor Carter?"

"I don't care how it looks. I don't want you out alone—day or night."

"I understand."

Decker paused. "Okay. That went well."

"How about Karen?" Rina said. "She'll be helpful in the kitchen."

"I need Karen to watch Carter, Rina. That much I know. She worked a lot of undercover before she came here. How about Kevin Butterfield?"

"Don't you need Kevin for the investigation?"

"He's been taking a backseat since he was the original detective on Delilah Occum's case and it went nowhere. He's reading and rereading the files on all three bodies. He can read at our house as well as at the station house."

"Sure. Put Kevin on me. He's a nice guy. He likes my coffee cake."

"Thank you for being reasonable."

"Thanks, but I really don't know why I need him."

"Rina—"

"If I can handle Chris Donatti, Hank Carter should be a breeze." When Rina saw Peter's eyes get wide, she said, "No, Peter. No, no, no, no, no—"

"He owes us."

"Are you hearing me, Peter? Involving him is opening up a whole 'nother can of worms. At the moment, he's worse than Carter because we know beyond a reasonable doubt that Chris is a bad man."

"Yeah, but he's our bad man."

"Peter!"

"I hear you, Rina. You're right. No Donatti. I'll send Kevin over to the house at around eight in the morning, okay?"

"Fine." She stared at her husband. "Are you okay?"

"Not really. I need to figure out how to turn the tables on Carter . . . let the bastard know who's the predator and who's the prey."

Thursday morning at quarter to seven, the doorbell rang. Rina was expecting Kevin Butterfield, even though he was early. Since Peter was in the shower, she looked through the peephole and then let out an involuntary groan.

She opened the door. "Oh my God! I can't *believe* he called you. This is patently ridiculous!"

"Nice to see you, too, Rina." Donatti sashayed across the threshold. He was carrying a large duffel and a backpack. He went down the hallway and surveyed the available space. "This room will do."

"Take the one across the hall," Rina said. "That room is reserved for Tyler."

"Who the fuck is he?"

"He's a detective on the force who's now in school full-time. But he comes down on the weekends to help Peter out."

"Which school?"

"Harvard Law."

"So he's a twit."

"A bit of a twit, but he took a bullet for Peter, so he's on our good side . . . like you."

Wordlessly, Donatti went into the guest room across the hall and slung his duffel on the bed. He then returned to the living room and looked around, lowering his backpack off his shoulders. "I can't work on your couch. I'll set up at your dining room table."

"That's fine," Rina said. "Coffee?"

"Yes." Donatti sat down, opened the rucksack, and immediately spread out on the table with his laptop. "Password?" Rina gave it to him. Within a few minutes, he was deep in concentration.

Donatti was now in his forties and Rina thought he looked every bit his age. His hair was predominately white, although there was still plenty of it. The stubble on his face retained some natural strawberry blond, but the white was creeping in there as well. His piercing blue eyes were bloodless as usual, but his face was still handsome—strong features, including great cheekbones. At six four, he was too tall and too lanky to be mistaken for a bouncer, but he could pass for a pro wrestler with his broad chest and the muscle from his arms straining the long-sleeved shirt. Muscles weren't anything compared to a gun. She was sure that Chris had plenty of those as well. She poured him coffee and started back to the kitchen.

He said, "Leave the pot."

Decker came out, towel drying his head. "Hey, Chris. Thanks for coming."

Donatti looked up. "You look old."

"So do you," Decker said. "Your hair is whiter than mine."

"That's what happens when you're a natural blond."

Decker stared at him. "You look . . . evil, Chris."

"That's *exactly* what I was thinking," Rina said. "Perfect casting for the bad guy in a James Bond film. You know the psychopathic, albino hit man?"

"I'm not albino," Chris said. "Are you done?"

"I'm just saying . . ."

Donatti had gone back to staring at his laptop. "This couldn't have come at a worse time. I am so behind in all my shit. It would really be nice to have a kid to help me out. Instead I got Mr. Artsy Fartsy touring around the world like some hotshot."

Rina said, "He is a hotshot."

"He's an asshole."

Decker said, "Kids don't always follow in the way of their parents. Look at mine."

"What the hell are you talking about, Decker. Your daughter's a cop."

"Yeah, you're right." When Decker started to pour himself a cup of coffee, Donatti said, "That's mine."

"I'll make you a fresh pot, Chris. You deserve that much."

"And I'll come with you," Rina said.

Once they were in the kitchen, she bit her lip and told herself to calm down before she started in on him. "You completely disregarded my feelings."

"I disregarded your feelings, but I regarded your safety. Safety won out. With him around, I will truly not worry about you, and that means I can concentrate on my job."

"When did you even *call* him?"

"Around one in the morning, our time. I just couldn't fall asleep I was so preoccupied. I did what I did because Carter was eating at my soul, and I didn't want to do something dumb."

"This was dumb."

"No, it wasn't. This way, if need be, Chris can be the enforcer and I can be the reasonable cop and stay on the case. It was eleven in Elko when I called him. I don't think he gave the matter more than two seconds' thought before he jumped on his private jet and came out here." Decker measured out coffee and poured fresh water into the tank. "I know he's a loose cannon, but he'll protect you and that's my primary concern right now."

By the time they returned, Donatti had taken out three guns and placed them on the dining room table: an SW 357 Magnum; a Glock G22 semiautomatic pistol; and a Mossberg Persuader 12-gauge shotgun with a pistol grip. He picked up the Mossberg. He looked like a commando off to the Afghani caves. "This one's just for show. But it's got a convincing personality. Tell me what happened again."

Decker explained it to him. Donatti neither interrupted nor asked questions. At the end, all he said was "Got it."

Rina said, "I don't think you're going to need the arsenal."

Chris looked at her. "Did I call you or did you call me?"

"I didn't call anyone. I'm going to start cooking for the holidays." Donatti said nothing. "I may have to go to the market." Silence. "Like in about two hours. Is that okay?"

"Give me ten minutes' lead time." Back to his work.

Rina paused. "Thanks for coming out on such short notice, Chris. I really do appreciate it. It should only be for a couple of days." No answer. "I know you're busy."

"Always."

"Thanks."

"Fine."

Decker placed the pot in front of him. "I'm going to work. Need anything else?"

"Nope."

"Take care of her."

"Yep."

Donatti had never been loquacious. But the years seemed to have turned him into a man of even fewer words. His actions, however, always spoke volumes.

⚡30

McAdams's outrage was apparent even over the phone. "That is utterly appalling. I'll kill the man myself. Is Rina okay?"

"I've got someone watching her for a day or two until I can figure out my next move."

"Who?"

"Someone."

"Obviously you don't want to get specific. How can I help, Peter?"

"You can't, McAdams. You've got school to worry about. But I didn't want you to hear any of this sec-ondhand."

"Let me do something." Silence over the phone. "Come on, Old Man. I feel so useless. Come up with something."

"Okay, this was on my to-do list. It's monoto-nous, I'm warning you. Do you have a pencil?"

"I do. I've been finding that lo-tech is better for taking notes. I don't write as much, but I hear what's being said and remember it much better. Tell me what I can do."

"I was interested in Hank Carter not only be-cause he was charismatic, but because Yvette Jones was last seen leaving his lecture. By that same token, Delilah Occum was last seen leaving a party at Morse McKinley, right?"

"Right."

"I'm interested in who was at that party. I know we have a list, and I know that Carter and Pallek are *not* on it. But I also know that the list is incomplete. Let's use it as a jumping-off point."

"I'll call everyone on the list, recheck their alibis."

"Yes, that, too, but this is my thinking. Kids take pictures of everything—from keggers to the food they're eating. I'd like you to ask everyone on the list if they have photographs from that night."

"That was three years ago."

"Do you have photographs from three years ago on your phone?"

"Actually, I do. If not on my phone, they're in the cloud."

"Exactly. Some of the people may have kept the pictures just out of ghoulish interest."

"I don't have the original file. As I recall there were photographs in it."

"You recall correctly. Kevin had amassed pictures of Delilah talking to various people at the party. Those were the first people he interviewed. Mostly she was hanging with Snowe and his buddies, who all alibied one another. I'm still not down with that. Buddies lie for one another. But they're not my main focus since Delilah was buried at Bogat with the others who were murdered long before any of Snowe and his buds was enrolled in school. I'm interested in who was at that party and whether or not they were captured talking to Delilah."

"You want to see if Carter was there."

"Anyone: student, faculty, employee, townie. And yes, Carter as well. I'm trying not to have tunnel vision, but after last night it's getting harder. Let's just see who we can place at the party."

"I'll start making calls. So once again, I ask you. Who's watching Rina?"

"I hired out."

"You hired a bodyguard? That doesn't sound like you. C'mon, fess up. Is it your ancient buddy from your L.A. days?"

"No, it's not Scott Oliver—who is now running a very successful security firm in Miami. It's just someone who was handy. Thanks, Harvard."

"No thanks necessary. I'm dying to nail the bastard. Any way I can help."

Decker hung up the phone. The first order of business was to find out as much as he could about Hank Carter and Michael Pallek before he interviewed Lydia Urbana—Pallek's wife and Carter's sister-in-law. An hour later, still engrossed in his computer, Decker jumped at the jangling ring tone of his cell. He looked at the screen—an out-of-town area code: 805.

"This is Decker."

"Hello, stranger."

Decker sat up. "Margie! How the hell are you?"

"Doing well."

"And Will?"

"Retired and happy. He's into bird-watching. He's kind of gotten me into it as well."

"I can see that. You both like to travel and you both like the outdoors."

"And we're both a little nuts."

"Aren't we all a little something? It's so good to hear your voice. It must be my week for old friends."

"Watch that adjective, Detective."

"However old you are, I'm older. Keep that in mind."

"What do you mean your week for old friends?"

"Oh boy. I tell you this with great reluctance." Decker took his time, relating what happened last night and his solution. When he was done, there was silence over the phone. "Are you still there?"

"I am," Marge said. "Exactly what made you think it was a good idea to involve Christopher Donatti in anything?"

"It is a reasonable question. Both Rina and I think that Carter is trying to make it personal to get me thrown off the case."

"I'll buy that."

"Donatti's my Hessian. He can fight the war so I can concentrate on the job."

"The British lost the war, Pete."

"He's only here for a day or two until I can catch my breath and figure out my next strategy with Carter. Once I calm down, I'll send him back. But we both know he'll take good care of Rina. Enough about my problems. What's going on, Sergeant?"

"That woman's picture you sent me? Erin Young? You thought she might be in L.A.?"

Decker sat up. "You found her?"

"Not sure. If I did, it's like a needle in a haystack. I'm going to scan the picture. I hate to be old-fashioned, but these pictures were taken without her knowledge. So they're not very good and the images don't scan well. Let me know what you think."

"Who is the woman in the pictures?"

"I know her as Elena Hardgreeves. She doesn't have a Facebook page or any kind of social media, which is suspicious in and of itself."

"Where'd you find her?"

"First just look at the pictures, okay?"

"Sure." Fifteen minutes later he was back on the phone with Marge. "It may be her, but it's hard to say. My captain is trying to get a warrant to see if anyone has been paying taxes under Erin Young's Social Security number, but that is slow going. Tell me what you know about Elena."

"She works as a waitress at a local fish restaurant in Old Town Ventura. She moved here about three years ago, which kind of fits with your time frame. It could be she originally moved to L.A., but then she got tired of the city that eats its own babies. I don't know what she did before she came to my city, but before she was a waitress, she worked as a live-in caregiver for a very nice old lady who died six months ago."

"Suspicious death?"

"Not at all. The woman was eighty-six and died of colon cancer. The woman had kids, but I think she left Elena some money. Obviously not enough to retire on, but it was enough for her to rent an apartment of her own."

"Have you talked to her yet?"

"No, I haven't. I thought you'd like to come out here and do it yourself—under my official guidance, of course."

"Of course." Decker thought quickly. If he hustled, he could arrange a trip to the West Coast before Shabbat tomorrow. Although they'd have to leave very early Friday morning, time was on their side. The spontaneous vacation would serve a multifold purpose. He could interview Elena, get Rina out of town and away from Carter, and they could spend a romantic weekend together in Ventura. As for Donatti, he'd be glad to crawl back under his rock.

"I can probably arrange to be there tomorrow right before the Sabbath so I wouldn't be able to talk to her until Sunday. What are Elena's hours?"

"I don't know, but I'll find out. You're bringing Rina, of course?"

"Absolutely. Where's the best place to stay for the weekend?"

"There are a couple of really nice places with ocean views. I'll book something for you."

"You're still my gal, Margie. Always will be my gal."

"I miss you, Pete. In my head, you talk to me all the time. Whenever I'm at a crossroads, I ask, 'What would Decker do?'"

"I hope it helps."

"It does."

"I'm glad. It's been a tough week, but it just got a lot better. I'll go phone Rina now. Thanks so much."

"Don't be a stranger."

"I could say the same for you," Decker told her. "You know we have guest bedrooms and we live in the woodlands. Lots of birds."

"Thank you, Peter. If the free accommodations

don't do it, the recent sighting of the 'flying rain-
bow' spotted bunting just might do the trick."

Even though the car was a Prius, Donatti heard it
pull up to the curb. His ears, sensitive to the slightest sound from birth, had become particularly acute
because over the years he had made enemies. It was
especially useful now because his sight wasn't what
it used to be. He stood up from the dining room
table and walked over to the picture window, hiding
himself in a corner, looking through the sheer
drapes. He walked over to the kitchen. "Come here
for a sec."

Rina knew the drill from Peter: cooperation first,
the questions later. Chris was as tall as Peter, but in
his boots he was easily six-six. He guided her to the
corner of the window. A man had gotten out of the
car, carrying a bouquet of flowers. "Is that your
Romeo?"

"Yes, that's Hank Carter. God, what does he
want?"

"Go in the back."

"I want to hear what he has to say."

"Then go in the hallway. Just don't be around
when I open the door."

Donatti untucked his shirt and stuck the Glock
in his jeans. Carter knocked and Donatti answered
the door, waiting until Carter spoke first. The guy
was around five ten with an average build and
looked to be around his age, maybe a couple years
older.

Carter said, "I'm looking for Rina Decker."

Donatti said nothing.

"Is she in?"

"Indisposed. What do you want?"

"That's between Mrs. Decker and myself."

"Well, now it's between Mrs. Decker, you, and me. What do you want?"

Slowly a smile came to Carter's lips. "Indisposed?"

Donatti said, "I'm her brother. What do you want?"

Carter shifted uncomfortably. "You don't look like her brother."

"Half brother. Look at the eyes." Donatti folded his hands in front of his chest. "What do you want with my sister? Why are you bringing her flowers? She's married and her husband isn't home. What are you doing here?"

"Nothing." Carter looked down. "It's a peace offering, that's all. I wanted to apologize."

"For what?"

"That's really not any of your business."

Donatti was silent.

Carter sighed. "She may have misconstrued my behavior yesterday as inappropriate."

"You're not helping your case coming here when her husband isn't home."

Rina stepped into Carter's line of vision. "What do you want?"

"May I come in, Ri— . . . Mrs. Decker?"

Rina rolled her eyes. "Let him in. It's all right."

Donatti didn't move. Carter had to step around him. He went into the living room and Rina relieved him of the flowers. "I'll put these in water." She disappeared into the kitchen.

Carter's eyes went to the two guns on the table. "Someone's a fan of the Second Amendment."

"I love guns but can't own any. Felony conviction. These are Rina's." Donatti made a show of retrieving the Glock from his waistband. "Sit down."

"What were you in for?" Carter sat down.

"Murder, but it was a misunderstanding."

Rina came out with a vase of flowers and put them on the table. Carter said, "You have a brother who was in the slammer for murder?"

"Half brother," Donatti corrected.

Without missing a beat, Rina laid a hand on Chris's shoulder. "There's always one in every family."

"What parent do you two have in common?"

Both Donatti and Rina said *father* in unison. Donatti gave her a look that said, *Let me talk.* Rina gave him a look that said, *I can talk for myself.* She said, "My parents' marriage was on the rocks and my dad was feeling his oats, I guess." She smiled.

Carter said, "You find that humorous."

Actually what Rina found humorous was the thought of her parents—both Holocaust survivors— ever straying. They had always been more in love with each other than anyone else, including their kids. "I didn't find the situation humorous, no. Just the result."

"He's a funny guy?" Carter asked.

"A barrel of laughs," Donatti answered.

Carter looked at the guns. His hand stretched out toward the Magnum and was instantly slammed down on the table by Donatti's palm. Carter yanked his hand away and waved it in the breeze. "Yeow! Jesus, are you crazy! I just wanted to look."

Donatti spoke mildly. "Looking isn't a problem. Touching is. I think you've overstayed your visit."

"You're *psycho*!" He glared at Rina. "He's not your brother. He's probably some goon that your husband hired to watch over you."

Rina stared at him. "Why in the world would Peter hire someone to watch over me?"

Silence. "With the murders and all."

"My husband was a homicide cop for thirty years. It never spilled over into our personal lives. I've never even thought about it."

Carter waved his hand in the air again. "You haven't heard the end of this." He got up and started toward the door.

Donatti said, "Hey, Carter. You may know where she lives. But I know where you live."

Carter said, "Are you trying to intimidate me?"

"That wasn't intimidation." Donatti ambled over to Carter, and closed in until their chests were touching. Chris absolutely towered over him. "*This* is intimidation."

Instinctively, Carter backed away and looked at Rina. "Your husband will hear about this." He turned around and slammed the door behind him. As soon as the car took off, Rina said, "Was it necessary to slap him that hard?"

"No. I just enjoyed hurting him." A pause. "I need coffee."

"Fine." Rina went back into the kitchen and retrieved the pot. When she poured Donatti a cup, he didn't even bother to look up. "You want me to leave you the pot?"

"Please." Donatti sipped coffee.

"Quick question, Chris. Why did you tell him that you were my brother?"

"Were you offended by it?"

"No. You're like a relative. But why tell him such an obvious lie?"

"Who are you talking to, Rina? I told him a lie because I like to lie. Any other stupid questions or can I get back to work?"

Rina paused before she spoke. Then she said, "I know you came out on a moment's notice just to protect me. And I really do appreciate it. But even so, you don't have to be rude, not to anyone, especially not to me."

Donatti looked up. "Understood."

"I just baked some brownies. Do you want one?"

"I'm actually a little hungry."

"I'll fix you something."

"Good." He paused. "Thanks."

"You're welcome."

Problem solved.

All men were psycho on empty stomachs.

Despite all the bluster, Carter was nervous. "I know what you did. And I know why you did it. But I'll tell you right now, it didn't work, Decker."

"What didn't work, Dr. Carter? I'm very confused. First off, why were you at my house?"

"That's my business."

"No, it's my business. Why?"

"Just to apologize if I scared Rina last night."

"You didn't. But it was weird."

"This is all beside the point. I'm going to report this to your captain. That goon you hired roughed me up."

"Why would I hire anyone to rough you up, Professor? And what goon are you talking about?"

"The ape at your house who's pretending to be your brother-in-law. You hired him to intimidate me. I'm taking this up with the civilian board. You and your captain are going to hear about this."

"Why would I want to intimidate you?"

"I'm not falling into that trap. You'll hear from my lawyer and so will that goon."

"Dr. Carter, I'm sorry if I intimidated you and I certainly didn't hire anyone to give you a hard time. But you're right about one thing. Chris isn't my brother-in-law. He's the biological father of our foster son, Gabriel. Chris comes into town now and again, wreaks havoc, and then leaves. I didn't even know he was coming in until this morning when he showed up at my door. What did he do to you by the way?"

"He assaulted me. He slammed my hand on the table. I'm filing charges. You'd better have him arrested or I'll make sure you'll regret that you didn't."

"You want me to arrest Chris for slamming your hand on the table?"

Carter looked momentarily sheepish. "He practically broke my pinkie. It's still swollen. I demand an apology from both of you."

"I didn't do anything to apologize for. And I know that Chris would rather spend time in jail than apologize for anything." Decker sighed. "But I'll arrest him if you insist."

"I insist."

"I'll do what you want, sir. But honestly, Donatti is not the type of guy you want on your bad side. Hold on. I want to show you something." Decker brought Donatti up on his computer screen. "Why don't you read this first and then make a decision."

As Carter read about Donatti, his eyes got wide. "He owns a whorehouse?"

"Several. One in Elko, a couple in Mexico in El Chapo's territory. Chris is a tough guy. He knows some evil people."

"He's *mob*?"

"His adopted dad was the head of a family, yes. But Chris is his own Cosa Nostra. He works solo, and that makes him even more dangerous."

"And you associate with this *psychopath*?"

"Chris and I have a relationship that goes back over two decades. I originally arrested him for murder. Then I exonerated him because the *one* murder I arrested him for he actually didn't do. I guess he harbors a soft spot for me. He is crazy, I'll grant you that. Both he and his wife are nuts. They abandoned their fourteen-year-old son, knowing full well that my wife and I would take him in. And we did. Gabe is terrific. He's a classical pianist, went to Juilliard, and is now touring the best concert halls in Europe. He's part of our family and I suppose that makes Chris a tiny part of our family as well. I will do whatever you want, Dr. Carter, even if it means hauling in Chris Donatti for slapping your hand. I promise you he won't hold it against *me*."

Carter didn't answer.

"Tell me what you want and I'll give you the paperwork to fill out," Decker said. "But I will say this. Once the charges have been filed, Chris's behavior is out of my hands."

"You're trying to get me to drop the charges."

"So far there are no charges to be dropped. I'm here to protect and serve and act as a public servant. Tell me what you want to do."

Carter jabbed a finger into Decker's chest. "You know what? I'm looking into you. And if I find even the tiniest item that compromises you as a cop, I swear I'll get you removed from Greenbury even if I have to take it all the way to the governor of this state—whom I have met more than once!"

"Suffice it to say, we're both on each other's radar. Would you like to press assault charges against Christopher Donatti for slapping your hand? In *my* home?"

The professor turned and walked away without another word.

Decker leaned back in his chair and tried not to appear too smug. Carter had been wounded, but not mortally. He'd be back as soon as he recouped his strategy.

Both on each other's radar.

For now, the score was one to zero, cop leading at the bottom of the first.

🪶31

Heading out to Kennedy Airport at one in the morning to catch a nonstop to L.A. at five A.M., neither Decker nor Rina went to sleep that night, opting to nap on the plane rather than awaken with that queasy feeling in the pit of the stomach. The flight arrived on time and they taxied into LAX at eight. After renting a car, they were in Los Angeles at nine A.M., right as the stores and markets on Pico Boulevard opened their shutters. The first order of business was a quick stop to get food for the weekend. Afterward, they stopped at Coffee Bean for to-go coffee and hit the road for the freeway drive to the city of Ventura.

"When's the interview?" Rina asked, sipping on a cappuccino.

"It was supposed to be Sunday," Decker replied. "But Marge thought sooner was better. If the waitress is Erin Young, she doesn't want her to bolt."

"What's your intuition?"

"Don't know on this one, Rina. I couldn't tell by the photos. It's been four years and the pics were taken on the sly so they weren't that clear." Decker entered the freeway ramp. "By the way, I'm not sure it was a good idea to let Donatti stay in our house without supervision."

"What's he going to do?"

"Steal my guns for one thing."

"Why would he do that? He's armed to the hilt."

"Just to say he did it."

"I'm more concerned about Hank Carter doing something evil rather than Chris Donatti stealing your guns. I think Gabe's coming down for the weekend."

"Poor kid."

"Gabe is no longer that abandoned fourteen-year-old we took in. He can take care of himself."

"Does he know the circumstances?"

"Chris told him when he asked him to come down. Maybe he actually misses his son."

"More likely Chris wants an extra set of hands. Gabe's a great shot."

"So cynical." Rina finished her coffee. As they took the curves through the canyon, she gazed out the passenger window, studying a day that promised heat and smog. When they crossed over into the valley, the temperature was already above eighty. "I forgot how hot September in Los Angeles is."

"Best time of the year in Greenbury and worst time of the year here. But the good news is, we're not going to be in L.A. We'll be seaside in Ventura with blue skies and six-foot waves in case you're interested in surfing."

Rina brightened. "You booked a hotel on the beach?"

"Marge handled everything. You can either thank her or blame her."

"So you had nothing to do with any of this?"

"I asked her for a romantic getaway near the ocean."

"Aw . . ." She patted his leg. "You still care."

"Least I could do after you put yourself out there for me."

"Don't blame yourself for that, Peter. Who knew that Carter would be a creep?"

"He's a suspect, Rina. I shouldn't have agreed when you asked to attend his lecture."

"If he was determined to spook me, he would have found me lecture or no lecture. At least I had backup." She nudged his rib gently. "Notice my spiffy cop lingo."

Decker smiled. "You've really been a help since we moved." A pause. "I mean your input was always welcome. But since we've been in Greenbury, you've picked up some of my slack when I'm short-staffed. You know you're working a nonpaid part-time job."

"Not to mention the never-ending coffeepot."

"That, too."

"Actually, I like nosing into your business. Maybe you should deputize me or something." When he didn't respond, Rina said, "I'm kidding."

"I'm wondering if that would be possible. Are you interested?"

She gave the question some thought. "I'm not, but I thank you for the compliment. Helping you is one thing. Doing it as a paid job . . . well, I'd rather cook for two hundred people."

"You'd be a terrific detective, darlin'. You've got a keen intuition and you're a crack shot."

"Thank you very much, but I'll still pass." She

patted his leg again. "So far, we've been a successful life team. Let's keep it that way."

Red and yellow roses, the attached card saying: *To my favorite partner.* Rina regarded her husband. "That could mean you talking about me or Marge talking about you."

Decker put the pastrami, smoked turkey, potato salad, and the coleslaw in the minibar to keep them fresh. He left the barbecued chicken on the counter. "They're for you, but I had Marge find the local florist. I told Marge to say: Love, Peter. She might have improvised."

Rina laughed and looked out the window. "What a view! This is perfect!"

The admiration for infinity was interrupted by the jangle of a phone. Decker depressed the button. "Hey there, Margie. Thanks so much. Wonderful accommodations. Everything's perfect. You did great!"

"Glad you like it."

"I liked the message on the flower card as well."

"Had to get my sentiments in. Hope Rina didn't mind."

"She was fine with it."

"Good." A pause. "Thanks."

Decker said, "Everything okay?"

"Why do you ask?" Marge said.

"Instinct after working with you for twenty-five years. What's going on?"

"Here's the thing—"

"Uh-oh."

"Not uh-oh quite yet." A beat. "She's vigilant,

Pete. She noticed me yesterday and she noticed me again today. Took a long hard look and didn't like what she saw. She's still working at the restaurant. I'm watching the front, and I've got someone at the back, but I'm using police time for a case that isn't ours."

"Hold on." He turned to Rina. "When is Shabbos?"

"About four hours."

To Marge: "How far away am I?"

"About a two-minute drive, fifteen-minute walk."

"I'll be right there."

"I'm sure you're tired, but I think that would be best."

"Of course. See you soon." He turned to Rina. "I'll be back as soon as I can."

"How far are you going?"

"Not far. Marge says it's a two-minute drive or a fifteen-minute walk."

"Give me directions and I'll meet you there. It's a beautiful day, and I want to stretch my legs."

"I don't know how I feel about your walking alone."

"Unless Hank Carter took off right after us, I'll be fine." When Decker didn't answer, Rina said, "Stop worrying. I'll check in with you when I get into town." She smiled and poked his ribs. "And if you don't see me in twenty, call the police."

Old Town Ventura Main Street was a palm-lined boulevard of cafés, boutiques, and secondhand stores housed in tile-and-brick buildings going back a century. Among its historical structures were an art deco theater, an original Beaux-Arts city hall, and the four-story Erle Stanley Gardner bank building where it was said that the writer was inspired to write his Perry Mason series in the second-floor law offices. With few of the typical clothing brands in sight, the retail sector harkened to a different time, when life was slower and people strolled instead of jogged. Decker found parking in one of the free lots and walked a block, passing a candle store, an olive oil store, several small eateries, a one-off coffee café and bakery, and a used clothing shop with a sign that said trade-ins were welcome.

The Rod and Reel restaurant was off the main road. The chalkboard outside advertised fresh fish, and being as the place was a few blocks from the ocean, Decker didn't doubt the claim. Marge was standing outside the door, checking phone messages. She looked up as she heard Decker approach and gave him a thousand-watt smile. A hug ensued and both were grinning. He held her at arm's length and looked her over. Marge was a tall woman with crinkles at the corners of her laughing brown eyes. Her skin was tan and she'd grown out her hair, now able to tie it in a ponytail. She was in a long-sleeved white shirt tucked into khaki slacks with rubber-soled oxfords on her feet. Decker nodded. "You're more blond and more buff."

"Livin' the dream, Rabbi," she told him. "Life in the slow lane is good. You look pretty handsome yourself."

"Thanks, Margie. I could use a bit of an ego

boost. I've got three dead bodies, and your Elena Hardgreeves is the closest I've gotten to anything resembling a breakthrough."

"Let's go in and find out if I'm a hero or zero."

Decker opened the door. "After you."

The place was packed with humanity: those waiting for tables, those waiting for stools at the raw fish bar, and those occupying said tables and stools. The restaurant was big and bright and nautical in theme—blue, aqua, and white glass spheres behind glass partitions mimicking bubbles. Mock game fish trophies, ship ropes, and life preservers hung on the walls. There were many servers scooting their way through the maze of flesh while carrying trays of food and drink. Marge pointed to a woman who was waiting on an elderly couple with young children. She was in her midthirties, around five six with a slim figure. She had short hair, a round face, and light eyes.

Decker said, "Watch this." He walked over to the woman's back and waited until she had finished serving. Then he shouted, "Hey, Erin!"

The woman turned around, then gasped and dropped her empty tray. Everyone turned to look at her. Decker picked up the tray, took her elbow, and led her away from the busy floor. "Where's the manager, Ms. Hardgreeves?" The woman remained speechless. Her face was ashen. He said, "I'm from the Greenbury Police. You're not in trouble, but I need your help."

Marge came over and showed Erin her identification. "We just want to talk to you, Ms. Hardgreeves."

The woman's eyes were terrified. She still couldn't speak. Decker said, "Let me talk to her manager."

"No, you stay with her and I'll talk to the manager. I'm the official, remember."

"I stand corrected."

After Marge walked away, Erin finally found her voice, which wasn't more than a whisper. "What do you want?"

"Let's wait until Sergeant Dunn comes back before we talk."

"Do I have to talk to you?"

"No, you don't. But in your hometown, there may be a serial killer on the loose. We've already dug up three bodies near Bogat Trail. I've got ideas, but that won't get me anywhere. I really need help."

"How'd you find me?"

"I talked to your mother. She said your dream was to go to Hollywood. I used to work in the LAPD. I still have contacts. Sergeant Dunn and I worked together for many years." When she didn't answer, Decker said, "I wouldn't be surprised if your mother knew where you were all along. I thought that much when I spoke to her. She pointed me in that direction, but she didn't give you away."

Erin said nothing. Both of them watched Marge walk toward them. "I got you a half-hour break but not a second more. Let's go to the Mission. It's quiet there."

The trio walked outside into the bright sunlight. In the distance was the Beaux-Arts city hall building, elevated and looking over Old Town like a guardian angel. Decker's phone rang. Over the line, Rina said, "Just checking in. Where are you?"

"Marge and I are going to the Mission, wherever that is."

"It's at the end of Main Street. You can't miss it," Marge said.

"I heard that," Rina said. "I take it the visit is business?"

"Correct."

"Then that must mean good news. I'll do a little shopping. Call me when you're done."

"Don't break the bank."

"Peter, don't you know the rule?" Rina laughed. "When you're on vacation, whatever you charge doesn't cost money and whatever you eat has no calories."

❧32

San Buenaventura Mission was erected in the late eighteenth century by Franciscans, the last of its kind to be founded by Father Junipero Serra, who was sainted in the twenty-first century. Most of the old structure had been destroyed by fire and earthquake, but the newly remodeled building still contained the original church with its painted crossbeams and hardwood floors. The place had been refashioned in the Monterey style with a peaked roof, white exterior walls, and dark trim. After paying an admission fee in the gift shop, Decker, Marge, and Erin walked through the shop and up a few steps into a tiny museum with histori-cal artifacts and then out into the grounds built around a tiled fountain with walkways in a T shape.

The magnificent gardens were irrigated by a duct system created by the indigenous Chumash Indi-ans. The beds were filled with native flowers still abloom in the warm California sun. The flora was especially lovely because the day was warm and cloudless with a gentle breeze wafting from the ocean blocks away. Choosing a bench at random—the place was empty—Marge sat and placed Erin between Decker and herself. Dressed in a white shirt and black pants, the restaurant uniform, Erin hung her head and had seemed to curl inward.

Decker regarded Marge and then took the lead. "Erin, I was really worried about you. I'm really glad you're alive and well." When she didn't respond, he said, "You know, you're not in any trouble."

Silence.

"He needs your help," Marge said.

"For what?" Her voice was soft.

Decker said, "Recently we've found some bodies near Bogat Trail. I realize that the pathway wasn't around when you lived in Greenbury. But it's near your mother's cabin and you know the area. I was terribly worried that you were among the bodies, so it's wonderful to find you not only alive, but in a new life. And I have no desire to uproot you or upend that life. But as Sergeant Dunn said, I need your help."

When she didn't talk, Decker continued. "I think you were brutally attacked. I think that's why you left so abruptly, without packing, without a word to anyone. You felt lucky to be alive and all you wanted to do was escape." Tears were streaming down her face. "Tell me about it."

She shook her head no.

"Please, Erin. There are three sets of parents who are looking for justice. Just tell me what happened."

"I'm not going back."

"Understood."

"*Ever.*"

"Understood."

She wiped her eyes with the backs of her hands. "I'm going to get fired if I don't get back."

Marge offered her a tissue. "No, you won't. I promise."

She sighed and took the Kleenex. She started shaking even though it wasn't cold. "It was Rick."

Decker narrowed his eyes and thought a moment. "Ricardo Diaz?"

She nodded. "You talked to him?"

"I interviewed him about you." He took out his notepad. "He said he fired you because your hands were in the till. Was that a lie?"

A long pause. "No. I did . . . take money." She rubbed her arms. "He said he wouldn't report me. And I was very grateful about it. But . . . afterward . . . he expected things." Her knee started bouncing up and down. "It wasn't any big deal at first. It wasn't like I was a Catholic schoolgirl or anything. But he got real controlling very quickly. Very demanding: who I was with, where I'd go. Things that weren't any of his business." She bit her lip. "When I tried to call it off, he threatened to tell my boss at the Circle M. So I told him I'd just tell my boss myself. And that made Rick furious."

"He had to be in control," Marge said.

She nodded.

Decker said, "What happened the night you disappeared?"

The tears flooded back. "It was warm and I decided to walk home. I'd done it hundreds of times. There was a car . . . his car. He pulled up beside me." Her voice was trembling and her breathing became shallow. "I told him to go away. He said he just wanted to talk." She was almost panting. She bit her lip again. "I knew better than to get inside the car. I started running . . . into the woods. He got out and ran after me." She tried to sniff back tears. "I tripped. Next thing I knew he was on top of me." She started sobbing. "He tore off my necklace. It sliced my neck. He started choking me."

Marge put a hand on her shoulder. "You must have been absolutely terrified!"

She nodded and wept. "I fought as hard as I could because I knew he was going to kill me. But . . . I couldn't get him off. I blacked out."

Both Decker and Marge waited for her to go on.

She wiped her eyes and blew her nose. Marge gave her another tissue. "Thanks." A long pause. "When I came to . . . it was still night. I remember feeling very, very cold although I remember having my clothes on. I was in the woods, lying on the ground. I was very confused."

Her eyes were far away.

"My throat was sore. My head was throbbing. I felt raw all over, like I'd been sanded. I couldn't move anything except my head. I saw a figure digging a hole . . . a deep hole." She looked at Decker. "I don't know where exactly it was, but I knew I was in the woods."

"You're doing great, Erin," Decker told her. "Just terrific."

"In my mind, it's very sketchy."

"Actually, for something so horrific, you have an amazing amount of detail."

She clasped her hands and hit her chin with her knuckles. "I forgot what I was saying."

"You saw a figure in the woods."

She nodded. "Digging a hole. I knew what it

meant. I knew . . . he thought I was dead. Or . . . he didn't care. I knew I had to get out, but I was very weak and confused."

She didn't talk for a long time. Decker said, "How'd you escape?"

"The good part was I wasn't tied up. Like I said, he must have thought I was dead. There was another shovel close to me. Maybe another person was supposed to come to help him dig the hole, I don't know. But I do remember reaching out my hand. I couldn't get it. I inched toward the handle . . . as quiet as I could be. I finally was able to grip it. I waited for a while . . . just holding the shovel while lying on the ground. I kept trying to clear my head."

"Of course," Marge said.

"At one point, he stopped digging. Started walking toward me . . . maybe walking to the other shovel, I don't know. So I knew I had to do something. I sprang up on my knees—that was as far as I could move—and bashed him in the back of his legs. His knees buckled. He fell. I stood up and tried to bash his head, but he rolled over and tried to pull the shovel away. Instead, I whacked him on his arm and on his back. I must have hit him with the sharp end of the blade because he started bleeding really bad. Just blood spurting all over. And then I just ran. I ran and ran and ran and ran. I don't even know how I got home. I certainly don't remember packing or anything and I don't remember riding my bike anywhere. But I must have ridden it to a bus stop because I do remember being on a bus to L.A. with a small bag of clothes and about five hundred dollars in cash. I felt dirty and awful and sick and scared. I didn't have my purse or a phone. Rick must have taken it . . . them." She checked her watch. "I need to get back."

"Erin, I know how hard this is for you," Decker said. "It has to be traumatic and painful. I remember when I was shot. So many things go through your mind."

She turned to him. "You were shot?"

"It's a danger of my job. But what happened to you should never, ever happen to you again or to anyone else. The scope of the horror is unimaginable."

She nodded.

"But you know, I can't arrest him without your help."

"I'm sorry, but I can't do it." Her voice faltered. "I just can't."

"Erin, I respect your decision and I respect that you may have your own timetable for recovery, but we can't let him do this to any other woman."

"My mother still lives there."

"We can protect her."

"Sorry, but I don't think you can."

"I can't get him without you, Erin."

"I'm not going to testify against him." When Decker was silent, she said, "So where does that leave me? Are you going to arrest me?"

"No." Decker shook his head. "No, I would never do that. You've suffered enough. But without you, it'll make it that much harder to get Diaz. I'll just have to put a watch on him and hope he trips up."

She nodded.

"We could videotape something if you're willing."

"No . . . not yet. I'll . . . think about it. That's as much as I can do right now. I'm sorry."

Decker said, "I understand."

Erin stood up. "So can I get back now?"

Marge and Decker stood as well. She said, "Sure, you can get back."

Decker said, "Thank you so much for talking to us."

"We'll give you our cards—cell numbers included," Marge said. "If you suddenly remember something, please call us anytime."

Erin nodded.

"I'm local," Marge said. "If you just want to talk, I'm available whenever you want."

"Thank you. I appreciate it."

Decker said, "Would you mind if I take down your phone number? I couldn't find one for you. I might need to call you if I have any more questions."

"I only use burner phones. And I never call anyone. If you have a question, call Sergeant Dunn and she'll get in contact with me."

"Sounds good," Decker said. "Thank you, Erin."

"Elena, please."

"Elena, then."

"Tell my mom I love her. But make sure no one's following you."

"I'll be sure to relay the message, and I'll be sure to be alone."

The trio walked a block in silence. Erin started to speak, but then stopped herself.

Decker caught it. "What is it, Elena?"

"The figure digging the hole . . ." She stopped talking.

Marge put her arm around her shoulder and talked softly. "What about him?"

"I might be wrong . . . I wasn't thinking clearly at all, but . . ."

"Go on," Marge said.

"I think . . . I'm not sure." She swallowed. "I think I remember seeing him without a shirt. I don't know why he'd be without a shirt. Maybe he worked up a sweat digging. Anyway, I could be making all this up. The mind plays tricks after you think about something over and over."

"Sometimes," Decker said. "But sometimes you remember details that have been pushed aside. Tell me what you're thinking."

"Well, like I said, it was very dark and I really never made out his face. I mean, I saw a face, but no features really. Like just this shadow."

"Okay."

"Like I said, I might be making this up, but I saw this guy shirtless. I remember in my mind now that he wasn't all that big and he wasn't all that muscular." She turned to Marge then to Decker. "I've seen Rick's body many times. I don't think the digger was Rick Diaz."

Back at the hotel room, Decker was pacing. "Two people. It's so obvious now. That's what happens when you get tunnel vision."

"Until now there was nothing to lead you in that direction," Marge said. "There are plenty of serial killers who bury bodies all by their lonesome."

"And how could I miss Diaz?" He turned to Rina. "Did he give off a weird vibe to you?"

"Actually, in retrospect, he did."

"How so?"

"Saying that he'd remember me because I was a pretty older woman." She made a face. "Almost identical to what Hank Carter said to me."

Decker slapped his forehead. "You're right. I betcha they're in cahoots."

Marge said, "Slow down, partner. I know you don't like Carter, but you might want to get something to tie him with Diaz before you reach conclusions."

"You're right. I don't like Carter so I'm putting him in the picture. But Rina's right. The phraseology was almost identical. It's something to consider."

"Of course," Marge said. "I'll keep an eye on Elena for you. Make sure she's okay and that she doesn't run. If she stays put, I'm betting I can get her to come around."

"How the hell did I miss Ricardo Diaz?" Decker was still admonishing himself. "I'm sure he didn't show up on any registered sex offender list in the area."

"Maybe he wasn't a registered sex offender," Rina said.

"No, you don't suddenly choke a woman to near death and not have done it before."

Marge said, "Maybe he hadn't been caught. Or he did it and scared the wits out of his victims. He certainly scared Elena. Or maybe he is a sex offender but when he came to Greenbury, he didn't register."

Abruptly, Rina said, "He dyes his hair."

Decker looked up at her. "What?"

"He had dyed blond hair. I remember noticing that he had dark roots."

"So much for my powers of observation."

"Women notice these things. I thought the color was an affectation—an attempt to be cool with the college kids. But in context, it could be he was changing his identity."

Decker pawed through his notes. "I'm rusty!"

Rina said, "Stop berating yourself. You found Erin Young when everyone else gave up."

"*She* found Erin Young." Decker cocked his head toward Marge.

"After you gave me the picture," Marge said. "Anyway, let's concentrate on Ricardo Diaz. What do you know about him?"

"Just what he told me about himself," Decker said. "Probably all lies." He continued to page through his notes. "Where the hell is that list?"

"What list?" Marge said.

"The registry of sex offenders in the area. I thought I brought it with me. I was planning to show it to Erin or Elena—ask her if she knew anyone on there, but it turned out to be irrelevant. I can't believe I left it at home. Shit. I bet Donatti's looking through it right now."

"Why would he do that?" Rina said.

"Because he can." A pause. "Maybe I can call him up and have him read it to me. There weren't that many names as I recall."

"Why don't you call Tyler?"

"Because that would be way too logical." Decker picked up his cell. A moment later, he was explaining the situation to the kid.

To Marge, Rina said, "You know, your help has been invaluable. You solved one case but maybe more."

"We got lucky. I'm just glad that Erin is alive. I'll work on her to give up Ricardo Diaz. These things take time, though. The big guy will need to keep track of him."

"I'm sure Pete will put a man on him. Most of the time, it's pretty quiet where we are."

Decker hung up. "Tyler's e-mailing me the sex offenders list as we speak."

"Good," Marge said. "I need to get back to work."

"Go, go. I've already wasted enough of your time."

"It certainly wasn't a waste of time to solve a missing person case. And I'm happy to be a part of it." She hugged Decker. "See you tomorrow night?"

"Eight o'clock. We'll be there."

"You'd better. I bought a whole new set of pots and pans and plastic dishes just for you."

Rina kissed her cheek. "Thank you."

"See you then." Marge gently closed the door as she left.

Decker kept his eyes glued to his iPad. He said, "She probably thinks I'm a doofus."

"She adores you and so do I."

"Ah. Thank you, Harvard!" The attachment was a list of thirty names. His phone rang: McAdams's cell. "Got the list. Thanks."

The kid said, "Ricardo Diaz isn't on it."

"That much I know. We'd remember if he was. We should look for possible aliases . . . like the one staring right in front of me."

"Richard Damon," McAdams said.

"You're one step ahead of me. I'll call Marge and ask her to run the name through the national register of sex offenders and NCIC for me. If Ricardo Diaz is the same guy as Richard Damon, it means that Diaz didn't register as a sex offender. I can bring him in. But I don't want to play that card until I have more information."

"Like what?"

"Like another open case with the same MO. We need to find out if Diaz had an alibi for the night Yvette Jones went missing."

"I thought he told us that he didn't arrive in Greenbury until after she disappeared."

"According to him."

McAdams said, "I could come down tomorrow, while you're still in Ventura, and question him myself. He's going to tell me that he can't remember back seven years ago. But I can find out where he was living and verify that."

"If you wouldn't mind, it would help. But don't ask him about the others, especially Erin Young. Don't want to let on that we found her. Just make like we're getting nowhere and this is just a routine follow-up."

"Interesting to see how he handles being questioned again."

"He knows Erin escaped. And we know that he had a partner. When I get off the phone with you, I'll call up Greenbury and have Kevin watch him. Let's see if he tries to contact someone."

"Want me to apply for his phone records?"

"Without Erin, we don't have enough evidence to

justify a warrant. But it would be interesting to see if he meets anyone. Keep a watch."

"What about the other two murders when he was living in Greenbury?"

"Don't mention those."

"You think he was involved?"

"Three bodies buried in the same place? Yes, I think he was involved. He admitted that he knew Pettigrew. And he admitted that he remembered Occum very well. Let me call the name Richard Damon in to Marge. I'd call Greenbury to look it up, but I know her department has a bigger database."

"Still using outside help, Old Man."

"Harvard, I'm using any help I can get."

❧33

The Sabbath couldn't come soon enough. Decker
needed Saturday to rest and to recoup his strength.
In the morning, he and Rina walked on the beach,
admiring the infinity of the ocean and the wheel of
life and, with God's help, how things had turned
out grand for both of them. After lunch, they re-
versed directions and walked into town: window
shopping and people watching with lots of couples
and families enjoying the weekend. By the time
they returned to the hotel, it was late afternoon.
Rina put her feet up on the couch and settled in to
read her book. Decker tried to follow suit. His brain
had been on hibernation. Now it was awakening
from its needed rest, and once the ideas started, he
couldn't stop them. It angered him that Ricardo
Diaz, who had attempted to murder Erin Young,
was a free bird, working in Decker's town, thinking
he got away with something.

Rina noticed that he was fidgety. "If McAdams
has something to tell you, he'll call you."

"I know, I know." A pause. "I'm fine."

"What's on your mind, Peter?" A shrug. "Like I
don't know? You're furious about Diaz. And without

Erin's help, you're stymied. It's okay. Something will break. You'll probably find Diaz in some kind of database. If Tyler or Marge found something out, you'd know."

"I'm assuming he isn't because neither of them has called me."

"Or maybe they just wanted you to enjoy the day without thinking about work. You'll find out tonight. I'm sure you two will have plenty to talk about. Will, too. He was in the job for a long time."

"We'll try not to bore you."

"It's not boring. I'm interested. I'm glad you have a case to talk about. It's probably a little more interesting than tales of bird-watching."

Decker smiled. "Maybe."

"So do yourself a favor and turn off your brain for just a few more hours."

"I've got a good way to do that."

Rina smiled. "I thought you'd never ask."

After drinks and chips and olives, Marge led Decker and Rina to a beautifully appointed dining room table.

"I'll just be a minute," Marge said.

"Can I help?" Rina asked.

"We're fine." Marge looked at her husband. "Right?"

"Oh sure," Will said. "Sit, Rina." He got up and followed his wife into the kitchen.

"This is lovely," Rina said.

Marge had really gone all out, from cleaning her oven to buying new cookware, plates, and silverware in order to comply with their rules for keeping kosher. The table was set with place mats and napkin rings and included silver bird decorations in the middle of a vintage trestle table. She and Will lived in a Victorian house in the mountains south of Old Town. The interior had light-painted walls, hardwood floors, and a paneled parlor. And while Marge had comfortable furniture, she had added a few antiques to give it an authentic touch. The decor was so quaint and charming, it could have been a movie set.

Marge came back holding a casserole dish. She set it down on a trivet, opened the lid, and steam poured out. "Ta da!"

"It smells wonderful," Decker said. "What is it?"

"Cassoulet," she crowed. "Will smoked the duck himself. He also made the sausage. Glatt kosher meat, Rina. I went to the butcher myself."

"You bought kosher *duck*?"

"She did." Will was carrying a large salad bowl and several baguettes. He placed the items on the table. "I won't tell you what it cost."

"Will!" Marge slugged him. "What's the matter with you?"

"If you're not used to kosher prices, it's sticker shock." Decker turned to Will. "We owe you, buddy."

"Dodger tickets would be a good start."

Marge slugged him again.

"Ow." William Tecumseh Barnes's blue eyes twinkled with mischief. He was a little over six feet and after retiring from the force, his weight had turned north of two hundred pounds. His thin hair was white as was his goatee. "Or if you don't do baseball, we could just come out to Greenbury and do some birding."

"Anytime," Rina said.

Decker pulled out a bottle of Herzog Reserve syrah that he and Rina had picked up on the way to Ventura. "Bottle opener, perchance?"

"Now you're talking my language," Will said.

"I'm starving." Marge started serving. After everyone had food and drink, she sat down.

Twenty minutes of table conversation spanned topics from police work and politics to the arts and fashion before Rina said, "I noticed no one has mentioned anything about the case. I'm very proud of all of you. Now you may talk shop."

"I was going to wait until after dinner, but as long as you brought it up . . ." Marge got up and came back with a sheet of paper a moment later. She handed it to Decker. "Is this your guy?"

Decker was looking at a mug shot of Richard Damon—six one, one ninety, brown hair, brown eyes. Distinguishing marks included tattoos on his arms, leg, and back, the most noticeable being a panther's head on his right bicep. His convictions included two assaults and one sexual assault in the Boston area that landed him a spot on the registry of sex offenders. He handed the mug shot to Rina.

She nodded. "That's our guy."

"You gave him a fifty on a thirty-two-dollar bill," Decker said.

"It was all part of the plan," Rina said.

"What plan? To bankrupt me?"

"No, to throw him off guard." Rina handed the

paper back to Decker. "With my being so generous, there's no way he thinks we're after him."

Decker wagged a finger at her.

"Sorry." Rina put her fork down. "I don't recall the panther tattoo, but he did have ink on his forearms."

"Yes, he did. And it's something I can check out easily." Decker put the sheet in his jacket pocket. "This is very, very helpful, Margie. Thank you. When did you find this out?"

"This afternoon. I could have dropped it off at the hotel, but why spoil your Sabbath?"

"Exactly right," Rina said. "Thanks so much."

Will said, "What's your next step?"

"Tyler went to Greenbury to talk to Diaz about Yvette Jones only," Decker told him. "Diaz told him that he was living in the Boston area when Jones disappeared, working in a bar near the Cambridge area—the Rock and Whale. McAdams will contact that bar tomorrow and let me know if he was working the night she disappeared."

"What was his demeanor when he was questioned?" Marge asked.

"Tyler said he was calm, but a bit put out. Not nearly as helpful as he was the first time." Decker smiled at Rina. "He was obviously distracted by your beauty."

"So many are."

Decker laughed. Then he grew serious. "We've got to nail this bastard."

"Patience," Marge said. "Isn't that what you always told me?"

"I'm old. I don't have time to be patient." Decker

paused. "I was thinking about distinguishing marks." He snapped his fingers. "Erin said she whacked the guy who was burying her with a shovel and that he was bleeding all over the place. I bet she gave him a nice gash."

Marge said, "You can check out the hospitals and see who came in that night. But you know that no one will tell you anything without a warrant."

"Probably not in a big city, but we live in a small town."

"It would be inadmissible without a warrant, Pete."

"I'm just after a direction . . . a name. Then I could find evidence."

"Poisoned fruit from a poisoned tree."

"Yeah, yeah."

"You bring up an interesting point, though," Rina said.

"About going to the hospital?" Decker asked.

"If the gash was bad enough that he had to go to the hospital, there should be a scar."

"Okay, that is an interesting thought. But I can't go around checking out bare backs. People have been arrested for a lot less."

"Don't you check out suspects' hands for scratches?"

"Not on something that happened four years ago."

She shrugged. "Just a thought."

Marge said, "If you have suspicions already, Pete, it's not a bad idea."

"How do I get them to remove their shirts?"

"You ask," Will said. "If they don't do it willingly, that tells you something."

"He's right about that." Rina pushed her plate aside. "I am stuffed. The meal was absolutely delicious."

Will said, "Wait until you see dessert." He paused. "You aren't thinking about leaving?"

"It's past eleven, Will," Marge said. "East Coast time, it's two in the morning. They're exhausted."

"But I baked a black forest cake using nondairy whipped cream that we got at the kosher market."

"Will, give them a slice to go."

Decker said to Rina, "I'm okay if you are."

"I'm great. I napped but I don't want to wear out our welcome." Rina stood up. "But I am truly full. I need to move. Let me help you clear."

"I'll do it, Rina," Marge said.

"You talk with your old partner. Will and I can take care of it."

"I'll make us some coffee," Will said. "We got nondairy creamer at the kosher market."

"Will, I'm sure you did everything by the book." She picked up the casserole dish, which was now just warm, and headed for the kitchen.

Will gathered up the dishes. "This is fun. Let's make sure we do it again."

"Absolutely," Decker said.

After Will left, Marge said, "I think he's a little bored. Actually, I'm a little bored. I haven't had this much fun in ages. Ventura must be a big city compared to Greenbury, but it's certainly not Los Angeles. It feels good to sink your teeth into a real whodunit. But then again, I'm on the outside of the case. You must be frustrated."

"Less frustrated than I was before I came here. I now have a directional arrow, thank you very much."

Marge smiled. "I shall point and with any luck, ye shall find."

ᔆ34

As long as they were in New York, Rina and Decker had dinner with the kids. Leaving later meant lighter traffic, especially since most New Yorkers were driving into the city rather than out. Rina took the wheel while Decker spoke on his cell to McAdams about Diaz.

"According to his time sheet, Diaz was definitely working at the Rock and Whale in Boston on the day Yvette Jones disappeared."

Decker said, "And you found someone to verify this?"

"Nobody remembers anything specific from seven years ago, but Diaz did sign in and out on his time sheet. He could have left and come back, but that's pushing it for a round-trip from Greenbury to Boston, adding in time for a murder and a burial."

"Agreed. How did Diaz act after you left?"

"The surveillance, you mean? Nothing unusual. He worked his entire shift. What he did during bathroom breaks, I couldn't tell you. If you could get Erin to speak up, we could get a warrant for his phone and find out if he called anyone after I spoke to him, provided that he's not using a burner."

"We can't get a warrant for his phone unless he's done something to justify it."

"He's a sex offender who didn't register. Maybe he's calling women."

"If he is bothering women, no one's complaining," Decker said.

"And we're sure that Diaz is Damon."

"I had a female officer go into the Grill and check out Diaz's forearms. Same tattoos, same guy. So we do have him for failure to register. But I don't want to waste my one shot at bringing him in, and failure to register isn't justification enough to open Diaz's phone records."

"So our best shot is Erin Young."

"She's our *only* shot right now. She's too terrified to speak up, but Marge will work on her. We have a couple of years before the statute of limitations runs out."

"I like your idea about looking for a scar on the back," McAdams said.

"It was Rina's idea. I don't know how we'd pull that off and it wouldn't mean anything without Erin's testimony." Decker paused. "Thanks for coming into town in our absence and speaking to Diaz, Harvard. I know you're busy."

"No prob. I take it that the big spooky guy at your house is Gabe's father?"

"Yes. Did you stop by my house?"

"I did. I wanted to give it a once-over since I knew you were out of town. When he answered the door, I was surprised. When I told him who I was, he asked for my ID. Since I'm the cop, I thought it should be the other way around, but I didn't want to start a pissing contest. Once he saw I was legit, I think he relaxed although I really couldn't tell. His face looks like it's been entirely Botoxed. He not only didn't crack a smile, he didn't move a muscle. He did ask me to buy him lunch. I bought him a tuna sandwich. He didn't thank me nor did he even offer recompense."

"I'll pay for the sandwich."

"Oh please. I'm just saying he was very weird."

"Tell me something I don't know. Anyway, he'll be gone soon. Are you coming down next weekend for Rosh Hashanah?"

"I'm planning on it if it's okay with you and the family."

"Harvard, you are family."

"Thanks, Old Man. That's nice of you to say since I'm not a member of the tribe."

"Just change the name from Tyler to Tevye and the transition is complete."

On Monday, Decker got a call just as he reached his desk at eight in the morning. It was Edie Aarons—the nurse who had been tending to Dana Berinson. The teen had awakened the previous night. She was still groggy and unclear on things—where she was and how she got there—but she knew her parents, which was truly remarkable.

"Has she been questioned by the police?"

"Not yet. Doctor won't allow it. I've contacted the local police and told them the same thing. You guys might want to coordinate so the poor girl doesn't have to repeat herself when she is interviewed."

"Thank you, I'll do just that."

As Decker hung up, Radar walked into the station house. He wore a dark suit and white shirt with no tie. "Good work with finding Erin Young. It's always wonderful to find a missing person alive and well."

"It is. Now the key is getting Erin to talk!" Decker poured himself a mug of coffee. "Erin told me that she was wearing a necklace when Diaz began choking her. What's happening with that necklace I got from Q? She said the necklace sliced her throat. If it is the same one, there's a good chance that her DNA is on it."

"I took it out of storage and sent it to the lab on Friday—once you found Erin. We've got her DNA on file. And now that we know that Ricardo Diaz is a registered sex offender, we'll have his profile as well. The necklace is four years old. Whatever was on there is probably degraded, but you found Erin, which was a needle in a haystack. Maybe we'll get lucky again."

"One can always hope." Decker sat down at his desk. "The week is starting off good. Dana Berinson regained consciousness."

"The college girl in the horrible car crash up north?"

"Yes."

"That *is* good news. You'll want to go up and talk to her, I suppose."

"I don't know how much she remembers if anything. And I'm not sure when the doctors will let her talk to the police. But since I'm not doing much here, I'd like to be there, yes."

"Did you okay it with the local police?"

"I was just about to do that."

"I'll call. It'll mean more coming from me." Radar rubbed his eyes.

"Long night?"

"Just a bad bout of insomnia. It doesn't happen a lot, but I don't sleep as well as I once did. Probably a combination of age and the Bogat case."

"I know the feeling. I'll sleep way better after Bogat is solved. Do we have enough people to be on Diaz twenty-four/seven?"

"We're figuring out the rotation," Radar said. "Don't worry about it. How's Rina by the way? Any more contact from the creep?"

"No." Decker started scratching a nonexistent itch. "Doesn't mean anything of course. Leaving her alone is nerve-racking."

"The mob guy left."

"Yes, the mob guy left. I told her I'd hire a body-guard, but she won't hear of it. She says if I do that, Carter wins. I told her I don't care about that, just that she's safe." Decker exhaled. "If Carter shows up again, I will do him bodily harm."

"We don't want that," Radar said. "What about that friend of yours? The one who worked on the Angeline Moreau case?"

"Scott Oliver?"

"Yeah, him. What's he doing?"

"He works as a PI. I have no idea what his schedule is like." Decker shrugged. "I could call him up. I know he'll come, but I hate to take advantage of his good nature."

"With us rotating people for Diaz, we could use

him to keep an eye on Carter. Can't pay him much, but he might be willing to come out. Could you put him up?"

"Yeah, the house is going to be open season for the holidays. Another person won't make a difference."

"Why don't you give him a call?"

Decker was quiet. Then he picked up his cell and did what he had to do despite Rina's protests.

Even a six-year-old knew the concept of safety first.

"If you can't meet me at the hospital, it's fine." Decker was driving while talking into the Bluetooth to McAdams. "St. Beatrice is a couple of hours away from you. But I just wanted to give you the option to come if you want."

"How long are you going to be there?"

"It'll probably take a while. Hours even."

"I understand. I'll come down. If you have a chance, we can look over the photos from the party. I printed them out so we'd have hard copies of them."

"What photos and what party?"

"The photos people sent me from the party where Delilah Occum disappeared."

"Oh, right." Decker mentally hit his head. "I've got too many loose threads going through my brain. You told me about this. Photos of the Morse McKinley party where you spotted Hank Carter among the students. Good work."

"Not only Hank Carter, but after sifting through

all these phone pictures, I spotted Michael Pallek there as well."

"Pallek never mentioned he was at that party."

"Neither did Hank Carter," McAdams said.

"Were their wives there?"

"If they were, they didn't make it into any of the photos."

"Those two are very disturbing."

"The common parlance would be pervy. Is Mr. Mob still around?"

"No, he went back this morning. But I know what you're thinking. Rina should be protected. Scott Oliver is coming out for a bit to keep an eye on Carter. It was Radar's idea. I should have thought of it myself."

"How's Scott doing?"

"He was thrilled to take the gig at minimum wage, so I guess his PI business is a little slow."

"Minimum wage will barely keep him in burger money. I take it he's staying with you through the weekend?"

"Most likely."

"And your kids will be there?"

"Just Jacob and Ilana—and the pugs."

"You can't possibly cram all of us into your house. I'll reserve a room at the Inn of the Colleges."

"You don't have to do that. We'll figure out some- thing."

"I'm allergic to cats."

"Pugs are dogs."

"They are animals that shed hair. I'll be fine at the Inn. It's right on campus, which will make it easy for me to spy on our growing cast of characters. What were those two old clowns doing at a college party?"

"I asked you for a list of charismatic teachers. Both Carter and Pallek made your cut. They may have been invited."

"I don't know. Seeing your prof at a party might be a buzzkill. But parties are usually open affairs. All sorts of people show up."

"Over the years, the boundaries between professors and students have really blurred. I was reading this book on the history of the teenager. It used to be that sophisticated young people imitated adults— they dressed like their parents, they danced to the same music, saw the same plays, and drank martinis when they went out. Teenagers, as we know and love them, came in the '50s along with rebellious rock and roll. Now adults are emulating teens. It's trickled down to universities. More and more, the students seem to be running the show. So it would make sense that profs would want to ingratiate themselves with the kids. They're the ones who pass judgment."

Silence over the line.

"Of course, that could be my old fogey brain talking."

"Your brain is old and fogey, but nonetheless, it's a pretty accurate assessment of the callow youth of today. Then again, I betcha all old fogeys from time immemorial consider youth callow."

"Absolutely."

"I'll see you at the hospital, Old Man."

"See you then, Harvard. And for the record, I don't consider you nearly as callow as I once did."

The kid hung up on him.

Decker laughed out loud, turning up the oldies radio station and singing along with the classics as he tooled down the highway. Sometimes he felt very old. Other times he felt like a callow youth himself. All it took was a car, a long stretch of open highway, and good old rock and roll.

Entering the small, square waiting room for the ICU, Decker saw a seated muscular guy straining the sleeves of his state trooper uniform with his shades dangling from his pocket. His head was down, and his eyes were concentrating on a notepad; he was flipping through it as if he were looking for a lost passage of something. There weren't a lot of chairs—a half dozen squeezed into the windowless space—so Decker dragged one over to the trooper. Byrd Hissops—the same trooper he had spoken with over the phone—introduced himself. The men shook hands. A moment later, McAdams came in, wearing a white shirt under a cashmere navy pullover and black slacks. There were more introductions until a doctor—the white coat and clipboard were the giveaway—came out a few minutes later. She was in her fifties with short gray hair and brown eyes behind tortoiseshell glasses. Her name tag said Alice Anders. She looked at the three men and shook her head. "Only two at a time in an ICU."

Decker said, "Any leeway on that?"

"None."

"Not even for cops?"

"Two at a time."

McAdams said, "I'll wait. I was just going to take notes so my boss can concentrate on asking questions."

"That's another thing," the doctor said. "Dana is still disoriented. She is up now, which is fortunate for you. Please don't tire her out."

"How long do we have?" Decker asked.

"Not more than a few minutes." She handed out two tags to Decker and Hissops. She looked at McAdams. "Sorry."

"I understand. It's fine."

"Wait here. I'll have to ask the parents to leave so you can come in. They're not going to be happy."

After Anders left, Decker turned to McAdams. "You know, you might want to stay and talk to the parents when they come out. We might learn something from them."

"I can do that."

Hissops was still paging through his notes. Decker said, "The official ruling is still attempted homicide?"

"The car was definitely set on fire," Hissops said. "Since we don't have a lot of time, I think one person should ask questions."

"Agreed. I know it's your territory, but if it's okay with you, I'd like to ask a couple of questions. I've spoken to her parents before. I know a little about Dana's life at college. She's not going to be able to tell me a detailed account, but maybe she can remember something."

"Fine with me. You're the homicide cop. If I think of something, I'll chime in."

Five minutes later, Larry and Jamie Berinson walked into the room, making a crowded space even more cramped. Decker shook Larry's hand and nodded to Jamie, who was dabbing her eyes. They both appeared to have lost weight and aged ten years: pale, gaunt faces and stooped shoulders.

"She recognized us right away," Jamie said.

"I heard the good news. That's great."

"Did you meet the doctor?"

"Alice Anders?" When Jamie nodded, Decker said, "She seems very caring and very competent."

"The nurses are very nice, too."

"Jamie, he doesn't care," Larry Berinson said.

"Actually, I do care. I'm very sorry you have to go through all this. I know it's very traumatic as well as taxing. Can I get either one of you a cup of coffee before we talk to your daughter?"

"I'll get it." McAdams gave an appropriate smile to the parents. "Can I get you something to eat as well? A donut or a pastry?"

Larry sat down and threw his head back. "Coffee, please. Black. A croissant if they still have them from this morning. If not, just coffee."

"And you, ma'am?"

Jamie sat next to her husband. "Coffee is fine. Cream. No sugar. Maybe a fruit bowl."

Larry sat up. "Actually fruit sounds good."

"Two coffees, one black, one with cream, two fruit bowls and a croissant. I'll be right back."

Before McAdams left, Larry said, "I suppose you'll want to talk to us?"

"Only if you're up to talking."

"Why not," Larry said. "It's better than staring at the walls . . . which is all we've been doing for the past week." His eyes watered. "Not that I'm not grateful for her recovery."

The room fell silent. Jamie dabbed her eyes again. "My husband has been a rock." Larry waved her off. "Yes, you have."

"It's good that you two are united," Decker said.

McAdams said, "I'll be back." He walked out of the room with Decker. "What should I ask them?"

"How they're doing, how they're feeling, have they gotten any sleep, things like that. Let them do the talking and if they don't feel like talking, don't push it. But I have a feeling they'll both be chatty. They haven't seen anyone in a while. You may have to direct conversation traffic so each one gets their say."

"Got it. Get them food, be caring, and just listen."

"Yep." Decker placed a hand on McAdams's shoulder. "It's like the old country song."

McAdams waited. "Okay, Old Man. What country song?"

"'You say it best when you say nothing at all.'"

35

Dana was hooked up to a spaghetti pile of tubes. They monitored her heart rate, her blood pressure, her pulse, and her oxygen level. The IV line fed her glucose and Demerol. She had an oxygen mask and was also on a catheter. She had broken bones, a bruised face, bandaged hands and arms, and greasy hair. Her brown eyes, though bloodshot, were alert.

Decker pulled up a chair close to her so if she talked, he could hear her. He said, "Hi, Dana. It's good to see you awake."

A nod.

"I'm Peter Decker and this is Byrd Hissops. We're the police. We'd like to ask you a couple of questions if you're up to answering them."

She was struggling to take off her oxygen mask. Decker helped her.

"Ber . . . ?" She made an attempt to flap her arms.

Hissops smiled. "B-Y-R-D. I think my mom was woozy from childbirth."

She tried to smile. It was lopsided and didn't last long.

"How are you, Dana?" Decker asked.

A tear came down from her eye.

"I realize this is very hard, but time is important. Do you have any memory of what happened to you?"

She nodded. "Little . . ."

"Do you know that you were in a car accident?"

She shook her head no.

"You don't remember that?"

"No . . ."

"Do you remember driving from the Boston area to go back to the colleges?"

She shook her head. "I . . ." Decker waited. Her voice was a whisper. "Not driving."

Hissops said, "You weren't driving?"

She nodded.

"So you were with someone," Decker said.

Again a nod.

"Do you remember who?"

"Snow . . ."

Hissops looked confused. "There was snow on the ground?" He turned to Decker. "It's way too early for snow."

Decker's eyes had gone wide. "That's not what she means." The bruises on Snowe's face suddenly made sense. "Were you with Cameron Snowe?"

She nodded.

"You know this guy?" Hissops asked.

"Yes. I'll fill you in later." To Dana, Decker said, "Did he drive with you up to Boston?"

She nodded. "He . . . okay?"

Dana may have been a dealer, but she wasn't a psychopath. "Yes, he's okay, Dana. Don't worry about him." Silence. "So Cameron Snowe was driving with you back to the colleges?"

A nod.

"In your car?"

"Yeah . . ."

"Okay," Decker said. "Anyone else with you in the car?"

She shook her head no.

"Great. That helps a lot, Dana. Were you and Cameron arguing about something? Did you two have a fight?"

Another shake of the head.

"No fighting, no arguments, no conflict over which route to take?"

"No."

"Okay. Do you remember getting into a car crash, Dana?"

"No." She closed her eyes.

Decker tried to pare down his questions because she was clearly getting tired. "You don't remember being in a car crash or the car stopping? Maybe there was car trouble? A flat tire?"

She shook her head no. "Don't . . . know."

"So the last thing you remember was being in the car with Cameron Snowe."

A nod.

"And he was driving you both back to the colleges."

Another nod.

"If you can't remember the crash, what's your next memory, Dana?"

She shrugged, eyes still closed.

"Do you remember how you got here? In the hospital?"

"No . . . tired."

"You did great," Decker said. "We'll go now, but I want you to know you've been a tremendous help."

She didn't answer. Her breathing became labored, so Decker placed the mask back over her face. After a minute, it was quieter and regular. Both men got up and left the room. Nurse Aarons was waiting on the other side of the window. She introduced herself.

Decker said, "Nice to meet you in person. Thanks for all your help."

"I haven't done anything."

"I'd debate that." Decker smiled. "I hope we didn't tire her too much. Can you tell me when she's up again and talking?"

"I'll try." The nurse went back into the ICU.

On the way to the waiting room, Hissops asked, "Are you staying over?"

"No, I have to get back to Greenbury. I'll try to come back when she's more awake. I've got to make a call. Excuse me."

Hissops said, "Who's this Cameron Snowe—besides now being our primary suspect in Dana's attempted murder?"

"Tell you in a minute." Decker called up the station house. Kevin Butterfield picked up the phone. After a brief recap, Decker said, "Pick Snowe up, pronto. Before he finds out that Dana Berinson is up and talking."

"I'm on it," Kevin said. "Unbelievable."

"Yes, it is. And call me when you have him in custody."

"Got it." Butterfield hung up.

Decker returned his attention to Hissops. "Deli-

lah Occum was one of the bodies we unearthed at
Bogat Trail. She was last seen leaving a party after
arguing with Cameron Snowe, her sometimes boyfriend. He took a leave of absence after she disappeared, but he came back to finish up his degree. I
interviewed him on Sunday afternoon around one.
So whatever took place on the road probably happened Saturday night. I had noticed Snowe had
some bruising."

"Do you think it was from an accident?"

"It was minor bruising, but sure it could have
been from getting smacked in the face with an
airbag."

"Dana's injuries were primarily from the car
going over the road and the arson. It's a miracle
she's alive, her brain is intact, and her burns are
minor."

"Incredible." Decker was puzzled. "Why would
Snowe want to kill her? She doesn't remember any
arguments between them."

"If she was a dealer, maybe he wanted the goods
all to himself."

"It seems like a very extreme measure to get some
weed and some pills. There had to be some bad
blood between them. Maybe they were arguing and
that's how he got the bruises and she doesn't remember."

"Do you remember any cuts on Snowe's hands?"

"No. But after I saw the bruises, I glanced at his
hands. If I'd seen something off, I'd have made a
note of it."

"And, again, when did you interview Snowe?"

"Sunday afternoon. I was interviewing him about

Delilah Occum. The next day, Monday, I got the call about Dana having disappeared. I haven't spoken to Snowe since then. He could be long gone by now."

"If he didn't run right after the accident, he probably thought he was safe, that Dana was dead."

"I'm sure at this point he knows that Dana isn't dead. The whole school knows." Decker thought a moment. "He probably doesn't know, though, that she is conscious and talking." He looked at Hissops. "You keep that cop on her. There's no way that Snowe handled the car and arson all by himself. Also, when we spoke over the phone, you said something about picking up CCTV of the toll roads to get a time frame for Dana's accident."

Hissops made a face. "I did pick them up because I didn't want them erased. But I haven't gone through them."

"As long as you have them. If they did go through toll roads, it would show who was behind the wheel."

"I'll get to it right away."

Decker was visibly trying to control his fury. "Man, that little prick was slick, especially considering he had just tried to murder Dana."

"He probably had practice with the first one. What is he? A serial killer?"

"He's a killer and the rest is semantics. One girl is dead and another is messed up, and both of them have Cameron Snowe in common."

"Just a bad egg then."

Decker nodded. "Rotten to the core."

As soon as Decker and Hissops came into the waiting room, Larry and Jamie Berinson stopped talking and stood up. Larry spoke first. "Did you find out anything?"

"Quite a bit," Decker said. "According to your daughter, she wasn't alone and she wasn't driv—"

"What?" Berinson blurted out. "Who was behind the wheel?"

Decker looked at McAdams and put his finger to his lips. "A young man named Cameron Snowe."

McAdams broke into a coughing fit. "Went down the wrong . . . pipe."

Decker said, "Has Dana ever talked about him before?"

Larry looked at his wife. "Not to me," Jamie said. "Who is he?"

"He's a senior at the colleges. His name has been brought to our attention before."

Berinson said, "In what capacity?"

"Various things. I want to hear what he has to say before I tell you anything else."

"Why is my daughter in the hospital in critical condition and this Snowe guy not even around?" Berinson raged. "If he was driving, it was his fault! Why isn't he here?"

"It's one of the things that Trooper Hissops and I need to find out—"

"What? The son of a bitch just left her to die?"

"We'll find out, Mr. Berinson. Dana's memory is very hazy. At this point, we all need to make sure that what she's telling me is what happened."

"You don't believe her?"

"Of course I believe her," Decker said. "We totally believe her. But it is possible that she's getting things confused. She had a very serious accident—"

"If it was an accident!" Larry thundered.

Hissops said, "We'll tell you the details once we're sure about what we have."

"Do you think it wasn't an accident?" Jamie asked.

"I can't say without knowing more," Decker said. "Dana told us one thing. I want to see what Snowe has to say. He's being picked up right now by one of my colleagues. I'm going down to interview him." *If he hasn't bolted.*

"What should we do?" Berinson asked.

"Stay right where you are and keep taking care of your daughter. She's doing better than anyone thought because you two are around her, giving her support and love."

Larry said, "You'd better keep me up to date. I want to know everything."

Hissops said, "Of course, sir. We understand."

Jamie took out a tissue and dabbed her eyes. She said, "We'd better be getting back, Larry. I don't want her waking up and not finding us there."

"You go. I'll be there in a minute." After his wife left, Larry said, "If this guy left her to die, I want him strung up by his balls."

"We will take care of it, sir," Decker said. "Just take care of your daughter."

"I'm just telling you what will happen."

"I get it. If he's guilty, he'll pay."

"I'll remember you said that."

"No problem." After Larry left, Decker looked at the kid. "Your throat okay?"

"I'm coming back with you, boss. Don't even try to talk me out of it."

Hissops said, "I'll stick around until we get a rotation for a cop on Dana. Besides, maybe she'll be up again. And I want to make sure that Larry Berinson stays put. Last thing we need is a vigilante."

"He's just venting," Decker said. "I'd feel the same way. But it doesn't hurt to keep an eye on him. If Dana does tell you something new, let me know. I'll bring you up to speed on Snowe after we're done with the interview. It may take some time."

"I know how that goes. Just make sure he doesn't give you a snow job."

Hissops smiled at his pun while Decker and McAdams groaned. But it broke the tension and for that Decker was very grateful.

🌱36

The ride back to Greenbury was silent and tense. Finally, Decker couldn't take it. "Call up the station house. Find out why it's taking so long to pick up Snowe."

McAdams took out his cell. "No reception."

"You're kidding me." Decker put pedal to the metal.

"Slow down," McAdams said. "When is Scott Oliver due into town?"

"Sometime tomorrow. I haven't told Rina yet. She'll think I'm silly."

"No, she won't. It's the right thing to do. Who's watching Rina now?"

"She's with people until I get back." Decker took a deep breath and let it out slowly. "You know, you're doing a lousy job of calming me down. Now I'm thinking about Snowe *and* Rina."

"I didn't know I was your Zen master."

"Okay. So I'm taking it out on you. Deal."

"No prob, boss."

Decker's cell rang through the Bluetooth. He depressed the button. The call came through the speaker. "Kevin?"

"We got him," Kevin said.

McAdams gave his hands a single clap. "We're about a half hour out of town."

"Is that you, kid?"

"Yeah, just can't get rid of me, Butterfield."

"Just as long as you're not my responsibility," Kevin said. "Do you want me to charge Snowe with something? Otherwise, we can't hold him."

"Right now all we're asking for is his cooperation."

"He's not in a cooperative mood. He's already asked for a lawyer. He insists that he's already told us everything he knows about Delilah Occum."

"He thinks it's about Delilah, then?"

"Yes, and I haven't told him differently."

"Obviously he doesn't know that Dana is talking. So let him think it's about Occum. Don't tell him about Dana."

"Decker, with regards to Occum we have nothing to hold him. What if the lawyer demands we charge him or let him go?"

"Okay. If it comes to that and you have to play our hand, yes, hold him on the car crash. And if you have to charge him, go full force: failure to report a near lethal accident, leaving the scene of a car crash, possession of controlled substances. Let him know he's not going anywhere soon."

"You can't talk to him without his legal eagle."

"We can't *question* him without his legal eagle. But I can talk to McAdams with Snowe in the room. And if he's the least bit interested, he can listen to what we're saying."

* * *

As Decker walked into the station house, Kevin Butterfield said, "Snowe's lawyer is with him now. She just arrived about five minutes ago." He turned to McAdams. "Good to have a resident lawyer on our side."

"Do you mean him or me?"

"God forbid he means me," Decker said.

"You, at least, graduated."

Butterfield said, "The woman's from Hamilton County. I doubt she went to Harvard Law School."

"Hate to break it to you, Butterfield, but sometimes those second-tier guys can run rings around the academics. Those guys and gals are on the battlefields." Decker was heading toward the interview room. McAdams took a couple of big strides to keep up with him. "Should I exaggerate my limp to make her feel sorry for me?"

"You don't limp."

"I do when it suits me."

Decker smiled and opened the door to the room. A gorgeous woman in her early thirties looked up— long brown hair, brown eyes, and a face perfectly made up to enhance her naturally good looks. She wore a black pants suit, white shirt, and heels. "Excuse me, we're not done."

"Sorry." Decker held up his hands. "Just letting you know I'm here—"

"Can you close the door behind you?" she said.

"And you are . . ."

"Felicia Estrella." Anglicized as the *L* sound instead of the *Y* sound. "Please leave."

"Sure." Decker closed the door. Softly he said, "I'm thinking she has some issues with the police."

"What better time to use the limp?"

Decker laughed. He went to his desk. "It might be a while, Harvard."

"Then now's the time to show you my party pictures including the two pervs."

"Yeah, right. That reminds me. I want to check up on Rina and see what Carter and Diaz have been up to." Decker sat at his desk and phoned his wife. "Hey, how are you?"

"Wading in pots of chicken soup."

"Where are you?"

"At Hillel. I'm cooking it here because everything is industrial size."

"Tell me you're not alone."

"I have anywhere from three to six people with me at all times except for bathroom breaks. I'm fine, Peter. Stop worrying."

"No sign of you know who?"

At that moment, Kevin came over. "They're waiting for you."

Decker stood up. "Honey, I have to go. I'll call when I'm free again. Don't you dare go anywhere without a posse." He hung up. "C'mon, Mr. Gimp. Let's get going."

"Just call me Chester."

"You're way too young to remember *Gunsmoke*."

"There are these things called classic TV channels. I used to love westerns."

"You? Westerns?"

"I loved anything that was diametrically opposed to my childhood: no brains and all brawn. Everything I wasn't, pard. I used to dream of being a real hero. Why do you think I became a cop?"

"I thought it was to spite your dad."

"That, too."

Snowe was dressed in jeans and a yellow T-shirt. A gray hoodie rested on the back of his chair. His facial bruises had faded. Decker took a quick glance at his hands. There was nothing to suggest that he had been in a pitched battle with another person. His manner seemed subdued compared to the last interview.

After he and McAdams introduced themselves, Felicia Estrella did the staredown. Her voice was still hard. "Mr. Snowe's days of cooperation are waning, Detective McAdams. The first time you talked to Mr. Snowe about the disappearance of Delilah Occum, he was very forthcoming. Now it's beginning to look like harassment. So either charge him or we're leaving."

"Decker." He pointed to the kid. "He's McAdams. New developments, Ms. Estrella. We need to ask your client a couple of questions."

Felicia was unfazed by her identification error. "What developments?"

"We'll talk about Delilah Occum, but not just yet." Decker sat down and zeroed in on Cameron Snowe. He kept his voice even and neutral. "Cameron, I want to talk to you about a near-fatal car accident involving a young woman who was almost killed. She came out of her coma last night." Decker waited. "Is this ringing any bells?"

The kid looked stunned.

To Estrella, Decker said, "Her name is Dana Berinson and she had something very interesting to say to us about your client."

Felicia looked at Cameron. "Do you know what they're talking about?"

Snowe had paled, but he managed to find his voice. "No idea."

Decker's voice was conversational. "Cameron, it's stupid to lie because this is what we're going to do." He looked at Felicia. "You might want to take notes." When she didn't answer, he said, "Cameron, we're going to subpoena your phone records to find out where you were and who you called for help Saturday night. We're also going over every single inch of Dana's Honda. We are in the process of finding a boatload of evidence that puts you at the scene of that accident."

Snowe stumbled over his words. "I heard the car exploded when it crashed."

"No, it did not explode," Decker explained. "It was set on fire and whoever did it did a lousy job. There is still plenty of evidence left inside the car, including controlled substances. So at the moment, you are facing a multitude of charges, including arson." Decker sighed. "You're not leaving here, Cameron. You're going to be arrested on charges ranging from reckless driving to attempted murder—"

"What are you talking about!" The kid was sitting up in his chair. "It was a fucking accident—"

Felicia blurted out, "I'd like a moment with my—"

Decker broke in. "You probably don't know about attempted murder—"

"You're crazy! The bitch took off her seat belt and that's my fault?"

Felicia said, "Cameron, stop talking!"

"I told her to keep it on! She did it to herself. Give me a fucking break!"

"I'd like a moment with my client."

"No way you're gonna pin murder on me!"

Decker said, "Cameron, you are under the misguided delusion that just because Dana did something stupid that it's not your fault. *You* were driving."

"You don't know that. It's her fucking word against mine."

"Cameron, the steering wheel was intact. Whose prints are we going to find?"

"It just meant I touched . . ." He paused, his eyes darting everywhere. "I drove on the way up, not on the way back. That's why you'll find my prints . . . if you do find them."

Decker leaned over and made his voice deliberately soft. "Cameron, you went past tollbooths. We have CCTV that shows you behind the wheel on the way back to the colleges. It would help your case if you just started telling me the truth."

"I am telling you the truth!"

"No, you're not. And that makes me think that you were far more involved than you claim. It makes me think that you pushed the car over the embankment—"

"I didn't push anything over anything!" His eyes started to water. "That is totally untrue."

"Okay. I can believe that." Decker nodded. "Because you probably weren't working alone. But someone pushed it over the embankment, attempting to make it look like an accident. And someone tried to burn the car up after it fell over. And just because you *weren't* there doesn't mean you won't be charged for attempted murder."

Snowe wiped tears from his eyes. "Fuck you!"

"That's your answer to all this?" McAdams said. "'Fuck you'? You're in deep shit, Cameron. Maybe you should listen to Detective Decker. He's your best option right now."

Felicia was scribbling as she spoke. "I need to talk to my client alone, please."

When the men started to rise, Cameron said, "Wait."

Decker sat back down. So did McAdams.

"Just listen a moment. I admit I was in the car, okay? And I admit I was behind the wheel *part* of the time. But I wasn't at the wheel when it happened. We switched places because I was getting tired."

"You switched positions so that she was behind the wheel when the accident happened."

"Yes."

"And she was driving without her seat belt?"

"Yeah, exactly. She got in the accident. Not me."

"And you want to go to a grand jury with that one, Cameron?"

"It's the truth and you can't prove otherwise unless you have CCTV of *that* moment."

"You know, Cameron, we wouldn't just take Dana's word for it. That's why we sent the wheel to forensics—"

"Of course my prints are going to be on it. I was driving."

"Look in the mirror, son. You have bruises on your forehead. And a little cut. If you go with that story, it better be the truth, because if there is an atom of your blood on the steering wheel, we shall find it. And then you'll be shown to be a liar, and then no one will believe anything you say even if it's the truth."

Snowe stuttered unintelligible words.

"I need to talk to him right now." Felicia sighed. "Can you please leave?"

Decker turned to Cameron. "Stay or go?"

"I swear to God, I didn't push any car over any embankment!"

"Cameron, listen to me." Decker's voice was soft. "We're going to find out who you called. And if the person you called pushed the car off the road, you'll be charged with attempted murder. If the person you called decided to call someone else to do it, it still doesn't matter. You will still be charged with attempted murder—"

"I didn't kill the bitch!"

"It doesn't matter if—"

"I didn't *kill* her!"

McAdams said to Estrella, "Perhaps you want to clue him in on the finer points of law?"

"I would if you two would leave so I can speak to him in confidence!"

"This is a setup," Cameron said. "A total frame!"

"Cameron, just shut up now!" Estrella stood up, trying to face off to Decker's six foot four inches of height. Her neck was craned upward. "I need to speak to my client alone! Now!"

"Take your time," Decker said mildly. "He's not going anywhere."

❦37

Radar walked into the station house. "What's going on with Snowe?"

Decker and McAdams were sorting through photos with magnifying glasses. Decker said, "He's still conferring with his lawyer."

"Have you charged him yet?"

"Not yet." Decker looked up from the desk. "I want him to labor under the delusion that if he tells us something, we might let him go."

"What are you doing now?"

McAdams said, "Looking at photos from the party where Delilah Occum disappeared."

"How'd you get those, McAdams?" Radar said.

"I asked for them."

"Direct and effective. Anything interesting?"

"Hank Carter and Michael Pallek were there. No photos of the wives. Pretty weird, huh?"

"I'll say. Any pictures of either of those guys talking to Delilah Occum?"

McAdams held up his magnifying glass. "That's what we're searching for, Captain."

Radar pulled up an empty chair. He plopped a

folder on Decker's desktop. "Forensics on Erin Young's necklace."

"That was fast," Decker said.

"I rushed the report."

As Decker read, McAdams peered over his shoulder. "You nailed it."

"Good start, but not quite," Decker said. "Diaz's DNA and Erin's DNA on the same necklace. But without her testimony, he can always claim it was a gift and he helped her put it on. They were an item for some time. What the blood on the necklace does is buttress Erin's testimony that he yanked it off her neck and tried to choke her."

Radar said, "What can we do to secure her cooperation?"

"I've got my former partner, Marge Dunn, working on her. I'll call her up and let her know that there's evidence to back up Erin's claim."

"Think that'll do it?"

"I don't know, Mike. Erin was pretty adamant about not testifying. I'm thinking that if we can find who she whacked with a shovel and put him behind bars, it might make her feel safe enough to go against Diaz."

Radar said, "Whoever tried to bury Erin had buried the others?"

"It's the only conclusion that makes sense."

Radar said, "How is Snowe looking for our gravedigger?"

"As far as I know, he wasn't around when Yvette Jones and Lawrence Pettigrew went missing. I don't think he's the digger. But that doesn't mean he wasn't involved in Occum's death. We have Snowe over a barrel, peering down Niagara Falls. Let's see what happens as we nudge him closer to the precipice."

When Decker and McAdams came back to the interview room, Felicia Estrella was looking downward at the tabletop, stacking her notes until the edges were all lined up. Cameron's face was slack. His eyes were red and tired. After officially arresting him, Decker listed the charges. The sheer amount of allegations leveled against him would have been enough to make even the most hardened felon wince. Cameron looked stunned.

"Let's get one thing straight, Counselor." Decker pulled up a chair and McAdams followed suit. "No talk of deals yet. I haven't talked to the D.A., and I don't know what he or she is willing to do, if anything." He looked at Snowe. "What you need to do is tell me the truth from start to end. Get it all out there so the D.A. knows you're not trying to con him or her. If you do that, you're much more likely to catch a break. Do you understand what I'm saying, Cameron?"

Snowe nodded. He turned to his lawyer. "Please leave."

Felicia looked bewildered. "Excuse me?"

"I spoke to my dad when I was in the head a few minutes ago. I explained that I needed a real defense lawyer. He's getting a top-notch attorney for me, not someone from a mediocre law school who earns her living defending people who can't speak English against DUIs. This case is way over your pay grade. I don't need you to tell me not to talk. I know what I'm doing. Please leave."

The woman's skin tone had deepened to an un-natural color. "Why didn't—"

"You're fired. Leave now!"

Felicia gathered up her papers. "Off the record, you're a little shit." She bolted from the interview room.

Decker said, "A little harsh."

"She doesn't know what's flying." Snowe drummed the table. "So what happens now?"

"What do you mean?"

"I mean, if I say I want my attorney present, what do you do with me?"

"Oh, you mean procedure. We begin to process you. We take you down to booking, print you, take a mug shot, take your clothes and valuables, and dress you in oranges. Then we put you in a cell until the time of your arraignment where we hope to set your bail at a very high number so it'll take your parents some time to raise it."

"And I stay in jail the whole time?"

"Yes."

"Unacceptable."

"No matter what you tell me or don't tell me, you're going to jail. How long you go to *prison* is another question. You've got to show a reason why the D.A. would want to plea-bargain. So far, you've said nothing, which of course is your right. I'm just letting you know what's likely to happen."

"So you really don't have much to do in this process."

"The police do all the procedures. We also present the evidence to the D.A. and make recommendations. The D.A. listens to our input. Our experience—and I've been at this for a very long time—counts. But our recommendations are not binding."

"So you don't make the ultimate deal."

"No."

"So even if I told you something good, you couldn't help me."

"Yes." Decker shrugged. "You are facing jail time, Snowe. It's up to you to determine how long."

"I didn't kill Dana."

"I know that. She's alive."

"I mean I didn't even *try* to kill her."

Decker paused a long time. "Do you want to talk to me without your lawyer?"

"I'm just saying."

"Yes or no, Snowe. Do you want to talk or wait for your lawyer?"

"I certainly don't want you to start the 'process.'" He made quotes with his fingers. "So yes, I'm talking to you without a lawyer. And I'm telling you I wasn't there when the car went over the cliff or whatever you call it."

"Embankment."

"Yeah, that."

"I need a time frame from you." Decker pulled out his notepad. "When did you and Dana leave to go up north together?"

"Friday around four in the afternoon."

"So you two came up from the colleges to the Boston area."

"Yeah."

"You came up to buy drugs—"

"Correction. *She* came up to buy drugs."

"I can totally believe that. She has a history. But drugs were found in her car, Cameron. And so were your prints. Plus, we'll get phone records—"

"Burner phones don't have records."

"They do have records."

"They have numbers but not who called."

"That is correct," Decker said.

McAdams said, "Tracing them isn't as impossible as you think it is."

"Bullshit."

Decker said, "Burner phones are hard to track, even harder to trace. You're right about that, Cameron. But nothing is impossible."

Cameron went silent. "I wasn't *there*."

"You were there when the car got into an accident."

"I'm pleading the Fifth on that one. I have no idea how the car flipped over."

Decker said, "You were at the wheel of Dana Berinson's Honda, driving Dana and yourself back to the colleges on Saturday night. We have CCTV."

"Can I talk to you off the record?"

"No. I've already arrested you and read you your rights."

"Not even if I have something to say that really might be of interest to you?"

"Everything is on the record, Cameron. But if you want to talk to me, you can talk theoretically."

"Like in the third person?"

"Yeah, like in the third person."

"And you won't record that?"

"We are recording everything you're saying." Decker folded his hands and put them on the table.

He leaned toward Snowe. "You're an intelligent boy, Cameron. I know you're constantly thinking about what's best for you. If you want my advice, the first step to a plea bargain is cooperation."

"It's really stupid for me to talk to you before my new lawyer gets here."

"It's up to you. I'm just here to listen."

The room was silent for thirty seconds. Then Snowe said, "I wasn't there when the car went over the embankment."

"I believe you."

Cameron leaned back in his chair. "It was a stupid accident."

"When Dana's car crashed, it was an accident?"

"Yeah, of course. What else would I be talking about?"

"I'm just clarifying." Decker filled the kid's water glass. "So you were there when the car got into an accident. And I'm sure it was an accident. You're off to a good start."

"I didn't even want to leave Saturday night, but the bitch was in such a hurry to play big shot with her stash." He hung his head in his hands, and then he looked up. "She was supposed to drive home. That was the deal. I'd drive there, she'd drive home. Ten, fifteen minutes into the ride home, she said she was tired. We're out of the Boston area in the middle of nowhere. We could either go back or go forward and like an idiot, I took the wheel and decided to drive back. It's stupid to deny that I wasn't driving because I did go through a tollbooth—two actually."

He emitted something that sounded like a growl.

"About ten minutes later, the dumb bitch decides

to take off her seat belt. Doesn't want to wear it because it was riding up on her face, bothering her
while she was trying to sleep. So she clicks it behind
her butt and proceeds to fall asleep."

"That was a dumb move."

"She's an idiot," Cameron said. "I shouldn't have
even gone with her."

"Why did you?" McAdams asked.

"Because I'm an idiot!"

Decker said, "What time did you leave from the
Boston area?"

"After dark but not too late. Maybe nine or ten."
He rubbed his neck and blew out air. "I was tired,
too. The road was dark and it was hard to stay
awake. I must have dozed off for a moment. Next
thing I knew I was headed for the railing. I swerved
and braked very hard. I didn't hit the railing head-
on. I hit it on the passenger-side front bumper,
enough to break through the metal so that the airbags deployed." He shook his head again and
pinched off a fraction of space between his thumb
and forefinger. "I was this close to going off the
edge. The front wheels were almost dangling."

"Scary," Decker said.

"Uh, yeah!"

"Airbags deploy?"

"Yep. But I hit my forehead on something. Could
have been the airbag hitting me. In any case, I was
wearing my seat belt so I was okay."

A long sigh.

"Dana knocked her head on the side window. I
guess since she wasn't wearing her seat belt, the

airbag knocked her sideways. The glass broke . . .
not shattered, but it broke like in that concentric
circle pattern. There was blood everywhere." A long
pause. "She never uttered a sound—not a groan, not
a moan, nothing. I thought for sure she was dead."

"Did you check?"

"I don't remember. I was in shock at that point.
And she wasn't moving."

Decker nodded. "What did you do next?"

"I eased myself out of the car. It was pitch-black. I
was scared and completely panicked. I didn't know
what to do."

The young man suddenly shut down. Softly,
Decker said, "You called someone for help."

"I don't think I should say anything else. This is
the deal part."

"The part when you called up a person to help
you out."

"Like I said, I use burner phones."

"*You* might have used a burner phone. But you
probably called a standard cell where we can access
phone logs and texts." Decker sat back and spoke
calmly. "There are only so many people you would
have called in that situation. How long do you think
it's going to take us to figure it out?"

"You can't randomly go around checking people's
cell-phone records."

"There is nothing random about our investigation, Cameron. We do everything properly and
we'll get our warrants. If you help us out now and
save us work, you can go a long way toward making
yourself look good. So who'd you call?"

"If I give you information that may have to do with some other crime, what can you do for me?"

"What will I recommend to the D.A., you mean?"

"Yes."

"Depends on the information. What ideally are you looking for in a plea bargain?"

"Ideally? All charges dropped."

"That's not going to happen."

"I've got good information."

"Is it about Delilah Occum?"

"I had nothing to do with her death. Nothing!"

"I believe you. You had nothing to do with her death. Tell me what you think happened to her. Have you heard rumors?"

"Maybe yes, maybe no." Snowe sat back in his seat. "I'm not saying anything more. Even when I get my lawyer, I'm not talking to you."

"That's your right, son. So stand up. Let's start the process."

"Can't I just wait here for my lawyer?"

"No, Cameron, you cannot wait in an interview room. We have to book you now."

Snowe didn't move. "How about no jail time?"

"You're controlling this interview, you know. You're a force to be reckoned with." Decker watched pride sweep across the kid's face. "Do you want to continue talking to me without a lawyer present? I need a yes or no answer to the question."

"Okay. Yes, I'll talk to you without my lawyer for a few more minutes. I'll tell you everything I know if you can recommend no jail time."

"Tell me what you have and I'll take it to the D.A."

"I need assurances that you'll take that recommendation to the D.A."

"I can't give you that," Decker said. "But I can tell you what will happen if you don't tell us the name of the third party who was involved in helping you out. The attempted murder falls on you. If you name a third party and we're able to prove it was him or her who pushed the car over the embankment, maybe a D.A. would plead down that charge to something lesser."

"To what?"

"I don't know," Decker said. "I'm not a lawyer." McAdams broke out in a coughing fit. "You really need to go to the doctor with that cough."

"Sorry." McAdams took a swig of water.

Snowe, also taking a drink of water, said, "I'm not going to prison."

"That's exactly where you're going unless you have something to bargain with." Decker waited for Snowe to finish his water. Then he refilled the cup.

Snowe said, "I've got to take a wicked piss."

"There's a bathroom down in booking," Decker said.

The kid made a face. McAdams said, "Right now . . . right at this moment . . . this is your best chance to save your neck, Snowe."

Snowe blew out air. "I called a friend."

"Who?" Decker said. "Casey Halpern? Marcus Craven? One of your other buddies who alibied you on the night that Delilah Occum died? We'll try them all, Cameron. It's going to take a while. And in the meantime, you're languishing in jail."

"I'll be out on bond. They have to grant me bail for a car accident."

"Not if you're a suspected murderer—for Dana Berinson as well as Delilah Occum—"

"I had nothing to do with Delilah's murder. Or Dana's attempted murder."

"But you *might* know something about both of them." Decker stood. "Look, Snowe. I can't keep questioning you if you have to go to the bathroom. Your lawyer will say I questioned you under duress. Let's go down to booking."

The kid remained seated. "I had nothing to do with Delilah Occum's murder."

"Fine. Do you want to take a piss or do you want to talk?"

"Give me a sec, okay. I'm thinking."

"Take your time. And if you want to help yourself, give me the name of the person you called the night of the accident."

A few moments passed. Then Snowe said, "I called someone who gave me the number of someone who had helped *him* out in the past."

"Who did you first call for help?"

Snowe's jaw was bulging. "What the hell? No honor among thieves, right?"

"Who'd you call, Cameron?"

"Casey Halpern."

"Good. Thank you. And who did you call after you called Casey Halpern?"

"I didn't call anyone. Casey called someone for me."

"So who came down to help you out, Cameron?"

"Dr. Pallek."

"Michael Pallek?"

"Do you know another Dr. Pallek?"

"Clarification, Cameron."

"Yes, it was Michael Pallek. Three hours later, he rode up in some dinky car without plates."

"So this was about two in the morning?" McAdams asked.

"About."

"Then what happened?"

"He gave me the keys to his car and a map of how to get back to the colleges without going through tollbooths."

"Okay," Decker said. "That's great. Do you still have the map by any chance?"

"It might be somewhere in my dorm room. I'd have to check."

"We'll check for you. Don't worry about it."

"It wasn't a very clear map. I got lost and had to use my GPS to make it home."

"Then if you used your GPS, you probably went through several tollbooths."

Snowe made a face. "Sometimes I'm not only a dick, I'm real stupid."

A rare moment of insight. Decker said, "Let's get back to what happened, Cameron. Michael Pallek gave you the keys to the car he was driving."

"Yes."

"And he gave you a map to avoid going through tollbooths."

"Yes."

"What did he say to you after he gave you the map and keys?"

"He told me where to leave the car and said he'd pick it up later."

"Where did he tell you to leave the car?"

"At Harvard and Fourth."

"A block away from campus then."

"Yes."

"Did he tell you anything else?"

"He told me that he'd take care of everything. He told me to go back to the colleges and not to stop for anything."

"Then what happened?"

"He told me to leave and I did. He didn't have to tell me twice. I really have to piss."

"Let's go," McAdams said.

"Are you taking me to booking?"

McAdams looked at Decker, who said, "Bring him back here. We're far from done."

❧38

As Decker regarded Snowe through the one-way mirror, he said, "Could someone go in and ask him if he wants something to eat or drink?"

"I'll do it." Kevin got up from the chair.

Radar said, "Do you personally want to pick up Pallek?"

"Send Kevin and Karen to do it when the time comes," Decker said.

"You want to wait on it?"

"I'd like to have something other than Snowe's word that Pallek was there. First thing I want to do is search Snowe's room and find the map that Pallek allegedly gave him."

"It'll take a while to get the warrant," Radar said. "Might be easier to ask Snowe for permission. He seems to be in a cooperative mood."

"Okay," Decker said. "The car that Snowe described Pallek as driving—it doesn't sound like his regular car."

"You think it was a rental," McAdams said. "I'll call up the local companies."

"Before we do it, let's check the DMV and find out what car is registered in his name."

"I'll do that as well," McAdams said.

Radar said, "What do you want to do about Casey Halpern?"

"We have to make sure that Snowe is telling the truth about Halpern. He's been lying from day one."

"So pick up Halpern and ask him."

"He's not local anymore. He graduated and I don't know where he lives. But I'm betting that Snowe does. Halpern is probably out of our jurisdiction. We'll be depending on another police department. I don't know if they'll be willing to pick him up just based on what Snowe says."

McAdams said, "If what Snowe says is true, we can get Pallek on attempted murder."

Decker said, "But we need something to tie Pallek to Snowe other than Snowe's confession. If Pallek avoided tollbooths, he probably avoided populated areas and CCTV. It's unlikely we'll pick him up on the road. We need the map."

McAdams said, "Do you want me to ask him for permission to search his dorm room and for his burner phone to corroborate what he just told us?"

"I can do it," Decker said.

"I'm less threatening. Let me do it."

"Fine."

"I'll also ask him where Casey Halpern lives so you know which police department to contact."

"Great."

"Question," Radar said. "Do you think that Snowe has already called Pallek and Halpern and warned them that he's being questioned?"

"I thought about that," Decker said. "My opinion? He hasn't told them anything. I think as soon as we started talking about Dana and attempted murder, Snowe knew he was in it up to his eyeballs. I think he decided that they were his get-out-of-jail-free card. So no, I don't think he's called either of them . . . yet. If we had his cell phone and his burner, we could check."

McAdams said, "You want me to ask him for his cell to see who he's been calling?"

"It would show good faith on our part to *ask* him for it. But once he's booked we'll get it anyway." Decker turned to Radar. "I don't know who else is involved in this mess, but I think we should keep watch on Carter and Diaz while we're interviewing Pallek."

"When's your buddy coming in to watch Carter?"

"Oliver? Tomorrow."

"I can spare someone until then. What about Rina?"

"She's supposed to be with someone at all times. I'll check in on her. Thanks for asking."

Radar said to McAdams, "Go in and ask Snowe for his cell and burner phones and permission to search his room. Let's see what he does."

Both of them watched as McAdams went into the interview room and sat down. "Is Detective Butterfield bringing you food?"

"The guy who just came in?"

"Yes."

"Yeah, I think he's bringing me a hamburger." Snowe sat back. "You know, I've been very cooperative."

"Yes, you have."

"I hope you guys will be equally cooperative with me. I really laid it on the line, you know. I'm bare assed in the wind right now."

"Cameron, we're thinking about what you told us and we're leaning toward believing you."

"You should. It's the truth."

"Right. I do have a few requests that'll help your case out considerably."

"I told you everything I have to say."

"I realize that. Now it's just about corroborating what you said."

The kid was quiet. Then he said, "Go ahead. I'm listening."

McAdams said, "You told us that Pallek gave you a map that night. You also said that the map might be in your dorm room."

"I don't know if I threw it away or not."

"Can Detective Decker and I search your dorm room?"

"For the map?"

"For the map and for anything else that might corroborate your story."

Cameron shrugged. "Sure."

"Okay. Thanks. A couple of other things. What about your burner phone? It would help our case if we had it and could corroborate the calls that you said you made."

Cameron sighed. "Well, you're too late for that. I threw it away."

McAdams said, "Where did you throw it?"

"I chucked it when I was on the road headed back."

"Okay. Do you remember the phone's number?"

"No idea."

"Where did you buy it?"

"I think I bought this one at Target."

"At which Target did you buy the burner that you tossed on the side of the road?"

"In Hamilton, I think."

"Do you remember *when* you bought it?"

"A month ago, maybe. It was almost used up when I decided to ditch it."

"Okay," McAdams said. "You bought the burner a month ago at Target in Hamilton. How did you pay for it?"

"In cash. It doesn't do you much good if your burner has a paper trail."

"And this was the phone that you used to call Casey Halpern?" When Cameron nodded, McAdams said, "Can you say yes or no for the recording?"

"Yes, I called Casey Halpern on it."

"Did you block your number when you called him?"

"No, I did not. I wanted it to register on his phone logs in case he tried to deny that I called him."

"Why would he deny that you called him?"

"I'm not saying he would. But I did call him, and then Dr. Pallek showed up. So you draw your own conclusions."

"Okay, that makes sense. So your burner's phone number would be on Casey Halpern's phone logs. Trouble is, I can't get into Halpern's phone logs until I verify that your burner called him. And I can't verify that unless I know your burner's number."

"I don't want you to pull up my burner because I don't want you knowing everyone I called on it."

"Cameron, I'm not working Vice. This is a Homicide case, and it would really help your case if we had the burner's number."

"I have to think about it."

"Don't take too long to come up with an answer."

"Anything else you want to squeeze out of me?"

"Yes, as a matter of fact. Do we have your permission to look at your cell phone?"

"No. It has my burner phone number in it. What are you looking for?"

McAdams said, "Just verifying your story."

Kevin Butterfield came back with a fast-food bag and a Coke. He set the bag in front of Snowe. "Here you go."

"No, you can't look at my phone." Cameron pulled out a hamburger. "Bon appétit." He took a bite.

McAdams said, "Where does Casey Halpern live?"

Snowe swallowed and wiped his mouth. "Last time I saw him, he was in New York."

"Okay," McAdams said. "Can you narrow that down?"

"Brooklyn."

"Do you know where in Brooklyn?"

"Nope. And I don't even know if he still lives there."

"Have you ever been to his place?"

"A few times but I couldn't tell you a thing about it."

"You've been there but you don't know his address?"

"I had it at one time. He texted it to me. It was a long time ago. I probably deleted it. I don't remember."

"Was it a posh area?"

Cameron thought a moment. "It had a lot of cafés, places where people hang out and check their phones and do nothing."

"That could be a lot of areas."

"I don't know what to tell you. I don't know Brooklyn."

"Okay. I'll be back."

"Yeah, I hope you remember that I've done nothing but cooperate with you." McAdams was about to leave when Snowe said, "It was near a lot of Jews. Where Halpern lived. You know the Jews I'm talking about—the ones with the curls and the long black coats."

"Did Halpern live in Williamsburg?"

The kid shrugged. "Don't know. You're the cop. You find him. Can I eat my hamburger in peace? Even a guy going to the gallows is entitled to his last meal."

"Sure."

"I'm kidding about going to the gallows," Snowe said. "But if I did go, my meal would be a whole lot better than a fucking hamburger."

Cameron Snowe's dorm room was a single and that meant no meddling roommate to worry about. It wasn't dirty, but it wasn't tidy—clothes scattered on the bed, a pile of papers on top of the desk, and a messy closet. The garbage had been emptied and there were no stray food containers or wrappers. He had several boxes of cereal, several bags of chips, and cans of beans, corn, and soup. There was a small fridge with dips, instant coffee, a carton of milk, and beer.

After searching through the desk drawers, McAdams despaired. "No map."

"Check again."

"I did it twice, but I'll go for the trifecta if you insist."

Decker was flipping through papers from the desktop. "Let's switch." He handed McAdams the papers and went to check the drawers. Twenty minutes later, he got up, his knees cracking.

"No luck. What about you?"

"Nothing." McAdams placed the papers back on the desk.

"Check the closet," Decker said. "It's been a little nippy at night. He was probably wearing a jacket. Maybe he folded the map and stuffed it in a pocket."

"Sure."

"When are you headed back?" Decker asked as he lifted off Snowe's crumpled bedcovers.

"What time is it?" McAdams checked his watch. It was almost six. "I'll go back after I've had some dinner. Hint, hint."

"I'll tell Rina you're coming over." Decker felt the covers, shook them out, and then laid them on the floor. He pulled out his phone. After a few rings, he said, "She's not picking up. That's not good." He sent her a text.

"I'm sure she's fine. Didn't you just speak to her?"

"A half hour ago." Decker's phone buzzed. "Okay. She's answered that you're welcome anytime, you don't even have to ask." He texted back for her to call him.

McAdams separated the coats from the rest of the clothes and began to check pockets.

Decker's cell rang. He said, "Just wanted to hear your voice."

Rina said, "I'm still at Hillel with around six students who are helping me cook. I'm going to pack it in at around seven."

"Perfect. I'll come pick you up."

"You don't have to do that."

"I'm at Morse McKinley. Do not step foot out the door until I get there."

"What are you doing there?"

"All in due time. Make sure you're with someone at all times."

"I'm fine, Peter."

"Nuh-uh. Just listen to me, okay?"

"What's wrong?"

"I can't get into it now, but I'll fill you in later, okay?"

"Son of a bitch!" McAdams announced.

"What?" Decker said.

"I didn't say anything," Rina said.

"Can I call you back in a bit?"

"Don't bother. I'll see you in an hour."

Decker hung up. McAdams was holding a folded plastic sleeve that contained a piece of paper. "It's not a map. It's directions from Morse McKinley to somewhere up north—presumably the accident spot."

"What kind of directions?"

"Very complicated directions." McAdams smiled.

"Back roads. Looks like he got them off a computer service. Why are you always right?"

"Tell that to my wife."

"Evidence bag, please?" McAdams shook his head. "That was a stroke of luck."

"It would have been better if the directions were handwritten."

"Decker, gift horse . . . mouth."

"I expect nothing except perfection." Decker was grinning. "You know what the best part of those directions is?"

"What?"

"It's hard to pull prints off paper." Decker handed McAdams a paper bag. "It's much easier to pull them off plastic."

🌭39

As soon as McAdams came to the station house, Radar said, "We've got eyes on Diaz and Pallek. We can't seem to locate Carter."

"Shit. What happened?"

"This is a walking town. He must have slipped away. And, yes, it is not good to lose visual with the creep. Where's Decker?"

"Picking up his wife at Hillel at Morse McKinley. He told me to drop this off and get it dusted immediately for prints."

"What is it?"

"The directions that Pallek allegedly gave to Cameron Snowe. I was going to copy them down and see what route Pallek took to the accident spot. See if there are CCTVs en route."

"And the paper was like that when you found it? In the plastic sleeve?"

"Yes. Let's cross our fingers that we've got Pallek's prints on the plastic. Do we have Pallek's prints on file?"

"I'll check for you. School would have them. It's part of the local ordinance that all faculty from the colleges are printed."

"Do you want me to get them?"

"They'll ask why and I don't want to open up that can of worms without proper papers. When we pull Pallek in for questioning, just lie and say we got them from the colleges and we found a match."

"Sure. When are you going to pick up Pallek?"

"Now, before he bolts. Call up Decker. Ask him when he's coming in."

"Sure." McAdams made the call. "He wants to know if he can eat dinner first. It'll take him about a half hour."

"That'll be fine. It'll take at least that long to process Pallek. Where are you eating dinner?"

"Pete invited me over."

"Go." Radar relieved him of the evidence bag with the sleeve. "I'll see you both back here in an hour or so. In the meantime, I'll see if Pallek's prints are in the system for any criminal reason."

"He doesn't have a record. Neither does Hank Carter. Are you sure you don't want me to go over to the college and ask for them?"

"They won't give them to us, Tyler. They're very private with their own. Have you had any luck calling up rental car agencies?"

"The local ones are closed." McAdams paused. "What about notaries, Captain?"

"What about them?"

"I don't think they have the duty of confidentiality like a lawyer or doctor or priest. And I know you give them a right thumbprint when you sign some types of notarized documents. It's only a right thumbprint but most people are right handed and most people use their thumbs. I could check with local notaries to see if Pallek has a print in their books."

"Okay. Good idea."

"I'll make some calls at Decker's house."

"Right," Radar said. "Go enjoy your dinner. It might be a while before you'll eat again."

"Have you found Carter yet?" When Radar shook his head, Decker began to pace. "How could this happen?"

"We can't bring him in anyway, Pete. We don't have anything on him other than being creepy. Where is Rina now?"

"She's with friends. She's okay, but I would feel so much better if I knew where that asshole was. He must be involved in something. Otherwise why would he bolt?"

"I don't know that he did," Radar said. "Your PI friend is coming tomorrow. I hired him to watch Carter. So let him use his PI skills and find Carter if he's still AWOL. Right now we have more pressing matters. Pallek needs to be interviewed before he asks for a lawyer and we lose our chance with him."

"I know, I know. Where's Snowe?"

Radar said, "He's in jail waiting for arraignment. I'm hoping bail is high enough to keep him overnight, but a judge may not consider him dangerous or a flight risk. If he's about to be cut loose, we'll parade him in front of Pallek to make him nervous. Let's get going, Pete."

"Right." Decker looked around. "Where's Tyler?"

"I sent him home to eat dinner with you." When Decker didn't answer, Radar said, "He didn't show up?"

"I thought he just decided to stay here. Damn it." Decker dialed McAdams's number.

The kid picked up. "Yo."

"Where the hell are you?"

"Hello to you, too, boss."

"Don't be a wiseass. You had me worried."

"Aw, you care," McAdams said. "Listen to this. I, through my doggedness and persistence, have managed to find a twenty-four-hour rent-a-car agency in Hamilton called Neweast Transportation. After a bit of bullying and lying, they finally opened the records for me for the night of the accident, which was actually Sunday by the time James Dellek rented a red Chevy Sonic at 1:17 A.M."

"Okay." Decker exhaled. "That's really good. And we know definitely that Dellek is Pallek because . . ."

"You've got to be kidding me."

"Did you show the rental agent a picture of Pallek?"

"Please. I know better than to bias her before we have a six-pack or a lineup. Besides, I don't even know if she was the one who rented to Pallek—or Dellek if you want to play it by the book, whatever the book is. Have you brought Pallek in yet?"

"I was just about to go into the interview room. I'll use the information you just gave me to put on the heat. Get your ass down here so you can be part of it."

"I've got a few more things to do."

"Like?"

"I'm trying to track down local notaries. Another

one of my brainstorms. Ask Radar about it. It may take me a while."

"Come in whenever you can, Harvard. We're in this for the long haul."

This time Pallek had drawn his thick hair back in a man bun. He was still slight and still short. Decker motioned the standing man to the chair, and both of them sat down. He put his notes on the table, poured two cups of water, and slid one in front of Pallek, who said, "What do you want?" He didn't wait for an answer. "I'm a really busy guy."

"I appreciate that, Dr. Pallek. Thanks for coming down."

"Like I had a choice? Why am I here?"

"I'm asking for your help."

"What help? I can't help you."

"You don't even know what I'm asking for."

"It can't be good. You don't drag a person down to the police station just to get help. So either arrest me for something or I'm going home."

"You want me to arrest you?"

"Well, no, I don't *want* you to arrest me. I didn't do anything arrestable. I don't even know if that's a word."

"Dr. Pallek, do you have any idea where your brother-in-law might be?"

"You mean Hank?"

"Yes, Hank Carter. Do you know where he is?"

"No, I don't. He's a grown man and I don't keep tabs on him."

"Think about it, sir. You have *no* idea where he is?"

"I answered your question already. Why? Is he missing?"

"We're looking for him just to chat and we can't seem to find him anywhere. He doesn't appear to be home, he's not in his office. I thought that was odd."

"It is odd, but . . ." Pallek stood up, and then he sat back down. "You didn't drag me down here to ask where my brother-in-law is. So if that's it . . ."

"I have a few more questions."

"Well, if you have a few questions, I might be willing to answer them. If you have more than a few questions, then I might have to get a lawyer."

"Up to you."

"So is it a few or is it more?"

"Let me start with a few, okay?"

"Fine." Pallek threw his hand up in the air and let it drop back down. "Ask your questions."

"Do you want a lawyer?"

"Am I under arrest?"

"Did I arrest you?"

Pallek exhaled. "Fine. Ask your *few* questions and then I'll decide if I want a lawyer."

"Sure. First let me give you a little background."

"So this isn't about Bogat."

"No."

Pallek seemed to visibly relax. "Okay. Give me background."

"A week ago I got a call about a missing Morse McKinley college student named Dana Berinson. I'm sure you heard about the incident."

"Yeah, of course." Eyes on the ground. "A car crash, right? Poor thing. I heard she's in critical condition . . . in a coma." When Decker nodded, Pallek said, "I heard she isn't going to survive."

"Who told you that?"

Pallek looked down again. "That's what I heard."

"Because the car went over the embankment."

"Exactly."

"And afterward, it caught on fire."

"Is that true?"

"Yes."

"Poor, poor thing. How do you survive that?"

"Only by a miracle." Decker paused. "But miracles do happen, Dr. Pallek. Dana has come out of her coma. She's groggy. She doesn't remember everything. But she does remember some things."

Pallek was quiet. Then he said, "Well, that's wonderful." He kneaded his hands. His eyes were everywhere except on Decker's face. "That's just great." Silence. "Anything else? I'm really very busy."

"I know. And I wouldn't drag you down here unless I thought you could help."

"Help? How?"

"Well . . ." Decker sat back and took a sip of water. "As we're looking into this horrific accident, your name came up."

"*My* name?"

"Yes, sir."

"I don't understand." Pallek was biting his lip. "How did my name come up?"

"Well . . . Dana mentioned it in a hazy fog. Now yours wasn't the only one, but she did say your name. I'm just wondering why."

Pallek didn't say anything.

Decker said, "Like I said, she's still in a fog. So if you could just tell me where you were a week ago very early Sunday morning between twelve-thirty and five A.M., I can strike you off my persons of interest list."

"That's easy." Pallek's eyes twitched. "At that time, I was undoubtedly home sleeping."

"Is there anyone who can verify that?"

"My wife, of course. I was home the entire evening."

"You're sure about that?"

"I mean, I might have gone out earlier in the evening, but I was definitely home later."

"And you're sure?"

"Of course I'm sure."

"Okay, thanks."

"Is that it?"

"A couple more questions."

"You said a *few* questions."

"So far I only asked you two questions—where your brother-in-law is and where you were in the wee hours of Sunday morning—and you answered them for me." Pallek was quiet. Decker said, "So if you were home that Sunday morning between twelve-thirty and five A.M., can you tell me something?"

"Depends on what."

"Why did a rental car agent at Neweast Transportation near Hamilton identify you as the man who rented a Chevy Sonic at 1:17 A.M. under the name of James Dellek?"

Pallek was momentarily stunned. "I am not James Dellek."

"No, you're not. That's why I brought you in . . . to help me clear this up."

"If James Dellek rented a car, you should contact him."

"But the agent identified you as James Dellek."

"Obviously, she made a mistake."

So the agent was a woman. Good to know. Decker thought about how to use it. "How'd you know it was a woman, Professor Pallek?"

Pallek stuttered. "You told me it was a woman."

"No, I didn't. I said an agent identified you as James Dellek."

"It's either a man or a woman and most of those rental car places are staffed with women. I don't like what you're implying. This isn't a fact-finding mission. This is a setup. So either arrest me or I'm leaving."

"Do you want me to arrest you?"

"No, I don't *want* you to arrest me. I don't even know why I'm here."

"That is what I'm telling you, Dr. Pallek. We're clearing up a few things. Like if you weren't posing as James Dellek, why is the handwriting on the car contract so similar to your own handwriting?"

"What do you know about my handwriting?"

"How hard do you think it would be to get a complete sample of your handwriting and match it to James Dellek's handwriting on the contract?"

"So you don't have a complete copy of my handwriting."

"I borrowed some tests from some of your students where you made comments. I have some samples."

"Look, Detective, I didn't rent any car and I'm not James Dellek. If you don't get to the point, I'm leaving."

"Another question. Why would Casey Halpern call you the Saturday night of the accident?"

Pallek turned pale. He stammered out, "He didn't call me."

"Your cell number is on his phone."

"That's impossible."

"Why's that?"

"Now I know you're lying to me. This is probably all lies."

"Why would you say that?"

"Because I know my cell number is not on his phone."

Decker said. "I meant your burner phone number. Casey gave the number to me, sir, so there's no sense denying it. If I call the number, will my cell ring in your house?"

Pallek was quiet. "I think I need to talk to a lawyer."

"That is certainly your right. And it's my right to arrest you for the attempted murder of Dana Berinson."

"You can't be serious!"

"I'm very serious."

"That's what you have on me? Some agent's misidentification and a phone number from a burner phone that no doubt can't be traced to me?"

"I can't talk to you anymore. You asked for a lawyer. I'm going to arrest you now and read you your rights—"

"Wait, wait, wait."

Decker paused. "If you want to keep talking to me, you have to say explicitly that you're willing to do so without legal representation. All this is being taped and I don't want it messed up by procedural errors."

Pallek was nervous, guilty, and furious all at the same time. Finally he said, "So what if Halpern called me? Is that a crime?"

"Are we still talking or do you want a lawyer?"

"Just listen, okay?"

"I can't because you asked for a lawyer."

"Okay. Forget the lawyer. What's the big deal if an old student calls me?"

"It's not a big deal. What did he call you about?"

"What he always calls me about," Pallek exploded. "Girl problems. He took a shine to me while he was here. I was his confidant. So he calls me whenever he has girl issues. That was it. I talked to him for a little bit. So what?"

"What time was that?"

"You should know. You're the one who claims I talked to him."

"It was a little past ten Saturday evening. How long did you talk to him?"

"You should know that, too."

"Just answer the question, Professor."

Pallek cleared his throat and took a sip of water. "Maybe twenty minutes . . . maybe a little longer."

"A little late to call about girl problems."

"Casey's a jerk. But like I said, he imprinted on me. He's always calling me. So I talked to him for around a half hour and then I suppose I futzed around the house until I went to bed. I don't know anything about James Dellek. I certainly didn't rent a car at that hour. I must have a doppelgänger."

"A doppelgänger with your handwriting."

"It's not my handwriting because I'm not James Dellek."

"Same handwriting, similar names . . ."

"It's not me!"

"Do you have an identical twin?"

"Maybe, because James Dellek isn't me. So unless you have other proof—"

There was a knock on the door. Both Decker and Pallek looked up as McAdams walked in. He was stifling a smile. "May I talk to you for a moment, sir?"

Decker got up and took his notes and folders. "Make yourself comfortable, Dr. Pallek. You're not going anywhere." He and McAdams went into another room and stared at a frantic man pacing behind a one-way mirror. "What's up?"

"I found the agent who rented to Pallek," McAdams said. "She lives about thirty minutes from here, but she's willing to come in, God bless her soul. Do we do a lineup or a six-pack?"

"I can't round up five guys who look like Pallek that soon. Go through the mug books and get a six-pack. Great job, Harvard. The case is going to rest on her ID."

"Not quite." McAdams broke into a wide smile. "Forensics got a few great prints off the plastic sleeve a half hour ago. We pulled in a fingerprint expert from Hamilton. She just arrived. First she's going to see if any of the prints match to Cameron Snowe."

"Are there other prints besides Cameron's?"

"Forensics wrote that there are at least two types of prints: two types of right *thumb*prints!" When he got no response, McAdams said, "Didn't you talk to Radar?"

"About what?"

"Oh man, you will truly appreciate my genius with this one. Pallek's prints aren't in any of our files because he doesn't have a criminal record. His prints *are* on file with the colleges, but to get them, Radar said we'd need to file all sorts of paperwork. So I got creative. Notaries take right thumbprints of their signatories and they don't have the official duty of confidentiality like lawyers and doctors."

"You got hold of Pallek's right thumbprint."

"Like I said, the expert is checking right now. I know you'll get Pallek's prints when we arrest him. But I thought it would be good to bag him while you're still interviewing him."

"A print and a witness ID. If it works out, we're gold. In the meantime, I'll use it. The guy is going to break. Would you like to come in and put the nail in the coffin with me?"

"I'd rather watch from behind the one-way mirror. It's great blood sport and no one dies."

❧40

Just as Decker came up from booking Pallek, Radar said, "We have Diaz behind bars."

Decker made a face. "What happened?"

"He had packed a suitcase and was ready to go somewhere. He said vacation, but I'm sure he heard about Pallek. I'll probably have to spring him in the morning, so think of something before we have to open the cage."

"As long as he's in custody, let's see if Diaz has a scar on his back."

"I thought Erin told you that it wasn't Diaz who tried to bury her."

"Well, it wasn't Pallek, either," Decker said. "When both he and Cameron were booked, they changed into their jail oranges. We checked them for both and neither one have any back scars or anything on their shoulders."

"Maybe it didn't leave a scar."

"If Erin hit the guy as hard as she said she did, there'd be a scar."

McAdams stated the obvious. "How about our phantom?"

Decker said, "Yeah, how about him? That's fucking great!"

"We'll find Carter," Radar said. "With Pallek and Snowe locked up for the night—"

"And Diaz," McAdams said.

"Now we can concentrate on finding Carter," Radar said.

"What's Snowe's bail?"

"Quarter mil. His parents should be able to get hold of the twenty-five grand by tomorrow."

Decker said, "What about Casey Halpern?"

Radar said, "He's been picked up by the NYPD on attempted murder, which of course won't stick, but it's enough to get him up here so you can question him. There's nothing more to do right now."

"I can look for Carter."

"You're better off going home, getting some rest, and taking care of Rina." To McAdams, Radar said, "You might as well go back to school."

"I'm not leaving until something is resolved." He turned to Decker. "Ready?"

"Yeah, let's get out of here."

It was ten by the time they sat down to dinner. Rina was quiet and Decker commented on it. She said, "Long day. Not only physical, but it's emotionally stressful to find someone to babysit me all the time. I feel like I'm imposing on everyone and I hate being an imposition."

"It'll be all over soon," Decker said.

"Yeah, especially since Oli—" McAdams was kicked under the table. He looked at Decker and stopped talking.

"Especially since what?" Rina said.

"Since all of us are pretty close to the end." Decker had yet to tell Rina about Oliver. He knew she'd resent the idea, and she would feel doubly bad about involving a friend. Decker just wasn't up to the arguing when he was clearly right.

"So Pallek doesn't have a scar on his back?" Rina said.

"No," McAdams said. "And neither does Snowe or Diaz."

"So it's Carter?"

"He's looking guiltier since he went missing." Decker managed a smile. "We're scouring the streets for him. We'll find him."

"I'm sure you will. I'm not worried, Peter. You know that."

"Of course. Neither am I."

"I have some cooking to do tomorrow in the house," Rina said. "I'll get way more done without another person to entertain."

"I would think another person would be an extra set of hands."

"It is nice having help, but cooking time is my thinking time. A few hours in the morning alone would go a long way. I'll keep the doors locked and my gun out."

Decker knew that Oliver would be in town around twelve. "We'll talk about it tomorrow."

"You're right. We'll talk about it in the morning." She speared a green bean and managed a weak smile. There was nothing left to say. The meal was functional and quick. Sleep was even quicker.

* * *

At seven in the morning, as Decker was sipping coffee and eating toast, his cell rang.

Radar said, "Casey Halpern is coming into the station house with his lawyer in about an hour."

"What's going on?" Decker put down his coffee cup. "I thought we'd have to fight tooth and nail to get him here."

"Something big must be on his mind. I haven't had a chance to read any briefs or statements, so I don't know what his angle is going to be. But I'm sure it's some sort of plea bargain."

"Who's our D.A.?"

"Melinda Message will be here in a half hour. I suggest we all confer to see what our strategy is going to be."

"I'll be right there with Tyler." Decker hung up and looked at McAdams. "Casey Halpern will be at the station house with his lawyer in an hour. I don't know the specifics."

"Delilah Occum?"

"He was in school when she died. He alibied Snowe. We can hope."

McAdams put down his coffee cup. "I'm ready."

Decker looked at Rina. "I'm going to have to leave you alone."

"I'm fine—"

"Can you invite someone over for the next couple of hours?"

"No, I can't. I'll be perfectly fine by myself. As a matter of fact, I'll be better off by myself because I'll only be thinking about myself. I'll lock the doors, take out my gun, and I'll phone you every hour."

"Don't open the door for anyone or anything. You don't even *answer* the door. Be vigilant and if you feel anything is off, call the police. I don't care how trivial it is. I'll go do a quick check of the windows—"

"I can do that. You go solve some murders." She was pushing him to the door. "I love you. And thank you for trusting me."

"This may not be my finest hour."

"Go!" After the two men left, Rina checked the doors, the windows, and anything else that might be a way into the house—like crawlspaces and attics. When she was satisfied, she took out a five-pound bag of sugar, a two-pound bag of brown sugar, two pounds of pareve margarine, salt, baking powder, vanilla, pareve chocolate chips, and ten pounds of all-purpose flour. When she finished, she'd have enough chocolate chip cookies to feed a small Caribbean island. She went back into the living room and peered out the windows for any signs of life.

All was quiet, all was still.

She went to her bedroom and took out a .22 from the gun safe. With care, she loaded the bullets and then took it back with her into the kitchen. She wasn't a gun fan. If she had her druthers, all guns— even recreational guns—would be destroyed. Go back to the bow and arrow if you wanted to hunt.

But, being a cop's wife, she did know how to shoot.

There was a time for idealism.

And there was a time for practicality.

❧41

During interviews Decker liked to keep it cordial: nothing personal but he had a job to do. Even so, interviews often became adversarial. Once in a blue moon there was that sweet spot where the suspect was clearly burdened by a past event. Such was the case with Casey Halpern. Like Snowe, he was a good-looking and athletically built young man. He had auburn hair and dark troubled eyes that looked at Decker without flinching. He sat with his lawyer—a young man in his twenties named Nathan Borstein—on one side of the table while Decker, McAdams, and Melinda Message—a handsome woman in her fifties—sat opposite them. When all the procedure was done with, the plea-bargain haggling started in earnest. Halpern raised his hand, and the lawyers stopped talking.

"I need you guys to work something out because I can't go on like this."

Decker spoke before anyone else could. "Ideally, what do you want to happen, Casey?"

Halpern thought a moment. "Ideally, no charges because I didn't do anything. I certainly didn't have anything to do with Dana Berry or whatever her name is. I don't even know her."

"That's ideally," Decker said. "What are you willing to live with?"

"I don't know because I don't know what you guys have in mind."

His lawyer spoke to Message. "What do you have in mind?"

"Give us something to work with," Melinda said.

Decker interrupted. "Casey, what can you live with?"

"I don't want any jail time, that's for sure. I didn't do anything."

"You helped Cameron Snowe."

"I took his phone call and then I called Pallek. I thought Pallek was going to pick him up and take him back to the colleges. That's it."

"I can believe that," Decker said. "It's not Dana Berinson that's troubling you, it's something else." When Halpern didn't answer, Decker said, "Cameron Snowe doesn't have a moral barometer, but you do. I could tell the moment you walked through that door."

Melinda Message said, "Casey, if it's a case that I think warrants no jail time—maybe probation and community service—I can make the recommendations to the judge. But I can't do anything until we hear what you have to say."

"That's the problem," Borstein said. "Once you hear what Mr. Halpern has to say, we no longer have any bargaining chips."

"Like Casey said, this isn't about Dana Berinson," McAdams said.

Decker said, "If he says he took a phone call from

Snowe and then called Pallek to help Snowe out—pick him up in the car—I'm willing to believe that." He turned to Melinda Message. "How about we deal with Dana Berinson's attempted murder *if* he gives us something in return?"

"As in drop the charges?" Halpern said. "I'll go with that."

"Nothing will be dropped until you tell us what you know," Melinda asked.

Halpern whispered to his lawyer, who nodded. "It's about Delilah Occum."

"Okay," Decker said. "You want to tell me about it?"

"I've been thinking about it since you guys picked me up. It's a sign."

And then he began his recitation.

"I was there—at the party when Cameron and Delilah got into a fight. They were both drunk and when Cameron gets loaded, he can be loud and abrasive. Delilah, who was no angel, I'm just saying, was also hammered. They started with words, but then the fight became a little physical. She was poking him in the chest. He flung his arm to push her away and wound up hitting her in the chest. She stalked off. It should have ended there, but he was still angry."

"Cameron was still angry at Delilah," Decker said.

"That's what I'm saying. He stuck around at the party for maybe another minute or two, but then he ran after her."

"So he left the party," McAdams said.

"Yeah, but not for too long. He came back around twenty minutes later."

"So he wasn't with you and your friends the entire time."

"No, we were covering for him." He closed his eyes. "It was a dumb thing to do but once you hear the whole story, maybe you'll understand why I did it."

Decker said, "Good that you're telling the truth. Please go on."

"Yeah. Where was I?"

"Cameron left to go after Delilah."

"Yeah, he was gone for about twenty minutes. Then when he came back, I asked him where he'd been. He told me he went after Delilah. He said that she was really agitated and he was trying to calm her down. Then suddenly she said she didn't feel well. He said she threw up and passed out . . . which I can totally believe. There were more than a few times that I found Delilah passed out on the floor of a party or in someone's bed."

"What did you do when you found her passed out?" Melinda asked.

"Nothing. She'd eventually wake up and go." He turned to McAdams. "Don't say that never happened to you, right?"

McAdams said, "No one is interested in me, Casey."

Decker said, "Let's get back to the party. What did Snowe say he did after Delilah passed out?"

Halpern sighed. "Nothing. Snowe said he just left her there to sleep it off."

"Left her where?"

"Outside not too far from her dorm behind some

bushes. He said he watched her for a moment, then she rolled over and started snoring. He went back to the party and then sometime in the evening, he hooked up with Eloise Braggen. I saw them leave together so that part is probably true."

"Okay," Decker said. "Tell me what you did."

"We left the party together—the guys, some girls, and me—and went back to my dorm and we continued to party there for another two, three hours. You know, drinking and fooling around. People started to pair off—Snowe with Eloise, for instance—and everyone was gone by about three in the morning. I didn't pair off with anyone. I waited until they left and then I went to bed."

"Where was Marcus Craven?" McAdams asked.

"Marcus had hooked up with Jennie Malley. I guess they went to her dorm and he spent the night there."

"Okay. Go on."

"Anyway, about an hour after I had gone to sleep, Snowe comes crashing into my space and shakes me awake. He was freaked, totally panicked."

"This is about four in the morning?" Decker asked.

"About. Maybe a little later."

"So he wasn't with Eloise Braggen the entire night."

"He sure wasn't with her when he woke me up. I was real groggy, trying to sleep off my own hangover. Snowe was pale. He was sweating beer and fear. It took me a few minutes to understand what he was saying."

Halpern paused. Everyone waited.

"Apparently he went back to check on Delilah, make sure she was okay or had left to go to her dorm . . . I forgot what he said exactly." He looked down. "What I do remember real clear is that he said she was at the same spot where he had left her and she wouldn't wake up. He kept shaking her. Finally, he realized she was dead."

Decker said, "That must have woken you up real quick."

"Scared the shit out of me. I, being a jerk, said, are you sure? He said he thought so because she wasn't moving or anything. And he couldn't feel a pulse. I told him to call an ambulance and the cops. He said that he couldn't do that without looking guilty and that we had to think of something."

"Cameron said that he couldn't call the cops without looking guilty."

"Yes. I said he needed to call the cops. I didn't want any part of being his alibi or anything. But then he begged me to go look at Delilah to make sure she was dead. I said I wasn't gonna have any part of that. But he looked so pathetic. I finally told him I'd go back with him, but eventually we'd have to call the cops. He said okay."

"He dragged you into it," McAdams said.

"Totally. I suppose I felt responsible a little because I didn't go back and help Delilah initially. And even though she wasn't my problem, I should have made sure she was sleeping it off somewhere safe. But then again, if someone had seen me carrying her, then they'd think that I did something. I was screwed no matter what.

"So . . ." He sighed. "So we went back to see if Delilah was dead or not. Halfway through—and I don't know if this was real or fake—Snowe's knees buckled. He began to barf. I felt sorry for him—idiot that I am. I told him to go back to the dorm and I'd check her out. I guess a part of me thought that Snowe was bullshitting and that Delilah was okay."

He stopped talking. He looked faraway and haunted.

"Her eyes were open. I couldn't tell if she'd been raped or not, but she had no pants on. I was about to get the hell out of there, but then out of nowhere, Dr. Pallek shows up. He's staring at the body and staring at me. He looks at me and says, 'You killed her.'

"And then I say, 'Man, I just got here.' And then I tell him about Cameron Snowe . . . that he woke me up in a panic. That he was the one who had left her in the bushes after she passed out. I told him I had nothing to do with it, that I was just gonna check on her. Then Pallek says, 'No one is going to believe that.'"

Halpern paused.

"That was probably true. Everything I just told him sounded so stupid."

"You were scared," Decker said.

"I was *terrified*. And super *pissed* at Snowe who had roped me into this."

He shook his head.

"I mean, why would *I* do anything to Delilah? Everyone saw Snowe arguing with her. Lots of people saw Snowe leave. Why would I hurt her? Pallek said the truth didn't matter. I was here and Snowe wasn't and I'd be held accountable."

"Do you think Snowe set you up?"

"That's exactly what I believed. But when I asked him later on, he claimed he didn't even *know* Michael Pallek. It really didn't matter. At that point, I was there and Snowe wasn't and it looked terrible for me."

"Must have put you in a panic."

"Beyond any fear I've ever felt in my life. But even so—even with all this shit in my face—I was still going to call the police."

"Smart thinking," McAdams said.

"Except I wasn't smart. Pallek gave me an out. He said . . ."

Halpern looked away and then looked back.

"Pallek said that he believed me and everything I said made total sense. It was Snowe who was arguing with Delilah. Everyone saw it. Then he added that it was stupid for him to ruin my life or Snowe's life for that matter, because Delilah was dead and there wasn't anything that anyone could do about that. He . . . he told me to go back to my dorm, that he'd take care of everything."

"You must have been relieved," Decker said.

"I was relieved . . . but I was still terrified and kind of suspicious. Like what was really going on? But . . . I didn't stick around to ask questions. This *wasn't* my problem." He looked at Decker. "In the end, it became my problem. I dropped out of the colleges after it happened, went to New York, and finished up in Brooklyn. But every once in a while

Pallek would call me . . . how was I, what was I doing. Never threatening me, but it was still very, very creepy."

"Letting you know he was still around," McAdams said.

"Exactly." He covered his face. "I thought about what had happened with Snowe, Delilah, and Pallek all that night and all the next day. I couldn't think about anything else. And the more I thought about it, the more I came to believe that Pallek killed her. But by the time I came to that definite conclusion, Delilah had been reported missing and I had no idea what Pallek did to her and with her. And I didn't know for *certain* who had killed her. It still could have been Snowe or maybe she just died of the cold or she ODed—she was a druggie. So I just let it go. The one thing I do know is that I didn't kill her."

"I believe you," Decker said.

McAdams said, "You know he—Dr. Pallek—and Dr. Carter were at the party."

"Yes, I knew that. I think he even said that he remembered Snowe leaving the party after Delilah did. So that's why he believed that I didn't hurt her."

"Did they come to a lot of parties?"

"I'd seen them at parties before. Everyone liked them . . . well, everyone liked Carter. I had a feeling that Pallek just came along for the ride. I know they are brothers-in-law. They hung out with each other a lot. Carter's a great guy, but Pallek has always been a little creepy."

Decker nodded, knowing another side of Carter. Two creepy guys finding each other, getting together. Halpern was still talking.

". . . couldn't exactly go accusing Pallek of anything. It would be his word against mine. I knew the police would think I had something to do with it. And since I didn't know the real truth, I just decided to keep quiet."

Decker said, "And then there were those creepy phone calls that Pallek made to you."

"Yeah, but those eventually stopped."

"Oh?" When Halpern nodded, Decker said, "Why do you think that happened?"

"Because I finally grew a set of balls." A pause. "Like I said, Pallek told me to leave, that he'd take care of everything. And I guess he did because no one knew what happened to Delilah until Bogat." He stopped talking.

"Go on," Decker said. "There's something else you want to say."

Halpern looked at the ceiling then at McAdams, then at Decker. "You're not going to believe me."

"Try me, Casey. I'm a very reasonable man."

"What happened next wasn't reasonable."

"If you keep it to yourself, it'll eat away at you."

"It's not that. I just think you won't believe me."

"Now I am curious. What's going on?"

Halpern said, "After Pallek told me to go and that he'd take care of everything, I ran back toward my dorm. But when I got there, I just didn't feel right. I kept thinking that this was gonna bite me in the ass and despite everything, we should call the police. So I went back to Pallek—to discuss it with him." He exhaled. "And then . . . oh God . . ."

"You're doing great, Casey. What happened next?"

"I was still conflicted. That's why I wanted to talk to him again."

"I understand," Decker said.

"When I approached—I was about ten yards away I guess—I saw that there was a body on top of Delilah. His pants were down. I could see his butt." He covered his mouth. "I couldn't absolutely swear it was Pallek, but I sure as hell knew what the guy was doing."

"That's revolting," Melissa said.

"It *was* revolting," Halpern said.

"Did he see you?" Decker said.

Halpern shook his head no.

"You have to answer out loud for the tape recorder."

"No, at that time Pallek didn't see that I'd come back."

Decker said, "So after enough of those creepy calls, you finally confronted him."

"Yeah, I told him what I saw . . . that he was on top of Delilah. There was this long pause and he said he had no idea what I was talking about and it would be good if we never brought up Delilah again. And I told him that I thoroughly agreed with that."

"And the calls stopped."

"Pretty much. Once in a while he checked in with me. But then once in a while, I also checked in with him. It's like we were locked in some kind of sadistic dance."

Decker said, "And what about Cameron Snowe? Do you think he put Pallek up to harassing you?"

"Sometimes I thought exactly that. Other times, I just thought Pallek was really weird."

"Casey, if Cameron bailed on you multiple times, why did you help him when he called you about the car accident? Up to this point, all he'd ever done was screw you over."

"You forget that we also shared the secret. Every time he needed something, he'd remind me that Pallek saw me and not him. And then I'd remind him that he was the one who fought with Delilah, not me. It was all real sick."

"It's good you finally got it off your chest."

"I don't know if it's good or not, but I can't deal with it anymore. It's ruining my life. I don't want to go to jail. I don't think I deserve jail. But I can't keep this in anymore."

"And yet you called Pallek when Snowe was in trouble," McAdams said.

"It wasn't my idea. Cameron *told* me to call Michael Pallek. He helped us out before, maybe he'd do it again."

"Cameron told us that you called Pallek on your own. That he was shocked to see Pallek drive up in his car."

"That's a total lie. Cameron texted me."

Decker said, "Do you have the text on your phone?"

"Of course not. I erased it. And I'm sure he erased it on his phone. But if you check his phone records . . . my phone records also . . . you'll see that he reached out to me before I reached out to Pallek. And like I said way before, I just thought that Pallek was gonna pick him up. I had no idea that there was another person involved in the accident and I had no idea that someone was gonna try to kill someone."

He stopped talking and blew out air.

"And that's why I'm here. I didn't kill anyone, I didn't hurt anyone, and I certainly didn't know anything about any attempted murder. I don't even know the victim."

Melinda Message said, "But you didn't do anything to *help* Delilah when you had the chance."

Halpern made a face. "All true."

"And you helped Snowe," Melinda said. "You helped him twice—with Delilah and with Dana Berinson."

"I never killed anyone, and I never *helped* anyone kill anyone."

Decker said, "Are you willing to take a lie detector test?"

A long pause. "What would you ask me?"

"If you killed Delilah or helped Snowe and Pallek kill Dana Berinson."

"I didn't."

"If you take a polygraph and you pass, it would go a long way toward having the police believe you. You're facing some bad charges right now, Casey. Passing it would only help your case."

"Then sure, I'll do it."

"I'll set up the questions myself," Decker said. "I want to ask you something."

"What?"

"You mentioned that Dr. Pallek and Dr. Carter used to show up at quite a few parties. Have you ever heard anything about Dr. Carter's involvement in Delilah Occum's murder?"

"Dr. Carter?" Halpern looked confused. "No. Why? *Is* he involved?"

"No evidence, but like you said, he and Pallek did hang around a lot. Also, we can't seem to locate him."

"Who? Pallek?"

"Pallek's in custody. He isn't going anywhere. We also have Snowe on attempted murder charges. But we'd like to ask Hank Carter a few questions and we can't find him. Any ideas?"

"No . . . nothing. So you're assuming that Carter's involved in Delilah's death?"

"I'm not paid to assume," Decker said. "I'm paid to prove things. And your testimony will go a long way with that."

"If I testify, what will I get in return?"

Decker shrugged. "Maybe a lighter sentence and no doubt a clearer conscience."

42

It was around ten in the morning, just as the third batch of cookies was coming out of the oven, when Rina heard a knock at the door. It was a harmless knock, but it set her heart racing, and her breathing quickened. The simplest thing to do was to see who it was by parting the drawn drapes and peeking out the living room window. But doing that would let the person on the other side know she was home. So she remained in the kitchen, vigilant and on edge.

The knocking stopped. But then the doorbell rang.

One ring.

Two rings.

Then several times in rapid succession: impatient and hostile. Then the rapping started up again, growing angrier and louder.

Rina's heart was hammering in her chest. She was having trouble breathing. Her hands started shaking.

A muffled voice—Carter's—from behind the door said, "I know you're in there, Rina! Open up. I just want to talk to you without that goon around!"

She didn't know if he was referring to Peter or

Chris, but it really didn't matter. She didn't want to leave the safety of her kitchen, but her cell phone and gun were in the living room.

More pounding.

Thank God for old-fashioned kitchen landlines. She picked up the receiver from the cradle of the wall mount and punched in 911.

She was trembling so badly she dropped the phone just as the operator answered. She managed to pick the receiver up and ask for immediate assistance. She felt better as soon as the responder said the police were on their way. It emboldened her. She went into the living room and retrieved her gun.

"I see you!" he said.

Rina stationed herself between the wall and her front door. If he should somehow manage to get inside, she'd be behind the door when it was flung open.

She held the gun in shaky hands.

He kept pummeling the wood. And then he started screaming.

Vile things that became louder and louder.

She felt tears coming from her eyes—so wet and fast she couldn't see through the veil of water. She admonished herself. She had the gun. She was a good shot.

He kept on with the vicious words. Through all the noise, her heightened sense of hearing detected a car pulling up in front of her house. She would have thought it was the police but had heard no sirens.

She waited.

"Hey!" It was a male voice, angry but assured.

Not Peter's voice, but familiar. In her anxiety she couldn't place it. He said, "Get the hell away from there!"

Without warning, deafening gunshots rang out, coming directly from the other side of the front door. She ran to the front window and looked outside. The maniac was shooting at the parked car. With the gun cocked and ready to spit fire, Rina threw open the front door. Before Carter had a chance to fully absorb that she was now visible, she pumped a couple of bullets into his body—his arm and chest. He looked at her wide-eyed, with his knees giving way. As he fell forward, the gun slipped from his hand. In a flash, Rina kicked it into the nearby bushes.

She ran over to the parked car. The driver's door was still open and the passenger's door was riddled with bullet holes. She was pale and sick and out of breath. "Everyone okay?"

From behind the driver's door, an elderly man stood up, knees cracking as he did. Full head of gray hair and dressed in a dapper blue suit with a contrasting red silk tie. "I'm fine, Rina. Call the police."

Rina stared at him. "Scott?"

"Yeah. Is the guy alive?"

"I don't know. I'll go check—"

"I'll check him out, Rina. You call for an ambulance."

She did as told. Afterward, she rushed over to Oliver, who was bent over and ministering aid to the man as he lay on his back. Rina could hear horrid groans. "Is he alive?"

"So far."

"What are you *doing* here?"

"Besides trying to keep this guy from bleeding to death?"

"How can I help?"

"Put pressure on this spot." Oliver directed her hands over a leaky bullet wound. "I was hired to keep an eye on a guy named Carter. Looks like I found him, yeah?"

"Yes, that's him. You saved my life."

"No, actually you saved my life because he was shooting at me, not you." Blood was oozing from between his fingers. They could both hear several sirens. "Do you have a permit for your gun?"

"Yes."

"You're sure?"

"Positive."

"And it's up to date?"

"I think so."

"If there's any doubt, I'll take your gun and claim that I shot him."

"Scott, I have a permit and I'm pretty sure it's current. Carter's been stalking me for over a week. Let's just tell it as it happened."

"The truth is usually easier to remember, I'll give you that. I'm just saying that if you need it, I'll fall on the sword."

"I appreciate the chivalry." Tears were streaming down her face. She started trembling uncontrollably.

Oliver regarded her pallid face. "Sit down, Rina, and catch your breath, honey. I've got this one."

The ambulance had arrived. Seconds later, Hank Carter was surrounded by paramedics. As Rina sat on the front porch steps watching and wiping her eyes, a car zoomed up into the driveway. Decker and McAdams jumped out and rushed over. Sitting down next to his wife, Decker pulled her to his chest as she sobbed deep, thick inhalations that were filled with tears.

He whispered, "It's okay. You're safe now."

"I'm fine, I'm fine, I'm fine," she kept repeating. Her hands were wet and sticky with blood. Mucus was pouring from her nose.

"I know," Decker whispered. "I can see that you're just fine." He took his jacket and wiped her face. He kissed her cheek. "You're fine."

Oliver came over to them, wiping his hands on a paper towel. He looked at Tyler and said, "Hey, kid."

"Looks like you showed up just in time."

"I didn't do anything." He regarded Decker, who was holding his wife. "Rina says that she has a permit for the gun."

"She does."

"Then I'll tell you what happened. I had just pulled my car up when I saw this dude pounding on her door. I got out of my car, but didn't approach right away, using the car for a shield. I shouted at him to leave and without warning, he opened fire. At that point, Rina saw my life was in danger. So she opened the front door and shot him out of fear for my safety, and fear for her own life. And that's all she wrote."

"Great timing, Scott," McAdams said.

Decker was still stunned. All he could say was, "I thought you were coming in later in the day."

"I made good time," Oliver said. "I might have been speeding. If I get a ticket from one of those machines, I'll send it your way."

"Not a problem." Decker felt his throat clog up. "Thanks for . . ."

"Thanks for what?" Oliver smiled. "For showing up? Easiest money I've ever earned. Unfortunately, someone will have to pay for the rental car damage. I didn't take out insurance for bullet holes."

Rina smiled through her copious tears.

The EMTs worked for several minutes on Carter as he lay on the ground. Eventually they took out the gurney to load him up. Decker bolted from the porch step. "I'll be right back."

Oliver stared at him. "What's that about? I hope he isn't thinking of doing anything stupid."

"I'll go check on him," McAdams said.

"No, you stay here with Rina."

Oliver went over to Decker, who was talking to one of the medics. On the gurney, Carter lay on his back. His shirt had been ripped off, and his chest was bandaged and patched and leaking pools of blood. There was an oxygen mask over his face and an IV in his vein.

Decker was still talking to the EMT. Pleading with him. "It'll just take a sec. I just want to peek at his back."

"And I'm telling you, we need to get him in stat."

"I know but this is a police matter."

"And we have a medical matter."

Oliver said, "In the time you two are talking, it could have been done. This guy just tried to kill me. Do what he asks, please?"

Again, the medic frowned. But he slowly lifted his right shoulder. Decker peeked underneath. "The other one?"

The left shoulder was lifted.

And there it was: a six- to seven-inch gash that had been healed over into a keloid scar.

By five in the afternoon, Carter was out of surgery and out of danger. He was listed in guarded condition. The two bullets had missed major blood vessels, but he was suffering from a collapsed lung and pleural bleeding. He had tubes coming in and out of his body and was high on Demerol. But for some odd reason, in post-op he asked to talk to Decker and to Decker only. Because Carter was in such a compromised state, anything he'd say was automatically suspect. He couldn't be Mirandized because he really wasn't in a state to give consent. But Decker figured that if Carter asked for him, it was better to hear him than to ignore him.

By the time Decker made it to the hospital, Carter had been transferred to a room. Angry eyes greeted Decker when he walked in. Carter was surrounded by his wife, Lydia Urbana—a petite woman with a helmet of curly hair and smoky eyes—and two teen-aged boys who had inherited their mother's hair and eyes.

"I'll come back later."

Carter started talking from behind the oxygen mask. No one could understand a thing. He yanked it off and called out to Decker. "Stay . . ."

Decker turned around. He looked at the family. "Can we have a minute?"

"So you can take advantage of him?" his wife said. "Go to hell!"

"Dr. Urbana, he asked me to come. So I came. What do you want me to do?"

"Stay . . ." Carter said.

Decker said, "You probably shouldn't be talking, sir."

He grimaced. "I thou . . . was tha maniac. He's . . . gonna kill me."

"You thought that man in the parked car was Christopher Donatti?"

"Yah . . ."

"Okay. Good to know. But you can't randomly shoot at people based on a hunch. You really should rest, Dr. Carter. We'll have plenty of time to talk later."

"No . . ."

"It's okay, sir. Rest."

Carter took Decker's arm. "Never kill . . . befor . . ."

"Okay. I believe you."

"No one."

Decker put the mask back over his face. "Rest."

But Carter held on to his arm. "Sit . . ."

"Hank, stop that," Lydia said.

Again, he took off the mask. "Fu . . . you."

Lydia winced at the words. "Anything he tells you won't stick because he's drugged up."

Decker said, "Five minutes. That's it. I don't want to push him any more than you do."

Without answering, Lydia left with the boys. Carter said, "Fu-ing cun . . ."

"Dr. Carter you really shouldn't be talking."

"Didn't kill anyon . . . just help . . ."

"I understand. You're just helping, right?"

He nodded.

Decker put the mask back on. "I hope you recover really soon."

Carter smiled and then he closed his eyes.

Over the phone, Decker said, "We've got Carter for attempted murder. He isn't going anywhere. All Erin has to do is testify that he's the guy who tried to bury her alive."

Marge said, "She didn't see him clearly enough."

"So just get her to say she whacked him on the back."

"And she's going to say, unless you have Diaz wrapped up with a bow, she's not going to want to testify against anyone."

"But I can't get him wrapped up with a bow without her testimony."

"Pete, I'm trying my best. I took her out for coffee yesterday and talked to her, but I'm not pushing. I can't push. You know how these things work. She's like a turtle. She's not going to stick her neck out if I keep prodding her."

"Just tell her that we have Carter in custody. And that we have Diaz's DNA along with her DNA on the necklace. I'm going to push for Carter's medical records to see if he got the gash sewn up on the night Erin disappeared. If I can get that through, we've got a very good chance of putting Diaz away. I'll convince both of them—Diaz and Carter—that they're pointing the finger at each other. If she doesn't testify, I have to spring Diaz tomorrow."

There was a long pause over the line. "Charge Diaz with murder," Marge said.

"Now how is that going to stick? And if it doesn't stick, I'm going to have a real hard time making it stick the next time I charge him."

"Don't spring him, Pete. Hold him on murder. If I can get Erin to show up and talk, you can reduce it to attempted murder. With Carter now in custody, I'll see if I can use that and work some magic. If I tell her that Diaz has been arrested and charged, and it won't go through without her, maybe she'll cave. It's our best shot. How long can you hold him if you charge him?"

"If I say I have a witness . . . maybe three days."

"So that's by Friday. Can you stall it until Monday?"

"I think so. If I charge him tomorrow, I don't think Diaz has enough money to hire a private lawyer. So maybe we can stall getting a county defense attorney for a day or two. And then maybe another day for defense to prepare for the arraignment. I'll do my best, but if Erin doesn't show by Sunday for Monday-morning arraignment, I'm cooked. I don't have enough evidence to take to a grand jury. I'll have to let him out and he'll bolt to Mexico where I'll never find him."

"Let me make a few phone calls. I'll get back to you."

"When?"

"When I have something to tell you. Pete, I want this felon as much as you do. And I certainly don't want to make you look like an ass. Just . . . give me a little time and space and we'll both hope for the best."

"Thank you, Margie. That's about as reasonable as one can expect."

"On another note, how's Rina?"

"She's drowning her anxiety in cooking rice pilaf and noodle pudding for about a hundred kids. Rosh Hashanah is this weekend. She's invited a million kids over."

"I remember the holidays very well. I don't think I ever left a meal at your house where I didn't feel like a stuffed goose."

"Where are my manners? I don't think I ever thanked you for that wonderful meal and all the trouble you went to. That was way beyond, Margie. I really do appreciate it."

"Rina sent me a thank-you card."

"Of course she did." Decker paused. "You know you're always welcome here. Free meals and enough birds to occupy even the most avid of watchers."

"I know. Thanks."

"Marge, don't worry about Erin Young. I don't want to traumatize the poor girl. She's already been through enough."

"Giving testimony will be traumatizing. It's always traumatizing. But it also can be liberating and empowering. Maybe she's tired of living in a shadow. I'm hoping there's a part of her that would love to see the sun again."

43

Three days had passed without a word from Marge. During that period, Decker sent McAdams back to school, Oliver went back to Miami, Snowe and Pallek were charged, Carter was still alive, and Diaz was arrested on murder charges. So all was not lost except maybe Diaz, and Decker, in a career spanning well over three decades, had dealt with a lot bigger blows.

In that seventy-two-hour period—as Decker waited for Marge to call—Hank Carter had been recuperating nicely. He had become more awake and more coherent and had asked to speak to Decker again. As soon as Decker walked into the hospital room, the professor shooed away his family with a wave of his arm. Carter was aware enough to hear his rights, aware enough to waive the right to an attorney, and aware enough to sign the Miranda card *and* allow himself to be recorded.

He had a story to tell.

He insisted he had never murdered anyone. Quite the contrary: he was a do-gooder, just helping people out. He always had been a people person, oriented toward social causes. Look at his foundation, how many people he had helped overcome adverse circumstances. With that self-serving prelude out of the way, Decker said, "Why don't you start at the beginning?"

It was still painful for the professor to talk, but the oxygen mask was no longer over his face. Instead, he had two little tubes feeding the gas into his nose. His arm still held an IV, but his bleeding was controlled. He was clearly on the mend because the doctor was talking about discharging him over the weekend. His hair was greasy and his complexion was wan, but his eyes were open and he spoke clearly. "What beginning?"

"I think it starts with Yvette Jones. What do you know about her murder?"

"You'll have to talk to Michael for the details, but it's all going to come out anyway, so . . .." His breathing was shallow. "I'll tell you what I know."

"Please."

"Michael called me in a panic. The guy always left ruin in his wake and he was always calling me to clean up his messes. On top of being a jerk, he can't keep it in his pants." A shrug. "But what can I do? He's family. His wife and my wife are sisters."

"Tell me about Yvette."

"Michael calls me up and says he has a problem . . . a big problem."

"When was this?"

"I don't remember the exact date. You'd know it. I remember I had just given one of my free talks. I do it as a community service."

"Like the one my wife went to."

"Yeah . . . like that." His smile was unnerving.

"The girl—Yvette—had been at the talk. She sat next to Michael. They talked and Michael claimed she was coming on to him. He says she became flirtatious and asked him if he wanted to go somewhere private to talk some more. At first, he said no and they went their separate ways. But then Michael changed his mind and decided to catch up with her after my talk."

Stalk her, Decker thought.

"She started getting physical with him—kissing and stuff like that."

"Where did this happen?"

"Michael told me they took a walk together on the edge of campus bordering the nature preserve. He said they talked and then it started getting passionate. After a few minutes, he realized he was being an idiot and he broke it off. He told me she got angry. She started yelling and hitting him. I don't know what really happened, but the upshot is, she wound up dead."

"That's a big step, going from yelling to dead."

"I wasn't there. I don't know the details. I just know what he told me."

"Did you believe him?"

"I wanted to, but did I?" A pause. "I'll circle back to you on that one." Carter winced in pain. "Anyway, when he called me, as I said, he was in a panic. What should he do? I told him to call the police . . . say it was an accident. The idiot was blubbering over the phone. He said he couldn't go to the police."

"Because . . ."

"He had had sex with her—unprotected sex . . .

DNA and all that. He said it was consensual but it would look bad. So he couldn't call the police. He begged me to help him."

"So you helped him."

"I like helping people because I like people." Carter looked at Decker. "I'm sorry about your wife, by the way. I just wanted to talk to her."

While carrying a gun. Decker said, "I understand."

"Do you?"

"I do. You felt misrepresented and you wanted to explain your case."

Carter nodded. "Exactly. And I had to take the gun because of that maniac. You know yourself he's a maniac."

"I understand," Decker said. "How did you help your brother-in-law with Yvette Jones?"

"We waited until it was very late . . . around three, four in the morning. I'm a night owl, and I do my best thinking when everyone else sleeps. We put the body in a trash bag and carried it to the trunk of Michael's car. I told Michael to go home. He was too shaken up to be of any use. I took it into the woods near Bogat Trail . . . before it was Bogat . . . and buried it."

Decker nodded.

"She was dead," Carter said. "Nothing was going to change that. I really felt that it was kinder to the parents to think that maybe she was still alive, right?"

Decker didn't answer.

"Anyway, that was my rationale at the time," Carter said. "Everything was going okay until I got a call from Lawrence Pettigrew a couple of days later. Who was, by the way, a good guy: a little crazy and a little showy, but very smart."

"That's what everyone says. Why did he call you?"

"He was walking around the nature preserve near Morse McKinley coming back from somewhere the night that Yvette disappeared." Carter swore under his breath. "He told me he saw Michael and me moving a large trash bag into the trunk of Michael's car. He wondered what that was about."

"I see where this is going."

"Yes, and so did I. I told him we were getting some firewood from an old dead tree."

"At four in the morning."

"It was the only thing I could think of on the spur of the moment. He knew it was a lie and he didn't probe it further. But a few weeks later, Lawrence did mention to me that he wanted to quit college to undergo sex reassignment surgery and that it was very expensive."

"You gave him money."

"Michael did. I was just the delivery guy. I believe it was around ten thousand dollars. I told him the money was his to do whatever he wanted with, but he wouldn't get a dime more. He said that was fine. He thanked me profusely. He said he considered it a loan. I told him it was a gift. He wouldn't ask any more questions. He didn't want trouble. He said he was going for a new identity and it would be a fresh start for all of us."

Decker noticed that Carter was panting. "Do you want a break?"

Carter waved him off. "Naively, I thought that it was the last I'd hear from him. And for two years, all was going smoothly."

"Then Pettigrew suddenly showed up at the colleges."

"Dressed like some drag queen." Carter sighed. "He had called and said he needed to talk to me. We set up a meeting over the weekend."

"Okay." Decker was writing notes. "Where?"

"In my office, of course. First thing I did was pat him down. I wanted to make sure that it wasn't a setup. The guy had real breasts but he still had a penis. How weird is that?"

"Go on, Professor."

"He was psychologically confused. And that's why I took the time to listen to him. I really do care about people."

"What did he tell you?"

"Not what I expected. I expected to be hit up again. What happened was that he said he had a change of heart. That he was becoming a father and he needed to clear his conscience. He had a bag of money with him. He shoved it in my face, saying it was blood money. He told us to go to the police and tell them what happened. If we didn't, he would. That was the problem with Lawrence. He was always pushy if not downright self-righteous."

"What did you tell him?"

"I said I wasn't about to turn my family in. And I knew that Michael wouldn't go to the police. I told him to do whatever his conscience dictated. But we would deny everything and it would be his word against ours. There was no body. Police would see him as a mixed-up transgender woman who hadn't even transitioned all the way. Who was the most believable?"

"Got it."

"But Pettigrew just wouldn't give up." Carter adjusted his hospital bed. "He said that I should at least tell the police where the body was. It was terrible for the parents not to know. I said I didn't know where the body was. I told him to go back to New York and live his life. He left. I thought I got through to him or her."

"Obviously not," Decker said. "Pettigrew wound up dead."

"After he left me, he approached Michael."

"And . . ."

"And what do you think?"

"What do I think?"

"Michael talked to him on the phone and arranged a meeting with him later in the evening around eleven. Very late so no one else was around. He had asked me to come, but I said no. I told him to blow Pettigrew off. He couldn't harm us because there was no body and if he went to the police, no one would take him seriously."

Carter rolled his eyes and again adjusted the bed.

"Pettigrew tried to convince Michael to tell him where we buried the body. He said he wouldn't report us, just give an anonymous tip to the police so the parents could bury their daughter. Michael said he couldn't describe the spot—it was too wooded—but he'd show him the spot where Yvette was buried."

"Did he know where you buried Yvette?"

"Not a clue. I wanted it that way. Michael buckles under pressure. That's why I knew I'd better tell you my story because it's all going to come out. I know I was an accessory after the fact with Yvette, but I didn't kill her. I just did Mike a favor."

"I believe you," Decker said. "So what did Pettigrew say after Michael offered to show him the spot?"

"The kid wasn't dumb. He wasn't going to follow a murderer into the forest. This is what Michael said happened, okay? He said they started arguing. It got heated very quickly. Pettigrew pushed him and Michael, out of self-defense, picked up a paperweight and smashed it over his head. Next thing he knew, Pettigrew was dead."

"Michael argues with Yvette. Then he argues with Pettigrew. Then they both wind up dead."

"I'm just telling you what Michael told me."

"You know forensics said that Pettigrew was bashed in the back of the head. That indicates that Pettigrew had his back to Pallek when he hit him."

Carter shrugged.

"Go on," Decker said.

"I took the body—again in Michael's car—and buried it near Yvette. I figured if someone was to find them, they'd think it was the work of a crazed serial killer."

Which it was, Decker thought. "Why'd you keep helping your loser brother-in-law out?"

"Family is family."

Even if Carter didn't kill anyone—and Decker had his doubts—he clearly enjoyed burying dead bodies. He said, "Tell me about Delilah Occum."

"Michael swears that he found her dead, that either Cameron Snowe or Casey Halpern had killed her and just left her there to rot. He stumbled upon her accidentally and he felt bad about that."

"Why didn't he just call the police?"

"After killing two people, I don't think Michael wanted to have anything to do with the police. Plus . . ." Carter sighed. "My brother-in-law has some very peculiar habits."

"Tell me," Decker said. He was pretty sure where this was going.

"Well, let me put it this way. He was horny and she was young and pretty and warm."

"But dead."

Carter was silent. Then he said, "So you see why he couldn't go to the police."

"DNA and all that."

"Don't look at me," Carter said. "I'm not enamored with necrophilia."

"But you helped your brother-in-law out and buried her with the others."

"Every person should have a proper burial." Carter looked quite pleased with himself.

"I know Michael is in very bad shape especially with Dana Berinson being alive. I had absolutely nothing to do with that."

Decker thought for a moment. "You know he's being accused of setting up the accident, of pushing the car over the embankment."

"Yes, I'm aware of that."

"By any chance, before he pushed the car . . . did he tell you that he thought she was dead and . . . you know, DNA and all that."

"No, he didn't tell me. But I wouldn't be a bit surprised."

Decker felt sick to his stomach. The act was just vile. Then, deliberating like a cop, Decker thought to himself that it was unlikely that when Dana was brought in that any doctor performed a rape analysis on her. It was doubtful that any biological evidence had survived. But if something did survive, it would absolutely tie Michael Pallek to Dana Berinson. He'd have to talk to the parents first.

Carter said, "I know that I'm going to get a few slaps on the wrist. I deserve it. I shouldn't have tried to protect him. I'll be charged with accessory after the fact. But I'm telling you straight out. I never harmed a soul."

"You stalked my wife. And you shot at a perfect stranger."

"I didn't stalk her. She bumped into me. As far as the stranger, I thought it was that Donatti guy. I thought he was going to kill me. It was as much self-defense as Rina shooting me. It was all one big misunderstanding. Look, right now I'm not going to press charges against your wife, either civilly or criminally, although I reserve the right to do it later on if you give me a hard time. I never hurt anyone."

"You buried three *bodies*."

"They were dead. Nothing anyone could do

about that. I might as well have given them the re-spect of a place to rest."

"And you'd swear under oath that they were dead?"

"Yes, of course they were dead!"

"Just like Erin Young was dead?" Decker asked.

Carter's eyes clouded with fury. "Who?"

"She was a cashier at a local convenience store who went missing four years ago. The poor woman was attacked and then someone tried to bury her while she was still alive."

"I don't know who you're talking about."

"Dr. Carter, that gash on your back says you know very well who she is."

Carter was silent. Then he said, "Yeah, I hurt myself a long time ago. I backed into a barbed-wire fence. I tore up my back."

"You're not very good at making up spur-of-the-moment stories." When Carter didn't answer, Decker said, "So if I were to look at your health records on the night Erin Young went missing, I wouldn't find an emergency room where you happened to get your back sewn up?"

Carter weighed his words. "The missing girl. What's her name?"

"Erin Young."

"You found her?"

"Nope."

"Then how do you know that she was attacked and left for dead?"

Decker covered his goof. "You'd be surprised by what I know, Dr. Carter."

"But you don't know if she's alive or dead."

"True," Decker lied. "You know we have Ricardo

Diaz in custody. I've charged him with Erin's murder."

"Who's Ricardo Diaz?"

The guy was a smooth operator. Decker said, "He's a bartender at the College Grill."

"Oh . . . yes. We've spoken a couple of times. He murdered the girl?"

"We've charged him with the murder, yes."

"So if you have your man, why are you talking to me about this?"

"I've heard that you might have been helping him out—the same way that you've helped out Michael Pallek."

"Why would I help him out?" Carter asked.

"Because you're a night owl and you prowl the streets, looking for prey."

Carter smiled broadly. "Did you find this woman's body up at Bogat?"

"I've already told you that we don't have a body. But I heard that you went a little overboard in helping Diaz out and that's how you got the gash."

"I don't know what you're talking about." Carter stared at him. "Has he admitted killing this girl?"

"No."

"Do you have evidence against Diaz?"

"Of course we have evidence."

"But if you don't have the girl and you don't have a body, all you must have is circumstantial evidence. You're on a fishing expedition."

Decker said, "You have a good grasp of the law, but I've been at this longer than you have."

"I still think that you're going to have a very hard time making your case."

"I don't know about that. Diaz seems pretty weak-willed. He'll start talking."

"I doubt it. And if he doesn't talk, you'll have to prove your case without him." Carter lowered the hospital bed, closed his eyes, and smiled. "Good luck with that."

🦢44

By the time the last of the holiday lunch guests had left the house, it was close to six in the evening. The students had tried to clean up as best as they could, but there were paper plates and cups scattered throughout the living room and dining room and a slew of dirty serving platters. It was depressing to look at, even more depressing to know it was going to happen all over again tomorrow. But in keeping with the Rosh Hashanah, Decker tried to maintain a positive attitude. His stepson, Jacob, and his wife, Ilana, came out of the bedroom with their three pugs. Jacob was a heartthrob with his big blue eyes, black hair, and athletic build. Ilana was petite with curly hair, wide brown eyes, and a perpetual smile. They both were in their midthirties and were now *thinking* about children of the human kind. The two of them were very deliberate.

"They've been cooped up all afternoon," Jacob said. "We're taking them for a walk. Want to come?"

"Love to, but I think I need to clean this up."

Rina said, "Go, Peter, I'll take care of it."

Decker said, "Why don't you go and I'll take care of it?"

"I'll help you," McAdams offered.

"No." Decker smiled. "Don't need it. You all go. I'll be fine."

"Someone needs his alone time," Jacob said.

"Someone is right." Decker fluffed out a trash bag and began to dump paper goods inside. It would soon join the other ten trash bags already sitting in the garage. And they still had another lunch to go. "It's going to get dark soon."

"Are you sure you don't want to come?" Rina tried again. "It's so lovely outside."

"Let me make a dent in this first." Decker smiled. "Really, I need to unwind."

"Fair enough," Rina said. "If you feel like it, you can set the table for dinner. I'll warm up the food as soon as Shabbos is over."

"Rina, we just finished lunch."

"We should at least make Kiddush. It's Rosh Hashanah. And I for one have a lot to be thankful for."

"How about we talk about it later?" McAdams was ushering everyone out the door. "Want me to take one of the dogs, guys?"

"Take Pogo," Ilana said. "She likes you."

"That's me—a real lady killer."

As soon as the front door clicked shut, Decker breathed a sigh of relief. It was wonderful to be doing something concrete. His brain had been on all afternoon and it immediately shut down without words to stimulate it. The first thing he did was throw away all the disposables. After he did that, he began to gather up the dirty platters and take them into the kitchen. When that was done, he collected items left behind, mostly sunglasses but a few yarmulkes and hats and several sweaters. After he established the lost and found in the front closet, he washed down the tables, brushed the crumbs from the chairs and couches, and took out a broom. He really didn't even know why he bothered because it was only going to get messed up again tomorrow, but cleanliness and godliness and all that jazz. He'd vacuum the area rugs after the holidays.

He was working on his second pile of crumbs on the dining room floor when he heard a knock at the door. Rina and the gang had keys so it had to be a student who forgot something. He put down the broom and peered through the living room picture window, the drapes now wide open since Carter was in custody. He stared through the picture window as Marge waved to him. He flung the door open. With her were Will and Erin Young a.k.a. Elena Hardgreeves dressed demurely in a knee-length skirt and a pink blouse with ballet flats on her feet. She was looking at the ground.

"Come in, please," Decker said.

Will spoke first as he stepped inside. "Since my wife needed to see you, I decided to take you up on the bird-watching invite." He paused. "Something smells good."

Decker could barely contain his excitement. He said, "You're just in time for dinner."

"That's good because I'm starved," Will said.

"Will!" Marge said.

"No, it really is good. We just finished eating two hours ago."

"And you're going to eat again?" Will asked.

"He doesn't understand yet," Marge said. "I'll explain it to him."

"Anyway, you're all invited." Decker looked at Elena. "Ms. Hardgreeves. It's nice to see you again."

She didn't answer. Marge said, "I think at some point, it would be truly useful if you let Elena know precisely what's going on and what charges you have."

"I'd be happy to do that." Decker paused. "Right now if you want to."

"Maybe in an hour or two," Marge said. "We just got off the plane and had a long car ride over."

"Of course, of course. What can I get everybody to drink?"

"Martini," Will said. "Or is that not allowed on the holiday?"

"It's not only allowed, at times it's mandatory," Decker said. "Marge?"

"Glass of white wine."

"Ms. Hardgreeves?"

"Wine sounds good." Her voice was soft.

"Right away." A minute later, Decker came out with the drinks and served them. "Everyone sit and relax."

Marge sat on the couch. Decker was really glad he had cleaned everything so thoroughly. "Where are you staying?" he asked.

"We booked rooms at the Ramada Inn."

"That's great. It's just a few blocks away."

"Right. We figured it would be convenient for you. Elena is in the room right next door. I'm assuming the department will pay for the accommodations?"

"Of course. No problem." Decker smiled. "And again, all of you are invited for dinner."

"We don't want to impose." Marge sipped wine.

"Oh, please. I'm the one who has imposed on all of you."

Marge said, "You're just doing your job. So am I. It's Elena who's bearing the brunt of all this."

Decker nodded. "I can only imagine how hard this is for you. Your bravery and your commitment to justice will save lives, Elena. Diaz is a very bad man and your testimony will put him away. It will also add charges to Hank Carter. Serious charges."

"I thought he was behind bars."

"He is. He's already been charged with attempted murder along with a slew of other things."

"Yeah, how is Rina?" Will asked. Then he turned to Elena. "Rina is Detective Decker's wife. That Carter guy was stalking her."

"Oh God." Elena put her hands to her mouth. "That's terrible!"

"It worked out," Will said. "She shot him."

"Will!" Marge said.

"It's the truth. And within these four walls, everyone's happy about it."

Softly, Elena said, "He's right."

"Yes, he is, but we can't admit things like that out loud," Marge said.

"I'll fill you in on everything, Elena," Decker said. "But right now all I want to do is thank you for coming forward. You're doing the right thing. You're preventing this monster from doing something horrible to someone else."

"That makes me sound very righteous."

"You are very righteous."

"The fact is, Detective, I can't go on living in fear anymore. Detective Dunn and I talked about this and she's right. If I hope to live a normal life ever again—whatever normal now means—I have to reclaim myself."

At that moment, the door opened and the family came spilling inside. Rina's eyes widened when she saw Marge and Will. "My goodness, twice in a month?" She gave them each a hug.

Marge said, "Hey, Jake."

"Margie . . ." Jacob hugged her and shook Will's hand. "You guys remember Ilana from the wedding."

"I remember her," Will said. "I'm sure she doesn't remember me."

"I do," Ilana said. "You were a cop up in Berkeley and you met Marge and Dad—my father-in-law—on an assignment. Then you came down south to be with her."

"Whoa," Will said. "I stand corrected."

Marge stuck out her hand to McAdams. "You must be the kid."

Tyler shook hands and smiled. "And you must be the ex-partner that the Old Man is constantly comparing me to—invidiously, I might add."

"I do not," Decker said. Tyler cleared his throat. "Well, maybe a little."

"I should hope so," Marge said.

"Everyone," Decker said. "This brave young woman who has come here to help put away a bad guy is Elena Hardgreeves."

She smiled. "Actually, Detective, my name is Erin Young."

FAYE KELLERMAN

THE BEAST

978-0-06-212176-9

Peter Decker's latest case with the LAPD is the most bizarre of his storied career. When the elderly, eccentric billionaire Hobart Penny is found dead in his apartment, the cops think his pet Bengal tiger must have turned against him. But as Decker and his colleagues dig into the victim's life, it soon becomes clear that the beast that killed the peculiar inventor is all too human.

MURDER 101

978-0-06-227019-1

Former LAPD detective lieutenant Peter Decker and his wife, Rina Lazarus, are ready to enjoy the quiet beauty of upstate New York, with Decker working for the Greenbury Police department. But a reported break-in at a local cemetery draws Decker and his newest partner, Harvard-educated Tyler McAdams, into a web of dark secrets, cold case crimes, international intrigue, and ruthless people who kill for sport.

THE THEORY OF DEATH

978-0-06-227022-1

The slow pace of Peter Decker's new job with the Greenbury police is upended when an unidentified nude male body is found deep within the local woods. When the body is finally identified, Decker and Tyler McAdams must penetrate the indecipherable upper echelons of mathematics at Kneed Loft College, where even harmless nerds can morph into depraved, evil masterminds.

FK3 0817